The Faerie Door

The
Faerie
Door

B. E. MAXWELL

Harcourt, Inc.

Orlando   Austin   New York   San Diego   London

Requests for permission to make copies of any part of the work should be
submitted online at www.harcourt.com/contact or mailed to the following address:
Permissions Department, Houghton Mifflin Harcourt Publishing Company,
6277 Sea Harbor Drive, Orlando, Florida 32887-6777.

www.HarcourtBooks.com

Library of Congress Cataloging-in-Publication Data
Maxwell, Bruce (Bruce Edward), 1957–
The faerie door/Bruce Maxwell.
p.   cm.
Summary: Victoria Deveny is transported from her Northumberland,
England, home in 1890 to 1966 Alton Bay, New Hampshire, where she meets
Elliot Good and they agree to help the Faerie Queen defeat the Shadow Knight,
who is trying to close the portals that allow fairies to help humans in time of need.
[1. Space and time—Fiction.   2. Fairies—Fiction.   3. Magic—Fiction.
4. Adventure and adventurers—Fiction.]   I. Title.
PZ7.M446513Fae   2008
[Fic]—dc22   2007051848
ISBN 978-0-15-206345-0

Text set in Adobe Jenson Pro
Designed by Lydia D'moch

First edition
A C E G H F D B

Printed in the United States of America

To my daughter Erinn and my niece Deborah,
my first listeners, who loved the story before it grew,
when both it and they were small

The
Faerie
Door

Prologue

EVER SO LONG AGO, high in the treetops of her hidden city, Edwina, Queen of the Faeries, held council with her court. Intent seriousness was etched upon the features of each wild and lovely face in her retinue. Radiance from faintly luminous leaves upon the overhanging boughs bathed everything in a soft, silvery light. A circular platform, situated high in the treetops above the tallest palace spire, served as her council chamber.

"I see dark forces with sinister intent reaching into the mortal world to wreak havoc and impose their designs of chaos and wickedness," declared the Faerie Queen. "Were they to succeed, the course of human history would be profoundly and terribly altered, and light and happiness eclipsed."

As if to punctuate her words, a fragrant wind sighed through the boughs above and about them, softly moving the leaves to and fro.

"And so, in ancient times interconnecting gates were fashioned—portals between our world and theirs—for a total separation shall never be permitted. Our fate is intertwined with theirs, after all, and any ill befalling them weakens us also in the end."

The Faerie Queen unfolded a velvet cloth that lay on the table before her. Her court gasped to see the glitter of lovely rings, their gemstones sparkling with subtle crimson fire. "These rings have great magical power, and can open the portals between worlds. I shall dispatch troops of you into the mortal world to find a suitable hiding place for each ring."

And so it was that faeries entered our world in nocturnal processions. They moved through wild moorlands, their silver and blue garments sparkling in the moonlight; they crept along the eaves of dark woods, their lanterns dimly aglow, danced through starlit pastures, and walked cloaked through snowy meadows. Most came quite close indeed to human habitation, while a few even moved silently through the hushed upstairs corridors of sleeping households. They kept at their task until they fulfilled their mission. Each and every ring was hidden to await the child who would find it in due time.

When they were finished their queen was pleased and said, "For each ring there is a child destined to find it in times of trouble. And the children who find the rings shall have their imagination take wing, for they shall cross between worlds. And so shall evil and darkness be diminished—for the heart of each child shall call out to us and we shall answer every call."

Chapter 1

Northumberland, England, 1890

VICTORIA DEVENY was very cross. She stood beside her bags on the platform of the small railway station at Cotby, watching the Blue Comet Limited puff away into the distance, until the black smoke from the locomotive's stack dissipated against the far-off treetops.

Victoria scowled and twirled her parasol in annoyance. She tried fixing the porter with a contemptuous look, but her efforts were wasted. He continued to nap in his chair behind the ticket window, his green visor pulled down low over his eyes.

Victoria folded her arms, sighed, and prodded one of her brown leather bags with her toe. After a bit she sighed once more and sat down on the wooden bench in the shade beneath a posted railway timetable. Uncle Dexter had probably forgotten all about her! How dare he! Her eyes narrowed menacingly. If he really had forgotten, he would regret it.

Finally, she heard the rattle of an approaching carriage. Her uncle's driver was very apologetic, thrice regretting his tardiness and twice begging her pardon. Victoria tossed her head and stepped disdainfully past him up into the carriage, her nose high in the air.

"Fetch all my bags and hurry, if you please," she said as she settled into the velvet cushions. "I have been waiting quite long enough. And do be careful—there are breakables."

In a moment they were off, down a long wooded lane leading from Cotby toward Summerwind, her uncle's estate.

As they drove, Victoria found her anger fading. The day was beautiful and her summer holidays had barely begun. No more French conjugations or Latin verbs for three whole months! And best of all, no grueling ballet practices under the exacting eye of Mademoiselle Andre, repeating the same postures at the bar and the same formal steps over and over again.

The carriage moved between sunlit fields and shaded hedgerows. After following a slow curving rise, they reached thickets of purple lilac and the scent of the blossoms filled the interior. Victoria heard the drowsy hum of bumblebees, even over the rattle of the wheels. One especially large bee buzzed in through the carriage window and flew about aimlessly for a moment before realizing its mistake and flying out again, without so much as a how-do-you-do.

Despite all her efforts to the contrary, Victoria smiled at the beauty of the day. The carriage descended into a hollow and rumbled across the stone bridge that spanned one corner of a dappled pond. A dragonfly flitted alongside and then abruptly darted away to disappear across the water.

Victoria felt a thrill as they reached a bright meadow brimming full of blue cornflowers. She could finally glimpse the rooftops and chimneys of Summerwind just ahead.

Out in the meadow, a hundred feet from the carriage, Victoria's uncle Dexter sprang into view, butterfly net in hand. He was gesturing enthusiastically, wearing field tweeds, pith helmet, and thick-soled expedition oxfords. Her uncle did not even seem to notice her carriage, but continued leaping eagerly toward a large butterfly, whose meandering flight was taking it farther afield by the second.

Victoria rolled her eyes. And to make matters worse—if that were even possible—Penrod Periwinkle and his bookish sister Adelaide burst from the undergrowth to join her uncle. They, too, were armed with huge butterfly nets. Adelaide clutched her hat to her head with one hand and waved her net at Victoria with the other. She was the only one who bothered to notice Victoria's arrival at all. Then, with shrill cries of "Nymphalidae" and "Camberwell Beauty," all three madly dashed off.

Victoria shook her head and shut her eyes to blot out the sight of her uncle and his ridiculous friends. "Whatever butterfly that is, I am positive that it is quite safe indeed— especially from them!" she muttered to herself. Victoria had noticed, however, that the butterfly sported an exceptionally large wingspan. In fact, she hadn't ever seen one quite half as large!

By the time the carriage passed through the wrought iron archway, Victoria already had its door half open. Before the wheels had crunched to a halt on the gravel drive, she was halfway up the steps to the formal entrance doors, where Summerwind servants awaited her arrival.

First in line was Mrs. Hampstead, her uncle's housekeeper, head of the maids and kitchen staff. Beside Mrs. Hampstead stood Sheffington, the butler and chief of the menservants. Accompanying them was Ellen, an upstairs maid.

At least I have a welcoming committee among the staff, thought Victoria.

Mrs. Hampstead greeted Victoria formally. Although the housekeeper seemed incapable of exhibiting affection in the customary sense, she had two traits that Victoria admired above all. She was both punctual and predictable. One could set a railway timepiece by Mrs. Hampstead's activities. If Victoria wished to prowl the house at night, or explore its attics at odd hours, she had only to memorize Mrs. Hampstead's unvarying schedule to know precisely where she would be at any given moment. This knowledge had served Victoria well in times past.

Sheffington bowed stiffly, hands held rigidly at his sides, his thumbs aligned precisely to his trouser seams. Victoria was always amazed at how he could fasten his collar so tightly and keep his tie so perfectly straight. Sheffington had lines of seriousness permanently etched in his face, but his genuine fondness for Victoria was revealed by the slight smile that appeared only when she was present.

Victoria said a polite hello to Mrs. Hampstead, but as she reached out to shake Sheffington's hand, she quite shocked him by quickly embracing him instead. "Hello, Sheffington. I hope you are well!" she said solemnly in her deepest and most serious tone, which was neither very deep nor too serious. Sheffington coughed, then beamed. He replied that he hoped she would have a delightful summer holiday.

Ellen smiled at Victoria as she curtsied, properly clad in her starched uniform, lace apron, and prim ribboned cap. Victoria greeted her affectionately, and as the two of them disappeared into the house, a footman was summoned to help with her things.

"I am going to have many adventures this summer, Ellen, and explore all the secrets of this house!" Victoria promised. As they ascended the first flight of stairs, she paused, dancing on alternating feet, to tug off her side-buttoned boots.

"Has Mrs. Hampstead excused you from your other duties so you can be devoted to me?"

"Yes, miss, just as usual for your holidays," Ellen replied. "And I have set out some suitable clothes for you."

"Thank you, Ellen. Have you seen any of the strange lights out in the wood, like we glimpsed last autumn, before I had to return to horrid old Prosingham?"

"Yes, miss, I saw them once, and Clara saw them a second time. The last time was perhaps a fortnight ago."

"I will get to the bottom of this," Victoria declared. "And you must cover for me when I disappear on my excursions."

Ellen smiled. "I am at your service, miss."

As they climbed the last few steps, a clock struck the Windsor chimes in a distant corner of the house. They entered a short hallway that led to Victoria's suite of rooms. To the right was the door to Victoria's bedchamber, and to the left was the nursery. Some of Victoria's earliest memories were of playing in that nursery. Nothing ever changed at Summerwind. If she rummaged about in the toy chest, she was certain she would find some of her favorite playthings.

But she would not find the big rocking horse. For it had frightened Victoria so much that her uncle had it taken away. It had alarming glass eyes, and once when she had a fever, it had vividly haunted her dreams. In her delirium it came alive, rocking down the nursery passage, mouth agape. But instead of neighing, it groaned a horrid human-sounding groan, and its eyes blazed crimson. When the maids awakened her from her dream, she realized that it was she herself who had been groaning.

Victoria took off her gloves and her boater, tossing them onto the plush cushions of her window seat. The window seat, where she often slept, was one of her two favorite things about the room, the other being the elaborately carved book-case completely filling one wall. Next to back issues of *Chatterbox Magazine*, rows and rows of leather-bound volumes lined the shelves. Victoria didn't remember most of the stories she had been read as a child. She was best at making up her own adventures as she went along.

After Ellen assisted Victoria with changing into a dove gray dress of summer wool, they crossed the little hallway and sat together at the nursery table, which was covered with blocks, school slates, bits of broken chalk, and a toy steamship.

"Tell me more about the lights, Ellen," Victoria insisted. "What color were they, and how many of them were there, and in what direction were they moving?"

"Well, miss," Ellen replied, "the first time there were only two or three of them, but the next time, when Clara and I both glimpsed them, there were five or six. And they were blue, just like the ones you and I saw last autumn. As for their direction, they seemed to be moving aimlessly, like fireflies do. At first I thought that they were right outside the windowpane, but then I realized they were farther away than they appeared. They were moving about, in and out of the willows, and then crossed the meadow to disappear into the poplars beyond."

Victoria nodded, deep in thought. As she glanced about the nursery, her eyes fell on a small framed painting that hung on the wall. She had seen it hundreds of times before, but now she really noticed it. She stepped over a rag doll and a tin soldier to study it more closely. The painting depicted a tiny, dark-haired beauty with gossamer wings and a wreath of wildflowers plaited in her hair. She was seated on the limb of a tree with the full moon rising behind her. The caption read, "Edwina, Queen of the Faeries."

Something about the painting stirred Victoria's imagination. The painter had conveyed the beauty and magnetism of his subject as convincingly as if she were real.

"Oh, Ellen, I am sure that the lights are faeries!" Victoria said. "I believe that the faeries at Summerwind are the blue faeries, quite like the faerie queen in this painting."

Victoria did not notice Ellen biting her lip as she tried not to smile. Just then a creak on the staircase warned them that someone was approaching. It was Clara, another upstairs maid, who curtsied and told them that Victoria was expected downstairs for luncheon with her uncle and the Periwinkles. Victoria scowled and kicked one of the tin soldiers, a green-coated Prussian fusilier. Its head promptly flew off and landed in a far corner of the room.

When Victoria entered the lesser dining room, her uncle Dexter rose to greet her. "My dear!" he said in his awkward yet affectionate way. "We are so glad to have you with us again for the summer holidays. I am truly sorry for not greeting you earlier, but my colleagues and I had a Camberwell Beauty nearly within our grasp and it was a stupendously large specimen!" The entire time her uncle was speaking, he was shaking her hand both warmly and absentmindedly—as if she were not only another adult, but one whose hand he had quite forgotten to stop shaking.

"Yes, of course, Uncle Dexter," Victoria said, withdrawing her hand with some difficulty. She patted her uncle's arm, and her expression was so sweet, and her tone so warm, that he ought to have instantly been on his guard. "There was no offense taken and I had quite forgotten about it!"

Victoria's uncle was attired in a velvet smoking jacket with wide quilted lapels. His hair was long and his face a trifle too sensitive for a proper lord. He wore a longish beard and mustache.

Certainly neither Victoria's uncle Dexter, nor his friends the Periwinkles, noticed Victoria's eyes flash as she took her seat at the table. Penrod Periwinkle sported spectacles with such thick lenses that he resembled an owl, his eyes blinking slowly. Victoria often amused the servants with pantomimes of his oddities. His sister Adelaide was a slender woman with a long neck, prominent nose, and high cheeks. She had a tiny downturned mouth and a high supercilious voice. She began by telling Victoria how truly splendid she looked.

As the meal progressed, Victoria heard all about their hobbies and research projects—primarily their efforts to capture every butterfly unfortunate enough to take wing in all of Northumberland. Victoria feigned interest only for so long, then could no longer hide the fact that she was bored beyond all imagining.

As the others discussed things that only the most stodgy of adults could find interesting, Victoria amused herself by picking every bit of turnip from her Cornish pasty. Then she removed her leeks and onions, setting them aside with a look of fastidious distaste. Next she ate the perfect golden crust of the pastry itself. Finally, separating each bit of potato and beef into two piles on opposite sides of her plate, she meticulously ate alternate bites from each pile, kicking her heels against her chair leg and wishing that the meal was over.

At last, when Victoria was done and the adults were sipping sherry from tiny glasses, she asked if she might be excused. As she got up from the table, her uncle interrupted his friends for a moment. "Oh, Victoria, you may eat supper belowstairs this evening. I will be out late, attending a dinner party down in Clewly."

Victoria sniffed with elaborate distaste and turned away.

Another affront to be avenged, she thought. *Imagine him not staying at home to entertain his newly arrived niece. At the very least he could take me along . . . though I daresay it would prove a dreadful bore!*

Then Victoria remembered the ginger beer she had enjoyed with her Cornish pasty, and it gave her a perfectly wicked idea. She hurried downstairs to the kitchens and begged a fresh bottle from the cook. On her way back, she crept into her uncle's study and tiptoed to the large table, which was covered with leather-bound books and star atlases. Here she found a full decanter of very expensive Madeira dozing pleasantly under an ornate stopper. This she carefully removed, and with a satisfied smile, poured nearly half her bottle of ginger beer into the decanter, spoiling a great deal of fine thirty-year-old Sandeman Malmsey.

Victoria left the study with an angelic expression illuminating her face.

IN THE AFTERNOON Victoria decided to go for a walk with Ellen through the enclosed garden behind the house. It was nearly an acre in size and surrounded by a high brick wall. A winding pathway led across the rear lawn to its gateway. A second gate led into the garden from the adjoining property, Mayweather. Victoria's uncle Dexter and the owner of Mayweather had been schoolmates and both properties shared the garden.

As they walked, Victoria chatted to Ellen about how she had cleverly gotten another girl blamed for one of her own pranks at Prosingham. Ellen found the courage to venture a timid "Perhaps you oughtn't have done it," to which Victoria replied, "Nonsense! It was a capital idea and I would have given a princely sum to see Honorine's face as it unfolded!"

When they passed beneath the archway of the gate, they found themselves in a different world altogether. Every view within the garden was calculated to please the eye. The lawns were well mowed and fragrant. The intricate brick pathways wound about miniature hills, descended through shady groves, and passed sun-dappled meadows full of wildflowers. All was in harmonious array.

Victoria suggested they take different paths to see where they might meet. Even in a private garden on this isolated estate, who knew what one might encounter around the next bend in the path?

And so it was that Victoria encountered the Mayweather nanny, who was seated on a stone bench, beside a small sunlit lawn, nigh a thicket of blooming Bradford pears. If Victoria had paid closer attention to her botany lessons at Prosingham, she would have known that Bradford pears should have stopped blooming a month ago.

This nanny was capped, aproned, and uniformed as was customary for her station. She sat on the bench, reading a small leather-bound volume, while gently rocking a pram to and fro with her free hand, soothing the unseen child within.

"How do you do?" Victoria said. The Mayweather nanny glanced up and smiled. There was something uncommon about her manner, although Victoria couldn't decide exactly what. A wisp of dark hair fell across her forehead. Her nose was upturned, and a hint of a smile made her appear imper-tinent, as if she was about to burst into laughter. The nanny reached up with a lace-cuffed hand to brush the stray lock back into place.

"How do you do! You are the niece of Lord Dexter Deveny, master of Summerwind, are you not?" she inquired.

Victoria's eyebrows raised a trifle. How had she known? "Yes, I'm Victoria Deveny—visiting my uncle for the summer holiday. What are you reading?"

"It is a volume of faerie stories, entitled *Glade of the Moon.* I find it quite mysterious."

The reference to faerie stories piqued Victoria's curiosity at once.

"Are you interested in faeries?" the nanny asked. "I have heard that there are some hereabouts, though I haven't seen any myself."

"My maid Ellen glimpsed strange blue lights moving down in the willows. Have you seen anything of that sort?" Victo-ria kept her tone casual, but it was obvious that she was most interested in the answer.

The Mayweather nanny regarded Victoria quietly. "I dare-say I have not," she said dismissively, then turned her atten-tion to her book once more. Victoria was about to bid her farewell and continue on her walk when the nanny spoke again.

"A bit of advice, Victoria! First, if you see a book of faerie stories titled *Glade of the Moon,* you would do well to pick it up, for it makes interesting reading indeed. Second, have you noticed the gazebo on the rise behind you? I have heard that there are surprising things to be glimpsed if one stands just beneath it."

Victoria did not much care for the familiar tone the Mayweather nanny used with her. It was not the place of a servant to be giving advice, after all. Nonetheless, she looked round, and was startled to see the little gazebo standing just where the nanny said it would be, on a grassy rise directly behind her. She was surprised because she hadn't noticed it before. Unlike everything else in the garden, it was decrepit and in good need of repair. The rise upon which it stood wasn't very high at all. Victoria couldn't imagine what she could possibly glimpse from there.

Victoria walked to the top of the rise and stood before the gazebo. The paint was peeling badly. Pieces of the lattice about the domed top and sides were coming apart. When she turned to glance back at the Mayweather nanny, she was astonished to find that both the nanny and her perambulator were gone! Victoria was certain she should have heard the wheels rattle on the bricks at least. *How strange*, she thought as she stepped up onto the sagging platform. *How very strange indeed! And the view is quite common after all!* There were trees, and more trees, then the rooftops and chimneys of Summerwind.

She stood still, peering intently, and that was when something caught her eye. A person taller than Victoria would not have seen it, for the view would have been obscured by the branches. A person shorter than Victoria wouldn't have been able to peer over the elderberry thicket at all. Nor would it have been visible from ground level, as it was nestled in a cleft between gables.

Victoria was gazing straight at the conical roof of the tower, directly above her rooms in the west wing. She squinted to be sure, but it was unmistakable! Where the slates of the tower roof curved round to blend into the steeply pitched roof of the house, she glimpsed a tiny, stained-glass window.

Victoria knew every nook and cranny of the rooms beneath the tower and she was certain none of them had a stained-glass window. That meant that there was a secret room hidden in the roof of the tower!

Breathless with excitement, she dashed down the little rise, so intent upon her discovery that she nearly collided with Ellen, who was coming the other way. They started back the way Ellen had come, descending a narrow side path where the frosts of many winters had jumbled the pattern of bricks. Victoria wasn't really listening to whatever it was that Ellen was saying. Her head was humming. That very night she would try to find the door to the hidden room!

"Ellen," she interrupted. "Are you acquainted with the Mayweather nanny? I had a pleasant chat with her. She was rocking a pram as we talked."

A puzzled look crossed Ellen's honest face. "Why, there hasn't been a child at Mayweather for years! The house is shut up; there's only a groundskeeper on the premises. The entire family is on extended holiday in Portobello!"

Victoria's heart thudded with a strange excitement. "Perhaps I was mistaken," she said casually.

"Oh, Victoria, you awful thing! I never know when you're playing one of your games." Ellen shook her head in an annoyance that was more feigned than genuine.

But Victoria's head was swimming with thoughts of adventure all the way back to the house.

WHEN VICTORIA JOINED the servants for supper below-stairs, they weren't as reluctant to behave normally as one might expect. They were accustomed to having her about in the summer and they quite liked her. Victoria could be snobbish in her way, yet in other respects she was anything but. Her uncle once said she was a curious mixture of sugar and sour balls, and one never knew what the ratio would be from one moment to the next.

She often amused the servants by making fun of their lord's stuffiest friends. Victoria ate little more than half her bacon and cabbage pie before launching into an impression of Adelaide Periwinkle. Anything to distract herself from her excitement—for later that night, she would find the secret room! Victoria could hardly bear the waiting.

"Adelaide Periwinkle has a very long neck!" she said, interrupting several side conversations about the table. Victoria pushed her shoulders down to elongate her own neck, stretching it to a ludicrous extent. Then she raised her chin just so. "Adelaide Periwinkle has a small mouth, too!" Victoria pursed her lips, even managing to turn down the corners of her mouth in a surprisingly accurate mimicry. "And Adelaide Periwinkle has a prominent nose!" Her voice, constricted by the shape of her lips, became an octave higher and more pene-trating. Victoria did not have a prominent nose herself, so she made the best of it by licking her spoon and sticking it to the tip.

Then she raised her head to regard the servants down the length of her now preposterous nose. She began lecturing them in the most solemn tones about the preparation of minced butterfly, a delicacy she was certain would be the culi-nary specialty at the Periwinkles'.

True to form, she soon had them all convulsing with laugh-ter. Clara clutched her napkin to her mouth and laughed until she cried, while Ellen put her head down on her arms and gasped for breath. Even Mrs. Hampstead, who was determined to show no amusement whatsoever, got up from the table and fled into the serving room. There she thrust her head into a dumbwaiter to burst into helpless merriment. Sheffington re-tained his composure best of all, but his face did redden, and the corners of his mouth twitched. Due to Victoria's presence, the supper was a rousing success.

Soon Victoria excused herself, for she was tired after her long railway journey. She promised them impressions of the staid headmistress and the fierce matrons who ruled at Pros-ingham next time.

Victoria and Ellen ascended the long flights of stairs to-gether. The house was solemn and empty when her uncle was away. The sun had set and all but a few of the gas jets had been lit. The ticking of a mantel clock from a distant room echoed in the stillness.

Victoria got into her nightclothes while Ellen folded her things. Then she knelt on the window seat, peering out into the dark while Ellen brushed her hair.

"Do you think we shall see the lights tonight, Ellen?" Victoria asked hopefully.

The willows were tall shadows against a darkling sky. Even the familiar lawns and hedges became mysterious in the nighttime. Victoria saw that the willow boughs were moving in a breeze that murmured about the corners of the house.

"This kind of wind that comes up from nowhere in the summertime has a name," Ellen observed.

"What name is that?" asked Victoria.

"My old aunt Myrtle, rest her soul, always called it faerie wind," Ellen replied. "And she should know, for she spent her childhood at the foot of the Eildon Hills." Victoria nodded solemnly. Everyone knew that the Eildon Hills were nigh the doors of Faerieland.

Victoria stared intently into the darkness until her eyes grew heavy. She was determined to stay awake until Ellen went to bed. But she was steadily losing her battle with sleep. By the time Ellen finished brushing Victoria's hair, she had drifted off. Ellen covered her with a quilted counterpane, then carefully blew out the candle and tiptoed from Victoria's room, closing the door softly behind her.

As Victoria slept, she had the most peculiar dream. She was slowly stealing into a cavern in total darkness. She crept cautiously forward, feeling her way along the wall with her hand. At last she came to a vaulted chamber. She knew it to be large by the change in air currents, but she couldn't see a thing. All was inky black. Then she heard the sound of breathing, and it was most unpleasant. She could tell straightaway that the breathing was far too loud to be human, and that it was the breath of something very large indeed!

Victoria noticed the cavern was frightfully cold. She groped forward in the darkness until her hand touched something that wasn't rock. It was ice cold and scaly. The scales were immense. Suddenly, thirty feet above her head, two great pale eyes flickered open. In the luminescent glow of the eyes, Victoria could see that she was in a cavern filled with the coils of a vast dragon. It lowered its massive head until its icy breath made her shiver.

"How do you do?" the creature said pleasantly enough, which only added to its air of menace. "I am the Ice Dragon. And you shall not have what is mine!"

Victoria awoke from her dream with a start. She sat up groggily, but then remembered her task, and her heart leaped with excitement. She sprang to her feet, casting off her covers.

Victoria found where Ellen put the lucifers and was trying to strike one to light a candle, when something outside caught her eye. Blue lights were moving above the hedges, near the willows. She stared in rapt fascination as they moved to and fro. They were larger than fireflies, and when they approached the trees, their dim illumination cast enough light to play off the leaves.

Victoria watched intently, her nose pressed to the glass. She thought she could even distinguish graceful forms and twinkling wings as they hovered. Eager for a closer view, she determined to run down the dark silent stairs, rush outside, and dash across the dewy lawn in her bare feet. She had just pulled on her dressing gown, her hands shaking with anticipation, when the clouds obscuring the moon parted to bathe the lawn in ethereal light.

At that precise moment, she heard the crunch of her uncle's carriage wheels on the drive. She rushed to the window again, only to see the blue lights slowly disappearing beyond the willows.

Victoria slid off her dressing gown, letting it fall to the floor. Her disappointment was tempered by the knowledge that at least she could still search for the secret room. She decided to put on her finest clothes for her adventure. After all, it simply would not do to meet faeries dressed in anything but her finest. She rummaged about in the steamer trunk for her petticoats and her fanciest dress. It was white, with a high collar, long sleeves, and a snowy lace front.

She changed quickly, her fingers awkward at the buttons. *There must be at least twenty!* she thought with great impatience. It was a much easier process when Ellen assisted her. But at last she finished fastening nearly all of them.

She quickly rebrushed her hair—Ellen's careful earlier work saving her time—and slipped on her best pair of embroidered silken hose. She gave up trying to find her white shoes, after a chaotic rummaging under her bed revealed only her satin ballet slippers, which were, of course, completely unsuitable for adventures. She would simply embark upon the unknown in her stocking feet!

Victoria struck a lucifer to light the candle. Holding it carefully, she crept softly across the corridor to the nursery. There she spent the next hour rapping on wall panels, tugging on every sconce, and wiggling each shelf, expecting at any moment to hear the sound of a secret lock giving way.

Finally, she permitted herself respite, sitting in the rocking chair where Summerwind nursemaids had soothed her to sleep when she was little. She surveyed the room. By now she was sure that the entrance to the secret room wasn't in the nursery. Her search had been thorough.

She went back to her bedroom to repeat the same process, making a mess that would certainly have Ellen cross with her come morning. She tapped on the panels below the window seat, investigated the cedar-scented depths of her wardrobe, and pressed every knot in the wainscot.

She was close to abandoning her efforts entirely when something caught her eye. One of the books on the highest shelf was out of place. All the others were as neat as a pin. She drew closer and remembered what the Mayweather nanny had said. A peculiar feeling stole over her as she saw that the out-of-place volume was titled *Glade of the Moon*. She stood on tiptoe, reaching high to press it back into place.

Victoria's heart skipped a beat when she heard a soft click, and saw the bookshelf silently turn sideways in its frame. A set of tight spiral stairs curved upward into the darkness. As Victoria stepped closer, the flame of her candle danced fitfully in the breath of stale air that swept down the dusty passage. She took a deep breath and ascended the stairs.

She did not hear the bookshelf silently swivel shut to close the way behind her.

Victoria's shadow glided along the wall as she crept up the steps, going round in tight spiral turns. It seemed to be a very long way, and she was afraid that the candle would blow out and leave her in darkness.

Finally, it grew brighter as she came around the last turn into an open space. She stood wide-eyed, one hand clutching the banister at the top of the stair, the other trembling as she held her candle high aloft. The room in which she found herself was larger than she expected. Bright beams of moonlight cascaded in through its stained-glass window, bathing everything in a strange ethereal glow.

Victoria gazed at the ceiling high above her head, where wooden beams were expertly joined to form the peak. She was standing in a circular library! Shelves containing thousands of leather-bound books were ranked all around the walls. Glass cabinets contained volumes with ribbed spines crumbling with age. A table stood nearby on lion-paw legs, more books scattered across its dusty surface. A high-backed chair was placed at one end of the table. In the exact center of the room loomed a fantastical wooden arch carved with endlessly repeating elaborate designs of mythical creatures and spiral patterns.

On each side of the arch was a pedestal, connected by low railings. One held a large silver candlestick bearing a thick half-melted candle. On the other danced a lifelike statue of a faerie poised frozen in midstep. Her wings were a masterwork of intricacy; and how the artist had rendered wood into shapes so fine and delicate made Victoria marvel.

She stepped across the dusty floor and carefully lit the candle in the silver candlestick with her own, then blew hers out. She sat down in the high-backed chair, and discovered that her feet wouldn't even reach the floor. Victoria's eyes were immediately drawn to the large volume closest to her. It lay open on the table, its pages cracked with age. The printing appeared to have been inked by hand long ago, but Victoria found that she could still read the words if she concentrated. She bent closer. *Poems and Verses from the Realms of Magic,* read the title page. She swallowed hard and turned the page.

Victoria noticed that the right-hand pages of the book contained verses, but the left-hand pages appeared blank. She began to read the first poem aloud in a low voice.

"When the sun sets crimson through the trees,
And fragrant comes the sighing breeze;
Then magic walks the eventide,
And myths take shape and live."

Suddenly, tiny flecks of light and darker spots of ink swirled about the surface of the left-hand page. She watched with fascination as shapes and colors took form before her very eyes! In a moment an illustration materialized, fully composed on the page.

It was a scene of a sunset beyond tall trees in a wood. The red hue of the sunset highlighted the tree branches with an almost photographic clarity. It made her long to explore strange realms and seek forgotten treasures. Victoria was captivated for quite some time. Then she took a deep breath, and ever so carefully turned the crumbling page. Her fingers were gentle, almost reverent, for she was convinced that she was reading a magical text.

The poem on the following page gave Victoria pause.

The realm of winter night conceals
The ice drake dreaming deep.
The firedrake lies coiled upon red gold,
His ceaseless vigil to keep.

She knew from her lessons at Prosingham that the word *drake* was an archaic term for dragon. Remembering her unpleasant dream, Victoria turned her gaze to the left-hand page, where flecks of light and bits of ink were already transforming before her eyes at dazzling speed.

A moment later the image of a pale dragon took shape, like the one she had glimpsed in her dream earlier that night. She shuddered. The image was so real she could feel the icy vapor of its breath. She turned the page quickly, afraid that the dragon might actually address her if she lingered.

The poem on the third page perplexed her at first. It sounded like a riddle. But it seemed natural that there might be riddles, puzzles, and mysteries concealed in magical books, in secret rooms, at the top of hidden staircases. So she read the poem slowly, studying each word.

Beneath the faerie's dancing feet sleeps power beyond
  compare;
A ring to charge the mystic gate—step through it if you dare.

Victoria watched in silent anticipation as the flecks of light and bits of ink swirled to arrange themselves on the opposite page. When the image was fully composed, Victoria bent low, studying it closely. This image reminded her of a type of photograph called a silver oxide daguerreotype taken with a box camera.

There was a mysterious sunlit meadow, all grown up to wildflowers. A long lattice wall covered in ivy sagged along one side. In the middle of the wall stood a little lattice gate leaning to one side. She studied the picture closely, then turned the page. The fourth poem read as follows:

Two kindred spirits and two rings,
Two gates that find the fey;
From sundered times the orbs they'll bring,
And with power the shadow gainsay.

This time the image that appeared was quite different. At first Victoria couldn't tell what it was, but as it became clearer, she saw it was a perfectly round orb, fashioned of the bluest crystal. The orb was absolutely smooth, about two inches in diameter. The beauty of its translucent hue, and the way it reflected light, was mesmerizing.

Victoria left the book lying open and got to her feet and peered about the room. She had the strangest feeling that something even more mysterious than a secret stair or a magic book awaited her. She was certain the verses and images were clues. The third poem kept echoing over and over in her mind.

Beneath the faerie's dancing feet sleeps power beyond compare . . .

She crept toward the beautifully carved image of the dancing faerie. She studied the wooden statue very closely, noticing with a thrill that it was the same likeness that hung on her nursery wall. It reminded her strongly of the Mayweather nanny!

Victoria wondered if there was something for her to find beneath the faerie's feet. She rapped on the fan-shaped base of the pedestal and didn't think it sounded hollow. But when she reached out a tentative fingertip to touch the smooth form of the faerie's heel there was a faint click, and Victoria gasped. Her hands shook as she reached out again, this time with two quivering fingertips, to press the heel more firmly. The statue swiveled from its pedestal and silently swung off to the side. To her astonishment, she saw that there was a velvet-lined compartment built into the base of the pedestal, directly beneath the faerie.

Despite the candlelight, Victoria had difficulty peering into the depths of the compartment. She took a deep breath, reaching down as far as she could, hoping there were no spiders. Her fingertips touched something round and cool. She drew her hand free and was amazed to discover the most beautiful ring she had ever laid eyes upon.

It was fashioned from two interlocking silver bands, joining to uphold a dark crimson gemstone. She slipped it onto her finger. To her surprise, it fit perfectly. Victoria held her hand up, turning it this way and that. The gemstone sparkled in the candlelight.

Once again the words of the third poem came to mind.

A ring to charge the mystic gate—step through it if you dare.

She glanced at the ring on her finger, then up at the arch. Could the "mystic gate" be looming there before her now, scarcely two steps away? And where might it lead? Victoria's mouth went dry and her heart fluttered. She took a deep quivering breath, steeling herself for high adventure. Then she stepped bravely forward and stood directly below the arch of the gate.

"Why, nothing has happened after all!" she said to herself, in a mixture of disappointment and relief.

A split second later Victoria vanished in a flash of brilliant light.

Chapter 2

Alton Bay, New Hampshire, 1966

IN THE DEAD OF NIGHT, a wind from nowhere began to roil the waters of the lake that bordered the little town of Alton Bay. The water changed from midnight blue to charcoal gray beneath vanishing stars, and the waves churned into whitecaps. Thunder muttered sullenly back and forth between the steep wooded hills that hemmed in the bay upon all sides. A dark rag of cloud detached from its massive thunderhead and floated toward the sleeping town. As it drew near, lightning flashed from its depths.

There were no boats out on the bay at that hour, which was fortunate. They were all safely moored at their docks or secure in boathouses. The water grew turbulent and tossed against the pilings. The motorboats and light sailboats rocked and bumped at their moorings. Soon the cloud grew larger and darker still, seething and boiling. Those who were awakened by the thunder shut their windows, slammed their doors, and went back to bed. They did not see the strange black cloud twisting in the air like a wicked genie. For it was no normal storm that had come to Alton Bay.

The cloud tore open, revealing its black insides, flickering with purple lightning. A shadow took shape within the cloud, forming the likeness of a great rearing horse. This was no placid workhorse, nor even a spirited racehorse, but a huge, heavily armored charger—a beast equipped for war. And upon its wide back, this horse bore the shape of a dark knight!

Both horse and rider grew larger and more menacing still as the churning cloud expanded. The hulking knight was clad in black armor, and rose high in his stirrups to brandish a broadsword. Lightning crackled down its blade. His black helm was equipped with horns and his eyes glowed baleful red. The knight's charcoal gray shield was emblazoned with a black star with sharply defined rays projecting outward in all directions. This ensign was no twinkling emblem of light, but a black hole.

An opposing wind sighed down from the hills behind the bay to clash with the storm. A bright mass of fireflies appeared in the trees along the edge of the water, as if defending the town from the dreadful apparition.

The fresh wind from the hills began breaking the dark cloud into fragments. Within moments the night sky cleared enough to reveal a few tentative stars. Soon the shrinking cloud had been pushed far out over the center of the lake. With a final crash of thunder—and perhaps what could be imagined as a distant screaming neigh—the apparition faded altogether. The fireflies and the wind from the hills had driven it away.

THE FOLLOWING DAY did not begin well for Elliot Good. His legs churned on the pedals of his bicycle as he shifted into third gear. Elliot's mother had splurged when she bought him the Chopper. It was candy red and had a long black leather seat with a high back. It came equipped with raised handlebars, a stick shift, and a little front wheel. It was Elliot's pride and joy.

He practically flew over a rise in the road as he made an abrupt left turn, skidding down a small overgrown lane, under the overshadowing boughs of tall pines. His heart was pounding in his chest. The bullies had threatened to kill him if they caught him again, and Elliot believed them. As far as he knew, he was pedaling for his very life.

It had all started when Elliot and his mother moved into the big Victorian house on the hill above Alton Bay. When the moving van had pulled away from the driveway, there they were—three boys, sitting on their bicycles.

Stevie St. Michael, their ringleader, smiled and seemed friendly at first. But even though his mother had urged him to go down and introduce himself, Elliot hung back. He sensed something contemptuous behind their smiles . . . something mean.

One day not long after, as he rode his Chopper down the hill from their home to the Alton Bay beach to buy a Green Hornet comic book at the little newsstand, the bullies found him. They were sitting on a low stone wall, waiting. Stevie said that if Elliot paid fifty cents a day, he would be safe. Otherwise, he warned, something very bad might happen.

The next time Elliot encountered them, he tried to stand

up for himself, but it was no use. Stevie punched him hard and split his lip. The others mocked him and pushed him down, grinding his face into the dirt. It was three against one and they were older, bigger, and stronger than Elliot.

When he returned home bleeding, Elliot told his mother, Janet Good, that he had run over a rock in the road and been thrown from his bicycle. He felt bad about the lie, but she had more than enough to worry about. He had gotten the mail frequently enough to know that it was nothing but bills and late notices. His mother's paintings weren't selling well and money was tight. Elliot knew she worried all the time.

Now the bullies had found him again, and he was praying that his bike would save his life. He flashed down the lane under the trees, pedaling madly. His heart was in his throat. He was dismayed to hear triumphant yells and the skid of bicycle tires on the pavement behind him.

Elliot risked a glance back over his shoulder. Maybe if he could just get far enough ahead he would have time to break off a branch and defend himself. That was when the front wheel of his bicycle caught a pine root and turned sideways. Before he knew what was happening, he was flung headlong over the handlebars and landed in the lane with a thud.

Elliot lay gasping, his fear replaced with pain. Suddenly, things became dreamlike and vague. He saw a young woman come striding toward him down the lane, as if she had just materialized from nowhere. She wore flat shoes, capri pants, and a plain short-sleeved blouse. Her dark hair was pulled back in a ponytail and one lock of it kept getting in her eyes.

The woman bent down to study him, her expression a mixture of concern and fondness. Elliot didn't know why she seemed so pleased to see him, as he had never set eyes on her before. She patted his shoulder. "Hello, Elliot Good," she whispered. She even knew his name! Elliot's mind registered that the bullies had come skidding to a halt behind him. He heard the creak of their bicycles, the scuff of their sneakers, and their heavy breathing. The kind lady ignored them for a moment.

"Just lie still, Elliot, and I'm sure you'll feel better presently!" Then she stepped lightly over him and walked to where the bullies sat waiting. They were now shifting uneasily in their seats.

All at once Elliot heard his tormentors cry out in unison, their voices terror-stricken. He pushed himself up on his elbows, peering back over his shoulder to see them pedaling away as fast as they could go. There was fear and desperation in each panic-stricken motion, as if a horrible apparition was foaming at their heels. The mysterious young woman stood watching them go, slowly shaking her head. Then she turned round and smiled as she stepped over Elliot once more to retrieve his Chopper from the bushes.

"Your bicycle is quite unharmed, Elliot. See? Just one little scratch," she said as she extended the kickstand with her foot and helped him up. Elliot gazed at her in awe.

"Thank you, ma'am," he said quietly, then hesitated. "Why did they all run away?"

The stranger smiled as she tousled his hair. "Who can say? Perhaps they glimpsed their true likenesses reflected in my face. Cruel and mean-spirited minds tend to have fearful corners in them, Elliot," she said cryptically. "I doubt they will bother you in the future, but if one of them still proves troublesome, I am acquainted with someone who may help you." Then she held the handlebars while Elliot carefully climbed back onto his bicycle.

"I see that it's made in England," she said in her curiously precise voice. "I lived there once, a long time ago—in Northumberland." Then she suggested that he pedal ahead for a dozen yards or so, to make certain that all was working properly.

As Elliot obeyed he was suddenly taken with an urge to invite her home for lunch as a thank-you. After all, she had practically saved his life, and he sensed that his mother would take to her.

Elliot stopped pedaling, and as he turned to extend his invitation, his eyes widened with astonishment. For there was no trace of the mysterious stranger! It was as if she had vanished into thin air.

THAT NIGHT AT DINNER, Elliot and his mother sat in the dining room of their home, scarcely a mile from Alton Bay. It was a large clapboard house with a wraparound veranda, tall chimneys, lots of fancy scrollwork, and a wide central staircase. They loved the house, but it required a great deal of upkeep. It badly needed a fresh coat of paint, as its appearance had become quite dingy. It was rather dark inside, because of the tall trees surrounding it, but Elliot's mother had done clever things with curtains and wallpaper to brighten it up.

There were lots of rooms upstairs, though many of them were unused. Elliot's room was at the rear of the house, and he loved his cushioned window seat. It overlooked a walled garden that had grown up to weeds. Beyond the garden wall, a dark thicket of solemn trees almost entirely concealed an old abandoned house—even larger and once far more elaborate than their own.

Elliot's mother had converted a bright room at the front of the house into her studio. It was full of easels and canvases. Cluttered tables were covered with half-empty tubes of paint, turpentine, linseed oil, and dozens of paintbrushes.

Elliot's mother often worked late into the night to complete her latest series of paintings. The art show was only days away and she wasn't quite finished. That was why they sat down to a supper of TV dinners. As they ate, Elliot thought of the mysterious woman in the lane. He had no idea how she had disappeared so abruptly. He wondered if she might possibly be a ghost.

"Our house isn't scary at all, is it?" he observed out of the blue. His mother paused, her fork raised halfway to her lips.

"What do you mean, dear?" she asked.

"Well, even though it's big, and old, and surrounded by trees, it doesn't really seem frightening. It's as though the house likes people. It's nothing like that old house up in the woods! You know, the one that's all sagging down, ready to collapse.

I think that house is haunted!" Elliot added the last bit almost hopefully.

His mother smiled. "I know what you mean. The real estate agent told me the history of both houses before we moved in. Would you like to hear about it?"

Elliot nodded.

"An Englishman named Mr. Murchison built the larger house in the center of what was then a field, high up on a hill, overlooking the town. There was more pastureland and less forest a hundred years ago. Mr. Murchison was rich, and many thought that he was titled, or perhaps that he had been a member of Parliament back in England. But there were others who suspected he was part of a secret magical order. Anyway, he was a very mysterious man. He always wore a black top hat and carried a walking stick with a fantastically carved handle. I'm told that his portrait still hangs above the mantelpiece in that old house up on the hill.

"Mr. Murchison wasn't exactly unfriendly, but he kept to himself as far as his neighbors were concerned. But it seems he was fond of costume parties, for both he and the guests he brought back from his excursions were frequently clad in clothes from another time. Several years went by. Neighbors noticed other strange things—lights moving to and fro in the wood and carriages driving up the old lake road after midnight.

"Then one day, Mr. Murchison suddenly decided the house was too large, so he had another, smaller house constructed, down at the foot of the hill—our house. It was the talk of the town when he didn't sell or lease his larger, older house, which was still in lovely condition then. He simply closed it up, locked the door, and abandoned it fully furnished. Afterward, Mr. Murchison lived in our house off and on for several years, still frequently entertaining guests at odd hours. He was often away for long periods of time. The strange thing was that his trips usually took him away in the summertime. You'd think he would choose to spend his summers here, but on the contrary, it was usually on a winter night, often during a driving snowstorm, that his carriage would return.

"Finally, Mr. Murchison departed and never returned. Eventually there was an inquest to be sure there had been no foul play. The house remained empty for nearly five more years until the legalities were taken care of. Since there were no heirs, the smaller house was sold. The larger house had fallen into such disrepair by then that no buyer would consider it. The rumors that it was haunted didn't help, either. And so it's been derelict ever since. As for Mr. Murchison, he was never seen or heard from again!"

Elliot was captivated. "I would love to explore that house!" he exclaimed.

His mother frowned. "I don't think that would be wise. The house isn't safe. It's practically falling down now."

Elliot didn't respond, but he noted that his mother hadn't actually forbidden him to do it.

They finished their dinner just before seven thirty, and Elliot begged his mother to let him watch *Batman*. It was Wednesday night and Batman and Robin had to escape from the Mad Hatter's diabolical predicament.

After *Batman* was over, Elliot's mother sent him up to bed. Janet Good had recently purchased three boxes of used hardcover books at a street fair. One of them was a collection of faerie stories called *Glade of the Moon*, which she had given to Elliot. He had a fondness for faerie stories and was a very good reader. The stories came alive to him.

The walls of Elliot's bedroom were covered with drawings of the things that captivated him most—dragons, faeries, sorcerers in dark towers, and heavily armored knights. Elliot put on his pajamas and got into bed with *Glade of the Moon*. The night was warm and his window was wide open. A breeze came up off the lake, making the curtains dance and wave.

He noticed a poem inscribed in the frontispiece of the book. It had been handwritten with an old dip pen and the ink had faded to a pale brown color. Elliot had trouble reading it at first because the style of writing was so old-fashioned, with fancy swirls and embellishments.

Beyond the dancing faerie's wings sleeps power beyond
*   compare;*
A ring to charge the mystic gate—step through it if you dare.

Elliot puzzled over the meaning of the verse, and then proceeded to read.

It was a tale about a knight, aided in his adventures by a faerie maiden who counseled him and kept him from danger. The story was excellent, but Elliot kept thinking about the mysterious verse until he fell asleep.

As the curtains waved in the soft breeze, Elliot had a strange dream. He was walking down a garden path, overshadowed by tall trees. Up ahead he saw a girl about his own age. She came toward him, pushing a baby carriage. The carriage was an antique, with large spoked wheels and a curved shape to its wicker sides. Her lacy blouse had a high collar and long puffy sleeves. She also wore a fancy hat that was covered in white silk flowers. But the girl had on plain denim shorts as well, like any girl from Elliot's own time.

"Hello!" said Elliot.

"Hello yourself!" said the girl.

At first she seemed conceited and snobbish, but they walked together for a while anyway. Elliot could see that she was upset about something. Finally she said, "I am having so much trouble with the little dragon in the perambulator! I simply don't know what to do, and I can't find anyone to advise me!"

Elliot reminded the girl that she was pushing a baby carriage and not a dragon carriage. He pulled back the retractable hood to show her that there was no dragon inside. But to his surprise, a small red dragon did lay coiled among the cushions of the carriage, fast asleep. The girl's loud exclamation, "See! I told you so!" awakened it.

The little dragon gazed up at them with eyes that were startlingly intelligent. A wisp of smoke curled up from each nostril. Then, as if it were irate at being disturbed, it uncoiled itself, stood upright, flapped its batlike wings, and flew up and out of the carriage.

As it flew beyond the treetops it grew larger and larger.

Soon it was very high and had grown to nearly a hundred feet in length. Elliot was relieved when it disappeared into the distance.

"Now look what you've done, you frightful boy!" said the girl.

And suddenly, Elliot noticed that a beautiful vase of the most vivid cobalt color had materialized in her hands. She removed the lid, and blue pinpoints of light swept into the air, pursuing the dragon.

"Oh, I do hope the fireflies catch him before he realizes he's a fire breather," she said.

Elliot awakened with a start. He didn't know what to make of his dream. It was the strangest one he had ever had. It was very dark in his bedroom. According to the noisy old clock on the wall it was a quarter to one. The tree limbs outside projected fantastic shadows. Elliot went to his window seat and sat down to peer out over the wall into the little garden.

He sat very still for a long time. His elbows rested on his drawn-up knees, his hands folded beneath his chin. He was beginning to nod off, when all at once a flash of motion startled him to complete wakefulness.

He was astonished at what he saw. Hundreds of fireflies were flying about the garden and over the wall. But instead of the usual pale green phosphorescence, these fireflies shone blue—a color so vivid it was almost purple. They darted around the garden haphazardly, the blinking of their little lights intermittent. As they began congregating, Elliot realized with amazement there were now thousands of them.

They formed a luminescent cloud and settled atop the garden wall. He blinked and rubbed his eyes in disbelief. When he looked again, the bright cluster of fireflies had transformed into a faerie maiden!

Her moonlit dress was sprinkled with silver stars. She wore a braided belt and her slippers were tiny. Her hair was long and dark. She danced along the top of the wall, moving gracefully on her toes like a ballerina. Her wings swept upward behind, translucent, sparkling in the night.

As her delicate steps brought her closer, Elliot caught a glimpse of her face. He was in for yet another surprise—for the face that gazed up into his own was the face of the mysterious lady who saved him from the bullies! Elliot watched in rapt fascination as her dance continued. The verse in the frontispiece of the storybook flooded into his mind.

Beyond the dancing faerie's wings sleeps power beyond
  compare;
A ring to charge the mystic gate—step through it if you dare.

Elliot's heart pounded as he gazed beyond her wings. He could just make out, in the lurid light of the waning moon now rising low over the treetops, the dark blank windows of the old abandoned house, looming like an ominous shadow in its thicket of trees.

When Elliot glanced back down into the garden, the faerie had vanished. But her message was clear: He knew beyond all shadow of doubt that he must explore that house. He would begin tomorrow morning.

ELLIOT REMAINED SLEEPING on the window seat all night. When his mother awakened him the next morning it was much later than he had planned. He was anxious to begin his adventure exploring the old abandoned house. He put on his Batman T-shirt and his PF Flyers sneakers. He would have been happy with Froot Loops for breakfast, but his mother still felt guilty about TV dinners the night before, so she fixed him scrambled eggs and toast.

Soon she went upstairs to work in her studio. Elliot's heart was already racing. He went outside and walked along the veranda to the back steps. On his way to the garage, he passed the garden wall and peered up at the spot where he had seen the faerie dancing, just below his window. In the bright sunshine of a summer morning it all seemed so unreal. He even wondered if it had been a figment of his imagination.

Elliot retrieved his bicycle from the garage and pedaled quickly down the rear driveway, but instead of taking the turn leading down to the main road, he continued on, coasting along a short pathway to the lane where he had met the mysterious woman. When he reached the lane, he looked both ways, but saw nothing unusual.

He rode along toward the summit of the hill where the huge abandoned house stood. The fir trees grew taller here, with lots of dead lower branches and dark shadows beneath. Elliot pedaled slowly now, as the lane had turned into more of a path. The sharp limbs scraped and tugged at his dungarees, but he continued on.

Soon he was forced to dismount his bike and walk, pushing his Chopper, so that its red paint wouldn't be scratched by the branches. He could no longer see the house and worried that he had lost it altogether—as if it were possible to misplace something that large—when he glimpsed faded gray clapboards up ahead through the trees.

Elliot stopped, leaning his Chopper against an old iron lamppost long since deprived of any lamp at the top. His heart was in his throat as he approached the derelict house. It grew larger and more foreboding as he drew closer. Despite its advanced state of decay, it was obvious that the house had once been beautiful. There was fancy woodwork everywhere and the tall windows were arched at the top. The fact that the house had once been so lovely made it all the more frightening in its present state.

There was a turret at the top of the house, just below the tips of the tallest trees, between two crooked brick chimneys. Elliot thought it peculiar that, unlike the turrets in most old houses, this one didn't have a single window. All it had was a short spire protruding from the center of its pointed roof with a faceted glass orb set at the top.

Several large gray moths were startled as he drew nearer. Everything in the vicinity of the house was stifling, dim, and eerie. He crept up three granite steps onto the wooden veranda—the part that hadn't yet collapsed—and gingerly stepped across the squeaking, groaning wooden planks to the front door. Amazingly, its frosted-glass window was still intact. Meticulous patterns of sphinx moths and butterflies were etched around its edge. Perhaps it was something his mother might want to paint if he told her about it.

Elliot tried the tarnished brass doorknob. The door creaked

halfway open, grinding to a halt on the uneven floorboards. He stepped inside, breathless with fear and wonder.

He found himself in a huge, dimly lit room. There were cobwebs everywhere. He saw the curve of a banister railing and staircase leading upward. Elliot carefully stepped around a place where the floor sagged like a big oblong bowl. He knew that if he stepped there he would fall all the way down into the basement. The very thought made him shudder.

At first he thought the floor was covered with moss, but then he realized that it was the remains of an old carpet. Long ago it had been a very expensive Turkish rug, but now it was dull and dirty. The fireplace was long cold, but Elliot could see from the braided columns on each side that it had once been luxurious. An oil painting still hung over the elaborate mantelpiece.

That must be Mr. Murchison himself, Elliot thought, studying the portrait for a moment. The subject was a man in old-fashioned dress with a turned collar, waistcoat, and tie. His face was artistic and sensitive and he had a mustache and beard.

Elliot summoned all his courage and began to ascend the rickety stairs with great trepidation. He felt as if each step was taking him into a part of the house that was older and more mysterious than the last. He jumped when part of the railing gave way in his hand with a crackle of rotting wood. Twice he had to step over stair treads that were obviously too weak to support him. Elliot continued up the creaking staircase, rounding the first turn of the landing. At last he came to the second floor.

It was very dark, as most of the doors to the rooms were closed. He wished that he had thought to bring a flashlight. A tall candlestick upon a side table loomed at him out of the gloom, but he had no matches. He opened each door he passed and glimpsed luxuriously appointed rooms with curtained beds, cherrywood armoires, high-backed chairs, ornate fireplaces with tattered silk screens, mahogany wardrobes, and scroll-topped writing desks, some still equipped with dip pens and dusty bottles of dried ink. He passed a room that must have once been an upstairs parlor. It was furnished with rickety divans and leather armchairs, their upholstery cracked and mildewed.

Elliot walked on and rounded a turn in the hallway. Up ahead, he could see the ceiling was sagging and the floor was crooked, leaning drunkenly to one side as though it were about to cave in. He opened every door that would open. His half-formed plan was to keep going upward in the house, but a third-floor stair was nowhere to be found.

He retraced his steps, glad that his sneakers gave him sure footing on the slippery old carpets and rotting boards. A loud groan from a distant part of the house made him worry it was about to fall in on him. He would never be seen again! He realized that he should have told someone where he was going. He crept back around the corner, eventually returning to the little upstairs parlor.

At the rear of the parlor, he found a doorway, half concealed behind a pillar. It led into a music room where he discovered an old grand piano, still gleaming darkly, although it leaned at a precarious angle. One of its legs was broken and its once pristine ivory keys were jumbled in disarray.

Beyond the piano, he discovered another almost completely hidden doorway. His heart almost stopped as he turned the crystal knob and the narrow door creaked open to reveal a spiral staircase.

Elliot drew a deep quivering breath and attempted the first step. The boards groaned, but bore his weight. The spiral stairway was enclosed within a tall cylinder of paneled wood, which rose through all levels of the house like a great column. Elliot felt his way upward in the darkness, going round and round.

Suddenly, he felt the steps beneath his feet tremble. Then he heard a loud rumbling and a creaking noise that rapidly got louder. He froze, fighting down waves of terror, the palms of his hands pressed against the wall. The old house was collapsing—and Elliot was trapped inside!

Elliot cried out in panic. He looked back, desperate for a glimpse of the doorway, but it had vanished, leaving him in absolute darkness. He realized that the spiral staircase was in fact turning upward like a gigantic corkscrew, or some strange form of escalator.

Finally, to his great relief, the turning slowed, then stopped with a shuddering groan. Above him a small opening appeared. He was surrounded by a curious pallid light that came cascading down the stair, casting slanted beams through dancing dust motes that had been shaken loose by the disturbance. Elliot coughed as he climbed up the steps and went through the doorway. He found himself standing in the windowless turret room at the very top of the house.

Above his head was a high domed ceiling aglow with the light of countless stars. He had learned two or three dozen constellations, and knew nearly a hundred stars by name, but these patterns were unfamiliar. He saw that the door leading from the turning stair was built into the base of a high circular platform. He walked about the circumference of the platform, gazing up in wonder at the stars as they flamed down at him, as if from a great distance. He found the illusion spellbinding.

Then he remembered the glass sphere atop the spire, above the turret's pointed roof. Could it be the source of the constellations? Maybe it conveyed sunlight to pinhole lenses in the dome to vividly re-create the night sky. Elliot wondered with a thrill if Mr. Murchison had journeyed to other worlds and replicated their constellations on the underside of the dome. Perhaps he had gone to one of those other worlds in the end—and stayed forever!

Elliot had gone almost all the way around the platform when he saw a set of wrought iron steps leading to the top. He climbed cautiously, his hand trembling as it slid smoothly up the banister rail. At the top of the platform stood a carved lectern, holding a huge open book. The cover of the book was very thick and its pages were cracked with age. Elliot bent low to examine the book, but found the pages were all blank.

However, something very odd transpired. Curious letters of fire, in an ancient and elaborate script that he could not read, began swirling and dancing across the page. The letters appeared to be the characters of an ancient alphabet. And yet somehow, although the letters remained unrecognizable, Elliot could hear the book speaking its verses directly to his mind.

Betwixt the worlds of are and could be,
Faeries on a summer's night
Assume firefly forms for mortals to see
And cloak their masquerade in light.

Elliot thought of the cloud of fireflies that had been the blue faerie's disguise. Had it been real after all? Surely that must be what the verse meant. Breathlessly he turned his attention to the right-hand page and the flaming letters spoke to his mind once more.

The ice drake dreams through the winter night,
His is the rune of cold.
The firedrake lies coiled upon treasure bright
To watch the ages unfold.

Elliot once read a story where comets were referred to as firedrakes, because in medieval times they were thought to be dragons. He remembered his dream of the girl pushing the carriage, in which a small dragon lay sleeping. His heart pounded as he reached out to turn the page. The next verse read:

Beyond the dancing faerie's wings sleeps power beyond
  compare;
A ring to charge the mystic gate—step through it if you dare.

He stood quite still, his heart thudding. Here, in a magic
book, below a starlit dome at the very top of the old house,
written in swirling letters of fire, was the very same verse he
had found inscribed in the faerie storybook!

Elliot looked expectantly at the right-hand page, but no
new letters or verses appeared. He glanced about the platform, but it was quite empty apart from the lectern and the
book. Then he stepped back, gazing up into the starlit dome,
where a sudden motion caught his eye. One of the thousands
of blue stars slid down the sky like a meteor. He watched
amazed as the shooting star came to rest, glowing like a fire-
brand, directly upon the right-hand page of the book.

And then, right before his eyes, more shooting stars fell
onto the page and began swirling in a counterclockwise motion, faster and faster, till their light blended to form a wheel
of fire. Elliot watched wide-eyed, the vivid light flickering on
his face. Suddenly, the spinning circle of stars blurred, then
flared to a brief incandescence so intense that he was momentarily blinded. When he recovered, the fallen stars were
all gone. And where they had been lay a silver ring with a brilliant red gemstone.

A ring to charge the mystic gate! Elliot tried it on, and found
that it fit the middle finger of his right hand perfectly. He
was in a daze as he made his way back to the staircase. He

wondered if the door to the spiral stair was the "mystic gate," and he half expected something magical to happen as he stepped through, but nothing did. Nothing, that is, except the heart-stopping rumble as the stairs turned once more, conveying him down to the doorway through which he had entered the stairway.

Elliot slowly retraced his steps along the corridors and down the creaking main staircase of the house. He had enough presence of mind to check for gates and doorways on his way out—anything that might possibly be magical. But he found nothing. As he walked through the old house to the front door, the far-off creaks and groans no longer terrified him. He felt that somehow the ring would keep him safe from harm.

As he stepped out onto the veranda, the etched glass in the door again caught his eye. He realized that the butterflies and moths about the edge of the frosted panel had transformed into faeries! Elliot stared long and hard. He was certain the window had displayed butterfly patterns before. He peered at his ring, then back at the looming bulk of the abandoned house.

"I was wrong about you," he whispered, as if the house could hear him. "You're not haunted—just magic!"

He retrieved his Chopper from the lamppost and walked it carefully through the trees. When the wood thinned out, he left the path, heading for the half-overgrown meadow. The tufts of grass were too high and thick for him to pedal through, so he walked along in the sunshine, pushing his Chopper, as he whistled the theme from *Robin Hood*.

Elliot was now walking along the edge of the meadow, where

an old lattice wall, nearly covered in ivy, ran under the shade of tall trees. Soon he passed an old arbor gate, nearly concealed beneath the growth of years. The wall on each side of the gate leaned at a precarious angle. Perhaps his mother would paint the gate once she was finished with her latest paintings. The gate and wall must have been beautiful when they were new.

Elliot was distracted by a large dragonfly darting low over the grass to disappear into the trees on the opposite side of the meadow. When he turned back again, he was startled by a burst of light. As the bright flecks swirling in his vision gradually subsided, he was astonished to see a girl his own age standing below the arch of the arbor gate looking bewildered.

She was dressed as if she had just come from a costume party, in a fancy frock with delicate lace tights. She appeared to have forgotten her shoes. She had materialized from nowhere, but the most amazing thing of all was that Elliot recognized her! She was the very same girl from his dream— the girl who pushed the perambulator.

He was temporarily speechless. A flash of crimson made him notice that she wore a ring very like his own. She stood still, attempting to get her bearings. Her eyes passed over Elliot dismissively. Finally he came to his senses and remembered his manners.

"Hello!" he said tentatively. The girl gave him a look bordering on contempt.

"Hello yourself!" she said.

Chapter 3

VICTORIA TOOK IN her new surroundings—the ivy-covered arbor gate, the sagging lattice wall, the thicket of trees looming high overhead. "Extraordinary!" she exclaimed. What she saw before her was the exact same scene she first glimpsed in the pages of the magic book, opposite the third poem.

Her ring had actually transported her through a magic portal! But her amazement was tempered with a twinge of disappointment. She could see that she was not in Faerieland, which was what she'd been hoping for. Indeed, this place was quite ordinary, and the boy who stood gaping at her seemed possibly even tiresome. The only unusual thing about him was the strange velocipede he was pushing. It was gleaming red and terribly extravagant, though its wheels were very small.

When Victoria was disappointed, it often made her cross. And when Victoria was feeling cross, she sometimes wasn't nice. Her eyes narrowed. The boy's shoes weren't even leather. They were fashioned from some sort of sail canvas, and the soles were composed of India rubber. Moreover, his haircut was much too short and he had no curls to speak of. Victoria decided that he was a simple serving lad, perhaps the groundskeeper's son. He couldn't possibly be anyone important—after all, he had a large fruit bat emblazoned on the front of his shirt!

Brimming with insolent superiority, she declared, "I am Victoria Deveny," forming the words curtly as if it was beneath her dignity to address such a boy.

"I'm Elliot." He reached out his hand, trying to be friendly. But Victoria was having none of this improper familiarity, so he stood awkwardly for some moments, his hand extended to thin air.

Victoria sniffed. "Elliot who?" she inquired in her pronounced English accent. "What is your surname, if you please?"

"Elliot Good," he replied.

"Good?" she said disdainfully. "Well then, you are nobody in particular, are you! For that is not a name in any peerage ranking, nor is it even noteworthy." Victoria turned and began striding away as though she had somewhere important to be or knew precisely where she was going.

"Hey, wait a minute!" exclaimed Elliot. "Wait! Didn't you just come through that gate back there? I mean, you appeared out of nowhere—and there was a blue flash! Hold on, will you please?" Victoria was walking along, her nose in the air. She glanced over her shoulder to see that he was trying to catch up. A part of her felt sorry for him. Another part of her was curious about the ticking sound his velocipede made as he pushed it. Velocipedes, in Victoria's experience, had only one gear and no shifting mechanism. They made no sound when their wheels turned. Relenting a little, Victoria walked slower. Besides, the uneven tufts of coarse grass had begun hurting her feet.

"Thanks for waiting, Vicky," Elliot said breathlessly as he caught up. She fixed him with a scathing glare.

"I am not acquainted with anyone with the Christian name of Vicky. My name is Victoria. And my *friends*"—here she placed a pronounced yet doubtful emphasis on the word—"at least those intelligent enough to know what's good for them, call me Victoria."

"Sorry, Victoria," Elliot said, repeating her name politely, to show that he had gotten it right. He wondered why she was wearing lace tights and no shoes, why her dress was so old-fashioned and had so many bows and buttons. Victoria, for her part, thought Elliot to be a simple member of the serving class and he was getting on her nerves more than a trifle.

But Victoria began to realize that she really hadn't any idea where she was, so when Elliot suggested they take a short path out of the meadow, which would eventually lead to a roadway, she reluctantly agreed. Five minutes later they were seated on a mossy embankment, overlooking the lane where Elliot had been rescued by the mysterious lady the day before. Victoria took off her hat and sat rubbing her toes contentedly. Elliot sat down beside her, glad to rest. He picked a long stalk of grass and began chewing on it. His bicycle was leaning against a nearby tree. The bullies would probably never come down this road again, so he considered it quite safe.

"I can give you a ride on my bike to wherever it is you need to go," Elliot offered.

Something about Elliot made Victoria begin to like him a little, despite herself. He seemed unassuming, rather kind, and surprisingly intelligent, at least for a groundskeeper's boy. "Why do you call your velocipede a bike?" she asked curiously.

Elliot shrugged. "It's a bicycle. What's a velocipede?"

A look of understanding crossed Victoria's face. "Oh yes," she said excitedly, "Adelaide Periwinkle says that there is a new kind of velocipede called a safety bicycle, which will soon replace penny-farthings. She says that they are simply the best for healthy constitutional cycling. So your contraption is some sort of safety bicycle, Elliot! That is it, isn't it?"

Elliot took the well-chewed stem from his mouth for a moment as he pondered what Victoria had said. "Yes, I'm sure you're right," he said agreeably. He started to place the stem in his mouth again, but Victoria snatched it from his fingertips. She tossed it away with an expression of fastidious distaste.

"Don't chew on timothy grass, Elliot," she said. "It's vulgar."

Elliot smiled at her. He had to admit that for all her peculiarities, she was very pretty, if perhaps a bit conceited. She even smelled nice, like an old perfume that his mother had purchased at an antiques auction. It came in a cut-crystal bottle and was so old that she had been surprised to find any scent remaining in it.

Elliot glanced down at Victoria's ring, and then at his own. Both were silver and set with vivid red gemstones. Hers had a round stone and a smooth, swirling band, while his had a teardrop-shaped stone and a patterned band. Elliot wondered if both rings were magical and if Victoria's ring had transported her here somehow. Victoria was thoughtfully gazing at Elliot's ring with a similar question in her eyes. It became very quiet for a few moments.

Elliot approached the subject carefully. "Have you ever read the Narnia books?" he asked. Victoria shook her head. "They're about these children in England—during World War One, I think—who stay at this big house in the country and discover a wardrobe that opens into another world, where they have adventures with dwarfs, talking animals, fauns, and a very wicked witch."

Victoria noticed with irritation that a thorn had snagged her dress. "I'm from England, but I have never heard of 'World War One.' Perhaps you mean the Franco-Prussian War? Though the books do sound interesting . . . They remind me a bit of the Curdie books."

Elliot admitted never having heard of the Franco-Prussian War or the Curdie books. Victoria explained, "The Curdie books tell the story of a little princess whose father is away. She lives in a great house in the country with a magical upstairs and her grandmother is some sort of enchanted queen. She meets a miner and they fight goblins who are invading from tunnels deep underground. They have all sorts of adventures." She paused and leaned closer. "Elliot, do you want to know a secret? I live in a big house in the country with a magical upstairs! It is my uncle Dexter's house, and it has a secret staircase and a hidden room!"

Elliot's heart thrilled. "I live in a big country house, too, but there is an even bigger house back there, over in the trees. It's very old and tumbling down, but it has a magical turning staircase and that's where I found—"

"Your ring! I just knew it!" Victoria recalled the verses of the fourth poem.

Two kindred spirits and two rings,
Two gates that find the fey . . .

Then both children talked excitedly, each relating the adventure they had had so far. Finally, something unsettling occurred to Victoria. "Then where are we now?" she asked.

"We're in America, in the state of New Hampshire, in a town called Alton Bay."

"Then I've somehow crossed the sea, haven't I?" Victoria breathed deeply, and then she was quiet for a long time. At length she said, "Elliot, you mentioned something called World War One. Did England fight in it?"

"Yes," said Elliot. "England, France, and Germany, and later America as well."

"What year was this war fought?" she asked, her voice quavering slightly.

"I think it was 1914 or 1918, something like that. A long, long time ago."

For a moment Victoria looked as though she was about to cry. Then she steeled herself and put on her bravest face.

"Elliot, I am eleven years old. Three or four hours ago, when I went to bed in Northumberland, it was 1890. What year is it now?"

Elliot swallowed hard. "It is 1966," he said.

"That means that I'm practically a hundred years old!" said Victoria softly, shaking her head in bewilderment. Then her eyes grew suddenly mischievous. "So then, if I am a hundred years old, that means I should be the captain of our adventures together!" she exclaimed. "For I am the eldest!"

"You're not a hundred years old at all! You're only about eighty-seven," Elliot retorted. "So there!"

Elliot and Victoria both found themselves laughing. Pulse-pounding excitement coursed through their veins. "I think you were destined to come," Elliot exclaimed.

ELLIOT'S PLAN was to take Victoria home with him. They couldn't exactly tell Elliot's mother that Victoria lived an ocean and a century away, and Elliot doubted he could come up with an explanation to satisfy her, but Victoria didn't concern herself with particulars. Such things were best left to household servants, and she was sure that Elliot would think of something.

Elliot tried not to laugh, watching Victoria swing her leg up onto the Chopper's seat. She was having difficulty, encumbered as she was by her lace dress with all its ribbons, ties, and bows. When she caught Elliot trying not to smile, she tossed her head defiantly, fixing him with another scathing glare. She tugged her skirts to her knees, admonishing him not to look because she was being "unavoidably improper." Finally she succeeded in getting herself settled on the seat. Elliot climbed up in front of her and they were off, coasting bumpily down the mossy embankment onto the path, then veering left onto the lane.

The lane led downhill toward the paved road, the most direct route to Elliot's house. The bicycle picked up speed as Elliot pedaled more quickly and Victoria wrapped her arms about his waist. She thought his modern velocipede to be quite splendid indeed, and she wished she had one like it to pedal about the grounds of Summerwind.

Suddenly, the wind began to moan in the trees. It began as a gentle murmur, but the sky darkened rapidly as the branches began to sway overhead. Scarcely a moment later, a full gale was blowing, its sound rising to a frightful howl. Tree limbs were tossing and bending above their heads in a truly alarming fashion.

Elliot squeezed his brakes to bring the bicycle to a skidding halt on the pine needles of the lane. The wind now filled the wood with the loud, unnerving roar that very powerful storms have, usually only the most intense nor'easters of midwinter. They heard loud creaking sounds and the crack of distant branches snapping. Soon clouds of green leaves were flying past.

"Do you always have storms like this in New Hampshire?" Victoria asked, shouting to be heard above the tumult.

"No! I've never seen anything like this! I hope it's not a tornado!"

"A tor-*what?*" yelled Victoria. The wind was now a shattering roar, and the sky had darkened to near pitch-black. Elliot was about to swallow his fear and pedal for home as fast as possible, when he and Victoria heard something that chilled them to the bone.

A screaming neigh sounded from directly ahead, down the lane. It rose to an ear-piercing pitch, then tumbled down the octaves, terminating in a low rumble that shook the ground beneath them. This was immediately followed by a drumming that sounded like approaching thunder. It grew louder and louder, even above the roar of the wind.

Having lived around horses all her life, and being an accomplished rider herself, Victoria recognized the noise right away. The rhythmic hoofbeats grew louder, and then, around a bend in the lane, appeared an apparition that made the children gasp with fright. They sat frozen in place as an immense black horse thundered down on them, its nostrils flaring, its breath steaming like exhaust from a locomotive's stack. It was far larger than any horse they had ever seen, and its face was covered with shaped armor plate, fashioned of dark metal and equipped with sinister eyeholes. Its mane rippled in the wind as its huge ironshod hooves thudded violently onto the soft earth, churning up chunks of turf.

But it was the creature who sat astride the huge black horse that was the most terrifying sight of all. A massive, heavily armored knight, clad all in black with a huge horned helmet, bore down on them at tremendous speed. His eyes glowed red like two smoldering coals and his air was one of unmistakable menace. A charcoal gray shield hung at his shoulder, with a sinister black star emblazoned at its center. Something about the black star gave Victoria the chills. It was as though there was a void behind it, for it gave off an unlight of darkness just as the summer sun gives off wholesome rays.

The knight's spurred heels kicked at the horse's steaming flanks, and it bore down on them with even more ferocity. Its lips were drawn back from its teeth and it rolled its bit with a pale, forked tongue. More screaming neighs assaulted their eardrums. The beating of its hooves was close enough now to drown out the roar of the wind.

Victoria and Elliot were sure they must be seconds from their doom, and that the thing would ride them down without pity or remorse. Elliot glimpsed the Shadow Knight's sword hanging from his side in a black scabbard. Its hilt was encrusted with jewels. The knight's iron-studded gloves grasped the reins, and his eyes bored straight through them, seething with malice.

Elliot and Victoria cried out in terror, braced for a horrific impact. There was no time even to leap from their seat. The black horse leaped high into the air as the grim figure on its back bent forward, poised to plunge directly down upon them!

But the deadly crash never came. Instead, the horse and its shadow rider disappeared in midstride, vanishing from directly above their heads.

The sky brightened abruptly and the wind eased from a sustained gale to intermittent gusts. Elliot and Victoria drew deep breaths and found that they were trembling. In a few moments, the summer day had become fair again, as though nothing had happened.

They sat still for some time, collecting their wits. Elliot's knees were shaking dreadfully. Had they really seen the apparition at all? It seemed unbelievable with the sun shining so brightly, now in a flawless sky. But when Elliot recovered enough to resume pedaling, the sight of the enormous iron-shod hoofprints that stopped yards from where they had cowered was proof enough. Elliot pedaled slowly down the lane, while Victoria studied the prints intently.

When they rounded the first bend in the path, all traces disappeared. "It didn't frighten me!" Victoria exclaimed, but the quaver of her voice belied her words.

Elliot skidded to a stop when they reached the asphalt of the paved road. They peered both ways warily, half surprised not to see a spectral knight hurtling toward them. The road led downhill for three-quarters of a mile, directly to Elliot's own driveway, and then down to the center of Alton Bay.

Elliot found the going easier now and the ride smoother on the pavement. Victoria was starting to calm down, when a rushing sound made her glance backward over her shoulder. She was about to receive her second fright in as many minutes.

A huge behemoth of shining steel was bearing down on them at an impossible rate of speed. It rolled along on thick black wheels, with a menacing roar as it drew rapidly nearer. Victoria's eyes widened as she cried out to warn Elliot to turn aside and save them before it was too late. In her fear she gripped Elliot tightly, her sharp nails digging into his sides. He gasped with pain and surprise.

The behemoth was on top of them now, and its thunderous commotion had grown louder. Victoria saw the smoke of its black breath belching from a thick pipe protruding from its top. Worst of all, Elliot was ignoring her warning, as if he cared nothing for their peril.

She gritted her teeth, preparing to be crushed. But then the huge thing roared past them with a gust of hot wind and a blast of its horn.

"Good Lord! What was that awful, loud, foul-smelling thing?" she asked. Elliot was about to say something not particularly nice about why Victoria found it necessary to claw him to ribbons, when a sudden realization swept over him.

"I'm sorry, Victoria," he said. "I forgot that you wouldn't know. That was just a big diesel truck—a machine that carries cargo from one place to another."

Victoria fixed him with a furious glare.

"Well! I daresay you could have told me to expect such things, Elliot Good! You really are a rude and thoughtless boy! Don't people here have enough sense to drive horse-drawn carriages and freight wagons?"

"Not in America, and hardly ever in England now, I imagine." Elliot's tone remained apologetic. "Only rich people can afford horses, Victoria. Everyone else drives around in smaller vehicles we call cars. My mother has one—a Chevrolet. You'll probably get to ride in it!"

Victoria sniffed, keeping a suspicious eye on the road ahead. "I am quite sure that I do not care to ride in one of those nasty things," she grumbled.

"ALL ANYONE WANTS now are abstracts!" Janet Good fumed in her second-floor studio. She had done abstract work at college but her heart was in traditional painting. She especially loved fanciful, nineteenth-century British works. She kept a large volume propped open in front of her as her inspiration. Two faerie paintings were side by side, one to each page. The first, by Arthur Rackham, featured several faeries cavorting above a Kensington garden pool at dusk. The second, by John Atkinson Grimshaw, showed a single faerie hovering on iridescent wings above a woodland pond in the twilight.

Janet Good had decided to try faerie painting. Of course, she would need a model. Elliot might agree to pose, but it would only be to please her, and she knew he would be mortified. She would think of something else.

She heard voices coming up the driveway and stepped to the lace curtain to peer outside. Perhaps Elliot had finally made friends with the neighbor boys. She spotted him just below the window, standing in the pedals of his bicycle as he struggled up the last few feet of the steepest rise. Sitting behind him was a girl about his own age.

"How very odd! I've never seen her before," Janet said quietly to herself. The girl was very pretty and there was something quaint about the way she carried herself. Her dress was so ornate that it was either a rare antique or an expensive reproduction. Oddly, she wore no shoes, only elaborate white lace tights. Janet noticed the girl's hair was wild and wind-blown. She wondered why she and Elliot weren't drenched from the sudden downpour that had accompanied the strange short-lived storm.

Janet quickly removed her smock, tossing it across the back of an old leather armchair. Her hands had a few dry smudges of paint on them, but they would have to do. Her fingers flitted about her hair to tidy it.

She came down the front stairs to greet Elliot and his new-found friend, just as they entered. "Hi, Mom," Elliot said.

"Hello, Elliot! Why aren't you all wet? We had such a dreadful downpour!" She ruffled his hair affectionately. Janet Good was pleased to see her son's new companion. He had made few friends since the move to Alton Bay.

"Hello, young lady. I'm Elliot's mother, Janet Good—and you are . . ."

"This is my new friend, Victoria," Elliot said nonchalantly. Victoria shook Janet Good's hand warmly.

"Yes, my name is Victoria Deveny. I must confess that I had thought you to be one of the servants at first. Or perhaps the only servant, as this little cottage is certainly not large enough to provide employment for many."

Janet Good couldn't tell for a moment whether Victoria was being deliberately rude. It was certainly the first time anyone had called her large, turreted Victorian home a "little cottage."

Elliot's mother laughed. "I can understand why you might

think that, Victoria. I have been painting all morning, so I'm a bit of a mess. And sometimes I do feel rather like 'the servant' around here!"

Janet put a hand on both their shoulders and Victoria bristled only slightly at the familiarity. "Well, come into the kitchen, both of you. I love your dress, Victoria—it's old-fashioned, but it suits you." She missed the startled look that passed between her son and his new friend. "Are either of you hungry?" she asked.

"I'll say!" exclaimed Elliot.

"Yes indeed, I am positively famished," agreed Victoria.

Elliot and Victoria sat at the kitchen table while Janet Good handed them ice-cold bottles of Wink soda from the fridge. Victoria stared suspiciously at the thick green bottle, bothered by the spiral twist of the glass. Elliot's mother noticed that she seemed to be at a loss with the bottle opener until Elliot showed her how to use it properly.

"What an odd metallic cork! And the bottle is as cold as ice!" Victoria exclaimed. "Does it contain medicine or patent elixir?"

Janet replied that it was a soft drink and Victoria's nose wrinkled in perplexity. She continued to study the open bottle.

Elliot explained, "It's a lemon-lime soda, Victoria. It's really very good—you'll like it." He took a long pull from the bottle himself and he sighed with exaggerated bliss. Victoria wasn't convinced.

"Do you mean bicarbonate of soda, the sort that they give old brigadiers who have apoplexy?" she asked.

Janet turned away to hide her amusement. Elliot tried a new tack. "I dare you to try it," he challenged. That was enough for Victoria. She raised the bottle to her lips and tried a tentative swallow.

"Oh! Elliot, it's simply splendid!" She took a second sip. "It's like ginger beer, only a jolly sight sweeter and not at all bitter."

As she busied herself at the counter making the children chicken salad sandwiches, Elliot's mother thought it all very perplexing. Where had this girl come from?

"Are you from England, Victoria?" she asked.

"Yes, I am," said Victoria, who had nearly finished her entire soda already.

"I adore your accent—it's so pleasant to the ear."

"Me, too," Elliot concurred, putting his own empty bottle down.

"But I haven't any accent at all," Victoria sniffed. "I simply speak English as it was meant to be." She drew her nostrils tight, and her voice turned nasal in an overemphasized imitation of an American accent. "On the contrary, it is you who have the oddest accent, talking as if you were all Yorkshiremen with messy colds scolding their pigs!"

Elliot interrupted his snicker, wondering if his mother might possibly have taken affront. Even though she faced the other direction, he could tell by her shoulders that she was trying to stifle her own laughter.

Janet Good brought them a plate of chicken salad sandwiches and two more Wink sodas. She joined them, sipping a cup of hot coffee, discreetly watching as they ate. She was very impressed with Victoria's proper table manners. The girl politely requested a knife and carefully cut her sandwich into elegant eighths, meticulously removing the crust from the bread as she did so.

It's almost like she's from another time altogether, Janet thought.

"So what brings you to Alton Bay, Victoria?" she asked. There was an awkward pause, and she noticed Victoria and Elliot exchanging uneasy glances. "Is your family vacationing on the lake for the summer?"

Relief swept across Victoria's features. "Yes, of course! We are on summer holiday on the lake. We have a punt and have picnics, and sometimes we go letterboxing in the hills as well!" Janet Good knew that a punt was a small, flat-bottomed boat. But oddly, she had just finished an article in the local newspaper about letterboxing, a quaint outdoor hobby from Victorian times.

"What part of England are you from?" Elliot's mother asked.

"Both from the north country and from London," Victoria replied. "My uncle Dexter has an estate in Northumberland called Summerwind. I always take my summer holidays there—until this year, when he decided to vacation in America. He also has a London town house where we spend Christmas holidays."

"And why are you all dressed up?" Janet asked. "I'm sure that your uncle Dexter would not want that lovely dress spoiled."

"A wedding, maybe?" Elliot suggested as he fidgeted in his seat. Victoria smiled.

"Why, yes! I just attended a wedding this very morning, in fact. I accompanied the bride to the altar and stood beside her in front of the vicar. I carried a lovely bouquet and wore a splendid nosegay."

"What's a vicar and what's a nosegay?" Elliot asked, rolling his eyes. Janet Good abandoned her inquiries for the moment and helped herself to one of the sandwiches. Then she noticed Elliot's ring.

"Elliot! Where on earth did you get that lovely ring?" Elliot was startled by her question, but told the truth.

"I found it—up at the old abandoned house."

"Oh, Elliot, I don't think you ought to go up there. The whole thing could collapse and tumble down around your ears! But hold up your ring so I can see it. Perhaps it once belonged to Mr. Murchison himself!" Elliot's mother studied the ring closely.

"It's very lovely. Don't lose it, dear. It might be a good idea if we had it appraised. An antique like that could be quite valuable. And how interesting that Victoria has one so similar!" Elliot and Victoria were far too busy eating to respond.

After lunch, Elliot asked if Victoria might stay for the afternoon and Janet Good said yes. *One hurdle down*, Elliot thought as he followed Victoria and his mother upstairs, where she was taking them to find Victoria some appropriate playclothes. Still, how would he get his mother to let her stay all night, maybe even for days? He couldn't just say that Victoria was from 1890 and had nowhere to go in 1966!

When they reached the attic Janet flicked on the light. "I

say, what lovely bright lights you have!" Victoria exclaimed. She seemed oddly fascinated with the naked bulb dangling from the peak of the ceiling. "How did they enclose the incandescent gas jets in these perfect little glass orbs? It certainly makes them brighter, doesn't it!"

Elliot's mother looked to him with questioning eyes, but he was suddenly preoccupied with a bit of yellowed newsprint that someone pasted onto the chimney bricks long ago.

Janet led them over to a steamer trunk that stood in the center of the attic. It was surrounded by old packing crates and dusty boxes. "I'm sure that your uncle Dexter would be unhappy if you ruined your beautiful bridesmaid's dress. Besides, it's a hot day, and I imagine we can find something much more comfortable!" She rummaged about in the trunk and pulled out two pairs of denim shorts for Victoria to try. She sent Elliot downstairs to get one of his many T-shirts.

Victoria stepped behind a tall wardrobe to change. She had difficulty with the buttons of her dress and asked Elliot's mother for help. Victoria saw Janet noticing her trouble with fastenings, and ventured, "Ellen or Clara always assist me in dressing."

By that time Elliot had returned with still another Batman T-shirt. A minute later, Victoria stepped out from behind the wardrobe and handed her dress and tights to Janet for safekeeping. She was blushing furiously, as she stood barefoot in her denim shorts and T-shirt. "Do all the girls in your ti—I mean, here—wear such things in public?" she inquired as though astounded.

Both Elliot and his mother assured her that it was perfectly appropriate summer attire. Victoria shook her head in disbelief. "This is scandalous! And perfectly improper as well!" she exclaimed with a defiant toss of her head.

On the way downstairs, Victoria asked Elliot a question that had been perplexing her. "Elliot, why do all your shirts have large fruit bats on them?"

"Because *Batman* is my favorite show," he replied.

"My uncle Dexter has a private box at the Duke of York Theatre, on St. Martin's Lane. It has a velvet balustrade and its own valet. Surely you don't mean that Alton Bay is prominent enough to have its own theater like the Duke of York or the Lyceum?"

Victoria was contemptuous when Elliot replied he watched the shows he liked downstairs in the living room.

Janet suggested that he and Victoria amuse themselves outside while she searched for a pair of Elliot's old sneakers for Victoria to wear. The children walked down the driveway together, heading for the garage.

"Sneakers?" Victoria repeated. "What are sneakers? The word itself sounds devious and underhanded!" Elliot noticed that Victoria kept tugging at the hem of her shorts, though with time she seemed more comfortable in them.

"Sneakers are lace-up shoes like mine."

"I must say they look rather like something an Oxfordshire gamekeeper would wear." Victoria sniffed. "Even cricket batsmen have sense enough to wear proper white oxfords."

They paused at the edge of a deep mud puddle left over

from the storm. It filled one entire rut of the driveway. "Let's jump in and splash about!" Victoria suggested with a gleam in her eye. She felt particularly free in her new clothes.

Elliot said that he'd rather not, so Victoria called him a sissy and a stick in the mud—or rather a dullard, afraid of being stuck in the mud.

"Can't you play in mud puddles where you come from?" he asked with a trace of exasperation. Elliot hated being called a sissy, perhaps because part of him was afraid it was true.

Victoria fixed him with a disdainful glare. "Certainly not, Elliot!" she said vehemently. "It is simply not permitted!" Then with a rebellious look on her face, she jumped into the center of the puddle, making a loud splash. Elliot sprang backward to avoid getting soaked as Victoria gleefully stomped about.

It was a relief when his mother called them in to say she had found Victoria some sneakers. Janet took one look at Victoria's muddy feet and had Elliot show her where the hose was at the side of the house. Victoria stood on tiptoe in the grass, laughing as the cold water splashed her clean. Then she begged Elliot for a turn. Of course, as soon as she had the hose, she promptly drenched herself first and then him.

Victoria tried on the sneakers and to her distaste, she found they fit perfectly. Then she asked where the facilities were. She was surprised to find the clean and well-lit bathroom right inside the house itself. She washed her hands carefully with the blueberry-scented soap and flushed the toilet three times because she was so impressed by how it worked.

As the afternoon wore on into evening, Janet Good suggested that Victoria call her uncle to ask if she might stay for dinner. Elliot finally got up enough courage to ask his mother if Victoria could stay for a day or two. Janet was hesitant at first, but reluctantly agreed—providing they obtained permission from her uncle Dexter.

Elliot had the presence of mind to take Victoria aside while his mother was in the studio and explain the telephone to her. He showed her how it worked, and Victoria giggled as she listened to neighborhood conversations on the three-party line. She shook her head regretfully.

"If I only had one of these at Prosingham! I could talk to my friend Rebecca all night long. The proctors and matrons would never know!"

After a good deal of practice, Elliot and Victoria were ready to stage a pantomime. They pretended to dial Victoria's lakeside vacation home. They began their charade prematurely three times, in each instance abandoning their effort when Elliot's mother didn't traverse the hall at the proper moment. Finally the timing was right, and just as Janet passed them in the hall, Victoria began.

"Oh hello, Mrs. Hampstead," she said, assuming that even if they had a vacation home in New Hampshire and a phone, it would be the housekeeper who answered it. "Yes, I am fine. I wonder if you would mind terribly asking my uncle if I might spend a day or two with my new friend Elliot Good and his mother?"

Victoria nodded as if listening to a reply. Then she covered the mouthpiece with her hand and added, "She says that Uncle Dexter left for England scarcely an hour ago. He is so dreadfully busy with pressing business matters after all. Mrs. Hampstead says she will be happy to be rid of me for a day or two!"

Victoria's pause at that very moment was truly unfortunate, for Janet recognized the distinctive voice of an elderly neighbor. Her shrill, penetrating words were all too audible.

"Will you please put the receiver down, young lady! Don't you realize that it is rude to listen to other people's conversations!"

Janet shook her head in disappointment, taking the phone from a suddenly crestfallen Victoria. She frowned at Elliot. "I don't know what you two are up to, but I'm displeased with you both! Victoria, you'd better go upstairs and get your dress. I'll take you home."

Elliot and Victoria slunk up the steps in disgrace. They moped about Elliot's room for nearly ten minutes when they heard the front doorbell. They paused to listen, and could just make out that Elliot's mother was talking to someone. Then Janet called them downstairs.

They were completely unprepared for who stood at the door. Both children recognized the face of the woman who peered at them from the doorway with a mischievous sparkle in her eye.

She was dressed in the uniform of a prim and proper English housekeeper, in a well-starched apron and a cap with a lock of dark hair peeking out from underneath. A large antique bicycle, with a wicker basket and a bell on its handlebars, leaned against the porch rail. Elliot and Victoria were tongue-tied, but fortunately the only prompting that was required came from Janet.

"Victoria, your uncle's housekeeper, Mrs. Hampstead, was good enough to come by to see how you are doing, so I took the liberty of asking her if you might stay with us for a day or two."

Victoria swallowed hard. "Is it all right, Mrs. Hampstead?" she asked, playing along as best she could.

The woman pursed her lips and grew thoughtful. Then she reached out to gently take Victoria's chin in her hand. "Well, if you are obedient, Victoria, and mind your p's and q's, there may be no harm in it."

She turned to Elliot's mother. "I must warn you that she does make a fearful mess and is much too noisy, so if she is any trouble at all, pack her off to us at once! She can be a difficult, strong-willed child at times!"

Then she turned her attention to Elliot. "You appear to be a fine young man," she said with a twinkle in her eye. "Try to be a good example, and don't let Victoria run you about. She can be quite forceful, you know!"

Then "Mrs. Hampstead" said good day, turned on her heels, walked down the front steps, got on her bicycle, and rode away, ringing its bell three times in succession for good measure.

"Whew!" breathed Janet Good. "I had heard that there is nothing quite so formidable as an English housekeeper and now that I've seen one in action I absolutely agree! She's much younger than I expected, but very no-nonsense nonetheless!"

Elliot and Victoria thanked Janet profusely and said they were sorry for the phone incident. Then they dashed upstairs, where they collapsed breathlessly on Elliot's window seat, their hair practically standing on end.

"I had no idea that the lady who saved me from the bullies, and who is the faerie that danced under my window, is also your uncle's housekeeper!" exclaimed Elliot.

Victoria rested her hand on his shoulder and regarded him in thoughtful wonder. "But don't you see—she isn't! The real Mrs. Hampstead is frightfully old. She was only pretending to be Mrs. Hampstead! Elliot, that was the Mayweather nanny!" Victoria felt torn between euphoria and fear. "Something very strange is happening here."

Chapter 4

JANET DECIDED they would have a barbecue for their evening meal. Elliot ate three hot dogs but Victoria spat out the first bite of hers and loudly declared it to be vile—then apologized to Elliot's mother, saying that she wasn't accustomed to being served that type of meat in England and just couldn't see past the name. Janet just laughed. She was getting used to Victoria's odd ways. Victoria did enjoy the potato salad, however, and helped herself to two portions. She declared it to have been a very fine meal indeed.

Night had fallen and both Elliot and Victoria were dismayed when the wind began blowing stronger as it whispered about the eaves of the house. They peered anxiously out the window, hoping it didn't portend the return of the Shadow Knight. Elliot's mother even remarked that it was very strange to have such an abrupt and forceful wind in the summer.

Janet had both children get ready for bed, lending Victoria one of her own freshly laundered nightgowns, which of course was much too long and nearly swallowed her whole. Elliot asked his mother to read to them from the faerie book, *Glade of the Moon*, and she promised that she would be up in a few minutes to do so. Elliot considered himself too grown-up to be read to, but since they had a guest who also loved faerie stories, it was different. And he loved his mother's reading voice.

While they waited for Janet, Victoria tugged at Elliot's sleeve. "Did you say that the book was *Glade of the Moon?*" she asked. Elliot nodded. Victoria asked to see it and studied it closely. "Elliot, I have the exact same book! Moving it in my shelf is what activated the doorway to the secret stair. It's the book that the Mayweather nanny told me about!" Elliot and Victoria whispered together, wondering what it could all mean.

When Elliot's mother arrived, Victoria sat cross-legged at the foot of his bed for the first half of the story. For the second half she crept over to the window seat to sit by Janet, who paused in her reading to move over and make a place for her.

Victoria said wistfully, "I do so miss my own window seat back at Summerwind." Janet smiled and put her arm around Victoria's shoulder.

After about twenty minutes or so, the story drew to a close. The pauper in the magical suit of armor had rescued the faerie maiden from the evil sorcerer's high tower, and all was well. Elliot and his mother smiled at each other. Victoria had fallen fast asleep, her head resting lightly on Janet's shoulder.

The next morning Elliot and Victoria met on the landing on their way down to breakfast. They were each wearing denim shorts, sneakers, and fresh Batman T-shirts from El- liot's seemingly inexhaustible supply. The day brought more culinary surprises when Victoria discovered that she quite liked the brightly colored sugary rings called Froot Loops that Elliot's mother served them for breakfast.

When they were finished, Elliot and Victoria went up- stairs to Janet's studio to see how her painting was getting on. They found her discouraged. She peered long and hard at Victoria.

"Victoria, I seem to be having painter's block this week, but I must produce something soon. I've been looking at fa- erie paintings by Sir Arthur Rackham and John Atkinson Grimshaw—my style with oils is perhaps a bit like theirs, al- though I wouldn't presume to match their talent.

"I recently borrowed a book by Cecily Mary Barker from the library. She did many faerie paintings, mostly based on children in her sister's kindergarten. I wonder if you might as- sist me and would consider being my model?"

Victoria thought for a moment, then smiled. "You mean that I might live on in one of your faerie paintings, long after I am old and dead?" Seeing the rather horrified expression that crossed both Elliot's and his mother's faces, she added hastily, "or rather, that I might live on in your work, even when I am, say . . . a feeble old woman of eighty-seven?" She gave Elliot a wicked look. They both knew that eighty-seven was the age that Victoria would be now, even perhaps still was, somewhere across the sea in England.

Janet laughed. "Well yes, I suppose so."

She suggested that Victoria and Elliot amuse themselves

for two or three hours while she sewed a faerie costume for Victoria. They went outside and proceeded to the back of the house, arriving at the little walled garden that had all grown up to weeds.

"Let's search for another magic gate," suggested Victoria. "There must be one here as well or you wouldn't have found your ring."

They began their search by following the route that Elliot had taken to the old house. They walked through the wood, cut over to the lane, and soon they reached the quiet meadow with its tall tufts of grass. When they passed the gate where Victoria had first appeared, she felt a brief surge of homesickness and even considered taking Elliot back through the gate and showing him her rooms at Summerwind. But in the end they decided it was far too risky. It would be difficult to explain Elliot's sudden presence at Summerwind, to say nothing of Victoria's scandalous attire. Young English ladies of 1890 simply did not wear T-shirts and short pants!

They continued on, cutting diagonally across the meadow, through a blooming patch of bright blue flowers where dragonflies darted about. Victoria wondered if the presence of dragonflies meant they were near a faerie gate. Elliot considered that an inspired idea, and suggested they follow any dragonfly that left the meadow.

But the dragonflies all darted off in different directions. All, that is, except the one with the iridescent wings, the widest wingspan, and the longest blue-green tail. It zigzagged back and forth, as they followed it down the hill to the thicket of trees, where the old abandoned house stood. They caught only intermittent glimpses of it as it sped into the firs. They ran after it, ducking under dead, protruding lower branches.

Victoria observed the large house in an alarming state of decay. Its sagging upper story, blank gaping windows, and crumbling porches did look quite ominous.

"Elliot, how did you ever summon courage enough to go in there?" she gasped. Elliot's heart was fairly bursting with pride. He knew that Victoria was more audacious by nature, and it made him feel good that he had done at least one bold and daring thing in his life.

They caught another distant glimpse of the dragonfly, enough to guide them down the hill, deeper into the back meadow, where even Elliot had never gone. They ran down the slope and turned sharply to the right, skirting another tangled thicket of trees.

Now the dragonfly was nowhere to be found, but there they saw another lattice wall, just beyond a tiny orchard of old, gnarled apple trees. The wall ran arrow straight for a hundred feet, and in the center of the wall stood another gate. Though its woodwork was gray and weathered, the perfect arch of its construction remained elegant and sound.

"Maybe *this* is the gate into Faerieland!" breathed Victoria, and then they were off, running across the meadow for all they were worth.

They paused in the shadow of the gate and grew very quiet. "Which ring shall we try first?" Victoria asked.

"Let's try mine. You've already activated a gate with yours," Elliot suggested. He extended his hand, gazing down at the crimson stone glittering on his finger. He was feeling anything but brave at that moment, but he stepped through the gateway anyway. He braced himself, but nothing happened. Both children were crestfallen.

"Try coming back the other way," Victoria said. "Perhaps it only works in one direction." Elliot came back through and still there was nothing. "Well, I'll try my ring, then!" said Victoria with a determined air. She stepped through the gate and nothing whatsoever happened.

"I have an idea!" Elliot exclaimed. "Let's try going through it together!"

Victoria agreed it was worth a try. "Perhaps it takes double magic to activate this gate." They took a deep breath, held hands tightly, and stepped through. Their disappointment was palpable when once again nothing happened.

"You vile, stupid dragonfly!" Victoria said bitterly. "You have led us on a wild goose chase!"

"I thought for sure that this was the one," said Elliot in dismay. They spent the next hour and a half scouring the woods and meadows around the old house, but found nothing.

Finally, they made their way back to Elliot's house to see how Victoria's faerie costume was coming along. They were amazed to find it nearly complete.

It was very elaborate. The lower portion consisted of a puffy rounded skirt with crimson berry-shaped blossoms hanging from its hem. The bodice was formed like an open flower, with scarlet petals flaring out to each side. A thin wire network provided the framework for the translucent pink and violet wings. Janet had even used watercolors to give the wings their proper tint.

Janet showed them an open book, propped up in front of her. "I modeled it on the fuchsia faerie's costume."

"Wow!" said Elliot. "That's the most amazing dress I've ever seen!"

"It's not just a dress—it's an awe-inspiring creation of wonder and beauty," Victoria breathed. She couldn't wait to try the costume on.

Elliot's mother asked him to wait downstairs while Victoria changed. Janet would need to make a few final adjustments. She told Elliot that there was money on the coffee table for him to take Victoria down to the Dairy Swirl for lunch.

A few minutes later Victoria came downstairs, once again wearing her shorts and T-shirt. She sat on the bottom step to finish tying her sneakers. Elliot asked her if she could manage without an upstairs maid to assist her, and she fixed him with a scathing glare.

"Of course, you dreadful simpleton! My white summer dress boots have eleven eyelets down each side and I sometimes fasten the laces all by myself, if the maids get it all wrong and either make them too tight or too loose."

Elliot declared that it was silly to have maids employed just to lace one's boots, and Victoria said that they did many other things besides that. Elliot said that was even more ridiculous. Then Victoria stuck her tongue out and made a really rather horrid face, and then they were ready to go.

Victoria kept a wary eye on the road behind as they coasted down the hill on Elliot's bike. She kept glancing backward, dreading the sound of drumming hoofbeats or the screeching neigh of the Shadow Knight's horse. They breathed easier once they reached the lakeside cottages at the outskirts of town.

The day was warm. Scattered piles of fluffy clouds drifted across a radiant blue sky. They rode down into the center of Alton Bay, passing the reptile house with a python silhouette as its sign.

"Should we see how much it costs to tour the snake house?" Elliot asked reluctantly. He was trying to be a good host.

"Not for my sake, if you please! I do not at all care for reptiles," Victoria retorted, much to Elliot's relief.

They lingered at the little newsstand, because Elliot was anxious to buy the latest issue of the Green Hornet comic book. Victoria stood gaping at the lurid covers of detective magazines lining the lower shelves.

"Elliot, look at these awful periodicals. All the people on the covers, even the ladies, look so frightfully wicked! Have they nothing better to do than lie about and point weapons at people? We have similar things, but we call them penny dreadfuls. One Prosingham matron caught the gardener's boy with one. She told him that if he read such things he would grow up to be a simply awful boy, and then threatened to box his ears!"

Elliot laughed. He was ready to go on to the Dairy Swirl, but Victoria had turned her attention to the upper shelves. "Are you looking for a penny dreadful, Victoria?" he teased.

"No, I am most certainly not!" came her indignant reply. "I wanted to see if they sell *Chatterbox Magazine*, or at least perhaps an issue of the *Strand*." She spoke so wistfully that Elliot stopped teasing. "The *Strand* is a bit too stuffy for me, but it would be so nice to see just one familiar thing!"

Five minutes later the children were seated at a Dairy Swirl picnic table, in the shade of a striped awning. Victoria tried a malted while Elliot had an ice-cream soda. She nudged him and said, "Elliot! Will you look at those two great hulking savages over there!" Elliot whispered for Victoria to be polite and not point at people in public.

Victoria huffily informed him that comportment and demeanor training were highly emphasized at Prosingham Academy and that she required no lessons in manners from him. But Elliot was more concerned that she might have offended the large unshaven men with skull patches on their vests than he was with matters of formal etiquette.

But then a new concern presented itself. Victoria saw Elliot suddenly turn pale, and she knew by his face that someone was approaching—someone he was afraid of.

It was Stevie St. Michael, the ringleader of the bullies. He sat down beside Victoria, grinning at her. There was something unpleasant in the way he carried himself. Elliot told Stevie that he and Victoria were just leaving.

"So, Elliot," Stevie said, smirking. "Where's your lady friend—you know, the one on the path, with the pretty face that suddenly turned awful? She scared my friends half to death, but she didn't scare me! I don't see her anywhere, so who's going to protect you now?"

Victoria finished her malted with a slurp, then scraped her straw across the bottom of her glass. Stevie put his arm around her.

"Leave her alone!" Elliot said fiercely, rising from his seat on the other side of the table.

"*Leave her alone!*" mocked Stevie. He reached across the table to dip a dirty fingertip in what remained of Elliot's soda. Then he flicked it into Elliot's face. He laughed and turned to Victoria. "Why be friends with him when you can hang around with me? I'll take you for a ride over to the beach on Elliot's bike. He won't miss it, and anyway, he can always go home blubbering to his mommy!"

Victoria rolled her eyes elaborately. She made a disdainful face, as though a most distasteful odor assailed her. "Hang around! What a vulgar expression!" she declared, studying her fingernails intently, as if even turning her gaze on Stevie was far beneath her dignity. "Besides," she said, "I do not find dirty louts with flat noses to be pleasant companions!"

Stevie's eyes narrowed. He wasn't sure what "lout" meant, but he realized that it wasn't a compliment, especially when coupled with the word *dirty*. He decided to dispute the latter part of her insult, perhaps because it was the only part he fully understood.

"I do not have a flat nose!" he declared.

Victoria's eyes narrowed into her most scathing glare of all. In a single heartbeat, she stopped studying her fingernails, clenched her hand into a fist, and spun sideways in her seat. Then Victoria punched Stevie with all her might, her fist landing with a solid splat on the very center of his nose!

"You do now!" she said. A second later she jabbed her elbow into the pit of his stomach, knocking the wind from his lungs.

Stevie toppled off the end of the bench right into the mess of someone's previously spilled ice cream as he gasped for air. When he could finally suck enough breath back into his lungs, his first sound was a loud bleat of pain.

Victoria and Elliot were surprised at the sound of clapping. The other customers at the Dairy Swirl apparently all believed that the bully had gotten his deserts. Even the two "great hulking savages" endeared themselves to Victoria by cheering, before riding away on their loud motorcycles.

As Stevie slunk away, sniffling loudly, clutching his bloody nose and his stomach, Victoria noticed Elliot regarding her in awe. She read a silent thank-you in his eyes. Then he lowered his glance, grown suddenly shy, and picked at the dregs of his soda with his spoon.

"Don't have any more of that, Elliot," Victoria advised him. "Someone's dirty finger has been in it."

Victoria wondered if it might have been better to let Elliot fight his own battles, but on the other hand, the humiliation of being beaten by a girl would likely make Stevie much less of a menace in the future. And he did mend his ways afterward, and although still not exactly the nicest person, he was, for the most part, almost tolerable.

Back at Elliot's house, most of the afternoon was spent in the little walled garden behind the house. Janet set up her easel and brought out a wide assortment of brushes and paints. She declared over and over how lovely and elfin Victoria looked in her costume.

As she stood on tiptoes in the grass, one hand resting on

the wooden wall, Victoria seemed like a different person altogether—certainly quite unlike the girl who had just given
a bully a bloody nose!

Finally, Janet said that she had done enough painting for
today. She offered to drive Elliot and Victoria down to the
beach for a swim. Both eagerly accepted.

Janet had recently purchased a bathing suit for one of Elliot's female cousins who was just about Victoria's size. She
sent Elliot and Victoria upstairs to change. Elliot was waiting in the hall in his bathing suit with a towel draped across
his shoulders when Victoria emerged from the guest room.
The stylish plaid swimsuit fit her perfectly. Although it was
a one-piece, her face was beet red, and she was determinedly
tugging at the elasticized leg bands.

"Do stop gaping, Elliot!" she said fiercely. "This horrid thing
is the most indecent garment I have ever worn. I would be less
exposed in my petticoats!" She paused to look Elliot up and
down. "And you are no better," she declared, her voice bristling
with outrage. "Where is your sailor blouse? I can see your legs
high above the knee and you should be wearing alpaca
knickerbockers over those scanties!"

Elliot's amusement only further infuriated Victoria and she
flounced downstairs still seething. Janet assured Victoria that
everyone at the beach would be dressed the same way, but it
didn't do much to appease her.

"Well, this would certainly not do in the parts of England
I come from!" Victoria declared with a scandalized sniff.

Victoria followed Elliot and his mother into the garage behind the house and studied the car doubtfully. It was vaguely shaped like a coach, but it was low to the ground, and fashioned all of steel and gleaming glass. Even its tires were wide and thick, at least when compared to the high narrow wheels of carriages.

Victoria determined not to show fear or hesitation. She grasped the passenger door handle, attempting to turn it, just as one would unlatch a carriage door. It didn't budge. To Victoria's annoyance, Elliot brushed past her, pressed his thumb to the button at the side of the latch, and opened it for her.

"Sit up front, Victoria, and I'll ride in the back. That way you'll have a better view," he said cheerfully. Victoria sniffed.

"Indeed I shall not! I shall ride in the rear, if you please, as befits my station."

That annoyed Elliot and he made a face. His mother hadn't noticed their exchange and was already settled in the driver's seat, fitting the key in the ignition. Elliot tipped the seat forward so Victoria could climb in behind. Then he got in, and his mother started the automobile.

Victoria was startled by the sound of the motor, and she gave a barely perceptible flinch as Janet shifted into reverse, backing out onto the driveway. The rapid backward motion of reverse was something Victoria was not accustomed to. She felt sealed in, much more enclosed than in lightly constructed carriages. Even the most finely crafted coaches were flimsy by compare.

But by the time Janet had eased the car carefully down the steep drive to the road, Victoria felt much safer. Elliot rolled down his window, and Victoria enjoyed the sensation of wind in her hair. She was fascinated by how Janet operated the steering wheel and the shift lever. She leaned forward in her seat to watch Janet use the pedals. The gleaming instruments in the dash were intriguing. She asked lots of questions about driving and Janet patiently answered all of them.

As they drove down through the center of Alton Bay, approaching the bathing beach, they passed a row of large motorcycles. Victoria flinched when one was kick-started into thunderous life.

"Looks like some of your friends, Victoria," Elliot teased.

Victoria laughed. "My friends all have loud motorized velocipedes!" Janet studied Victoria in the rearview mirror. She was growing more perplexed by the minute.

When they parked at the beach, Victoria's jaw dropped. She was astonished at what people were wearing and said a few rather self-righteous and unkind things. Soon, however, she and Elliot were splashing about in the water and enjoying themselves, violations of nineteenth-century propriety all but forgotten.

Victoria declared that bathing at Portobello Pier was far superior. When Elliot asked why, she said that there were splendid bathing machines there, and donkeys to ride, too. Victoria boasted how she had once driven off two girls who were gingering up a sad little donkey and striking it with a mooring cord.

Elliot said he was glad there were no donkeys here because people might step in unpleasant things. Victoria sniffed indignantly and replied that donkeys and bathing machines were precisely what made bathing fun.

"What are bathing machines, anyway?" Elliot asked. "Are they robots with big metal hands that dip people in the water?" Victoria laughed, even though she hadn't the foggiest notion what a robot was.

"No, silly," she said condescendingly. "Bathing machines are enclosed carts with great high wheels. You give the attendant a bob or two and have it all to yourself for the afternoon. They draw the bathing machines down into the sea with ropes. Then you can change in privacy *and with decency*, neither of which you appear familiar with! When you are ready, you go down the steps from the door of your machine into the water."

Elliot said that bathing machines were the most ridiculous thing he had ever heard of. Victoria glared at him.

On the drive back to Elliot's house, Victoria was eager to sit up front. Once again she intently studied how Janet operated the controls. She thought the lights on the instrument panel were lovely. Elliot kept watch out the back window, hoping not to glimpse a large black horse galloping up behind them. To his relief, there was nothing.

Scarcely a half hour after arriving home, Victoria reluctantly joined Elliot on the living room carpet in front of the television. Both were wearing shorts and Batman T-shirts. Elliot insisted they had to be properly attired to watch the show. Janet Good had made fried chicken, and decided to *just this once* let them eat while watching TV.

Victoria declared that only beasts sat on the floor, and now she knew how her uncle's bulldog, Mr. Gladstone, felt. She also stated that television could not possibly be as exciting as a magic lantern show she once saw at Prosingham.

Then Elliot reached forward and turned the TV on.

Victoria watched as a tiny bright dot grew to engulf the entire screen. Her eyes widened in wonder as the music and video of the animated introduction began. Victoria's jaw dropped as the animation switched to live acting. She was obviously amazed.

Elliot's mother sat on the sofa behind them and thought it the strangest thing. Janet Good knew that England was no technological backwater. Hadn't they even invented television? She couldn't understand why Victoria not only acted like she had never watched television before, but didn't even seem familiar with the concept. Surely, even if she lived in an isolated British manor house, Victoria would have at least heard of TV.

The archvillain in tonight's episode of *Batman* was the hysterically demented Riddler. Victoria watched, a mixture of fascination and distaste for the Riddler's antics plain upon her face. Elliot explained that there were other villains, too, like the Joker and the Mad Hatter.

"My uncle Dexter has a hatter on St. James's Street and he isn't at all mad. Although he is a trifle fussy and rather peculiar," Victoria said between bites.

When the Riddler told Batman and Robin of the horrible fate that was in store for them, Victoria shook her head. "All of Batman's enemies must have escaped from an asylum," she said. "Couldn't the physicians see they were not cured?"

Later that night, when the children were changed into their pajamas and huddled on Elliot's window seat, they were both alarmed to find that the trees outside were tossing and waving in a sudden wind. Even the little enclosed garden appeared ominous in the nighttime. The sun-dappled grass where Victoria had posed in her faerie costume was now cloaked in shadow.

Janet sat on Elliot's bed to read to them from *Glade of the Moon*. She smiled at the sight Elliot and Victoria made, curled up, facing each other on the window seat, their knees drawn up, chins in hand, elbows resting on the window ledge, peering intently into the night. Of course she had no way of knowing that they were keeping a wary eye out for the Shadow Knight. Both children felt as though a great danger was approaching, and there was nothing they could do.

Elliot's mother read them a story about the Queen of the Snow Faeries, who rescued a mortal boy who became lost in a forest. She brought him to the faeries' hall of a thousand lamps, in the bower of a giant tree. There, he was warmed and fed, and then guided safely home again. It was a fine story, but neither Victoria nor Elliot paid very close attention.

They anxiously probed the darkness beyond the window, until at last, they fell asleep. Janet closed the book softly and tiptoed from the room. She saw no harm in letting them remain where they were, nestled among the cushions of the window seat.

Scarcely two hours later, Elliot's mother was watching an old movie downstairs when she felt a sudden sensation that made her blood run cold. She paused, her teacup raised halfway to her lips, and then jumped, startled by the drumming of hoofbeats down on the lake road. *That horse must be immense*, she thought. A moment later she heard a strange drawn-out sound—a harsh neigh more like a scream.

Janet sat still, her face ashen, her heart pounding. Suddenly the boards of the veranda creaked as if under massive weight, as heavy footsteps approached the door with a clanking tread. She saw a huge shadow pass across the curtains and then three slow, thunderous crashes pounded on her door.

Before she could respond, the glass panel shattered and a gauntleted hand groped inward, metal-clad fingers feeling for the latch. It seemed to Janet that her heart completely stopped as she ran for the staircase. Her only thought was to get between the children and the horror that was invading her home. She fled up the stairs. As she paused for a panicked moment at the turn of the banister, the front door was torn from its hinges and hurled violently against the opposite wall. There was a crash of splintered wood and a jangle of shattered glass.

The Shadow Knight stood upon the doorstep, his black armor glittering beneath his cloak. He stooped to enter the room, and Janet noticed how the light of the table lamp sparkled off red jewels in the hilt of his sword. Strangely, she noticed there were two empty holes just above the pommel, as if two jewels were missing. She thought of the crimson stones in the children's rings and clutched her chest intuitively as the great horned head lifted to meet her gaze. She felt the malice of its eyes burn through her senses like fire.

The Shadow Knight spoke. The bass rumble of his voice shook the house, as if it came up out of the ground.

"Stand aside, or give me what I seek."

The house quaked beneath his tread as he advanced toward the stairs. Janet was half fainting with terror. She felt small and helpless next to the towering spectral form, but she resolutely stood her ground.

"Stop!" she shouted, her voice quavering. "Stay where you are!" The Shadow Knight did pause, his eyes glowing with sullen hatred.

By now the commotion had brought Elliot and Victoria to the top of the stairs. Their faces blanched at the sight that greeted them.

"Run!" Elliot's mother hissed at them. "For god's sake, run for your lives!" Both children were too fear-stricken to move. The Shadow Knight reached beneath his cloak and withdrew a strange black orb. It lay gleaming in his palm, sparkling and flaring with a fitful inner fire. It seemed imbued with evil. They did not have to wonder about the orb's purpose for long. In one fluid motion, the Shadow Knight flung it directly at Janet!

The light in the room wavered as eerie gusts of unlight crackled from the depths of the black orb. Elliot and Victoria felt a sudden wave of vertigo, as if the whole orientation of the house had been altered.

Janet staggered backward, nearly losing her balance, frantically clutching the banister railing with both hands, her knuckles gone white. The orb flickered, sending out black tendrils that lapped and curled about her. To the children's absolute horror, her form wavered and she suddenly appeared two-dimensional. Then with a scream of sheer terror, Janet's body folded in upon itself and was sucked into the black orb!

The stairs groaned under the Shadow Knight as he rounded the banister and kept coming. Victoria and Elliot ran, their feet thudding down the carpeted hall.

Chapter 5

"Run, Elliot! He's coming!" Victoria screamed. "He's reached the top of the stairs! Oh, do hurry! Faster!"

She dashed into Elliot's room, desperate to open the window. The rug slid from beneath her feet and she fell, skidding halfway across the floor.

She leaped up, tugging frantically at the window sash. It finally creaked open, like old stubborn windows do, just as Elliot came stumbling through the doorway. His eyes were wide with despair and his lower lip was trembling.

"Hush, Elliot," Victoria whispered. "Don't even *think* about anything but escaping! Hurry!" She reached out her hand and grasped his.

"Elliot, we've got to jump—right *now*!" Her last word terminated in a scream as a hulking form filled the doorway, looming directly behind Elliot.

Victoria dragged Elliot up onto the window ledge beside her and then she jumped first. She landed atop the narrow garden wall, one of her feet slipping off. She managed to steady herself, her nails scraping across the chipped paint of the clapboards. Elliot was astride the window ledge now, one leg dangling. The Shadow Knight lunged forward. The cold steel of his fingers raked Elliot's shoulder as he jumped. By some miracle he landed on his feet, atop the wall, beside Victoria. She wrapped her arms tight about his waist till he recovered his balance. Above them, Elliot's bedroom window was more than filled by the frightful figure.

The children ran along the wall like acrobats, their arms outstretched for balance. They needed a safe place to jump down. They ran around the corner and came to where a large lilac bush offered minimal cushioning. They held hands and leaped. For a heart-stopping moment they seemed to hang in midair, and then they were scraping and bumping their way down through the lilac bush to land relatively unscathed.

Elliot wanted to flee to the garage, so they could make their escape on his bicycle. They ran out the gate and turned sharply right. There on the driveway, to their dismay, they saw what was left of his Chopper. Pieces were scattered everywhere. Both tires were flat, their rims squashed. The frame had been torn in half. The twisted handlebars dangled from a tree and the shredded seat was high on the porch roof.

The horrible screeching neigh of the Shadow Knight's horse tore the air as the beast thundered toward them at full gallop from around the corner. It was riderless, careening toward them at breakneck speed, its skull armor gleaming. The earth shook beneath the horse's hooves and its mane rippled in the tempest that had arisen from nowhere to shriek and roar in the treetops.

Elliot and Victoria headed for the garage as fast as their legs could carry them, and managed to slip inside the doorway, just inches ahead of the awful thing. Victoria jumped as high as she could to grab the hanging loop and pull the garage door closed. She succeeded on her second attempt, tugging the loop so hard the door crashed down, shattering the little four-paned window in the center with a tinkle of glass.

Elliot and Victoria were doubled over now, trying to catch their breaths. When Victoria recovered enough to stand on her toes, she risked a peek out the broken window. The screaming neigh came from so close it was earsplitting. The long forked tongue of the Shadow Knight's horse squirmed in, sampling the air just inches from the tip of her nose! Victoria screamed and threw herself backward in revulsion.

The horse reared up on its hind legs, crashing its ironshod hooves against the garage door. It was such a violent onslaught that Elliot knew it would soon give way.

"Elliot!" Victoria screamed. "Get in the automobile!"

Elliot was beside himself, overwhelmed with grief and fear. He clutched his head in his hands. "It won't stop him," he moaned. "He'll just smash the windows if we try to hide in the car."

"Who said anything about *hiding* in your mother's automobile, Elliot?" Victoria whispered fiercely, her expression resolute. "It is our escape vehicle!"

"You can't drive, Victoria!" Elliot protested, even as he

opened the passenger door and climbed inside. After her performance at the Dairy Swirl earlier, he half believed she could do anything. Victoria was already seated behind the wheel groping for the keys, which fortunately Janet usually left in the ignition.

"Perhaps I can," she said desperately. "At any rate I've watched your mother drive when we rode with her. And besides, it's our only hope of escape!" She turned the key and the engine sputtered to life. Victoria's bare feet barely reached the pedals. There was an awful grinding sound as the car lurched forward, crashing into the tool bench.

"The other way! The other way!" Elliot shouted. "Put it in reverse!"

The gears gnashed again, and Victoria pressed on the accelerator with a very determined look on her face. The car rocketed backward, smashing out through the closed door with a violent crash. For the moment there was no sign either of the Shadow Knight or his dreadful horse.

The car flashed past the corner of the house, then came to a dip in the driveway, its rear bumper scraping the gravel in a screeching shower of sparks. Elliot held on for dear life as Victoria spun the steering wheel and they skidded sideways, demolishing the lower step and part of the porch railing.

They decided to drive down to the main road and flee into town, but an immense shape blocked their way. The Shadow Knight was mounted once more!

"The lane! We'll make for the lane instead!" Elliot urged. "We can get back to the main road that way!" The tires kicked up copious amounts of dirt as they sped forward, veering sharply to the side, careening down the part of the driveway that cut toward the cross path leading to the lane. Victoria oversteered, causing the car to sideswipe a tall pine as it sped past, still spinning its tires in a shower of pebbles and roots.

"When we get to the lane we'll turn left and head for the paved road." Elliot's eyes were haunted as he searched the rearview mirror for danger. Victoria's knuckles gleamed white on the wheel. She stretched forward as far she could, reaching the pedals with her toes, at the same time keeping her head high enough to see out over the hood.

It was difficult to see what lay ahead of them in the dark. Suddenly, Elliot remembered—"The lights!" He groped for the knob, fussing with it anxiously till the headlamps clicked on. Victoria's concentration was thrown off, and they sideswiped a tree on Elliot's side with a screech of crumpled metal. He was flung across the seat into Victoria as his door dented inward. The car glanced off the tree, skidding back into the lane at full speed.

"Do get off me, Elliot, get off me at once!" she screamed. "I can barely operate this infernal contraption as it is!" The car skidded halfway across the intersection of the cross path and the lane before Victoria managed to stop by pressing both feet down on the brake pedal with all her might.

There in front of them lay the giant trunk of a fallen tree blocking the left branch of the lane, leading to the paved road and safety. They heard hoofbeats behind them and the screaming neigh of the Shadow Knight's horse. Victoria burst into tears and covered her ears with her hands. "Oh, Elliot, I can't stand that dreadful noise!"

Elliot did his best to summon their flagging courage. "We'll go back toward the woods—maybe we can hide in the old house." He noticed the dismay on Victoria's face when he mentioned the house. She could think of nothing worse than the Shadow Knight stalking them in there. "We have no choice," he said. "At least his horse is far too large to fit through the front door!"

Expressions of terror and desperation mingled on their faces as the screeching neigh sounded once more—much closer this time. The gears gnashed again and the tires spun as Victoria pressed the gas pedal and turned hard to the right. The car swerved as it accelerated, veering sideways before she regained control.

Elliot knelt on the seat peering backward. He saw that the Shadow Knight was directly behind them and gaining rapidly. "Go faster, Victoria!" he shouted. "Faster! He's getting closer!" The engine roared as the car zoomed down the narrow lane, the beams of its headlights bouncing. Their speed was truly dangerous, but they succeeded in distancing themselves from their pursuer.

As the car roared up the same embankment where the children had talked when they first met, the Shadow Knight could no longer be seen out the back window and even the pounding hoofbeats had faded. Still, Victoria didn't dare slow down.

The car bottomed out as it crested the embankment, and then went airborne from the momentum. For a terrifying moment, the tires spun in thin air, the engine roared, and the headlights stabbed upward, probing the treetops. Then the car plummeted back down again with a crash, two of the three remaining hubcaps flying off. Now they were bouncing out onto the meadow.

"I think the old house is that way!" shouted Elliot. Victoria cried out in alarm as she turned too sharply and the car skidded sideways, kicking up a choking cloud of dirt. She had to slow down as the trees grew thicker. They eased forward until they reached the edge of the wood. They could only crawl now, branches scraping their windows like gaunt fingers in the darkness.

Victoria steered carefully as they moved along between increasingly large trees. Soon, billows of steam rose from under the hood, accompanied by a loud hissing gurgle. The car could go no farther.

The children leaped from the automobile, leaving the doors open and the motor running. Using the headlights, penetrating eerily behind them through radiator steam, as a guide, Elliot and Victoria headed deep into the tangled trees surrounding the old house.

They ran till they couldn't see the headlights anymore, and then they walked, stumbling over roots and branches in the dark. When Elliot collided with the lamppost, he grabbed Victoria's arm and brought them both to a halt. "We're going the wrong way! I know by the lamppost that the old house is over there."

Elliot led Victoria forward by the hand, but even he was not sure of his way in the dark. Both children were in a state of dread each time a twig snapped beneath their feet, for fear that it would alert the Shadow Knight to their position in the darkness. When at last the clouds parted once more to let a shaft of moonlight through, the decrepit house loomed directly before them.

Victoria stopped in her tracks. "Oh, it looks so awful, doesn't it, Elliot? I don't like it at all!" But almost against their will, they crept forward, knowing the old house was their only refuge. They climbed the veranda steps and tiptoed across the creaking boards. The front door was sagging open and they stepped in, moving across the threshold. They crept slowly into the dark interior of the house. As they paused to permit their eyes to adjust to the gloom, Victoria clutched Elliot's arm, her fingers digging into him. "Why is there a painting of my uncle Dexter over the mantelpiece?" she asked, alarmed.

"That's Mr. Murchison, from England—the man who had this house built a hundred years ago. I'm sure he's not your uncle, Victoria."

"But he *is*, Elliot, he simply is. It is my uncle Dexter! I'm quite certain of it. I would wager a thousand pounds on it!"

Just then, something furry with luminescent eyes scuttled backward in the dimness and Victoria stifled a shriek. Elliot jumped half out of his skin. "Maybe we should go upstairs and find the room I told you about, at the top of the turning stair, where I found the ring," he whispered. "Perhaps its magic will hold back the Shadow Knight!"

They tiptoed to the stairs and had gone up only two or three steps when they both glanced backward to see the hulk-

ing figure coming in the door behind them! He strode forward, the floorboards creaking and groaning under his weight.

Victoria's eyes widened as he drew nearer, reaching out his
gauntleted hand. Suddenly, there was a sickening crack. The
Shadow Knight peered downward just as the ancient boards
gave way and he fell headlong through the rotten floor to land
with a clamor of armor and weaponry deep in the basement
below.

Safe for the moment, the children bolted up the stairs and
around the corner into the upstairs hallway. They ran, passing ghostly portraits that Elliot couldn't remember from his
last visit. An owl glided past, so close they could feel the wind
from its wings. Finally, Elliot found the room containing the
doorway to the turning stair and was frantically tugging at
the knob when Victoria shouted, "Look, Elliot! Out there in
the meadow!" They peered through the window to see the lattice wall with its gateway shining faintly in the light of the
waning moon—the very one they had spent so much time
trying to activate.

Even as they watched, they saw one of the mysterious blue
fireflies flit out across the meadow toward the gate.

"Watch the firefly, Elliot," Victoria breathed. It flew haphazardly at first and then straight, its course becoming more
and more direct as it approached the gate. Then, as both
children watched, it flew under the arch and disappeared.

Victoria was exultant. "It *is* the magic gate! It is! Perhaps
moonlight activated it," she whispered hopefully.

Their joy was short-lived. They both froze at the sound of
heavy armored footsteps treading up the creaking stairs and

moving down the corridor toward them, drawing nearer by the second. The Shadow Knight had apparently freed himself from the cellar below.

"Quick—we've got to get to the gate," Elliot said.

They struggled to lift a sagging chair by its broken legs and used it to shatter the window, then swept the shards of broken glass from the frame as best they could. Then they crept carefully out, standing on the mossy shingles of the veranda's ancient roof. Both feared it would give way beneath their feet.

"If we go back to where the roof sags into the trees we might be able to climb down and run across the meadow," Elliot suggested. They gingerly made their way across the treacherous roof, holding hands so they wouldn't lose their balance. Then they reached out to grasp the branches of a fir tree and clambered down, scraping and bruising themselves in the process.

And then Victoria and Elliot were running as fast as their legs would carry them, out across the meadow, the screaming neigh and the thunder of hooves close behind. As they approached the gate, the lopsided moon peeped out from behind the clouds to light their way.

They both fingered their rings instinctively as they passed beneath the archway of the gate, still running like the wind. A moment later they vanished in a sparkling cascade of blue light. A fading thunderclap of sound was all that was left behind.

Chapter 6

Elliot and Victoria had a very brief sensation of spinning and tumbling, accompanied by a sound like breaking surf. A split second later they found themselves standing, disheveled and breathless, below a huge gateway.

The gateway was plain and stark, composed of interlocking granite blocks. A wide set of stone stairs, whose balustrades were lined with tall lamps, descended onto a perfectly smooth meadow sprinkled with star-shaped blossoms.

The lamps had just begun to glow as Elliot and Victoria moved down the steps and walked across the meadow toward the fading crimson sunset. Victoria had just remarked that the meadow was as well tended and far smoother than even the nicest parts of Hampstead Heath when both children stopped short. Elliot grasped Victoria's arm to keep her from stepping forward, for a three-hundred-foot drop yawned before their feet. The treetops far below sloped down to a mysterious land full of half-glimpsed rivers, shadowy glens, and shining lakes.

Already the sunset had faded to a pastel pink with overtones of subdued violet. It was growing dark and the lamps had brightened considerably.

It was then that Elliot collapsed, overcome with grief. He dropped to his knees, his head in his hands, his body wracked with sobs. Victoria gazed down at him, her eyes full of sympathy. She gently placed her hand on his shoulder.

Then she knelt alongside Elliot and remained with him quietly while he expressed his sorrow. She, too, was overcome, for though they seemed to be safe where they were—at least for the time being—they did not yet have the faintest idea what awaited them.

Victoria tried her best to be a comfort. "This is without doubt Faerieland," she said gently. "At least we have come this far!" Then she smiled. "We were indefatigable, you know, and nothing could stop us! I expect that we'll meet someone who will help us save your mother."

Here it must be confessed that Victoria herself had grave doubts, having seen the horrid tendrils of unlight billow from the Shadow Knight's orb and draw Janet in, apparently dragging her down to her doom. The way her body had become two-dimensional before disappearing still disturbed Victoria deeply—and she was quite certain that it haunted Elliot even more. In her heart of hearts Victoria sensed that Janet had died trying to save them, but she could not bear to express this feeling to her friend.

"There is strong magic here in Faerieland, Elliot. One has only to look back at the gate that brought us here to realize that. Remember that your mother placed herself between us and the Shadow Knight and it is because of her bravery that we must have courage and carry on—no matter what!"

Elliot wiped his puffy eyes and stumbled to his feet. They retraced their steps away from the precipice and sat side by side on the stairs, below the comforting light of the lamps. The wind had begun to blow softly, and it became chilly for them in their nightclothes.

Victoria's brow furrowed with perplexity. "I simply cannot wait to return to Summerwind, Elliot. It was my uncle Dexter's likeness hanging above the mantelpiece in that old house. I am certain of it! I shall compel him to explain what he was doing there—and if he doesn't explain it properly, to my satisfaction, I shall be adamant and insist upon it! I shan't permit him any peace until he relents. Perhaps there is more to him than a silly butterfly collector after all!"

As the sky grew darker still, thousands of brilliant stars blazed down in a breathtaking display of dazzling light. Elliot and Victoria gazed in silent fascination, their faces uplifted to view star clusters, fields of nebulae, and dizzying constellations by the score. It made the night sky of their own world seem dim and empty by compare.

"Elliot, this is truly stunning! I have never seen anything half as lovely!" Victoria said, when she had found her voice.

"I have, Victoria!" Elliot exclaimed. "I have! This is the same sky that I saw under the turret dome, in the old house, where my ring formed of falling stars." He marveled that Mr. Murchison had somehow represented the night sky of Faerieland so accurately. He must have really visited here after all!

Suddenly, Victoria grew tense beside him. "Elliot, look," she whispered. "There are lights coming toward us—down from the forest!" As they watched, their hearts thudding with anticipation, and just a touch of fear as well, dim blue lights could clearly be glimpsed, moving to and fro in the eaves of the wood at the edge of the meadow. They were larger than firefly lights, and drawing nearer. Soon the children discerned shapes within the lights, forms with sweet faces and wings that fluttered whisper quiet. The faeries had come at last!

They had long hair and their garments twinkled as though woven from a blend of silk and starlight. Their cuffs were fashioned like turned blossoms, and silver slippers twinkled upon their feet.

They flew toward the children, in groups of two and three, hovering briefly, then moving forward, passing low over the grass. Their wings were a blur of effortless motion as they stood upon the very air itself, gently riding its whispering, sighing currents toward Elliot and Victoria. The children stood up and moved from the foot of the stairs to greet them. The faeries alighted one by one upon the grass, touching gently down among the star-shaped blossoms to form a ring about them.

There was silence for several moments until a faerie maiden of breathtaking radiance stepped forward. Elliot and Victoria noticed that her feet were neither trampling blossoms nor crushing blades of grass. She smiled, extending her hands to each child in a courtly gesture.

"I am Sindl, captain and guardian of the Faerie Realm's easternmost gate, and I bid you welcome, Elliot Good and

Victoria Deveny. I greet you on behalf of Edwina, Queen of the Faeries and Empress of the Hidden Realms!" Her voice was as sweet and bewitching as her form.

Victoria curtsied, feeling a curious mixture of solemnity and joy. Elliot managed to stammer something about being honored to meet her, and then, perhaps moved by some archaic impulse he did not even quite know he possessed, he kissed the faerie leader's hand, his cheeks flushing crimson. Then he finally found the courage to ask, "Why is this side of the gate so different than the plain old wooden gate we see from our world?"

Sindl stepped forward, resting one hand upon his shoulder as she studied his face intently. "The gate in your world is exactly the same as this, but it is under enchantment so that it will not be recognized for what it truly is. Many things in your world, Elliot—even people—are under similar enchantment and not recognized for what they are."

Sindl summoned a boy faerie forward and introduced him to the children as Aeron. He smiled, bowing gracefully.

"The Faerie Queen expects you to be her guests this very night," Aeron announced. "Her palace is a long way off, for it lies in the foothills of the westernmost mountains—and we must make haste."

"Neither of you are afraid of heights, are you?" Sindl inquired. Victoria declared emphatically that she was most certainly not afraid of anything, but Elliot hesitated and looked uncomfortable. Sindl took his chin in her hand and smiled. "Do not worry, friend Elliot. I am charged with your safekeeping—and at any rate, you are braver than you think!"

The faeries drew Elliot and Victoria forward until they stood at the very edge of the precipice at the far end of the meadow. The world far below was dark now, only faintly illuminated by the vast blue vault of starlight high above. Most of the faeries in Sindl's band waved farewell and silently melted back into the trees.

Ten faeries were left standing with the children, Aeron and Sindl chief among them. Five moved to stand close by Victoria, with Aeron and another taking her hands. Five others joined Elliot, as Sindl and another took his hands.

Then Sindl whispered a magic word of great power and portent. The wind strengthened steadily until everyone's clothes were rippling and their hair was streaming out behind them. "Come ride the wind with us!" cried Sindl, and a heart-stopping moment later Elliot, Victoria, and the faeries accompanying them stepped off the edge of the precipice into thin air.

At first it seemed they were plummeting downward, but only for a second—and then they were flying!

Elliot thought that the feeling was very like the one you get when the car you are riding in goes over a little rise on a country road. It reminded Victoria of the feeling she had when her horse leaped over a fence or a hedgerow. They all were leaning forward, holding hands, forming a long line as the treetops rushed past far below.

Elliot glanced backward over his shoulder to see that the gate was now tiny and receding rapidly. Its lamps were only twinkling points of light, fading among the distant trees. He quickly decided that it was a mistake to look backward and so he directed his gaze downward instead, which proved to be no better. There, far below, fields and forests sped past. It felt absurd to be riding the wind in pajamas.

Elliot clutched the faeries' hands for dear life. He glanced over at Victoria, who was three faeries away, and saw her with his mother's too-big nightgown flapping in the wind. Her eyes sparkled and she smiled at him with absolute delight. He noticed that the faeries at the outer edges of the group were trailing behind them small blue lamps on long silver chains.

"Elliot, it is best to look straight ahead!" advised Sindl. He looked briefly into the faerie's lovely smiling face and then he followed her advice, confident that she would permit no harm to befall them.

Victoria had no such apprehension about flying, and felt perfectly comfortable observing the landscape below. She noticed that they were much lower now, scarcely a hundred feet above the tallest treetops. They were gliding over a picturesque valley, and she could make out a river sparkling through the trees in the starlight. She glimpsed castles and cottages every so often as they passed overhead. Victoria had the strange sensation that they were passing above the landscape of the faerie tales that had been read to her as a young child, and that giants' castles, princesses' towers, and realms of high adventure and wonder were all there in their entirety.

Eventually, Elliot grew more confident. He scrutinized the landscape below with more fascination than fear. He swung his legs, leaning forward and trusting the wind that bore them. The children's hair rippled and their eyes watered from the swiftness of their passage through the cool night air.

Finally, Sindl pointed out the looming shadow of the westernmost mountains and they realized that they were almost at their journey's end. They were rising again now, gliding up into the foothills, and soon they were flying above a long, narrow lake that sparkled in the blue starlight. It was rimmed upon each side by the craggy outcroppings of the mountains.

Both Elliot and Victoria watched breathlessly as their destination drew nearer. At the head of the lake, in the tall silvery trees of a vast forest, they could see thousands of twinkling lights—the lights of the hidden city of the Faerie Queen.

They were descending steadily, the waters of the lovely starlit lake streaming past below their feet. At last they alighted upon a lawn that was as smooth as velvet.

Victoria realized that though the surrounding trees most resembled beeches, they were actually quite unlike any tree she had ever seen. Their trunks were thick, rising to tremendous heights. Their leaves, rustling in the soft evening wind, were noticeably luminescent.

But what amazed the children most of all was the fact that the Faerie Queen's city was constructed inside the trunks of the trees themselves. The trees had not been hollowed out or carved to accommodate the faerie city—rather, they appeared to have grown that way, with openings in their bark and vast interconnected hollows in their trunks. There were lamplit stairs rising into the boughs, and high bridges led from trunk to trunk across dizzying spans. There were hundreds of windows in every tree, even far up where they were veiled by boughs and branches.

Elliot and Victoria craned their necks upward to see faerie sentinels standing upon platforms high in the treetops.

Two faerie squires greeted them. "Come with us," they commanded. Elliot, Victoria, Sindl, and Aeron accompanied them, while the other faeries mingled with their companions in a formal yet joyous dance to wild, stirring music that swept about the foot of the trees.

Victoria watched the intricate steps of the faeries as they swept to and fro, until she ascended the broad stairs that led into the faerie city. For the very first time since leaving Prosingham Academy she was possessed of a mad desire to put on her ballet slippers and dance. Perhaps even to dance all through the night!

Chapter 7

AFTER ASCENDING a dizzying array of stairs, Elliot and Victoria found themselves in the royal palace of the faerie kingdom. They were led along a passage that sloped ever upward through the interior of one of the hollow trees with occasional smooth polished steps to ease them over the steepest ascent.

Faeries frequently flitted past as they went about palace business. The children noticed dozens of side passages and stairways that branched off in all directions. They would have become hopelessly lost had they attempted to find the way on their own.

Sindl and Aeron led them between two imposing sentinel statues and through an archway that had hidden lamps illuminating its hollow carvings from within. And thus it was that Elliot Good and Victoria Deveny first entered the great hall of the Faerie Queen.

The children could not help but blink their eyes and gaze in wonder at the scene of splendor that lay before them. The great hall was long and high, encompassing the hollow center of the most massive tree of all. An open hearth was surrounded by inlaid tiles set in flowing patterns. Only the most fragrant woods burned in the grate and the children thought the smell to be most heavenly. Many faerie courtiers sat all about the hearth while others reclined on tiers of high cushioned seats that rose upward on each side.

Fantastically formed archways upheld the high ceiling on stalwart pillars with fanning buttressed tops. The carvings reminded Victoria of the enchanted gate in the secret tower room at Summerwind.

From each pillar silver lamp stands of amazing detail protruded, supporting green and amber lamps that filled the hall with soothing light. "Rather like Christmastime at Harrods!" Victoria whispered to herself, recalling her holiday visits to the grand London department store.

Inside the pillars of the great hall, broad staircases spiraled upward to minstrels' galleries where musicians played poetic music full of longing. The music mingled with the merry voices and sounds of the faerie court.

Sindl and Aeron bade Victoria and Elliot come forward, leading them down alongside one edge of the hearth, close by its fragrant smoke. The children were trembling a little, self-conscious that they were still in their nightclothes and disheveled from their flight. Elliot tugged at the cuffs and collar of his pajamas in an effort to straighten them while Victoria swept her hair from her eyes and held the hem of Janet Good's nightgown up a bit lest it entangle her feet. But the faeries smiled at them graciously and seemed not to mind at all that they were not at their best appearance.

Elliot and Victoria stood awestruck before the steps that led up to the silver throne of the Faerie Queen. Victoria beheld her in amazement, for she saw that she had met her before—in the guise of the Mayweather nanny, and later, disguised as Mrs. Hampstead!

Elliot, too, had to blink back his astonishment, for there smiling at him, radiantly lovely in her gracious apparel, was the very same woman who had saved him from the bullies, and indeed, had danced atop the garden wall below his window seat.

The Faerie Queen was infinitely more beautiful in her true form than in any of the aspects under which she had previously appeared. She wore her hair high, set with a star-shaped diadem, and her gown was trimmed with blue and sprinkled with star sapphires at her cuffs, collar, and breast. She stepped lightly down from her silver throne to smile at both Aeron and Sindl and then she took Elliot and Victoria each by the hand.

"Hello, Elliot Good and Victoria Deveny! I am Edwina, Queen of the Faeries." Her voice was sweet with lilting inflections. "You have braved many perils to arrive here in my hall and I bid you most heartily welcome indeed!" She led Victoria and Elliot up the steps of the dais, making room for them on the sumptuous cushions of her throne, one on each side. The faerie folk who were gathered expectantly about the hearth drew nearer. Close beside the Faerie Queen stood her young daughter Mischil, an impish little faerie maid with short golden hair, an upturned nose, and a mischievous sprinkling of light freckles across her cheeks.

The Faerie Queen clapped her hands and earthenware bowls of cool water were brought for Elliot and Victoria to wash their hands and faces in, and then refreshments were served. Here, as in many of their experiences in Faerieland, the children later disagreed in their recollections. Elliot swore that the cool drink that was served in exquisite jeweled goblets was the most refreshing springwater he had ever tasted, while Victoria declared that it was the most delicious red wine, not dry and horrid like her uncle Dexter's claret, nor was it sickening and vile like his aged Madeira. Elliot said that the food was a kind of flavorful meat, and Victoria said that it was a lovely light bread, baked with honey.

After a bit, Victoria turned to earnestly gaze into the Faerie Queen's face. "Please, Your Majesty! We need your help desperately. Can you tell us why that dreadful Shadow Knight is pursuing us?"

"He threw his awful black orb that sucked my mother in and gave off this frightful black light and I'm afraid that she is . . ." and here Elliot found himself unable to finish and fought the urge to cry. A hush momentarily fell across the hall, and the fire in the long hearth darkened a trifle. Even little Mischil looked solemn and concerned. Sindl rested her hand supportively upon Elliot's knee.

The Faerie Queen answered softly, "The Shadow Knight covets your rings—indeed all others besides—on behalf of another who has sent him. For a wicked sorcerer queen, who can easily move between worlds herself, is endeavoring to make certain that others are prevented from doing so. She is determined to control all the doors between your world and ours, and if she succeeds, none of us will be safe any longer and darkness will triumph."

Victoria looked puzzled. "But if the doors are meant to go between our world and Faerieland, then why did I just end up in another country, in another time, when I went through the one in the tower at Summerwind?"

The Faerie Queen smiled. "Surely you've noticed by now that your rings have great magical power. In the hands of the right bearer—one who knows their capabilities and how to wield their magic—they can be used to create other doors, like the one that took you through time." Here the Faerie Queen paused, and frowned. "Of course, that is the problem with the Shadow Knight. He knows the power of these rings and will use the ones he has to open the doors to other interwoven worlds and allow terrible things into yours."

"Who is the Shadow Knight?" Elliot asked tremulously.

"Queen Ulricke of Lorinshar, who wields sorceries from her dark tower of Pendrongor, has brought him into being for her own purposes," replied the Faerie Queen.

"How can Queen Ulricke be stopped?" Victoria asked.

"It is not yet time for Queen Ulricke to be resisted directly," the Faerie Queen answered after a moment of consideration. "That battle will be fought in another world and in another time. But you, Elliot, and you, Victoria, must defeat the Shadow Knight now, for peril draws nigh."

"But how can we possibly defeat the Shadow Knight?" asked Elliot, his eyes wide with dismay.

"You must each embark upon a separate quest. Elliot's road

will take him into the very realm of Queen Ulricke herself. For he must find the red orb, the Orb of Fire that is in the possession of the Fire Dragon. And Victoria's quest will bring her into the Realm of Winter Night. She must there find the blue orb, the Orb of Ice, that only the Ice Dragon possesses.

"The orbs are sigils of tremendous magical portent, for they store the energies unleashed long ago in ancient battles between good and evil. These wars were titanic upheavals waged when the grandsires of these dragons were scarcely more than eggs and the world was young. Once you obtain the enchanted orbs, you must return to face the Shadow Knight together in Elliot's world—for it is the only hope of saving all the interwoven realms from falling under a perpetual shade of profound darkness and evil."

"Oh, no!" Victoria exclaimed in dismay. "I have seen the Ice Dragon, in a dream and beginning to materialize upon the page of a magic book—and I cannot bear him, not even his voice! Can no one retrieve these orbs but us? After all, Your Majesty, you have magical power to wield!"

Queen Edwina shook her head. "I'm sorry, Victoria, but only the finders of the rings may claim the orbs." Victoria felt a twinge of regret for being so eager to search out the secret room at Summerwind, but it was mixed with excitement as well. She had always wanted to go on a quest of the sort she'd read about in storybooks.

"Not only do we have to face the Shadow Knight," echoed Elliot in protest, "but we must go on our quests alone? By ourselves?"

The Faerie Queen regarded them thoughtfully. "You each have your rings, and they will give you magical aid. You will find friends and sustenance among the horrors you will face, and many surprises along your path!

"But for now, you are our guests and you must listen to our music and attend our convocation, for it will give you courage and joyfulness of heart. And then you may bathe and sleep, and thereafter your quests will commence."

"Our quests must begin tomorrow morning?" asked Victoria, clearly alarmed. She had hoped they would get to spend more time in the extraordinary faerie city.

"In this season in Faerieland, the days and nights are each a fortnight long," explained the queen. "And when you arrived at my eastern gate, the sun had just set, so your quest must begin well before morning, I'm afraid. But you will have time for sleeping nonetheless. Take courage, dear ones."

Now the great hall was filling with faerie folk of many types, not just blue faeries like the Faerie Queen and Aeron and Sindl's band. There were wild green faeries; sweetly solemn silver faeries; extravagantly beautiful, though somewhat haughty purple faeries; mischievous crimson faeries; and noble, poetic amber faeries.

The minstrels in the gallery above struck up merry music that coursed through the children's blood like stirring tonic, and soon they joined the faeries out on the open floor about the hearth. It may be that the faerie food and drink made them all the more fleet of foot, and it may be that faerie folk are the best dance teachers that ever could be. At any rate, both

Elliot and Victoria found themselves swept away with the faerie troupe. They whirled, twirled, and stepped in cadence with the others, all at breathtaking speed.

Sometimes the dancers took rapid wing, flitting into the air through the clouds of fragrant hearth smoke, to frolic up among the arches and lamps of the vaulted ceiling. Then the Faerie Queen's little daughter Mischil took them by the hand, joining them in giddy flight.

When Victoria and Elliot finally became tired, Aeron and Sindl led them from the convocation—where the dancing and music continued apace—out through a side doorway. They climbed a long spiral staircase leading into the uppermost treetops, where a guest room had been prepared especially for them. Its central chamber was perfectly round, consisting mostly of a luxurious window seat covered with soft cushions and thick counterpanes. The window's stained-glass panels glowed in the soft comfort of firelight from a nearby hearth. A teakettle had just begun to sing on the hob.

On each side of their sleeping chamber two separate screened bathing nooks awaited them. Hot scented water filled two scallop-shaped tubs, and thick warm towels were set out nearby. Aeron and Sindl poured their guests hot tea and then bade them good night as Elliot and Victoria each climbed into their baths and were soon soaking away their cares.

When they met again at the window-seat room, they had toweled dry and were clad in the softest nightclothes imaginable—faerie nightshirts that had been set out for them. The fire in their hearth had burned low and crackled softly on its bed of coals. The children climbed exhausted onto their window-seat bed, each collecting a pile of cushions to sleep among. They opened the stained-glass window to admit the softest of night breezes. It whispered in from across the lake, rustling the luminescent leaves of the palace trees.

Elliot and Victoria reached out their ring hands to touch fingertips and said that they would miss each other desperately in their separate quests.

Elliot made a very determined face. "Victoria, my quest shall be one of vengeance! The Shadow Knight killed my mother. But you don't have to be dragged into this. You can tell the Faerie Queen that you just want to go home!"

Victoria pressed her fingertip to his lips to quiet him. "There is always hope, Elliot," she said fiercely, though in her heart she had deep misgivings. "But you and I are adventurers, and although we must embark upon separate quests, we are friends forever and in it till the end! And besides, I do not yet want to go home!"

Their conversation continued until they grew sleepy. As Elliot drifted off, he noticed faerie sentries standing upon tiny lamplit platforms, high in the nearby treetops. Victoria thought that she saw other children flying overhead, hand in hand with faeries trailing lamps from silver chains. She wondered briefly if other children had been summoned into Faerieland to embark upon other adventures.

Soon both Elliot and Victoria were fast asleep as the soft wind from the foothills of the mountains soothingly ruffled their hair and gently drew them into a deeper and yet more peaceful slumber.

∽

ELLIOT WAS MUTTERING in his sleep—something to do with his shattered bicycle—when a gentle hand shook him awake and he opened his eyes to see Sindl gazing down. Her face was serious. Nearby, Aeron was shaking Victoria awake and was startled when Victoria, still half asleep, said something really rather rude.

"Time to get ready," said Sindl. "Queen Edwina will meet us at the postern gate." Elliot's heart was pounding. A profound sense of excitement, mingled with dread, was stealing over him. He looked to Victoria. He could see she was feeling similar by the bright look in her eyes as she stood up and stretched.

Aeron and Sindl brought basins of cool, clear water for the children to wash up. Then they were sent to separate chambers where they found clothes set out for them: for Victoria, items suitable for the Realm of Winter Night, and for Elliot, garments appropriate for the Realm of Lorinshar—the perilous kingdom of the wicked queen.

Victoria didn't like her clothes and bluntly said so. The fabric was plain and, worst of all, itchy, though it was thick and warm. The sturdy leather shoes were graceless and Victoria informed Sindl that the square buckles on her toes were hopelessly out of style. Shoe buckles were so eighteenth century, after all, and certainly not something one would expect Lord Deveny's niece to wear!

Elliot didn't mind his clothes quite so much. He wore a linen tunic under a thick doublet equipped with leather shoulder pads. Beneath the tunic he wore coarsely woven hose tucked into short brown boots. A plaid cloak completed his ensemble—and to his delight he found a small, sheathed dagger hanging from the belt they gave him.

As Aeron and Sindl led them from their room into the corridor, both Elliot and Victoria looked back longingly at the soft cushions of their window seat. They couldn't help but wonder if they would ever enjoy such accommodations again.

As the children followed Aeron and Sindl up the twisting staircases and down the narrow passages of the palace, they passed faerie courtiers of all kinds who smiled and wished them well.

"Evidently they are attempting to put a bold face on it, Elliot, but I daresay they know that we are in well over our heads," Victoria whispered.

"Don't say things like that, Victoria!" Elliot gulped. It was quite hard enough for him to keep his courage up as it was.

Finally they came to a perfectly round room lit by dozens of tall candlesticks. In another moment, they were led out a low doorway to find themselves standing on the porch of the upper postern gate, which faced the mountains.

Elliot and Victoria stood with their hands upon the railing gazing up into the splendor of the heavens. They were transfixed by the countless array of blazing stars.

"It is as if we are at the seashore and every grain of sand's a star," Victoria breathed.

"Look, Victoria—a falling star!" Elliot exclaimed. A second later the children gasped in wonder as a hundred more slid silently down the sky to burst like fireworks into cascades of celestial light out over the foothills.

It was then that the children heard the soft rustling of robes behind them. They turned about and saw that Queen Edwina had joined them.

"I have come from the convocation to give you last-minute counsel," she said softly.

"The faerie convocation is still going on!" Victoria exclaimed with astonishment. "Don't faeries ever get weary?"

Queen Edwina smiled. "Not in the way mortals do, Victoria, though when we rest it is because we wish to, not because we must." Her expression immediately grew solemn. "I see that Aeron and Sindl did their work well and that you are both equipped for your respective adventures. But there are one or two more things yet to accomplish."

The queen bade Elliot hold out his hand, and then she took the finger that held his ring between her own thumb and forefinger. The queen softly uttered a magic word. Both children's eyes widened, for Elliot's ring had transformed into a plain silver band—its stone had disappeared altogether.

"Do not worry, Elliot," said the Faerie Queen. "Your ring is still exactly as it was. I have simply laid a strong masking spell upon it. It will appear as an unimportant band to everyone who sees it—perhaps even to Queen Ulricke herself, although her powers have grown dreadfully since I last knew her, when she was scarcely more than a child!"

Elliot turned rather pale. "You mean I might have to actually meet her?"

"Perhaps," replied the Faerie Queen. "And the enchantments may not deceive her, for she is cunning. But it may fool others you meet along the way—those who don't have your best interests at heart." Elliot had little idea what the Faerie Queen meant exactly, but he did not care for the sound of it at all.

Then the queen had Victoria come forward and she took Victoria's ring finger in her hand and intoned another magic word. Victoria was shocked to see her ring vanish totally. All that was left upon her finger was a ring-shaped green stain— as if a cheap copper band had recently been worn there, then removed.

"It is but another enchantment," the queen explained. "Your ring is still there, but none will see it." Queen Edwina grew even more serious as she laid her hand gently on Victoria's shoulder. "I fear that if I made it appear, even as a plain silver band like Elliot's, it would be taken from you where you are going!"

"How perfectly beastly!" exclaimed Victoria, now more certain than ever that she did not like the sound of the Realm of Winter Night.

The Faerie Queen embraced Elliot and Victoria, holding them close to her heart as she wished them well. Her final words to the children were "Remember, do not be deceived by the offer of power tainted with evil." And then Queen Edwina left Victoria and Elliot on the postern porch.

Sindl announced, "Come. It is time for us to journey to the gate that will take Victoria to the Realm of Winter Night and Elliot to the Realm of Lorinshar."

"It is a gate of high air, for it is situated far above our palace," added Aeron.

Aeron and Sindl leaped up, to stand poised atop the silver railing, their wings twinkling in the starlight. They reached down to help Elliot and Victoria up, and in a moment they were hand in hand with the faeries, their legs trembling.

"Ready?" asked Sindl.

"Ready!" declared Victoria.

"R-ready," stammered Elliot.

And a second later, with a dizzying dip and a heart-stopping swoop, they were off, in full flight. They glided high into the starlit night, moving in great circles. They flew higher and higher, until even the massive palace tree grew smaller and smaller among its fellow trees, its luminescent leaves soon lost in the sparkling forest far below. The lake with its smooth lawn at one end now appeared as a tiny pond.

Elliot peered upward in the direction of their steadily rising progress. He noticed what he first thought to be a cluster of bright blue stars, but then he realized, as they drew near, that he was seeing the lamps upon the stairs of the gate. A structure similar to the one that was their portal into Faerieland was floating, suspended in thin air.

Its platform was shaped like an upside-down V with a rising staircase on each side and an archway at the very top. Aeron and Sindl guided the children to a soft landing on the steps. The gate was guarded by a troop of faeries standing poised straight and tall, two upon each stair, wings shimmering in the starlight, their garments and hair streaming out behind them in the freshening wind.

Aeron and Sindl led them slowly up the stairs, until they stood apprehensively before the archway. Sindl placed her hands on Victoria's shoulders and smiled at her. "You will go first, Victoria."

Aeron added, "Remember that I will come to aid you as often as I can. And because of the manner in which different worlds effect different forms, I will likely appear smaller in the Realm of Winter Night. But that may make it easier for me to aid you in secret."

Victoria smiled, thanking him, her hair whipping across her face. She threw her arms impulsively around Sindl and Aeron. Then she turned her attention to Elliot. When they embraced, each held the other tightly and neither child's eyes were dry.

"Good-bye and be careful, Victoria!" Elliot said earnestly.

"It's not a good-bye, it's only a see-you-later, so there!" Victoria said defiantly. Then she steeled herself and stepped quickly through the gate to vanish in a burst of sparkling radiance.

Aeron and Sindl moved to stand close by Elliot. He looked rather lost and forlorn without Victoria. Sindl smiled at him and ruffled his hair reassuringly. He regarded her solemnly.

"Remember that I will come to your aid," she said. "Your ring will help me locate you."

"Like Tinkerbell," said Elliot, then he felt silly, but of course neither Aeron nor Sindl knew what he meant. The faeries embraced him, and urged him to be brave. Then Elliot took a deep breath and stepped quickly through the gate—before he lost his nerve entirely. A moment later, he, too, disappeared in an abrupt burst of light.

Chapter 8

VICTORIA HAD A momentary dizzying sensation. She felt as though she were tumbling head over heels for a bit, then swirling about and falling, all at the same time. Despite her innate bravery, it was a feeling that she did not much care for. But within a minute or so, she found herself gliding earthward in a heavy twilight, through thickly falling snow. She had half expected that she would plummet earthward at breakneck speed, slowing down at the last possible moment before reaching the ground—but the magical power of the gate was all about her, upholding her and easing her down as gently as the falling snowflakes.

She was soon glad of her clothes, plain as they might be, for despite their homeliness they did keep her warm. She clutched her heavy cloak about herself more snugly. She looked down past her feet—clad in those silly shoes with the ridiculous square buckle on each toe—peering beyond the countless snowflakes for some sign of the ground. At last she glimpsed vague lights a good way off, down through the blurry dimness.

Victoria's heart began to beat more rapidly, for she knew that her real adventure was now just beginning. Soon she saw that the illumination came from tall lampposts. These were not lovely blue and silver lampposts like those in Faerieland, but a plainer variety made of wrought iron. Next she saw wooden buildings rising up toward her in the gloom.

The folds of Victoria's outer cloak whipped about her as the wind increased its velocity. Everywhere now she saw streets lined with lamps, and tall, weather-beaten wooden buildings—structures so narrow and so high that it appeared as though they were leaning forward and quite ready to topple into one another.

She glided to a gentle landing, alighting in the middle of a narrow street overshadowed by houses and shops, many of which had yellow lights shining through snowy windowpanes. The thick leather soles of her shoes crunched into the fresh snow.

Victoria stood rather forlornly for a minute or so, alone in the street. The wind was tugging at her clothes more persistently now. She pulled her collar up close about her chin, tucked her hands deep into her pockets, and began trudging forward. She did not notice that behind her, her footprints led backward for a few paces, then stopped abruptly at the point where she had landed. The snow was quickly obscuring them—and that was fortunate, for it would have appeared quite peculiar if anyone had seen them.

At first Victoria didn't realize she was hearing bells at all, but then the jangling grew more insistent, and she turned to see a horse pulling a small sleigh.

The sleigh pulled up alongside Victoria, swishing to a halt in the snow. The portly gentleman driving it had yanked rather sharply on the reins, heedless of the bit in his horse's mouth. He was a fleshy, well-dressed man with a florid face and longish white hair that fell to his collar at the sides. Victoria saw that he was quite bald on top when he doffed his tricornered hat in an exaggerated gesture of formal politeness.

His lips were full and complacent, but his eyes remained narrow and cold. Victoria did not like the look of him one little bit, so she simply tossed her head and kept walking. The man flicked the reins in his gloved hands and made a disagreeable clicking noise with his tongue. The horse began plodding slowly forward, to match Victoria's pace, the bells of its harness jangling halfheartedly.

"And who might you be, child?" the man inquired, his hearty baritone voice booming. Victoria rather liked his voice; she wished that it went with someone nicer. She was still uncertain what to do, so she ignored the man for the time being and kept walking.

"I am Clericor Demyin," he said pleasantly enough, though Victoria could detect self-importance in his tone and perhaps the beginning of annoyance as well. "I daresay that you are a stranger hereabouts, and I must warn you that you will die of exposure if you spend the night in the street. It is quite cold, and due to get colder still, I'll be bound!"

When he received no reply, he continued. "You will not find a single door open to you this night, or any night for that matter, for there is a strict curfew and the watch will enforce it most vigorously indeed with stout cudgels!"

"Why are you out and about, then?" Victoria asked bluntly. The man seemed only momentarily taken aback by her spirited reply, but she could detect a flash of anger dying quickly behind his eyes and it was impossible to tell if his subsequent boom of laughter was natural or artfully contrived.

"In my capacity as Clericor, I am good enough to patrol hereabouts from time to time, warning any wayward souls of their transgression—lest the watch fall upon them and give them a good sound drubbing. We must be perilously careful, you see, child, for we live very nigh to the Great Frozen Inland Sea, which is haunted—tainted with the very presence of evil! Good righteous, hardworking folk must all be safe abed when twilight ends and darkness falls!"

Victoria hesitated, not liking the sound of the "Great Frozen Inland Sea" or the terms "tainted with evil" or "haunted" very much at all. Clericor Demyin pursed his smug lips and pressed home his advantage.

"Child, you will indeed freeze to death if you stay the night outside. I can take you to the Black Swan Inn, where you would receive a warm supper and a bed, too, if you like. Of course you will have to work for your keep—for idleness is not tolerated hereabouts, and neither are vagabonds or beggars!"

"Very well then," Victoria said wearily. She stopped and

stood quietly waiting, still suspiciously studying Clericor Demyin, and not liking the look of him. But the thought of a warm supper and a bed—maybe even a fire—at an inn, or anywhere, for that matter, did make her realize that she was by now very nearly chilled to the bone.

Clericor Demyin invited Victoria up into his sleigh and she climbed aboard, sitting as far from him as possible. He offered her a spare lap blanket, which she tucked about her knees and found that it proved to be a substantial help against the wind. He took up the reins once more, shaking them impatiently, while making another unpleasant noise with his tongue, and they were off, the brass bells of the harness all ajangle once again.

Victoria noticed that the horse's ears had flattened to its head at the disagreeable sound that Clericor Demyin made, and she got the distinct impression that his horse disliked him even more than she did. She shifted in her seat uneasily when she noticed that the man was chuckling to himself, as if only he knew of some private little joke.

Clericor Demyin skillfully guided the sleigh through the snowy streets, then over the stone arc of a bridge spanning a frozen canal, and down at least a half dozen more narrow byways. The ceaselessly falling snow caused all the streets to look very much alike, crammed with high wooden buildings with diamond-paned windows, steep roofs, tall chimneys, and overhanging upper stories.

At one point they passed the watch—five burly men in snowy tricornered hats and thick greatcoats who carried lanterns and clubs. They appeared brutal and surly. Nonetheless, they tipped their hats respectfully to Clericor Demyin, who smiled at them indulgently.

"These are wonderful lads, brave and stalwart fellows, who keep our streets safe at night for good honest, decent folk," he boasted, his chest swelling with pomposity and pride. Victoria had to stifle an almost overpowering urge to reply that if the watch and Clericor Demyin were the most honest and decent folk about, this village must be a wretched place indeed, but she bit her tongue.

Finally the sleigh swished to a halt before the front of a building that was substantially more sizable than most. The sign reading BLACK SWAN INN AND BAKERY, adorned with a chipped swan painting, swayed creaking in the wind. But what Victoria noticed most of all was the delightful smell of freshly baked bread.

Clericor Demyin glanced sideways at her, his lips curled into an expression that was almost a sneer. "Wait here if you please, dear child," he said abruptly, after tucking the reins about an iron hook in the front curve of the sleigh's dash. Then he stepped down, trudging through the snow and up the steps to knock twice upon the inn's heavy door. He admitted himself without waiting for a response.

Victoria sat huddled forlornly, temporarily abandoned in the sleigh. She looked longingly at the warm yellow light from the interior of the inn when the door briefly opened, then slammed shut again behind Clericor Demyin.

She shivered as she waited, but soon the door opened once more and Clericor Demyin beckoned her to join him on the step. "And be quick about it, girl," he said peevishly, all pretense of kindliness forgotten. "These good folk have a business to run, and shouldn't be kept waiting by the likes of you!"

Victoria stepped down from the sleigh, picking her way carefully through the deepening snow, and went up the steps to the inn. A man and woman had joined Clericor Demyin in the doorway. The woman was dark haired and hard-eyed, and looked rather ferocious. The man was tall, heavily set, and wore a greasy apron that apparently hadn't been washed in ages. When Victoria got to the second step she found herself stiff with cold, and Clericor Demyin grasped her arm, pulling her up impatiently.

"What is your name, child?" he demanded.

"I am Victoria Deveny," she said, putting on a brave face and drawing herself up to her full height, trying to appear much larger and more formidable than in fact she was.

"Victoria, is it?" Clericor Demyin spat, accompanied by a disagreeable snicker from the man and a positively venomous glare from the woman. "Victoria, I want you to meet your new benefactors, Vidal and Nastya, from whom you will receive gainful employment, and who are kind and benevolent enough to take you in."

Vidal offered Victoria a thick-fingered greasy hand to shake and she did so reluctantly, not wishing to appear rude or ungrateful, for she was most anxious to get to the warm firelight of the low-ceilinged room she glimpsed beyond. The woman glared down at Victoria as she stepped closer, shaking a gaunt finger scarcely an inch from the tip of her nose.

"You'll get a supper, don't you worry," she hissed. "But you'll earn your keep at the Black Swan Inn, make no mistake. We're not a charity. Frankly, I doubt that you've done much honest work in all your life—so far!"

Her husband and Clericor Demyin both laughed heartily. Then the Clericor bade Nastya and Vidal good night. He showed himself out still chuckling. Victoria was finally escorted into the delicious warmth of the room beyond. There was a bright fire burning in the hearth and tables with ladderback chairs were set all about the center of the room, with wooden booths at the sides and the rear. The room was full of guests, but none seemed friendly. Men and women heavily wrapped to ward off the chill lingering in the corners away from the fire sat grim faced and taciturn. The guests had mostly finished their meals and were either dabbing what was left of their bread into the remnants of their broth or finishing their drinks from pewter tankards. Two hulking men seated nearest the fire, who looked like they might be off-duty members of the watch, were smoking a foul-smelling tobacco in smudged clay pipes and talking among themselves in low voices.

A painfully thin girl with sunken cheeks, clad in a coarse dress and a threadbare apron, began gathering up the supper things from the tables.

"Constance!" barked Vidal. The thin girl jumped, trembling at the sound of his voice. "See that this new girl gets supper in the kitchen, and show her where you sleep. Just give her the turnip gruel. Mind, I can't spare the potato and mutton broth for the likes of either of you."

Victoria thought she saw a brief glint of camaraderie in Constance's eyes before they turned dull and hopeless again.

"Yes, sir," she said humbly, beckoning Victoria to follow her. Victoria could not help but notice that her fingers trembled, quivering as though she were ill.

Victoria was soon seated on a stool in the corner of the scullery, with a bowl of lukewarm turnip gruel on the rough planks before her. She looked longingly at the loaves of freshly baked bread hot from the oven. A harsh-faced woman in a flour-dusted apron was setting them in racks to cool.

Victoria was so looking forward to a slice of the nice fresh bread! But when Constance handed her a chipped plate with just a single rind of dry crust on it she almost cried. Constance's haunted eyes were eloquent in their expression of apology. "I am truly sorry," she whispered. "But they won't let us have the good bread, only the leftovers." Victoria was shocked—the servants in her uncle's household ate far better than this.

It was then that the door from the dining room opened to admit Nastya. Constance scurried away like a fearful little mouse, hurrying back to the drudgery of her unending labors.

"Please, ma'am," Victoria said politely. "I would much prefer some fresh bread!"

She was quite unprepared for the eye-smarting slap Nastya delivered to her still half-frozen right cheek.

Chapter 9

AT FIRST ELLIOT was overwhelmed by a confused sensation of spinning and whirling about, but after it subsided, he became less disoriented. He realized that he was falling—though in a controlled fashion—descending through a damp, cold mist. He had the strong feeling that it was morning wherever he was, well past dawn perhaps, but still morning nonetheless. Despite his fear of heights, he peered down, anxious to see what sort of landscape he was approaching.

Elliot discerned nebulous shapes sliding past but could not properly identify them for some time. He squinted, trying to penetrate his surroundings. Presently, he descended out of a layer of cloud and the mist grew thinner and the light about him brightened considerably. He was gliding slowly past huge outcroppings of rock, alongside the steep upper slopes of a vast mountain range. Not only was he nowhere near the ground at all, but he was still several thousand feet above the treetops of the forests down in the valley below.

As the magic of the high gate eased him gently to the valley floor, more of the mist dissipated to reveal the dizzying heights and perilous cliffs of the mountain slopes sliding past. Finally he drew out from under the cloud completely and glimpsed more of the features of the landscape below. It seemed a most pleasant place indeed. The glittering thread of a distant river wound through a landscape comprised of low grasslands, hill-crested forests, and lakes shining like lovely blue mirrors in the morning sun.

Great piles of white clouds loomed high overhead, and the brilliant patches of vivid sky dramatically affected the play of light and shadow in the valley below. He watched the shadows of clouds drift across the valley floor, momentarily dimming the light and muting the sparkle of the river and lakes. And then the clouds parted again, allowing rays of sunlight to penetrate once more, painting the valley with color.

Elliot had not directly glimpsed the sun until, in his diagonal descent, he passed the notch of a steep valley, which opened off in the distance. He gave an involuntary gasp of surprise—for the sun in this realm was impossibly huge, at least four or five times larger than the sun Elliot knew, and it was crimson red.

To his amazement he saw that the very center of the sun appeared to be missing, as though it was pierced by a dark hole. But he soon realized that its center was simply obscured, blotted out by a rounded shape. It occurred to Elliot that he was landing during a solar eclipse, and that the moon had begun moving across the disk of the sun. He was astonished, for as the sun of the Realm of Lorinshar was far larger than his own, so its moon was smaller.

As Elliot got closer to the ground, he found himself approaching a thicket of trees. He grew worried that he would land in their prickly tops, or worse still, be impaled on sharp branches. But the power of the gate was still about him, slowing his descent. The topmost branch of the tallest tree scraped across the sole of his boot, and then he was safely past, angling quickly toward his landing. A moment later Elliot was safe upon the ground and such was his elation that he felt ready for any adventure.

He clambered up the sloping side of a large boulder with some difficulty. Once up, he sat still to catch his breath and get his bearings. It was now much warmer, so he undid his tartan cloak, pinning it back on his shoulder. He scanned the surrounding landscape. To his disappointment, he saw no sign of castles, villages, or even cottages, for that matter— nor indeed of any human habitation at all—so he set out at once.

It took him a good deal longer than expected to clamber down the treacherous slopes, carefully picking his way across expanses of bare rock. By now he was hot and hungry. But what bothered him most was the thirst. It had come upon him suddenly and grew out of all proportion—mainly because he saw no immediate solace nearby. The river and lakes he glimpsed from the air were still miles off, and Elliot was quite certain that he would die of thirst long before reaching them.

As he trudged on, he heard a noise that gave him hope. He paused, standing still, listening carefully. He was delighted to hear the rushing sound of a small stream cascading down through the highlands. Elliot reached it in moments and knelt on the mossy bank, dipping his hands in the stream to draw the cold water to his lips. As he did, the quality of light about him suddenly dimmed. At first he thought that the sun had gone behind a cloud—but when he gazed upward, he saw that the sky was now completely clear.

However, once again the shadow of a moon was crossing the disk of the sun, and he realized with alarm that this world must have two moons—perhaps even more, who could say. This second moon was much larger than the first, and he could tell by the angle of its curve that when the second eclipse achieved totality, the world about him would grow very dark indeed. Elliot had no desire to stumble about a rock-strewn mountainside in total darkness, so once again he clambered up to sit on the edge of a flat boulder.

As the eclipse progressed, Elliot had a premonition of dread. It seemed that there was something sinister about this second eclipse—an aspect far more threatening than an astronomical event. Something frightful and malignant was creeping out from the shadows as the light slowly darkened.

First it grew chilly, then truly cold, and once again Elliot unpinned his cloak, drawing it about himself. He shivered against a bitter wind that sprang up to hiss about the rocks and trees around him.

Elliot sensed he was being watched. As the black disk of

the second moon swept across the great red sun, engulfing all light, he crept down from the boulder to sit with his back braced against its lichen-covered side. He was more uncomfortable than before, but at least he was sheltered from the direct force of the wind, and felt less exposed to peril.

It was at the very moment of totality, when the sun above his head appeared as a glowing red ring, with a final flash of gemstone radiance—and the eclipse became absolute—that Elliot heard a series of loud quivering booms, the sounds rolling and echoing toward him. A loud, bloodcurdling blast, as from a horn, pierced the darkness. It was a harsh sound that reverberated off the rocks and hillsides. Then he heard a dreadful clamor rapidly approaching, drawing nearer upon the wings of a malignant wind.

He also heard another sound, one he liked even less than the horn. It was a mournful, distorted baying. Elliot was seized with a spine-chilling certainty that whatever made those awful sounds would not only be dangerous, but ghastly to look upon.

He drew farther back, cowering against the rock, as if it could open to create a sanctuary for him. His face had grown deathly white. From the sound of the approaching beasts, Elliot pictured razor fangs and deadly claws. A profound horror of being devoured swept over him, a primitive fear of being torn limb from limb and left for dead in a strange world under a blotted-out sun.

The horn sounded harshly again and the dreadful baying sounds approached closer still. Elliot grasped the hilt of his dagger, drawing it from its sheath, thankful at least to have that meager defense to wield against whatever atrocity was upon him.

The nightmare shapes took form, faded, coalesced, and took shape once more before his terror-stricken gaze. Shaggy beasts with unhinged jaws and gory fangs half materialized in front of him. The beasts appeared to neither possess nor require eyes, for only twitching snouts probed their surroundings.

Their riders seemed barely able to control the beasts, and were even more vague and shadowy of form, appearing intermittently, as figures cloaked in menace. They were partially revealed, then concealed once more by pale fingers of cold gray mist. At last the evil horde passed by and the tumult slowly faded, its echoes moving farther away, up into the hills.

Elliot wondered if he was being hunted. He sat absolutely still for the longest time, all alone in the dark of the solar eclipse, his heart thudding, his hands trembling violently as they brandished the dagger before him.

THIRTY LEAGUES to the north of where Elliot waited, hoping desperately that the phantom riders and their dreadful creatures would not return, a tall tower of dark stone rose upward from the solid crags of a steep mountainside.

Its highest spire tapered to a needle point nine hundred feet above the massive fanning bulwarks of its base. At the summit of the spire were four arched doorways, each with its own balcony. The doors faced the cardinal points of the compass.

Fifty feet below the balconies, a crenellated battlement ran about the entire circumference of the spire.

A mighty walled citadel stood at the base of the tower, separated by a bridge of black stonework. Upon its walls stood heavily armored watchmen in masked helms, clad in dark cloaks concealing tunics of black chain mail. Their captains wore sinister iron masks, some owl-faced, while others had ominous protruding noses and still others had ghastly, horrified expressions frozen on their features.

As huge as the fortress was above ground, it was even more labyrinthine below, with countless dungeons, gaping crypts, and dark sealed chambers imprisoning hideous beasts. There were lightless hibernacula where the most horrid monstrosities imaginable slumbered like the dead, awaiting the command of their mistress to awaken and wreak havoc in the world.

From the topmost spire of Pendrongor a long black and purple pennant rippled in the chill wind of the eclipse. It was a signal that Ulricke, Queen of the Realm of Lorinshar, was present and holding court.

High in the queen's tower, two of her handmaidens stepped out from the eastern door onto the balcony, each carrying a large wicker basket. They were flawless young women, seemingly possessed of every grace, witticism, and sophistication that life at court could demand. They were clad in the costliest garments and the finest jewelry. Their hair was swept upward in a fashion both regal and becoming, affixed in place by pins and combs of sparkling gemstone.

But their hands were another matter entirely. If Victoria

had seen them she would have been reminded of a drawing of a wicked faerie she had once seen in a children's book. Just the image had given her unpleasant dreams for a week and even her unflappable governess had refused to read from it. For the hands of Ulricke's handmaidens were dirty, filthy even, and their clever, tapering fingers were grotesquely elongated, equipped with large bony knuckles and sharp black nails.

The handmaidens approached the railing, which overlooked the crenellated battlements. They rested their baskets upon the polished marble of the railing before them, then turned about to face the door, the lamps at each side of the doorway illuminating their serenely sweet faces.

Then Queen Ulricke stepped from the doorway, moving out upon the balcony to join her handmaidens. Upon her head was a black crown, fashioned of a metal strange to behold. She moved so smoothly that she appeared to be gliding rather than walking. Her long skirts rippled across the polished floor in all directions, terminating in long, ragged tendrils that seemed to have a life all their own. Her gown was such a deep shade of black that it made every other color of black seem but a shade of gray. Her sleeves were long, and as she walked she kept them tucked into each other, so that her hands were concealed. Her dress was trimmed with the finest embroidery and studded with black onyx. Pale moonstones graced every swirl of the patterns repeating at sleeve and hem.

But the most remarkable thing about Queen Ulricke's gown was the lamps that it bore. Five vertical points rose upward from folds that began about her knees, rising in high ripples of utter blackness all about her. At the peak of each of the five folds was a small pointed lamp, fashioned of the same dark metal as her crown. Each lamp enclosed a writhing black flame.

A long chain was fastened around Queen Ulricke's neck. Suspended from it was a black orb fixed in the center of a starburst pendant of purest silver. The orb grew larger as the queen stepped forward across the paving stones, in the darkness of the eclipse—and a purple flame at its center burned the more fiercely.

Queen Ulricke's face was youthful, possessed of an extreme and flawless loveliness. There was a sweet and fastidious quality to her beauty that at first glance appeared almost childlike. But her skin was extremely pale, especially in contrast to her long straight black hair, and her eyes were a vivid red. The combination made her appear quite alarming indeed.

"Ahh! The darkness of totality is by itself quite enough to delight one's soul!" she exclaimed in greeting her handmaidens, who curtsied deeply, holding their servile positions until Ulricke's small elegant hands emerged from her flowing sleeves to bid them rise. The five lamps upon her gown guttered and flickered as a chill and cheerless wind swept across the balcony between the iron rails. Queen Ulricke's hands sported contorting, twisting rings fashioned of the same black metal as her crown.

"And how are my dear sweet angels?" the queen inquired. "They must be simply famished!" She stepped farther forward, joining her maidens to peer over the polished balustrade. Each crenellation of the gallery below sported its own rusted iron ring, driven deeply into solid stone. From each ring ancient chains looped across the filthy straw-strewn flagstones. Imprisoned at the end of these chains were hideous beastly forms, some with their paws outstretched and their tongues lolling from gaping jaws. Others sat back on gaunt haunches, their huge heads hung low, but their furtive eyes directed upward toward their mistress.

These were Queen Ulricke's were-beasts. Many of her knights and lords had become werewolves and wereboars long ago, and some could become worse things during the various lunar phases. But during a total eclipse they were in beast form entirely and kept in chains—both for their own safety and for the safety of their queen's other subjects.

Off to the side by itself lurked a hulking shadow exhaling blue phosphorescent vapors with every icy breath. The more one looked directly at it, the more it wasn't there at all, but it loomed vast and frightful nonetheless, on the periphery of one's vision. It was an undefined form of menace, an apparition haunting the shadows of one's consciousness. Even Queen Ulricke's handmaidens feared it and were scarcely able to look upon it.

This creature was Lord Sarton, a being of such incredible power that he was ofttimes only half in the physical realm. Ages ago his sorcery had transformed him into an astral shape-shifter. He was bound with two chains, a physical one composed of iron links, and another, glowing and half transparent, that kept him from wreaking havoc in the astral realm.

"Oh my dears! My sweet children! My lovely angels!" exclaimed the queen, looking down upon her were-beasts fondly, her pale little hands resting delicately on the rail before her. "Feed them their dainty morsels at once," she ordered.

With angelic smiles the handmaidens reached down to grope in their baskets. Then, up from the depths of their baskets came their grotesque hands, bearing slick, jiggling bits of mystery flesh—quivering, dangling, and dripping blood.

The handmaidens relished the feel of the wet meats in their grasp as they held and squeezed them, making them squelch and pop before tossing them over the balcony rail. The uproar was immediate and intense. Growling, howling, yelping, and gnashing ensued as Queen Ulricke's famished beasts leaped into the air, snapping their fangs. They lunged and leaped to the limit of their chains, heedless of the bite of cruel iron about their necks.

Most of the foul morsels were devoured in midair before they even hit the straw-covered flagstones. The few pieces that did manage to reach the ground were fought over and torn to shreds by phosphorescent-eyed monsters that snapped and lunged at one another, slavering and roaring in their bloodlust.

"Oh, how simply lovely! How perfectly divine!" exclaimed Queen Ulricke. She laughed delightedly, extending her arms to embrace both handmaidens. The trio stood still, riveted by the spectacle below, beatific smiles pasted on their faces. After several minutes of relishing their sport, the queen stirred and reluctantly tore her eyes from the scene.

"And now to business! The sacred ceremony of the dark of the sun must never be neglected!"

Both handmaidens swiftly stepped aside, looking expectantly toward the door leading into the tower's private apartments. Queen Ulricke's face went very still as she stretched her slender hands out before her, palms upward, as if she was about to receive something. Then very slowly, gliding from the shadows of the doorway, came a huge black cauldron, floating through the air without so much as a sound.

A glowing fog brimmed over the cauldron's edge and bubbled from it to spill down its sides in pallid wisps. Queen Ulricke raised her hands again and the vessel paused before her. She made another sign with her fingers and bronze supports materialized below the cauldron, upholding it on a base composed of grinning half-moon faces, scorpions with interlocked tails, and knotted sea serpents.

The black flames in the queen's lamp gown wavered. Even her maids looked fearful as she stepped chanting round the cauldron until she faced the black disk of the eclipsed sun across its frothing rim. She grasped the pendant that was suspended about her neck, unfastening her orb from the grip of its tines. She held it high over the cauldron, then released it. It did not fall—rather it hovered, unmoving. The orb drew the vapor up from the cauldron, roiling it about itself, until it appeared as a rotating ball of glowing fog that only half concealed the black and purple flame of the orb within. Queen Ulricke grew taller and more alarming as her eyes flamed a more vivid crimson.

"The sigil of the dark sun tells me of one who approaches Lorinshar," she intoned, her voice quiet and steady, as if she were speaking from a deep sleep. "My shadow seekers and phantom sentries have sensed him and run him to ground beyond the outer frontiers of my realm. He cowers now in great fear, his puny dagger outstretched before him.

"He shall be my guest and choices shall be offered him. But I shall not send my servants for him yet. It will be an amusement to see how splendidly or miserably he does when confronted with what awaits him on the path."

Queen Ulricke paused and folded her hands before her as if in prayer, an expression of utter concentration upon her face. "Ah! There is one that would come to aid this wretched spineless boy! A mere sprite shall not defend him, nor shall I permit any meddlesome subject of the Faerie Queen entry into my realm!"

And then Queen Ulricke stretched out her hands before her to cast a green powder into the cauldron. The amount of fog immediately increased so that it flowed down from the cauldron's rim to expand across the paving stones of the balcony, seething all about the queen and her handmaidens' feet. The queen chanted a powerful spell to prevent anyone from entering her kingdom to either comfort or assist Elliot—as the black rings writhed and squirmed upon her fingers.

Chapter 10

THE NEXT SEVERAL WEEKS, or perhaps it was even months—Victoria soon lost count—were a nightmare of drudgery and toil. She and Constance were virtual slaves at the Black Swan Inn. They scoured pots, perpetually stirred great cauldrons of soup, endlessly cranked roasting meats on iron basting spits in the open hearth—meats they themselves were not permitted to taste. They scrubbed floors and stairways and waited on tables, catering to each demanding guest's whim. They cleaned the guest rooms—but never to the grudging satisfaction of Nastya. They laundered enormous piles of soiled linen, lit cookstoves and bakery ovens before anyone else was even awake, and got grimy emptying sooty dustbins.

But for Victoria, the hardest thing—and the most enjoyable at the same time—was assisting the surly baker with the bread. Kneading and pounding the dough was a titillation that made her stomach growl, and using the thick pot-holder gloves and flat long-handled pans to take fresh loaves from the oven was a refined torment, yet still a keen delight. It made her hunger all the more difficult to bear, but at least she reveled in the aromas, inhaling the intoxicating smell of the flour and dough, as well as the bewitching fragrance of newly baked loaves.

Victoria quickly grew to like and trust Constance, for Constance showed her the ropes in a thoughtful way that helped keep her out of trouble. Some people only partially show someone else how to do something, keeping the best secrets for themselves so they will look superior, but Constance wasn't like that. She was kind to Victoria, and the two became fast friends.

One evening Victoria was driven to fury by the fashion in which a table of pampered girls, very near their own age, treated Constance. They took delight in demeaning her, both with tone of voice and choice of words—making it quite plain that she was beneath them in wealth and station. They made her scurry back and forth from the kitchen to remedy alleged shortcomings with their meals and gleefully found fault with the cleanliness of the cutlery, repeatedly sending Constance off to replace crockery that they declared was cracked or stained.

They even made Constance spin about, as she stood hollow cheeked and worn to a frazzle, while they laughed at her shabby clothing. Victoria's heart thudded with anger and her fingers curled into two determined fists. In another instant she would have unleashed her rage upon them, when a single notion gave her pause. She cared nothing for the harsh punishment that Vidal and Nastya would mete out. But she knew, with reluctant intuition, that Constance, though blameless, would be severely punished as well—and that knowledge was all that stopped Victoria from giving the contemptuous young girls bloody noses.

Later Victoria found a moment to ask Constance who the girls were. "One is Tasha Primvet, Lord Primvet's youngest daughter. The second is Hortense Demyin, Clericor Demyin's niece, and the third is Darcy Pomfret—the daughter of those who own the Pomfret Workhouse."

Victoria rolled her eyes. "And their parents are the self-righteous ones who blather on about being honest, God-fearing folk. What sickening hypocrisy!"

Constance almost smiled then, her pale face lightening briefly—only to grow solemn once more.

"Victoria, you musn't say such things!" she chided. "They are our betters, you know." It was well that Victoria had turned away so Constance didn't see the anger that smoldered in her eyes.

Late at night, when the guests were either safe abed or smoking close round the dying hearth, and the linens had been ironed and folded, Victoria and Constance were permitted to retire. They climbed the rickety back staircase up to a cold plaster-and-lath garret high under the eaves at the top of the inn.

There, in their narrow room, they made themselves comfortable as best they could. They had tugged their threadbare blankets up close to the big curving chimney. The bricks gave off faint warmth, and they snuggled up alongside it.

They often had long talks, if they weren't too exhausted, until sleep would first take one—while the other would continue talking till the slow, even breathing of her companion told her that she alone was awake. It was always either twilight or dark in this realm, so the concepts of day and night began to lose all meaning for Victoria. Night was just the interval between their late chores and their early chores.

During the coldest nights, Constance sat up, leaning against the warm chimney bricks, her body wracked with a rasping cough. At first Victoria's annoyance at being kept awake drove her to say unkind things like "You are a dashed nuisance, Constance, making all that infernal noise when I'm trying to sleep!"

Constance would say she was sorry and do her best to stifle her cough with a frail fist pressed to her lips. But before long, Victoria became patient and concerned for her friend. Sometimes she even lent one of her own quilts to Constance, if she had an especially hard bout; other times she snuck all the way down to the kitchen to get Constance a cup of water.

And she told Constance stories. Victoria told Constance about Elliot and their magic rings—after first of course swearing her to absolute secrecy.

One night, as the wind whispered about the chimney pots and snowflakes rattled the window, Constance sat spellbound on her straw pallet, resting her elbows on her knees, listening to Victoria's latest tale with rapt fascination.

"I knew it! I just knew it," she burst out suddenly. There were tears streaming down Constance's gaunt face. "I knew that there was more to life than this, and that somewhere there were truly magical things and truly good people. Not the people who just say they are good but are really mean-spirited and make endless rules for others to follow! And not the people who use noble-sounding words to make others do wicked things on their behalf. But *good* people—people who are kind!"

Victoria felt sorry for Constance because she had never known any life other than one of loneliness and grinding labor. She had come to the Black Swan Inn from the Pomfret Work-house when she was just a small child. Constance said that she had never had any family, and no friends, either—not until Victoria came. Victoria smiled, and they solemnly promised to be friends forever. They meant it with all their hearts.

It seemed that it always snowed in the Realm of Winter Night, until one night when Victoria and Constance had been talking about faeries and other magical things for quite some time. "Victoria, do you think that I shall ever see faeries?"

"I am certain of it!" Victoria stated emphatically. She touched the green stain on her finger hopefully, wishing Aeron would appear to help them escape the Black Swan Inn. Victoria wondered if Elliot might already be finished with his quest.

It was at that moment that a sudden blue light swept into the attic room, and the girls' shadows loomed huge behind them against the rafters. Victoria jumped and turned toward the window in alarm.

Constance smiled. "It's only the moon, Victoria. I have missed it so! I haven't glimpsed it in ever so long!" Victoria disentangled herself from her quilt and walked shivering to the window. She knelt to peer out, her eyes wide with wonder, heedless of the shining bits of icy frost on the floor under her knees.

The sky had cleared, and an enormous blue moon seemed to be balanced precariously as it rolled atop the chimney pots of the adjoining rooftops. It was far larger than the moon of Victoria's own world and far bluer. Victoria looked straight into its bright face, taking in every detail.

Only rarely after that would they get glimpses of the great blue moon. Victoria told Constance that it looked like an immense stage-prop moon, similar to one she saw suspended from thin wire while attending a ballet performance of *Cendrillon* with her uncle Dexter at the Duke of York on St. Martin's Lane. Constance asked all about it and Victoria spent a good deal of time explaining about theaters and how they worked backstage with lifts, trapdoors, and flying harnesses.

Constance was unfamiliar with the concept of ballet and Victoria explained that it was a stylized form of dance, that she had special shoes for it, and that she had to endure lessons from Mademoiselle Andre at Prosingham Academy. Victoria was surprised to see stars in Constance's eyes from hearing about theaters and ballet, but then she remembered that Constance's entire life had been one of unending drudgery. Then Victoria got a lump in her throat and wished that she was back at horrid old Prosingham, because even the most toilsome day there was a lark by compare.

Constance asked Victoria to dance for her, and Victoria agreed. There in the attic room, in the stark winter cold, on the rough boards where bits of frost sparkled like diadems, Victoria performed a sequence of postures and steps, amazing Constance with her leaps, pirouettes, and twirls. Constance was delighted, clapping her work-worn hands enthusiastically when Victoria was finished.

Every week either Vidal or Nastya would make a great show of setting aside three silver coins each for Victoria and Constance as their wages. But then they would sweep two of the three from the tabletop back into their palms for room and board deductions, and even the third coin would disappear into their pockets as well—"against potential losses and damages, all too common with your kind!"

"We are their slaves, Constance, and that's all that we are!" Victoria exclaimed wearily after just such a false payday.

Victoria soundly despised both Vidal and Nastya, but Constance seemed pathetically driven to attempt to please them, which of course was impossible, and she often burst into tears when they berated her, calling her useless and indolent. Victoria gritted her teeth and stifled her anger, determined not to give them the satisfaction of making her cry. That enraged Nastya all the more, and she was merciless to Victoria and critical of everything she did. Both Vidal and Nastya—but Nastya especially—took tremendous delight in forcing Victoria to do things over and over, finding imaginary fault with how she did it the first time.

As more time passed and there was no sign of Aeron, Victoria began making impossibly wild, hair-raising plans for how she and Constance might escape and live a life in hiding on the rooftops or even out on the Great Frozen Inland Sea. But Constance shuddered and said that she was afraid of the Great Frozen Inland Sea, for it was haunted, and that Clericor Demyin and Lord Primvet did bad things to people out there on the ice, far from shore. And no matter how much Victoria pestered Constance or how much she begged, Constance wouldn't say more, but got a strange lost look in her eyes and appeared as though she was holding back tears.

And so Victoria's time at the Black Swan Inn passed in unremitting tedium, with the newfound friendship she had with Constance the only ray of hope in her life. Their talks in their attic room, huddled against the warm chimney bricks, were the only things that kept her sane and gave her courage.

Chapter 11

ELLIOT REMAINED frozen in place, dagger outstretched for what seemed like hours. He would have been tempted to despair had he realized Queen Ulricke was already aware of him, and even preparing to welcome him to her tower. Whether he would find himself her prisoner or her honored guest would depend upon her whim.

At last, the disk of the eclipsing moon slowly moved away from the sun and the light gradually brightened once more. Elliot sighed with relief. When he got to his feet, his knees were shaking. He carefully sheathed his dagger, determining to be brave as he continued his journey. He peered about for signs of danger as he went, drawing ever closer to the inviting valley floor that lay spread out in the distance below.

Scarcely an hour after he started out he glimpsed something far up on the slopes behind him. Whatever it was, it was moving in a thin glade of hemlocks. He stood still, his heart pounding. What would confront him now? Perhaps one of the spectral beasts had materialized after all—or perhaps it was something worse. Elliot could only wait. Whatever it was, it was keeping well uphill from him, just out of clear view.

Finally he caught sight of his pursuer. It was a black horse! Even from a distance, as it moved in and out of the hemlocks, Elliot saw that it was a splendid beast. It was as black as night, its head held high upon a thick, powerful neck. It pawed the earth with its hooves and tossed its mane impatiently. Then it stopped to stand stock-still, staring boldly back at him.

As Elliot watched the black horse, his alarm began to fade. This was no hideous shaggy beast of the sort that menaced him during the dark of the sun. He had been fearful at first that the horse was somehow kindred to the thing that bore the Shadow Knight, but as he peered more closely, he saw that it couldn't possibly be.

It gazed at him fixedly for quite some time. Then it tossed its head, stamped its hoof, and neighed. Elliot concluded that the black horse meant him no harm, so he continued his journey, moving slowly, pausing frequently—often just to see that the horse was following. He found its proximity reassuring.

"I think perhaps that horse is my guardian angel!" he said to himself.

Evening was approaching when Elliot stopped suddenly. He saw a house, up on the slope to his right, nestled in a thicket of trees. It was three stories tall, with a steeply pitched tile roof and a thick stone chimney. There were window boxes brimming with geraniums and cornflowers at every window. Off to one side was a goat shed and pen. On the other side of the house stood a smaller building that appeared to be a three-quarter-scale replica of the house itself, perhaps exaggerated a bit to the vertical, with a very steep roof and an extremely tall chimney.

Elliot hesitated a good while, then decided to boldly walk up to the front door and see if anyone was at home. He required lodging for the night and he hoped to be welcomed by decent people. He took comfort in the fact that the black horse was still keeping him company from a distance.

Elliot was a little alarmed to see that the door of the house was carved in the likeness of a wild man with tangled hair and a long shaggy beard. His heart beat rapidly as he summoned his courage and knocked. The white oak of the door was so thick that his knuckles barely made any perceptible noise. Then he noticed a thin braided cord protruding from a wooden disk set in the plaster nigh the door.

As the sun slowly sank behind the mountains, he pulled the rope. A bell tinkled distantly somewhere in the depths of the house. Suddenly, the door swung and there stood a very large man with a white beard. He wore a leather carpenter's apron that was heavily dusted with wood shavings and sawdust. His eyes were the palest blue that Elliot had ever seen and his cheeks were ruddy. Elliot could tell by the lines creasing the corners of his eyes that he was smiling, even though his thick mustache completely concealed his mouth from view.

Elliot looked up at the man, and found himself wondering how he ate or drank without his mustache dipping into his food. Then the man stepped to the side, beckoning Elliot inside with the wave of one immensely thick forearm.

"Come in, my boy! You are welcome here!" He turned from

Elliot and bawled into the depths of the house. "Petra, my dear, we have a guest!"

Elliot stepped tentatively into the entrance hall. A moment later a plump bespectacled woman with white hair appeared through a doorway at the rear, wiping her hands on her apron. She had obviously been in the middle of making supper.

Petra beamed when she saw Elliot, stepping forward to give him a smile and a pat on the shoulder. "We shall be delighted if you would be good enough to join us. You do look famished—and Hans, have you at least asked the boy his name?"

Elliot smiled, somehow feeling drawn to the couple, yet cautious at the same time. He had read too many faerie tales about people being welcomed to woodland homes by owners who seemed friendly, but actually meant them harm.

"My name is Elliot Good. Thank you for your kindness!"

"Come wash up, lad," said Hans. "We have an iron pump just outside our back door."

"And the same goes for you," said Petra to her husband. "Scrub well, my dear, and remove that apron, too. I don't want sawdust scattered all about my table!"

Elliot followed Hans down the central corridor. He glimpsed doorways opening into fascinating rooms as they passed, including a large kitchen where the fire crackled on the hearth and the teakettle sang. Elliot noticed that three places had already been set at the table. Somehow they knew he was coming! Once again he was torn between gratitude and a feeling of unease.

Hans led Elliot out the back door onto a wide porch. It was quite empty save for three sturdy rockers. "One for me, one for Petra, and one for any guest we might be fortunate enough to welcome!" said Hans, gesturing expansively to the chairs with a thick-fingered hand. "I carved these chairs last winter. We were snowbound here in the valley by the heaviest storm of many years. My toys were all finished, and I needed something to keep me busy during the long nights by the fire."

They stepped off the porch and moved to the iron pump. "Your toys?" Elliot asked curiously.

"Ah yes! I'm a toymaker, lad. That's my workshop yonder, behind the house. I make most of the toys that children play with in the kingdom of Telvenril—the Realm of King Venture."

"So this is Telvenril, then?" Elliot asked as he splashed cold water on his face.

"More properly stated," Hans corrected, as he worked the handle of the pump, "this entire land is the Realm of Lorinshar. Telvenril is a province of Lorinshar that split away long ago. While here, you are under the protection of our good king Venture and his brave knights, who keep our wicked neighbors at bay!"

"And who are your wicked neighbors?" Elliot asked, his voice quiet.

Hans stepped closer, leading him back up onto the porch, insisting that he sit in one of the rockers before answering.

"Why, our wicked neighbors are the knights of the Realm of Lorinshar—not far yonder, just to the north, over the mountains. Their ruler, Queen Ulricke, is perhaps the wickedest person in all the world."

It made Elliot shiver to see a formidable man like Hans speak the name of the evil queen with a note of dread creeping into his voice. He had an uneasy premonition that his quest would inevitably lead him to Queen Ulricke. Hans regarded him thoughtfully, then drew up his own chair to sit close beside him.

"My lad, I deem that you are a traveler from afar. Are you on a quest, perhaps?" After Elliot had remained silent for a moment, deciding how best to answer, Hans continued. "You needn't reveal anything you don't wish to, my boy! There are secrets best kept and secrets best revealed—and only their bearer can decide which is which."

"What makes you think I'm on a quest?" Elliot asked, worried that his mission might be equally obvious to less savory characters he might encounter on the way.

Hans paused, then broke into a smile. "Because of the horse that accompanies you! We know that horse—it is the Questing Beast!" He nodded toward the black horse now half hidden in the dark eaves of the fir wood close by the toy shop.

"It is an animal sprung from noble sires and foaled in King Venture's own stables. He sets watch about the borders of our realm, defending travelers and sounding the alarm if there are intruders with evil intent. I knew that I liked the look of you, my boy, and if the Questing Beast is keeping you company, why then you are well received indeed!"

"Do you think he will stay with me on my journey?" Elliot asked hopefully. As if in answer the black horse moved toward them, quickly breaking into a gallop. Elliot's eyes were wide as it swiftly drew nearer, its mane flowing, its nostrils flaring, and its hooves thundering on the turf. And then it flashed past them, tossing its head, and was gone into the gathering dusk.

Hans laughed. "That's a sign for you, all right!" he said. "When you continue on in the morning you'll find him with you. He'll guide you and defend you until you come safely to King Venture."

Elliot was still lost in wonder from the close-up sight of the great noble beast. "Is he a magical horse?" he asked. "Is he mortal?"

"I can't say for certain, lad. He may well have magic blood in his veins, but I do know that he's mortal enough to enjoy the oats and bran I put out for him when he is near!"

It was then that Petra called them to supper, standing outlined in the warmth and light that flowed out the back door.

The lanterns were turned low. The fire crackled merrily on the grate as they sat down to their supper. Elliot hadn't realized how famished he was. He had no idea what schnitzel was, but enjoyed it from the first bite. He felt safe in the dining nook, sitting on the high-backed bench across from Hans and Petra. There was ice-cold apple cider from the springhouse to drink, and fried potato dumplings. The only item Elliot did not like the look of was the shredded red cabbage, but he determined to be polite and try it anyway. To his surprise he found that it was quite good. He noticed the dinnerware and the tankard from which Hans drank were all decorated with the same motif: a wild man with tangled hair.

After supper Hans drew three chairs close about the inglenook. The fire had burned down low. The three of them sat round the dying coals, staring into the embers. The cozy comfort of Hans and Petra's house made Elliot feel wistful and lonely for his own home. He was so very far from Alton Bay.

Hans and Petra were waiting for Elliot to begin the conversation, and at length he did. Although he believed they were kind and trustworthy, he still didn't wish to divulge too much. But he was hoping they might advise him how to best cope with whatever lay ahead.

"Do you know anything of a fire dragon?" Elliot asked abruptly.

Petra pursed her lips and thought a moment before answering, while Hans set about reloading his pipe—the bowl of which was also carved in the likeness of the wild man— pressing the fragrant tobacco deep into the depths of the bowl with his huge thumb.

"As far as we know, the very last dragon was killed hundreds of years ago," Petra said. "Though some say when he was killed, his fire turned to ice, he lives on in another realm—a sort of dragon phantasm, ever more wicked now than when he lived. But despite rumors to the contrary, I'm afraid, my child, that there are no dragons hereabouts."

Hans stopped in the middle of his second attempt to properly light his pipe, the flame fitfully illuminating his face until the stout wooden match went out. "The only dragon that I can think of does lie in Queen Ulricke's realm, but it is not an actual living creature at all. It's a geological formation, a gigantic sheer-sided pinnacle, a spur of the ancient northernmost mountains. It's called the Pinnacle of the Red Dragon because at sunset, crimson light casts a glow upon it and it appears to come alive. But it lies far away, across the Silent Sea."

The Faerie Queen had told Elliot that his path would lie in the realm of Queen Ulricke, so he assumed that what Hans spoke of must be the "dragon" he sought. He was keenly disappointed to hear that his goal might not exist at all, but it was a disappointment mingled with relief. Perhaps the Red Dragon was not the dreadful fire breather he had expected. Perhaps it was just a tall spire of rock, so named because it resembled a fabled beast.

Nevertheless, Elliot thought it wise to find out as much about Queen Ulricke as he could before journeying into her realm. He asked Petra to tell him of the evil queen.

"Queen Ulricke is a mighty sorceress. She sits upon a black throne in a crystal chamber set in the highest spire of her Tower of Pendrongor, and from there commands ranks of nightmare beasts, legions of sinister soldiers, and troops of wicked knights who ride for plunder and pillage under her banner."

"It is only by the power of our good king Venture and the bravery of his knights that the Province of Telvenril is kept from her absolute sway," added Hans.

"Why is Queen Ulricke so wicked?" Elliot wondered.

"She was not always wicked," came the reply. "In her origin, hundreds of years ago, she was a sweet child, the youngest of two immortal sisters—though I do not know what befell the eldest. But Ulricke was highly curious and ambitious in the extreme. It is said that she befriended the last dragon, one that was slain long ago."

"The one that turned to ice and became undead," interrupted Elliot. He knew that Victoria was supposed to find the ice dragon in her quest, and worried that she might not survive her encounter with that awful-sounding creature.

"Yes, that very one exactly," said Hans. "It is said that the dragon filled her heart with hatred and a hunger for power, while at the same time teaching her long-forgotten magical arts. And so he enticed her to wickedness—by gradual degrees at first, inch by inch. Soon she became expert in casting evil spells, conjurings that gave her mastery over the will of others. And all this, mind you, when she was still just a little girl!"

"If she's hundreds of years old, she must be all wrinkly and horrible to look at," Elliot said with a shudder.

"Rather to the contrary," said Hans. "I am told that she appears young and exquisitely beautiful, possessed of every courtly grace."

"Only if she wants to be nice, for her own ends," added Petra ominously. "But there is no wickedness she won't stoop to, nor any depravity she won't attempt!"

"If your journey brings you into her realm you are in dire peril for certain," intoned Hans, his head now wreathed in plumes of fragrant smoke from his pipe.

"But since the Questing Beast has shown such interest in you, there are forces beyond our knowledge that are guiding and protecting you. So don't lose heart, my dear!" Petra patted Elliot's knee, saddened at the crestfallen expression that had darkened his young face in the firelight.

"And now it's off to bed, for we are all quite tired, aren't we," said Petra. The fire in the stone hearth had burned low, and only a few coals remained, glowing among the ashes. Hans and Petra led Elliot up a broad staircase, each post of which was carved in the artful likeness of a dancing Pan—each subsequent carving depicting a different posture and step. The guest room they showed him to had a bed covered with handmade quilts and piled with the softest eiderdown pillows.

As Elliot was about to climb into bed, he thought he heard the sound of hoofbeats passing below in the night. He sprang to the window in time to see a noble shadow thunder past. Just knowing the Questing Beast was still with him was a great comfort.

The next morning Elliot awakened to brilliant sunshine and found that a breakfast of cold goat's milk, spicy sausages, and leftover potato dumplings awaited. The black horse was still out in the yard, stomping impatiently. Elliot sensed it was time for him to go, that the demands of his quest beckoned him onward. Petra pressed a wineskin of goat's milk and a packet containing cheese, dried apples, and bread into his hands for the journey ahead. He felt only a little embarrassed when she pulled him close to hug him. "May all that is kind and good be with you on your way!" she whispered.

"There is one thing we must do before you go, Elliot," boomed Hans as they stepped out onto the porch and down onto the lawn. "You must see my toy shop!"

Hans was wearing his leather apron again, ready to begin another day of crafting toys. He led Elliot up the winding path to the eaves of the wood where his shop stood. Its massive chimney and steeply pitched roof looked precisely like something drawn for a children's storybook—especially with great piles of fluffy clouds towering up into the sky as backdrop.

Hans produced an ornate key from his vest pocket. The iron lock groaned and grated when the key was inserted and the heavy wooden door creaked open, moving slowly on its massive hinges. As Hans stepped to the side, with a proud smile enlivening his face, he gestured for Elliot to go in first. Elliot stepped over the threshold into a world of absolute wonder.

It seemed strangely as though Hans's toy shop was bigger on the inside than the outside. Outside, the toy shop appeared smaller than the main house, but inside it was vast and overwhelming. There was a gallery running all around the second level, which was open the entire way up to the wooden beams of the roof. A toy train that puffed actual steam from its stack ran about the room on a track suspended from the gallery ceiling, its course navigating through precisely crafted plaster landscapes.

There were workbenches piled high with all sorts of tools and the clean smell of sawdust was everywhere. Curled shavings were heaped knee-deep like snowdrifts, completely obscuring the floor in many places. A large black stovelike apparatus dominated the center of the room at the base of the stone chimney. Elliot could tell that it was a forge, judging from the leather apron, tongs, and thick gloves hanging nearby.

But what delighted Elliot most of all were the toys. They were everywhere he looked—dozens, no, hundreds, no, thousands, perhaps tens of thousands of toys!

There were clever articulated puppets with dozens of pin joints and confusing tangles of strings set in cross pieces that in the hands of a skilled puppeteer would control their every nuance of posture and expression. There were puppet theaters with curtains and balconies.

There were toy carousels with hand-painted horses, music boxes, and windup steamboats with whistles and paddle wheels that turned.

There were hobbyhorses, hobbydragons, and rocking sea serpents, some big enough for two or three children to ride on at a time. There was row upon row of tin soldiers, of all sorts of rank and dress. There were toy horses, toy hansom cabs, and toy cannons, bats, balls, and spinning tops, even toy balloons with people in top hats waving from their wicker gondolas.

There was a tree house made from a real tree trunk, nine feet tall, that had rooms and tunnels carved into it, with pirate figures perched upon its platforms and ladders. There were toy cutlasses, toy flintlocks, toy treasure galleons, and toy pirate ships with gunports that opened to reveal brass cannons inside.

There were stuffed toys of all description, baby dolls, and dress-up toys. There were amazing windup toys, articulated knights that carried on battles with one another or with windup dragons—all with the simple turn of a key. There were dollhouses, too, tiny ones and huge ones—some even taller than a child—with multiple stories featuring incredibly detailed rooms inside.

Elliot was absolutely awestruck at the breathtaking scope and detail of the toy shop. At long last he exclaimed, "If I have children someday, they must come here and see this place!"

"And so perhaps they shall," said Hans, smiling down at him from beneath his mustache. "Come," he said. "I think it is time you took up your quest again." Hans opened the door of the toy shop.

Elliot had taken only a single step forward when he stopped dead in his tracks. For looming huge upon the threshold was the Questing Beast. He tossed his head and then rose up on his hind legs to paw the air.

"Oh, my dear boy, you are most fortunate indeed!" exclaimed Hans. "For you will not be required to walk upon this part of your journey. I have never seen the Questing Beast do such a thing as this. He is offering to carry you upon his back, my boy!"

Chapter 12

VICTORIA HAD NOTICED occasionally that an old man would come to the Black Swan Inn and sit in a corner all by himself, huddled in his threadbare cloak and homespun scarf. He appeared to have very little money to spare, usually ordering a mug of warm broth, or more rarely, a cup of mulled wine, to ward off the chill. Vidal and Nastya always eyed him suspiciously and made a great show of being short on tables— whether they were or not—to hurry him all the more quickly on his way out into the darkness and cold. The other guests peered over their shoulders, glaring at him with barely disguised hostility as they whispered malicious gossip.

But Victoria found herself strangely drawn to the old man. He had a gentle face etched with careworn lines, and long white hair. His eyes were bright, clear blue, appearing much more youthful than his face. There was a profound shortage of kind faces in the Realm of Winter Night, and when Victoria waited on him, she made certain that his mug was brim full, or that his cup of mulled wine was brought promptly to ease his shivering.

Sadly, there was very little chance for Victoria to speak with him, for either Vidal, Nastya, or the sour-faced baker would be glaring daggers from the kitchen doorway. But whenever Victoria brought the old man his broth, she smiled and he would look up at her with gratitude as he cradled the warm cup with trembling hands. One especially bitter cold evening, she determined to steal a bit of bread for him since he never seemed to have enough means to order proper food.

The very next time she went into the kitchen to fetch one of the hulking members of Clericor Demyin's watch another heaping bowl of rich mutton stew, she snatched a slice of warm bread, concealing it in a fold of her apron. She walked close by the old man's table and slipped the bread out from her apron, placing it beside his mug with a mischievous smile. The eyes that looked up from his weathered face were eloquent in their gratitude. She smiled at him again, quickly turning away, back to her work once more.

The next time she passed his table she saw that he had gone. There was no trace of the bread she had given him, not even the merest crumb—and for that she was grateful, for there was nothing remaining to reveal her indiscretion. Nonetheless, Victoria was summoned to the kitchen scarcely a minute later. There stood Nastya, hands on hips, along with Vidal and the baker, all three looking down at her with venom in their eyes. Vidal seemed as enraged as Nastya for once and he called her an ungrateful wretch and asked her if that was how she repaid the kindnesses they had shown her since her arrival.

Victoria grew reckless with anger. "You are all miserable taskmasters!" she shouted. "You will pay for it someday! I am certain of it!"

Nastya sprang forward, her face a mask of livid fury, to deliver a series of ferocious slaps to both Victoria's cheeks. Vidal and the baker had to pull her back—for she was just getting started. Vidal muttered something under his breath that unsettled Victoria even more than Nastya's slap.

"We'll be rid of that sickly one soon enough, and since that new brat from the Pomfret Workhouse is soon to come, we can be done with this mouthy one, too, don't you worry! She'll not be so cheeky when she's out on the Great Frozen Inland Sea in the biting cold waiting for nameless horrors to come for her!"

Nastya smiled with malicious glee, and Victoria's heart filled with dread. She bit her lip, blinking back tears of shame. She was made to stand quite still in the middle of the kitchen floor while Vidal pried the silver buckles loose from her shoes—in payment for the bit of bread she had stolen. Even though Victoria always detested those silly square buckles, she was sorry to see them go. Extra tasks were assigned that kept her up half the night, long past her usual bedtime.

Tears were streaming down her cheeks as much, much later, she wearily climbed the creaking staircase to the high attic room. Constance had saved her the warmest chimney spot, turned down her quilts, and offered to put her things away so that she could go right to sleep, but Victoria was in the mood to talk. She asked Constance why nobody at the Black Swan Inn seemed to care for the old man. Constance's brow furrowed. She said the bakery woman had told the kitchen staff something strange about him.

It seemed that a fortnight ago, several members of the watch followed the old man's tracks through the snowy streets after he had departed the inn. They were assigned to find out where he lived. His tracks took a sudden turn down one street, then another but soon disappeared altogether.

"Perhaps he stepped into a house or took shelter in a doorway?" ventured Victoria.

"No—I mean that his tracks just disappeared!" said Constance in a hushed voice. "His footprints were in the middle of the street, far from any wall or doorway, and they simply vanished."

"Oh, how splendid! Just like Spring Heeled Jack, except that our friend is good and not wicked!" exclaimed Victoria admiringly, liking the old man even more. At Constance's puzzled expression she explained.

"Spring Heeled Jack is a frightful criminal, Constance—with a horrid mask! His exploits have been written up in the *Daily Telegraph*. He is a fire-breathing phantasm that can magically leap over people's heads and onto rooftops in a single bound. The Liverpool constables cannot catch him!"

Constance was far less amused with the whole matter than Victoria. "Clericor Demyin says that the old man is in league with the wicked spirits of the Great Frozen Inland Sea, and that he should be severely punished if the watch can catch him during one of his vanishing acts. So do be careful of him, Victoria . . . Victoria?"

Constance gazed down at her friend and smiled, for Victoria had fallen fast asleep.

Scarcely two hours later Victoria awakened, taken with a sudden icy chill. She had kicked off her covers and been shivering with cold, even as she slept. A strange feeling of dread came stealing over her. She crept to the window, where the huge blue moon was riding above the snowy rooftops and tall chimneys, drifting in and out of the dramatically illuminated clouds.

It was at that precise moment Victoria saw a flying shadow cross the moon. It was an ominous shape that instantly made her heart race and her blood run cold. For the silhouette that crossed the moon was that of an immense dragon! She could tell that it was far away, but its form loomed large enough against the moon to convey something of its size nonetheless. Victoria shuddered as she watched the beating of its great batlike wings and the sweep of its forked tail in the distance. She watched until it vanished from sight.

Afterward she sat shivering by the window for the longest time. At last she crawled once more into her pile of straw and quilts, snuggling up as close as she could to the faintly warm bricks. She was shaken by the sight of the dragon, but eventually Constance's slow, peaceful breathing from the adjoining pallet soothed her enough to fall asleep again. Her dreams were frightful and restless.

Early the next morning Victoria asked Constance if she had ever heard any legend of a dragon out in the Great Frozen Inland Sea. Constance shook her head vehemently no and declared, "Though I shouldn't be surprised if there was one. All sorts of awful things lie in wait out there."

Victoria and Constance came downstairs to find that the kitchen fires had been banked and that the day had been declared a high festival by Lord Primvet and Clericor Demyin. Every citizen in the village must abide by its regulations— which were many and impossibly tedious—on pain of death. Victoria did not understand why Constance was in a state of panic, bordering on terror.

The festival, like everything else in the village, proved to be grim and unpleasant. They were required to put on their cloaks and hats to join a procession bound for the assembly building. The building's main hall was ringed with balconies overflowing with the unfriendly folk of the village. Clericor Demyin held forth in stately form, his booming voice echoing from the high lectern. He warned the villagers that hauntings and dreadful spirits were everywhere, that they must all be on guard, must never smile frivolously or take pleasure in common things. Above all, children must never pretend!

He said that the spirits of the Great Frozen Inland Sea were angry and required propitiation, or the entire village would suffer. There would be famine, plagues, and evil signs in the heavens. He hinted that infernal strangers would appear among them, newcomers who were not to be trusted—and here he glared at Victoria until she felt very uncomfortable.

Constance sat trembling beside Victoria, her eyes watery with fear. Then everyone bowed low as the ruler of the town, Lord Primvet, entered the room. He wore robes trimmed with snow-white lace and his precise black beard was in stark contrast to his powdered wig. In his pudgy hands Lord Primvet carried an ornate official staff of smooth ebony, with a loathsomely lifelike serpent's head for its handle. The serpent's eyes sparkled with deeply set garnets and its mouth gaped wide, as if it were preparing to inject venom from its razor fangs. Lord Primvet spoke, advising the throng that his staff functioned as an oracle to identify the person who was the source of ill omen.

"There is one among us who is in league with the demons of the Great Frozen Inland Sea. Though of innocent appearance, she continually works spells of spite against her fellows. She may have already corrupted a companion, newly arrived in our midst, yet who can tell—this companion may yet prove true and steadfast if the influence that bewitches her is removed."

Victoria did not like the look of Lord Primvet one little bit, for she had seen his sort before in the person of a traveling showman who had come to Northumberland the previous summer. He presented an assortment of fake mermaids and grotesques, using them to fleece the elderly and separate them from their stipends.

Lord Primvet stepped forward, now standing on the projection at the front of the stage. He swept the folds of his robe out of the way with a dramatic gesture and raised his staff like a weapon, slowly sweeping it to and fro across the faces in the crowd. Everyone, Victoria included, got the eerie feeling that the serpent's hateful eyes were boring into their own and that they were being subjected to a fearsome scrutiny.

The staff passed over Victoria and Constance slowly, and then traversed the entire group from the Black Swan Inn once more, before wavering, then weaving slowly back again. Constance was beside herself with fear, but Victoria saw that Vidal and Nastya were quite calm, as though they knew what was about to happen.

The staff hovered above Constance's and Victoria's heads another time or two and then stopped, to point directly at Constance. Constance shrieked when the serpent-headed staff hissed, its eyes flaming.

Lord Primvet's voice was smooth as silk. "Apparently the oracle has chosen you, child," he said to Constance, false pity dripping from every word. "But to be just and fair we must try the oracle."

Lord Primvet spun about on his heels to smile benignly. "Bring in the children, our dear ones, who delight our hearts with their moral goodness! The children will either confirm or deny the oracle!"

Victoria's eyes flashed with anger as a door opened to admit Tasha Primvet, Darcy Pomfret, and Hortense Demyin. Unlike the times when they had tormented Constance, they were not clad in elegant finery now, rather wearing plain clothing to bespeak their piety. Their faces were timid and hesitant as they advanced, trembling. Then they recoiled, drawing back from Constance as though they had been stung.

Victoria was white-lipped with fury. "What disgusting little actresses they are!" she muttered under her breath.

Gasps were drawn from the crowd as moments later, all three girls rolled upon the floor, eyes wide with pantomimed horror. "Oh, do make her stop!" they squealed, pointing at Constance with quivering fingers. "She has put spells upon us and bewitched us!" The crowd roared its outrage, glaring down upon Constance until she collapsed in a sobbing heap.

"And thus the source of our blight is revealed," Lord Primvet declared, in his smoothest judicial voice. "The sacred oracle cannot lie or make an error of judgment. Seize that wretch at once!"

Victoria, even in her rage, didn't miss the quick look of triumph she saw flicker across the features of Constance's accusers. As burly members of the watch shouldered their way forward through the throng intent on dragging Constance away, Victoria shouted at the very top of her lungs, "He's making his walking stick do that! Can't you see? It's not a sacred oracle at all. Why, he's just a despicable, lying cheat!"

Victoria threw herself upon the watch, her fists flying in a fury, heedless that they were many and each far stronger than she alone. She was desperate to save her friend. The watchmen snarled in rage as she scratched and kicked, finally slapping Victoria hard and shoving her backward into the clutches of Vidal and Nastya, who dragged her, still struggling and shouting, out of the assembly building.

When they returned to the Black Swan Inn, Victoria demanded to know what had become of Constance and how soon she would return.

Vidal replied mockingly that she had been sent to live with her grandmother who lived far across the village, while Nastya snickered all the while as if she thought that her husband had made the funniest joke ever. Victoria was enraged and told them that Constance didn't have a grandmother, then they both told Victoria to be quiet if she knew what was good for her. They sent her upstairs to her now lonely room. She wasn't given even a single bite of supper. She cried herself to sleep holding Constance's threadbare quilt clutched close. Victoria was sure that something horrible had happened to her friend.

The next few weeks were the darkest of Victoria's entire life. Constance's three smirking tormentors reappeared to mock and belittle her now—but Victoria was so exhausted she hadn't the will to fight back. The workload was impossible with Constance gone and the loneliness unbearable. Victoria didn't even see the old man anymore. Her only companion was the big blue moon.

It was during one bleak night, when Victoria sat huddled in her quilts, gazing forlornly out her window at the moon, that a quick movement, glimpsed from the corner of her eye, caught her attention. She peered out across the rooftops and saw it again, a flicker of motion against the tall chimney shadows. A scant second later her heart leaped for joy to see Aeron—borne on vivid vibrating wings—hovering just outside the window, smiling and waving.

Her icy hands trembled as they eagerly tugged at the bit of old table linen that stood in for a broken pane. At last it came loose, allowing Aeron to leap through into her attic room.

Victoria was delighted, her eyes sparkling with wonder as her faerie friend alighted upon the palm of her hand.

"Oh, Aeron," she laughed, tears in her eyes. "You *are* tiny in this world, aren't you!"

Aeron nodded, standing with his arms folded across his chest. His wings had ceased their beating and were at rest against his back. He smiled up at Victoria. "I bring you two messages from our queen. The first is that you haven't gone astray, that you are precisely where you ought to be."

He paused to catch his breath. "Second, don't worry overmuch for your friend Constance. She is quite safe and you will see her again—for your time at the Black Swan Inn is nearly at an end!"

"Oh, I am so glad, Aeron! I have been ever so distraught; you have no inkling!" Victoria exclaimed. "I was sure that Clericor Demyin and Nastya meant Constance harm."

"Oh, they meant her harm all right," Aeron said grimly. "But no harm was allowed to befall her!"

Aeron told Victoria that he hadn't much time, because the Ice Dragon continually exerted great magical force in an attempt to drive him, or any other rescuer for that matter, back through the faerie gate and out of the Realm of Winter Night altogether. He continued. "You couldn't have faced the final part of your quest when you first arrived in Faerieland, Victoria, but you are nearly ready now. Your experiences here have transformed you and made you stronger."

As Victoria watched, Aeron's wings began moving so fast as to render them invisible. He lifted up off her palm to hover for a moment, and then sped away, veering out across the rooftops and chimney pots, at first glowing brightly like a falling star, then fading against the backdrop of the moon. Victoria's frozen fingers had trouble stuffing the old bit of linen back into the broken pane but she finally managed.

After that it took her the longest time to fall asleep, but her heart was full of relief and joy.

Chapter 13

〜

ELLIOT HAD NEVER BEEN on horseback before, and it seemed high and precarious to him. It would have been a far more familiar experience to Victoria, for she was an expert with horses—yet even she would have taken pause when it came to the Questing Beast, for there was no saddle or stirrups.

"How do I hold on?" asked Elliot.

"Simply grasp his mane and lean forward," Hans advised. "The faster he goes, lean forward the more. Take care to lie right against his neck when he goes all out! He is a noble and intelligent fellow. He won't permit harm to befall you!"

With that Hans passed up the wineskin of goat's milk and the food packet. He patted Elliot's knee affectionately. "Now then, be off, my lad, and may blessing go with thee. The Questing Beast will take you to good King Venture who will give you wise counsel."

Even before the word "good-bye" had left Elliot's lips he felt the horse's flanks tighten. And then, with a plunge forward and a clash of hooves on the flagstones, they were off! Elliot hung on for dear life, hoping for the best. As they rocketed past the front of the house, Elliot caught a fleeting glimpse of Petra waving from the doorstep. They moved like a flashing comet, speeding down the rolling hillsides to pound along the banks of the sparkling lake in the bottom of the valley. When Elliot looked back over his shoulder Hans and Petra's house had already disappeared into a fold of the hills. Elliot squeezed his legs tightly against the Questing Beast's flanks. That made him feel a tiny bit more secure, though he was still unaccustomed to the height and speed of a living animal running beneath him.

The hooves of the Questing Beast thundered across the waving grasses of the valley floor. Now and again, the great black horse came to a place where a stream tumbled down from the highlands. He didn't even hesitate, but ran full tilt through the water, making tremendous splashes, and sending up rainbow-hued cascades in all directions.

After a bit, the valley broadened. Here, the power of the Questing Beast was unleashed. With a nicker of warning for Elliot to hold tighter still and a proud toss of his head, the Questing Beast launched full out into his fastest run. Elliot's eyes watered from the rush of wind in his face. The horse's mane streamed back against his cheek and the pounding of its hooves thundered in his ears. He leaned farther forward, clutching the Questing Beast's mane with both fists, and held on, using his legs as best he could. He turned his head to the side and watched the hillsides flow past at an incredible rate of speed. The Questing Beast ran effortlessly on and on, as hours passed.

It was well past noontide when the Questing Beast approached a perfectly round pond situated in the bottom of a hollow. Elliot sensed that the horse was thirsty. He swung one leg over its back and—with a quick apology for accidentally tugging its mane—slid down to land awkwardly on an uneven hummock.

Elliot found a large flat rock, near the water's edge. It was the perfect place to eat his lunch. He ate some of his bread with the dried apples, and then nibbled at the cheese. He raised the wineskin, taking a sip or two of the goat's milk, deciding that he didn't really care for it at all.

He rested for a bit, and then the Questing Beast trotted over, nudging his shoulder with its nose. Elliot wondered how he would ever manage to climb back on the horse without help. The thought of being stranded on foot, with many miles to go, dismayed him.

Then he laughed. The horse had thought of that already! While Elliot was fretting, it had moved off to a nearby boulder, standing close to its steepest side, waiting patiently.

Elliot climbed to the top of the boulder, then carefully slid onto the horse's back. Once again they were off, running farther and farther into the higher, more dramatic uplands lying along the boundary between King Venture's land and Queen Ulricke's realm. Elliot could tell that they had gained altitude by the popping of his eardrums.

Finally evening drew nigh. The shadows lengthened, stealing down from the surrounding hills. The Questing Beast slowed to a canter, stamping and tossing its head as they crested the brow of a hill bathed in the crimson light of the setting sun. As they came to a full stop, Elliot gasped at the sight that lay before him.

There in the valley, spread out like a bright collection of toys, lay the summer encampment of King Venture. Hundreds of tents were ranked in concentric rings. Circular avenues were arranged about a bright cluster of tall, stately pavilions—each with a pennant and coat of arms rippling from its pinnacle. Off to one side, painted grandstands ran along the edge of the lists, forming the border of the jousting fields. Even from a distance, Elliot was astonished at the finery of the royal court he could see below the shaded awnings.

But what attracted his attention most of all were the knights themselves. Some were on horseback, awaiting their turn to joust. Some wore full plate armor, and others long coats of chain mail. There were clusters of knights with their helmets off, talking to one another as their squires polished their shields. Still others were mounted on horseback, testing their agility by tilting at the quintain—a cross-armed device, with a shield suspended from one side and a heavy sandbag dangling from the other. One knight struck the shield with his lance, but wasn't quick enough in his getaway. The cross arm creaked round and its swinging sandbag struck his shield, unhorsing him.

Elliot watched fascinated as two massive horses, each bearing formidable armored knights, whirled about, facing each other from opposite ends of the lists. A trumpet sounded its clear note. Still the knights waited, lances raised, while their horses stamped and curveted. Elliot saw what appeared as a tiny white speck drifting earthward, dropped by one of the ladies in the stands. Her handkerchief hadn't even finished fluttering down when the two armored knights lowered their visors and their lances and charged toward each other at full gallop.

The knights drew closer to each other, their lances at the ready. Elliot could hear the horses' hooves pounding on the sod. Then came a distant crash of lance on shield as the horses braced, faltered, and whirled about, speeding past each other in clouds of dust. Neither knight was unhorsed, but one's lance had been shattered. His squire darted forward with a fresh one. In a moment both knights were awaiting the signal to resume.

But the Questing Beast had other plans. Elliot was nearly pitched backward off its back as it leaped forward. It sped down from the brow of the hill, running full tilt toward the royal pavilions. The eyes of every page, nobleman, and lady in the stands turned to the noble beast that came thundering toward them. Even the knights who were about to joust turned in their saddles to watch the arrival of the Questing Beast. The crowd was all abuzz at the sight.

"The Questing Beast is coming!"

"The Questing Beast has come down from the mountains, and he bears a rider!"

"A traveler is coming to greet King Venture—and is so favored that the Questing Beast is bearing him upon its back!"

Rumors flew round the grandstands at the speed of light. Even knights who had been wounded in earlier jousts came limping from their pavilions, leaning on their squires to watch as the mighty horse bore its rider straight to the central grandstands.

And so it was that Elliot Good, all breathless, his heart pounding with excitement, found himself face to face with King Venture of Telvenril. The Questing Beast reared theatrically, stamping and pawing the earth with its hooves. Then it lowered its head to stand silently, its flanks heaving with its exertion.

King Venture sat scarcely ten feet from Elliot, who could not help but notice that his left eye was opaque and cloudy, and that a long scar bisected his left cheek. His shoulders were covered with an ermine-trimmed cape that, along with his crown, signified his office. He wore a ring bearing the royal signet of Telvenril upon his right hand.

One of King Venture's daughters, the lovely Princess Emmanuelle, sat beside him. She joined her father in the pavilions of his summer court while the queen held sway in the royal castle. Princess Emmanuelle wore a gown of mingled green and blue with expansive sleeves and a gathered velvet bodice. Her headdress was the tall, pointed, backward-angled sort, with a gossamer veil hanging from the top, draped in rich folds about her shoulders. Her brown hair was worn in the longest and thickest braid Elliot had ever seen.

Elliot slid down from the Questing Beast's back. He thought it only proper to bow. As he gazed up at the royal court above him, he said the only words that came to his mind.

"I am at your service, Your Majesty! My name is Elliot Good, and I have come from afar."

King Venture smiled and nodded. Elliot was a bit relieved to see that the smile enlivened his remarkable features and emphasized his kindliness—still kingly indeed, but now perhaps a bit more human and fatherly.

King Venture raised his scepter. "I hereby declare the lists to be closed for the remainder of this day. As to the joust that was ongoing before the arrival of the Questing Beast, I declare Sir Edrim the victor, for he shattered Sir Vincent's lance. Come, take your token of victory, Sir Edrim!"

With that a powerful knight galloped forward, reining in his armored steed at the very last moment so that it whirled about to pause alongside the Questing Beast. The knight lowered his lance in a courtly gesture toward the ladies. Princess Emmanuelle placed the victor's wreath about its tip. Then the knight galloped off, proudly bearing his trophy for all to see.

"And now we have a guest to entertain. Let us disperse for the evening. My court will retire to the royal pavilions. Let the finest fodder be set out for the Questing Beast and let him be well tended and brushed—but neither bind him nor fence him in, for he is to be unfettered like the wind and allowed to come and go at will."

Then the king turned to venerable Sir Mortimer, master of his knights. "I want a redoubled watch of armed men set about the perimeter of our encampment, and see that you don't neglect to place watchers on the surrounding hilltops. Give them each a horn to sound if peril should come by night."

And so Elliot joined the throng of King Venture's court. He walked between two splendidly liveried royal guardsmen assigned to serve as his escorts toward the tallest pavilion in the encampment. It was surrounded by a ring of halberd-bearing men-at-arms, all in identical black and crimson livery with shields bearing the royal crest of Telvenril.

Nobody, including Elliot himself, noticed the momentary flash of resentment that flickered across Sir Edrim's face as he gazed upon the boy whom the Questing Beast had delivered to their camp.

Chapter 14

THE DAY FOLLOWING Aeron's visit, Victoria went downstairs to find the Black Swan Inn's fires banked once more. When she was told that the day had been proclaimed a high festival, her face went pale.

Victoria was given a cast-off coat to wear for the cold walk to the assembly building. The well-made cloak that she'd been given in Faerieland had somehow "disappeared." The sour-faced baker and a member of the watch walked in front of Victoria, while Vidal, Nastya, and two more watchmen trudged along close behind. Nastya seemed in unusually high spirits and even smiled at Victoria.

As they went, Victoria became quite certain that she was about to discover what had become of Constance, for the same fate was sure to befall her. Truthfully, she was surprised that Nastya and Vidal hadn't gotten rid of her sooner, as displeased with her attitude and her work as they seemed to be. Another orphan from the Pomfret Workhouse could easily be obtained to replace her.

Crowds converged at the assembly building and everyone ascended the stone steps to enter its high vaulted chamber. The overhanging tiers teemed with disapproving and unfriendly faces. Victoria was not in the least bit surprised when—like a well-rehearsed play—the entire performance was repeated once more. Lord Primvet came out onto the central platform in his formal robes, sweeping his serpent-headed staff across the faces in the crowd. He pursed his full petulant lips, as if giving careful consideration to a weighty matter. Victoria rolled her eyes and stood, arms folded, knowing that it was only a matter of time before the charade would conclude and she would be condemned.

And so it was. The serpent-headed staff chose Victoria as she knew it would. When Clericor Demyin came down from his high seat to stand solemnly beside Lord Primvet, his eyes narrowed with hate as they met Victoria's, but she did not flinch and boldly returned his glare. Victoria was defiant as the serpent's mouth at the head of the staff gaped open, its eyes flaming venomously as it hissed its warning. She was sure she saw Lord Primvet's fingertip pressing a tiny lever recessed in the side of the staff.

Victoria found that the script had been slightly altered. Clericor Demyin declared that Tasha Primvet, Hortense Demyin, and Darcy Pomfret were far too terrified of Victoria to validate the judgment of the oracle. She stood unmoved, as the crowd reacted with well-rehearsed outrage.

"Apparently I am a most powerful witch indeed. I never realized how truly frightful I really am," Victoria murmured under her breath.

The crowd recoiled from Victoria on cue as though stung, and Vidal and Nastya joined in the finger-pointing and the universal loathing. Victoria protested her innocence, but of course it was futile, and in a moment she felt the iron grip of the watch on her wrists. She was quickly led out through a side door and bustled into a waiting sleigh, beneath the wavering flame of an overhead streetlamp. This sleigh was much larger than Clericor Demyin's, for it had ceremonial purpose and was used exclusively for official business. The heavily cloaked driver took up the reins. Two members of the watch sat behind the driver in backward-facing seats, one on each side of Victoria. Nastya held court in the high cushioned rearward seat between Clericor Demyin and Lord Primvet. Two additional members of the watch stood on side running boards. With a crack of the whip across the horse's flanks the sleigh swept off into the night. There were no bells.

The crowds returning to their homes were left behind. Victoria saw that they were headed downhill into an unfamiliar part of the village that was older and more dingy than the area close about the inn. At first she glimpsed dim lights behind the diamond-paned windows of the houses, smoke curled up from the chimneys, and all the lit streetlamps appeared almost pleasant in the falling snow. But as the sleigh continued, they descended to streets that were older still, and Victoria noticed that the buildings were darkened and silent and that their chimneys were cold and still, as if nobody had lived in those houses for a long while.

"We are now drawing nigh the Great Frozen Inland Sea," Lord Primvet declared solemnly. Victoria wondered if everything he said was just as solemn a declaration, and if perhaps he was even solemn when he asked someone to pass him the pepper.

"The wicked spirits who lurk out upon the icy reaches of the Great Frozen Inland Sea, waiting eagerly to devour lost souls, are now quite near enough to make this portion of town uninhabitable. Our little village has thus, by necessity, grown uphill away from the evil sea."

"Yes indeed," added Clericor Demyin. "The evil that resides in the hearts of people—like Victoria, for one, strangers who come to us uninvited—blights our village the more, and places our good folk in terrible danger. It empowers the hideous ice demon Paracelsus, who stalks the sea out in the cold and darkness!"

Nastya glared at Victoria, then threw back her head and laughed, a grating, triumphant sound. "And worse still, this brat Victoria gave false hope to those who would best be content to live out lives of service—minding their betters! I saw rebellion in Constance's eyes from the moment she first became acquainted with Victoria. But in due course we found a remedy for that!"

Victoria steeled herself, saying nothing. Her face took on a very defiant look—though if truth be told, she was trying hard not to cry.

It was almost a relief when the sleigh drove down a steep ramp between the curving stone walls of a shore embankment. There were bright lamps at each rounded turn, the only comforting lights in that entire district. And in a moment they were driving out onto the ice of the Great Frozen Inland

Sea. It was snowing even harder now. The wind's velocity had increased and it had grown very cold. There were no narrow streets or sharp turns to navigate, so the sleigh went rapidly, its runners cutting swiftly through the snow as the driver applied his whip to the horses. Victoria peered backward, squinting into the darkness. She could still discern the dim embankment lights, but the looming shadows of the buildings were lost from sight, swallowed up in the silent blankness of the snowfall.

It was at least thirty minutes later that the sleigh crunched to a halt. There was silence for a while but for the swishing sound of falling snow and an occasional stamp or snort from the horses. The burly watchmen dragged Victoria down from the sleigh and into the trackless snow. The driver helped Clericor Demyin, Lord Primvet, and Nastya clamber down and the three stood huddled in their warm cloaks, anxious to be on their way. Victoria stood before them, shivering.

"And so we part company. We must remove every blight from our midst. The good folk of our village will be safe to lead lives of moral diligence," intoned Clericor Demyin pompously. "There have been uprisings at the Pomfret Workhouse that coincided with your arrival among us. Well, it shall be no more! We shall put your evil far from us!"

Victoria knew for a certainty that she was to be left to die of exposure out upon the Great Frozen Inland Sea, alone in the cold and dark. She wondered what it had been like for poor Constance, and though the assurances of Aeron comforted her a bit, all things warm and bright seemed ever so far away.

"You will remain here to be consumed by the evil ice demon

Paracelsus—for you are one of his infernal changelings and not of us at all!" gloated Clericor Demyin. "Any attempt to follow us and save yourself would be futile, for the snow will quickly obscure the marks of our runners. You would perish miserably long before you could ever reach the village. For you are leagues and leagues out into the sea, far from the warmth and succor you will never experience again!"

Nastya stepped forward as Clericor Demyin and Lord Primvet returned gratefully to the shelter of the sleigh. The watch remained on alert close by. "These superstitious fools believe in magic and ice demons," she whispered, bending to hiss her venom into Victoria's ear directly. "You won't have even that comfort, you wicked, vile child. Nobody, good or evil, will come to you—not a soul! You'll simply die alone out here in the dark!"

Nastya turned on her heels and walked briskly back to the sleigh, pulling at her collar and clapping her gloved hands together for warmth. Halfway back she added, "Oh, and do be careful lest you trip over Constance's bones! They might be somewhere close hereabouts!" Then with a triumphant sneer, Nastya laughed and stepped up into the sleigh.

When everyone except Victoria was seated securely, and the two members of the watch once again took their positions on the side steps, the driver cracked his whip, and the horses swept round. The sleigh returned the way it had come. Its lamps soon dwindled to mere pinpoints, finally disappearing altogether in the gloom of falling snow. Victoria found herself utterly alone—out in the darkness, in the midst of the Great Frozen Inland Sea.

Chapter 15

IN THE AIRY dining room of the royal pavilion, Elliot was seated at the king's left hand while Princess Emmanuelle took her place on his right alongside Sir Mortimer and Sir Edrim, the victor of the last joust. Elliot saw that Sir Edrim was regarded with high esteem. He was one of their staunchest knights, defending the realm against invasion. The other seats were filled with guests of every noble rank and station. Elliot was simply in awe of it all.

Servers brought freshly baked bread and wine. Then there were trenchers of grilled fish: trout from mountain streams, baked tench, and even perch from the cool valley lakes. Plums, grapes, and melons were served as palate cleansers between courses.

Elliot, had he been asked, would never have thought that one could eat courteously from the point of a dagger, but after watching both lords and ladies accomplish it, he tried it himself, finding that he quite liked it—though he doubted his mother would permit him to continue this new fashion once he returned home.

Then he remembered that his mother wasn't at home at all and his feelings of grief and loss came flooding back, preventing his enjoyment of the sumptuous meal. Though he had plenty of company at the banquet table, Elliot suddenly felt very lonely.

Then the main courses came, carried by sedate butlers, heads held high, three to each immense serving dish. The platters were crafted of solid silver, fashioned in the shape of colossal swans, wings outstretched on each side. The swans were hollow and within their bodies were set pasties, game, and sweetmeats.

Elliot was politely included in most of the conversation, noticing that Princess Emmanuelle was careful to initiate it, but he was often uncertain how to reply when his opinion was sought on unfamiliar matters. He wondered why Sindl hadn't yet come to his aid, and he heartily wished she would appear to advise him on royal protocol—and also on how much to reveal of his quest, were they to question him.

Long after dark, the feast dispersed at last; King Venture dismissed his court until the first contest of the morrow. Elliot found himself walking with the king, Princess Emmanuelle, Sir Mortimer, and Sir Edrim down a long corridor between tall candlestands—and then into the king's private apartments.

There, in a circular room hung with tapestries and the banners of each knightly order that swore fealty to King Venture, they gathered about an oaken table. A single steward stood by to wait upon them if they required refreshment. Halberd-bearing men-at-arms stood in each corner of the room. King Venture unrolled a large vellum map.

"And now," said the king at length, "tell me, Elliot, from whence have you come and what is the purpose of your quest—for if you were not errant upon a matter of great import, the Questing Beast wouldn't have bore you. Do be kind enough to point out the place of your origin on this map."

Elliot swallowed hard. He scanned the map—scrutinizing each precisely inked kingdom, valley, lake, and mountain. But not only was everything on the map unrecognizable, but the descriptions in the margin and the place-names listed in the legend were inked in an archaic script.

"Sire," said Elliot, after careful consideration. "I can't show you the place where I have come from, and I hesitate to say where I am going, because I've heard that the Realm of Lorinshar is a dangerous place."

The room grew silent. A meaningful look was exchanged between King Venture and Sir Mortimer. Sir Edrim gazed at Elliot with newfound respect, while Princess Emmanuelle studied him thoughtfully. The men-at-arms stood like impassive statues, their faces expressionless.

Sir Mortimer spoke, his voice grave and serious. "My son," he said. "This much we can divine. You are on a mission of no little importance. You are a stranger to this realm and to this world as well, I deem. What is your purpose in Lorinshar?"

In the torchlight Elliot could see King Venture's sighted eye was regarding him intently. Though he was under intense scrutiny from all in the room and wished to please the king, Elliot sensed that it somehow wouldn't be wise for him to tell of his quest for the orb. "I'm sorry, sire, but I cannot reveal the purpose of my quest," he said warily. The king and his knights looked taken aback by his answer.

It was then Princess Emmanuelle who spoke. "My lords, though our visitor from another world keeps the purpose of his quest secret, we must remember what goes on in other realms plays a part in what transpires here—for we live in interwoven worlds, after all, and the veils between are not as thick as they seem." Princess Emmanuelle's eyes probed Elliot's face, searching it for truthfulness. Then she turned to the king.

"Father, for nearly a fortnight I have been troubled with the same vivid dream over and over. I see a peaceable, sleepy little town of white wooden homes, situated on a picturesque lake. And then, into this lovely town, comes a frightful form of supernatural dread, mounted on a spectral steed with a forked tongue. The figure is armored all in black. In my dream the power of this specter grows continuously, until the sun doesn't rise at all and it is permanent night in this place. Evil beings come to join him, and fell spirits of malice begin there to walk the earth," and here the princess paused as though there was more to be told but she didn't have the heart for it. "It is my belief that the peril I glimpsed in my dream is what brought this brave lad to us."

Elliot's heart was in his throat. He feared that Princess Emmanuelle's dream was about what was happening in Alton Bay.

"Well, if my daughter's premonition is correct—and I believe it is, for she has the gift of foresight—then perhaps we can assist you on your quest, my boy," the king offered. "After all, if this evil puts your world in danger, it may overflow upon us in due time and we must do what we can to protect ourselves!"

"But I'm meant to complete my quest alone," Elliot said hesitantly.

Sir Edrim spoke for the first time. "Well then, if in fact this brave lad's intention is to approach Queen Ulricke's realm, perhaps the best we can do is advise him of the best way to proceed with his journey."

It was settled when the king agreed. Everyone leaned forward for a better view of the map in the flickering candlelight. Elliot's heart was fairly bursting with pride. He had been called brave by a knight and a princess and he was intoxicated at the thought of it all. King Venture placed a fatherly hand on his shoulder while pointing out the features on the map.

"We are situated here," said the king, pointing to a wide, almost perfectly round valley. "This is the place of our summer encampment."

The king's finger moved northward, then across to the left center of the map. "This valley, which begins as a cleft in the rock then widens until the mountains open upon each side, is where my castle is situated—the Vale of Tinteron. There my queen holds court on the emerald throne as regent in my absence. Traversing this valley to its very end is the only safe way to Queen Ulricke's realm."

"Perhaps I could take a shortcut through this little valley here. It starts as a cleft in the rock, too, then angles north, leading directly to Lorinshar," Elliot suggested, his voice diffident.

The room grew ominously silent.

"That, my boy, is the Valley of Direfall, and if the path of your quest lies through that valley, you will need a great deal of protection indeed to ever come out upon the other side alive!"

"Why is it so dangerous?" Elliot asked.

"We don't know exactly what the peril is," said Sir Mortimer. "Queen Ulricke surrounds the frontiers of her realm with awful things as a defensive bulwark. But even she had no need to place her minions in Direfall. For something or someone was there already, haunting the valley, and whatever it may be, it is incredibly wicked!"

Then Princess Emmanuelle spoke. "All we know is that no travelers who enter Direfall ever come this way again. We do not know of a single soul who, once entering that valley, has come out again on the other side—though perhaps some do make it through and reach Queen Ulricke's realm, receiving whatever fate awaits them there!"

"Journeying through the Vale of Tinteron takes longer, make no mistake, but it is free of peril and well guarded. There is simply no alternative!" the king declared.

Elliot shuddered. "I will take the long way around, whatever it may add to my journey!"

King Venture looked to Sir Mortimer, who stood staring

fixedly at the map, as though by force of will he could dissipate its dangers. Elliot's gaze turned to Sir Edrim, who towered over the map, leaning forward, his weight resting on his huge splayed hands. Elliot thought that anyone who faced Sir Edrim in the jousting lists—to say nothing of in real pitched battle—must be very brave indeed.

"Sir Edrim," said King Venture. "You will accompany Elliot to the opening of the Vale of Tinteron tomorrow, and see him safely that far. Thereafter he must continue by himself. He will be quite safe until he comes out the other side in Lorinshar."

"Perhaps the Questing Beast will go with me?" Elliot said hopefully.

"Alas, my servants tell me that no sooner had they set out his fodder and he had eaten that he vanished off over the hills, called by the forces that guide him—off on some new mission. I believe his destiny was to guide you this far, but from here on I'm afraid you must go alone," said King Venture solemnly.

In the morning Sir Mortimer, King Venture, and Princess Emmanuelle saw Elliot and Sir Edrim off. Elliot was sore in dozens of places from his ride upon the Questing Beast. Princess Emmanuelle embraced Elliot, kissing him on both cheeks, and wished him well. Elliot was a bit embarrassed when Sir Edrim lifted him up to sit directly before him in the saddle. The formidable knight was in full plate armor, though the visor of his helm was open. Elliot marveled at the size of the armored horse Sir Edrim rode. It was thick limbed and massive, well-suited to bear a heavy rider in full gear.

Elliot was a little disappointed when the royal steward declared that they had not only replenished his supply of bread and cheese but even thought to refresh the goat's milk.

King Venture wished Elliot Godspeed and blessings in his quest and invited him to visit court again when circumstances permitted. Sir Mortimer waved solemnly, his face grave, thinking of the dangerous quest of his own youth that had earned him the sword of knighthood.

And then they were off! Sir Edrim guided his horse up into the rising meadows, away from the summer encampment, until once again it reminded Elliot of a toy city in miniature, with its bright pavilions diminishing far below. They traveled up onto the lower slopes of the mountains, sometimes skirting the edge of dark beech forests, then moving along the narrowest and faintest of game paths, through woods of pine and hemlock.

Finally, they saw a vast headwall spread out before them and high off to one side a narrow notch was visible, seemingly cut into the very mountain wall. Sir Edrim pointed it out. "That, my lad," he said, "is the entrance to the Vale of Tinteron—the safest path to Lorinshar."

Sir Edrim spurred the armored flanks of his horse and made a clicking sound with his tongue as they sped off, down across the rolling glens. The sensation of speed on the back of Sir Edrim's horse was less than it had been on the Questing Beast, but the feeling of height was more precarious, for this beast was taller and more heavily built. The weapons and the equipment of war, as well as the armor of both horse and rider, jangled and clanked.

When they reached the entrance to the vale an hour or so later, Elliot found himself wishing it had taken longer.

Elliot determined to dismount from the horse by himself and did so, to his surprise, landing rather easily on the springy upland turf. Sir Edrim handed down his food packet.

"I have absolutely no doubt that the experiences that befall you on your journey will prove you worthy of the high regard both my liege and the princess Emmanuelle have for you. For you are a great adventurer, are you not?" said Sir Edrim.

Elliot thanked the knight, but for a moment found himself wondering if perhaps the smile accompanying Sir Edrim's words wasn't more of a sneer.

Then with a courtly wave, Sir Edrim whirled his armored steed about and was gone in a thunder of hooves. Elliot watched him and his horse recede until they were just specks in the far distance.

The place where Sir Edrim left Elliot was sunny and bright. Golden fields down on the valley floor mingled with thickets of bracken sloping upward to the edge of thick forests where tall trees were overshadowed by the mountains. Butterflies zigzagged to and fro and bees hummed about their business in the blossoms nearby.

Two or three times great winged shadows swept across the sky, momentarily dimming the sun, and each time Elliot paused, shading his eyes to peer up at them. *They must be eagles,* he thought. But he knew little of bird lore and he recognized neither the jet-black leading edges of their wings nor the charcoal gray of their trailing flight feathers as sure signs they were huge vultures. They flew too high for him to recognize their bald heads and sharp beaks, for they spiraled even higher, watching him with greedy unblinking eyes.

Toward midday, Elliot realized he was making less progress than he thought. It was mostly because the valley floor sloped up and down all along its length. He was forced to cross and recross the spurs of the foothills over and over. Much of his energy was spent struggling up one hill after the other, only to plunge down again through the bracken into yet another tiny valley—with the next hill looming mockingly just beyond.

At length he stopped under the shade of a huge gnarled tree to have a bit of lunch. He finished his dried apples. He had already eaten all his bread by nibbling at the loaf all morning as he went. He concluded his meal with a drink of cold water from a stream that cascaded across the path. He raised his hand, taking comfort in the fact that his ring was still on his finger, though in disguise.

Elliot stirred when he saw a quick blur of motion down in the bracken. He peered intently into the tall undergrowth of the valley floor, directly below. At first he thought he had glimpsed a songbird or perhaps a butterfly of unusual size. But something about its approach made him uneasy and an indefinable apprehension seized him. He concentrated harder, trying to penetrate the foliage with his gaze. He was almost at the point of seeking a hiding place, when a figure resolved itself from the green backdrop.

Elliot nearly laughed, so great was his relief! For it was a girl—about his age, clad in a bright green dirndl. Her raven locks were mostly concealed by a kerchief knotted prettily in a bow below her chin. She carried a wicker basket and was picking something from the bushes as she moved toward him, apparently unaware of his presence. Finally Elliot realized what occupied her. She was picking blueberries! Elliot loved blueberries, and just now was realizing he had been surrounded by a feast. They grew on the bushes all about him.

He got to his feet, gathered his things, and abandoned the shade to join the girl. "Hello," he said, a trifle awkwardly, as he approached. At first the girl was silent, intent on stripping the last few berries from one particular branch.

Elliot worried that she might respond rudely to him, as Victoria had first done. But after a short pause, during which she wiped her stained fingers upon her apron, she turned to give him a dazzling smile. "How do you do," she said pleasantly. "Welcome to my valley!" Elliot returned her smile, trying his best to think of something polite to say in reply, when she added, "You *are* a city boy, aren't you?"

Elliot was taken aback. He couldn't help but wonder why she thought him to be from the city. "Actually I'm from a small town . . . far away. I'm just passing through," he replied, and then couldn't help but add, "But what makes you think I'm a city boy?"

The girl smiled at him. "Because you're wearing shoes, silly. There are no sharp rocks or thorns upon my valley floor. It's a lovely place that welcomes travelers. That's why

I thought you were from a city. And your clothes are different as well."

"Where I'm from we wear shoes all the time," Elliot attempted to explain.

Here the girl interrupted him with her sweetest smile, wiped her fingers on her apron again for good measure, and extended her hand for him to shake.

"It doesn't matter; I meant no offense. My name is Deirdre. What's yours?"

Elliot shook her hand and returned her smile. "My name is Elliot, Elliot Good."

Deirdre threw back her head and laughed. "What an odd sort of surname you have!" she exclaimed. "Imagine that, I have a new friend whose name is Good! Oh, how perfectly funny! Mother will be so amused when you come to our cottage for supper. For you will, won't you? Oh, do! You simply must!" Her merriment was infectious, so Elliot laughed along with her, though he didn't really understand what she found so amusing.

After they recovered, Elliot asked, "Do you live nearby, Deirdre?"

Deirdre astonished him with her reply. "My home is nearly two days' walk from here. You must come with me! We will hurry, for I know a wonderful place where we may sleep if we but reach it by nightfall!"

Elliot could scarcely believe his ears. "Your mother lets you travel a two days' walk from home all by yourself?" he asked, a taint of disbelief in his voice.

Deirdre smiled and laid a reassuring hand on Elliot's arm.

"Don't be silly!" she said. "Mother would never permit it if our valley weren't a safe place. Why, I am as secure out here as I am at home beside the hearth!"

"But why have you come all this way?" Elliot asked.

"My mother sent me, for the blueberries at this end of the valley are the best in all the world. I am to fill my basket and bring them home so she can make blueberry scones. Do you care for blueberries, Elliot Good?" The inflections of Deirdre's voice sounded musical to his ears.

"Oh yes! I love blueberries."

"Well, it is settled, then! You will travel with me, and you will help me fill my basket as we go. And when we arrive— why, you simply must stay at our cottage for a night or two! We have a soft feather bed in our guest room, and we will have tea with fresh cream and blueberry scones!"

Elliot was delighted with this turn of events, for he found Deirdre to be pleasant company, and he was glad he wouldn't have to cross the valley alone.

Chapter 16

VICTORIA HADN'T A CLUE what to do, but she knew she was very cold indeed and she had better keep moving. If she didn't, she would perish sooner rather than later. So she began walking in circles, stamping her feet. She sang nonsense songs she remembered from her childhood nursery at Summerwind to keep her courage up. When she ran out of those songs she sang one Elliot had taught her. It was called "Puff, the Magic Dragon" and she sang it over and over, high-stepping and waving her arms for warmth.

Victoria had no hat or gloves, and her toes and fingers were becoming frightfully cold. She did not attempt to go back the way they had come, in fact she would rather risk death than return to that dreadful village. She decided to walk in the opposite direction, moving toward the center of the Great Frozen Inland Sea, farther and farther out into the vast, empty darkness.

Suddenly, a loud booming noise echoed through the night and made her start. The noise reverberated for the longest time, and then all was silent again. Victoria walked in near total darkness, unsure if she was going in circles or heading in a straight line. Within a few more minutes the booming sounded again. This time she noticed that the ice beneath her feet trembled.

Victoria didn't really believe the stories of the ice sorcerer Paracelsus any more than Nastya did, but still, the thought of such a thing when shivering alone in the darkness is something else entirely than a story told in a bright drawing room close by the fire. There in her desperately lonely, weakened, and half-frozen state, Victoria wondered if Clericor Demyin's disturbing tales might have been true after all.

Then another low-pitched booming sound seemed to come from under the ice below her feet. Victoria cried out in alarm when, a moment later, a loud, almost human gulping noise echoed through the darkness. She tried to put her fear aside by singing another verse of "Puff, the Magic Dragon," and she laughed because she could never get the name of the land where the dragon lived right. She recalled teasing Elliot because he couldn't, either.

Victoria's pace slowed. She was in true peril now, but she was becoming less and less aware of it. She felt sluggish and a bit dreamy. The cold was bothering her a good deal less. She began to think of the sounds the Great Frozen Inland Sea made as the voice of a living, breathing thing and she talked to it. It seemed to her in her delirium that it replied, with booms and gulps—and that soon they were conversing like old friends.

Victoria grew so tired she finally decided to lie down. She intended to have just a short rest, then she would get up again and continue. In her befuddled state she imagined that her uncle Dexter's town house was just a few steps away and that she wasn't far from the door and a nice hot cup of tea.

As she lay on the ice, the falling flakes swished about her sleeping body and the wind blew and blew. Soon, she appeared as nothing more than a huddled white lump, scarcely recognizable as a person at all, rather more a feature of the landscape. She didn't know it, for by now she was sleeping deeply, but the ice boomed and gulped even more—as if it was anxious for its newfound friend's safety and wanted to awaken her.

And then Victoria was freezing cold again and somebody was shaking her awake. She looked up, brushing the snow from her eyes, realizing that her hand had grown numb. She was surrounded by light and Aeron was beside her. At first she was very cross with him for interrupting her warm sleep, and his words seemed senseless and garbled, but at length she awakened enough to see the alarm upon his face. She made a valiant effort to sit up and understand what he was saying.

"Your ring, Victoria! Look! Look to your ring!"

She held up her hand to gaze upon her ring. It was no longer just a copper stain, but the intricate silver band with its gemstone was there upon her finger once more. And then Aeron was gone, and she wasn't sure if he had been a dream, or perhaps a vivid hallucination, but she was now sitting up, and the stone in her ring was ablaze with light.

The ice was still booming and gulping. Victoria had the most peculiar feeling that it was really trying to summon help to her, in the only way it knew. Then it occurred to her that if help was coming, she should hold her ring aloft—and so she held it up even higher, pointing its stone in the direction she had been walking. She gasped to see her ring flash a strong beam of brilliant light, its startling rays stabbing far out into the snowy night like a beacon.

Victoria held her hand up as long as she could, till she grew too weak, and once more lay down upon the snow. She was just about to drift off again when she thought she heard the sound of approaching horses. With the greatest of efforts she opened her eyes. A silver sleigh carriage with blue tinted windows and green running lamps was coming toward her, drawn by ten high-stepping horses with tall plumes on their brow bands.

The driver steered close as footmen in ornate coats and powdered wigs stepped down, hurrying toward her through the drifting snow. *Or perhaps they don't have powdered wigs at all and it's just the snow in their hair*, Victoria thought as she once again slipped into slumber. But all about her the frozen sea had fallen silent and there were no booms or gulps anymore.

Victoria had the sensation of being picked up and carried. She felt gentle hands brushing the snow from her face and hair before she lost consciousness again. It was some time before she awoke to find herself gratefully nestled in warmth and comfort. She slowly opened her eyes to find herself wrapped in a snow-white fur instead of her cold wet things. Her hair had been dried and combed back from her face. Her bare heels rested upon a padded footrest directly before the grate of a tiny porcelain stove.

Her impression was that she was seated inside an elaborate jeweled Easter egg. The floor was covered in thick carpet and the walls were upholstered in fine brocade. Recessed lamps shone from each sidewall, half concealed within carved tulip blossoms.

Suddenly, Victoria remembered her magic ring and raised her hand to see if it was safe. To her relief it was there, its stone no longer blazing. But when she turned her gaze to the side she gave a start. A striking woman sat on the cushioned seat immediately beside her. She was clad all in gray and white. Her pale fingers were decorated with rings of amber. The woman's skin and hair were of the palest white, though she did not appear to be aged or in any way infirm. Her hair was piled high upon her head, graced with a silver diadem. But what Victoria found most startling were her eyes. They were precisely the same shade of amber as her jewelry!

Chapter 17

ELLIOT AND DEIRDRE walked through the valley picking blueberries as they went. Elliot found himself a bit in awe of Deirdre. There was something about her that seemed different, almost as though she might possess some hidden power. He had quite forgotten how, when he half glimpsed her through the bracken and the tangle of blueberry thickets, he had been filled with a peculiar sensation of dread. Deirdre soothed his fears, silencing any alarms sounding from the deepest corners of his mind with her buoyant personality. They chatted like old friends as they picked berries.

When Deirdre's basket was brim full and both children's hands were stained purple, they came upon a small pond. They swished their hands clean and Deirdre insisted upon wading in the shallows. She hiked up her skirts and stepped in, stamping and kicking bright splashes toward Elliot, who remained seated on the bank. He smiled, even when she drenched him a time or two, because it was in those moments she reminded him of Victoria, and he realized how much he missed her.

"Eeew! Oh, how simply vile!" Deirdre exclaimed. "The mud on the bottom over in the weeds is soft and gooey, and squishing between my toes! Eeew!"

Elliot laughed. Soon Deirdre had her fill of the muddy pond and climbed up onto the rock to sit beside him. Just then, high above, three winged shadows swept across the sky. Elliot asked Deirdre if they were eagles. Deirdre looked up, squinting because of the sun, shading her eyes with her hand. "No, Elliot," she laughed. "Those are vultures."

Elliot frowned. He couldn't help but feel there was something sinister about a place where vultures constantly circled overhead. The Vale of Tinteron wasn't quite like he expected.

"Don't worry, Elliot," said Deirdre soothingly. "There are very few vultures in this valley. Whenever I find a nest, I crush their eggs—doing my part to make them very scarce indeed."

Deirdre said this so lightheartedly that Elliot's stomach did a little flip. "You actually crush their eggs?" he asked incredulously. It seemed a thing so out of place for a seemingly kind young girl to do, or even think of.

Deirdre laughed aloud. "Oh, Elliot! You are funny!" she exclaimed. "You should see your face. Yes, it's true. When I find vultures' eggs I simply crush them in my hands. Why ever not? Don't look at me that way. You eat chickens' eggs, don't you? What do you think happens to them when they are cooked in a pan? And then they end up down inside your stomach. Besides, you dislike vultures as much as I do—so there."

Deirdre crept into the bracken close by where they sat. Soon she found what she was searching for. "Come here, Elliot, and I'll show you. Here's a perfect one." She moved the tangled branches aside to reveal a little nest containing three small blue eggs. "Look," Deirdre whispered. "Vultures' eggs."

Elliot frowned. "I thought that robins' eggs were blue like that," he said. "And aren't they awfully small to be a vulture's eggs?"

"Oh, Elliot, there is a great deal you simply do not know about birds," Deirdre replied. "First, robins' eggs are mint green like my dirndl, not blue at all. Second, it is a robin's nest, but the vultures came when the robins were away and tossed the robins' eggs on the ground. That's what they do. Then they put their own eggs in the nest for the robins to raise. And the vulture's eggs must be tiny to deceive the robins into caring for them. For you see, all robins are color-blind and can't tell that the new eggs are blue!"

"A huge vulture couldn't possibly climb into that tiny nest to lay eggs, I'm quite sure of that," Elliot said doubtfully.

"Elliot," Deirdre said with just the faintest tone of exasperation creeping into her voice, "I didn't say that the vultures laid their eggs in the robin's nest—that would be absurd. They lay them elsewhere, then take them in their beaks, creep to the robin's nest when they are away, and drop them in."

Elliot was now totally convinced that Deirdre had been right all along, for she was a very skilled persuader. "I hope the vultures aren't creeping up on the nest just now," he said with a shudder.

Deirdre laughed at him, a sweet musical sound. "No, silly, they already came. They have simply abandoned their eggs, leaving the task of raising their chicks to the robins! But here, watch—I'll take care of them right now."

Deirdre carefully reached into the nest. Elliot tried his best to convince her to leave the eggs alone, even if they were vultures' eggs. He turned away, his stomach cringing when he heard the soft crunching sounds as Deirdre took them in her fingers and crushed them one by one. She did so with a light-hearted smile. Then she put them back into the nest, wiping her messy hand on her apron. To Elliot, placing the eggs back in the nest after crushing them seemed almost worse than the act of crushing them itself.

"There, Elliot," Deirdre said smugly, obviously pleased with herself. "That serves them right—just for being vultures," she added with a self-righteous toss of her head.

Elliot did not see the crestfallen robin that hopped forlornly from branch to branch as they left the thicket—and if Deirdre noticed, she gave no sign.

ELLIOT AND DEIRDRE hurried on. Deirdre proved quite merciless in the rapid pace she set for them both, though she frequently paused, waiting for Elliot to catch up at various points along their path, sometimes dashing lightly down from some rocky outcropping she had effortlessly climbed to lend him a helping hand. He was amazed at the strength in her grasp. It came close to being painful.

But it was at these times, when she came back to guide him across a particularly treacherous spot, that Elliot couldn't help noticing how pretty Deirdre was—her eyes were so innocent and clear. Despite his feelings about what she did to the bird's eggs, Elliot was becoming a bit infatuated.

At last they reached a wide upland forest where the trees towered above them. The spaces between the massive trunks were carpeted by soft beds of moss and there was no longer any bracken to toil through. It was rather like walking upon a soft carpet in a cool dim temple, pillared and shaded by the trees that wove their tangle of intertwined branches high overhead. Deirdre was fairly brimming with pride, as if the mossy forest was a contrivance of her own making and she had been present when its very first saplings grew from seed.

"Well, Elliot Good," she declared, "how do you like my secret forest? Isn't it the most lovely place you have ever set your eyes upon?" Elliot couldn't help but agree. It was an enchanted sort of place. He did think it a trifle odd that she kept referring to the Vale of Tinteron as *her* valley—after all, this valley was where King Venture's castle was situated, so by rights it was actually his.

"Say, Elliot—if you ever come this way again, you must not tell a soul! This is a hidden place, for now it is known only to you and me."

Deirdre's confidence in him, illustrated by the act of bringing him to her most secret place, made Elliot's heart swell with pride. He assured her that he would rather die the most frightful death than reveal its whereabouts even to a single soul. Something about his statement apparently amused

Deirdre, for she laughed aloud, before once again quickly turning sweet to thank him for his good faith.

"We are almost there, Elliot," she declared at length. "We've only to find the stream and follow it to the cave. I will catch us crayfish to eat, and we'll cook them over a nice open fire."

Elliot was glad to hear that they had nearly reached their destination, and that there would soon be a good meal. He couldn't bear any more pungent goat's milk, and as much as he loved blueberries, he was really becoming rather tired of them. The thought of a crayfish supper made his mouth water.

The crimson light of the setting sun guided them now, permeating the forest floor all about them and casting long dramatic shadows from tree to tree. Elliot soon heard the tinkling of the stream rushing down between moss-covered banks. After following it for just a short distance, they came to the very base of the mountainside, looming like a dark wall directly ahead. And there before them yawned the mouth of Deirdre's cave.

She showed Elliot a place where he could step across the stream upon flat stones without drenching his leather boots. Deirdre herself was content to wade through the stream, the skirts of her dirndl tugged up high about her knees, and she pronounced its ice-cold water to be most refreshing indeed.

The floor of the cave was a layer of smooth sand. It sloped upward around a corner to the curve of the rear wall—which had a broad stone shelf rounding along its sides, ideal for two people to sleep on. Deirdre ran ahead to unfold two blankets, which she had left on the sleeping shelf during her last visit.

She assured Elliot that he would spend the night comfortably and placed both blankets on his side. Elliot suggested they might share. After all, he had a cloak to wrap about himself as well, but Deirdre told him not to be silly, and proudly reminded him that she was used to the outdoors, and immune to cold.

"Besides," Deirdre added, "Mother and I wouldn't want you to catch cold before you come to visit our cottage. It simply would not do if I brought you home to Mother all sickly—it simply wouldn't do at all! She likes all of our guests to be healthy!" Something about her choice of words gave Elliot the most peculiar feeling in the pit of his stomach. But it passed in a moment and he forgot about it.

By now it was almost dark. Deirdre busied herself by kindling a fire in the circle of stones at the mouth of the cave. She inserted a sharp pointed twig into a tiny knothole, penetrating a flat bit of broken bough. Then she collected little tufts of dry moss and worked the pointed piece of wood briskly back and forth, scuffing it between her palms until wisps of smoke curled up from the dry tinder.

And then it was time to catch some crayfish for their supper. Deirdre jumped into the deepest part of the stream, wading slowly forward without the merest flinch in icy water that came up to the middle of her thighs. She stood poised and still upon the slippery stones for quite some time.

Then, quick as a flash, she bent forward, submerging her hands deep into the water. A second later she stood up laughing triumphantly with a fine wriggling crayfish held securely in her grasp. "We shall have a wonderful supper tonight, Elliot!" she exclaimed delightedly. In no time at all she had caught six more fat crayfish. Then she and Elliot filled the cooking pot with water and placed it carefully upon the iron grate directly over the fire, which by now was crackling nicely.

Deirdre was ready to snap the crayfish claws off one by one, because she declared that she much preferred roasting the claws over an open fire on sharp sticks and boiling the tails. But Elliot was horrified, declaring that it would be far too cruel to break off their claws while they were still alive, so she reluctantly agreed not to—all the while regarding him rather strangely, as though his concern for crayfish well-being made no sense whatever.

So instead, Deirdre dropped the crayfish into the pot whole, which made Elliot feel only a little better—that is, until he realized she hadn't even waited till the water was at full boil. He was again disturbed by her cruelty. But soon her artful companionship drove such unpleasantness from his mind.

As the very last rays of the setting sun fanned out, piercing through a deep notch in the distant mountains to cast a surreal crimson glow throughout the forest, they sat down to their crayfish supper. Deirdre showed Elliot how to crack open the claws and the tails with a sharp stone and how to extract every bit of tender steaming flesh. Both children ate until they were content. They sat chatting by the fire for quite some time afterward, until the constellations of red stars materialized through the leafy boughs overhead.

Elliot grew very sleepy, and Deirdre laughed at him when his head kept bumping the tree trunk behind him each time he nodded off. Finally, she suggested that they retire into the cave for a good night's sleep. The fire had burned down to faintly glowing coals. As they left the entrance of the cave, Elliot saw dim gray airborne shapes flitting past through the trees. Deirdre declared them to be owls out hunting for mice—but he wasn't quite so sure. Something about the way they flew reminded him of great pale bats.

In the rear of the cave, the sleeping shelves were scarcely more than three feet apart, for the cave's passageway narrowed as it went. Elliot was glad for the blankets and he spread them atop his unpinned cloak to form a bed. Deirdre lay facing him. She looked warm and comfortable, lying on her stomach with her ankles crossed up behind. The wavering light of a stubby candle melted to the rock combined with the flicker of the dying fire to play tricks on Elliot's imagination—for it made Deirdre's eyes appear black and featureless. He did not like that effect at all, so he turned over to lie on his back.

Deirdre suggested that she tell stories, and boasted to Elliot that her mother frequently declared her to be the finest storyteller. Her voice was well suited for storytelling, being sweetly toned, well modulated, and full of expression. But nearly all the stories she told were not nice at all—rather frightful tales of lost children, wicked stepmothers, and hungry witches.

Finally, Elliot begged her to stop, while admitting that she did have quite a lovely voice for it. He simply couldn't bear to hear more stories of that sort. When at last he drifted off to sleep, he was plagued all night long by strange and vividly disturbing dreams. First he dreamed that he was lying on his back, wakeful, yet unable to move. Deirdre came crawling slowly toward him, spiderlike, her black eyes fixed on him.

In another dream he was a terrified wriggling crayfish, helplessly clicking his ineffectual claws, while Deirdre grasped him about the abdomen. She was laughing as she snapped off his claws one by one, then slowly dipped him into a pot of hot, bubbling water.

Elliot's third dream was the strangest of all. While he slept restlessly, Deirdre was having a conversation with someone at the mouth of the cave. A grotesque figure in a tall pointed hat sat opposite her, across the dying embers of the fire. The frightening figure then seemed to change shape, transforming itself into a pleasant, sweet-faced woman. The two of them went on chatting for quite some time until the woman took some powders from her apron pocket and cast them directly upon the flames.

She chanted something in a dead, hollow-sounding voice that made Elliot's flesh crawl. The powders made the fire resurrect violently from its embers and burn high, almost high enough to ignite the very treetops, while flaring to a strange green coloration—the precise color of Deirdre's dirndl. Elliot moaned, stirring in his sleep.

Chapter 18

THE WOMAN WITH the startling amber eyes smiled. "Ah, Victoria Deveny! At long last! We have waited for you to come to us. The Palace of Kalingalad is bustling with activity—everyone is anticipating your arrival."

Victoria's brow furrowed. Her voice quavered as she asked, "Am I dead? Perhaps I froze to death!"

The woman at her side laughed. "First things first. I am the Albino Contessa, and am very pleased indeed to make your acquaintance. And no, Victoria, you are most assuredly not dead, though I daresay you soon would have been, except for the way the gemstone in your ring shone like a beacon to guide us, and of course the Great Frozen Inland Sea itself did its best to bring us to you posthaste—before all was lost."

"I did think the gulping noises and the booming sounds were its way of summoning help for me!" Victoria exclaimed.

The Albino Contessa nodded. "The Great Frozen Inland Sea is a place of profound loveliness, as you shall soon discover."

Victoria drew her furs about herself more tightly, savoring the luxuriant warmth. She still was perplexed, though. "Not meaning to seem rude, ma'am," she said at length, "but Clericor Demyin says that the Great Frozen Inland Sea is a fearful place full of evil!"

"Clericor Demyin and Lord Primvet poison every mind they touch with the likeness of their own darkness of heart! They do not understand the Great Frozen Inland Sea, so they fear it and declare it evil. They engender their own fear in the hearts of others with clever deceits," said the Albino Contessa.

Then she rang a little silver bell. Two ladies-in-waiting stepped up from their seats in the sleigh carriage's lower level, bearing a small glass decanter filled with a golden cordial. They smiled at Victoria and poured out some for her in an eggshell-thin cup. She swallowed it and felt a warmth course through her entire body. Soon her head felt much clearer and she wondered if perhaps they had given her a magical elixir.

Victoria sighed in the comfort of her surroundings and crossed her ankles, savoring the warmth beneath her heels. By the motion of the sleigh carriage and the sound of its runners on the snow, she could tell they were moving across the icy sea at a high rate of speed.

"Where might we be going, if you please?" she inquired.

"We are bound for the Palace of Kalingalad—home of Paracelsus. I suppose Clericor Demyin told you all about him!"

Victoria laughed, but she felt uneasy at the mention of that name. "Paracelsus is not really an ice demon, is he?" she asked apprehensively.

"No, of course not," scoffed the Albino Contessa, "though I daresay it might amuse him to hear the things that people say. No, child, Paracelsus is but the benefactor of all those lost and alone out upon our icy sea. He is also a magician of surpassing skill."

"Does that mean . . . did Constance come to you safely?" Victoria asked, suddenly remembering and growing anxious for the well-being of her friend. "Nastya said that I might trip over her bones out on the ice in the darkness!"

The Albino Contessa shook her head in contempt at the mere mention of Nastya's name. "Nastya would be so terribly disappointed if she knew that Constance is the happiest she has ever been!"

The Albino Contessa smiled at Victoria, patting her arm gently. "You will meet her within a few hours and see for yourself how she is getting on. She talks of you day and night—worrying about you constantly."

"Oh, I am so glad!" exclaimed Victoria, and when the Albino Contessa raised her eyebrows ever so slightly Victoria laughed. "No! I am not glad that she is worried, but I am delighted she is happy and safe! How perfectly splendid! Why, I feel pounds better straightaway!" Warm, comfortable, and rejoicing to hear of her friend's safety, Victoria drifted off to sleep once more.

When she awoke she found the Albino Contessa and her ladies-in-waiting were peering out the windows into the night. To Victoria's surprise the snow had nearly stopped and the great blue moon was rising, suffusing everything with its pale breathtaking radiance.

They sat in luxury, watching towering snow-covered crags pass close by on each side. They passed islands covered with precipitous hills and snowy forests of tall frost-bound trees, and under an archway of rock spanning two crags like a bridge. At one point Victoria glimpsed the ruin of a crumbling tower in the stark moonlight. As they passed beneath its shadow, she saw that it was very tall, and ancient. Its blank windows, empty battlements, and dilapidated state gave Victoria the chills.

"Servants of my sister, Queen Ulricke, built that tower long ago, for she lived there in ages past. Now she dwells in another realm and has turned her heart to wickedness, I fear," said the contessa sadly.

"Oh, how perfectly dreadful!" Victoria replied, with perhaps more alarm than genuine sympathy in her voice, for she grew suddenly fearful. Had she been rescued only to find herself in danger once more? After all, she was now in the clutches of Queen Ulricke's sister! Victoria's eyes widened in apprehension and she clutched her wrap more tightly about herself, as one of the ladies-in-waiting bent forward to stir the coals in the grate.

"Oh dear," exclaimed Victoria. "Can my friend Elliot have any hope of safety if he journeys into your sister's realm?"

The Albino Contessa answered carefully. "If he is under protection of faerie magic like you, Victoria, he may be safe," she said, looking at Victoria's ring. "Though my sister is very powerful . . ." The Albino Contessa then lapsed into silence.

Victoria felt guilty of her suspicions. The Albino Contessa had spoken so wistfully and seemed to have grown suddenly grieved.

"My sister chose to be immortal and I am bound by her choice as well," said the Albino Contessa softly. "It seems my fate is mingled with hers—but I did not ask that it be so."

Victoria wondered if the Albino Contessa would also die if something befell her sister. She didn't know what to say in reply so she reached out her hand instead, her fingers seeking those of the contessa, who smiled at her and became a trifle less sad.

From her window, Victoria saw the elongated shadow of the sleigh carriage flitting across the ice, behind the fantastic, distorted shadows of the horses that drew it. She leaned forward in her seat, straining to discern the form of several colossal shadowed objects they were approaching. They were huge looming forms, and she had difficulty making them out for some time. Exactly what were they?

With a sudden pulse-racing thrill, she realized that the shapes were not natural forms at all. They were drawing near to an entire fleet of frozen ships!

Victoria temporarily abandoned her seat, kneeling upon the cushions closest to the curve of the window to view the spectacle. Her face was pressed so close to the cool glass that her warm breath decorated it with fanciful patterns of frost. Within moments, the carriage slowed considerably, and was carefully maneuvering its way among the mysterious ships.

High angled sterns towered overhead. Blue moonlight flickered to briefly illuminate banks of diamond-paned windows in stern cabins far above. Thick mooring lines hung from the upper decks, festooned with icicles. Victoria thought that the mooring ropes must still be connected to massive rust-encumbered anchors embedded deep in the seafloor—far beneath thick ice that lay thick upon the surface of the Great Frozen Inland Sea.

Rank upon rank and row upon row of cannon ports—some gaping open and some battened tightly closed—slipped past, arranged down the curving sides of the huge old hulks. The ice-plugged and frost-draped muzzles of ancient bronze cannons protruded from the upper gunports. The blue-black sails of most of the ships were still set, hanging heavily from the spars as though they had been dipped in water and flash-frozen. The braces, shrouds, and topmasts were covered in icicles gleaming in the moonlight as the sleigh glided silently past.

Victoria was astonished at both the size and number of the vessels. She wondered if perhaps ghostly crews were still present on their ships. She had a dreadful vision of sightless, ice-encrusted phantoms manning their stations, standing watch—still vigilant at their gunports. "Why, this whole fleet lies here—frozen fast in time!" she breathed, thinking of how much Elliot would like to have seen it with her.

As they drew away from the frozen fleet, it seemed as though the sleigh carriage was standing still, and that the great ships were rushing rapidly backward, speeding away into the rear distance. Victoria watched spellbound, until at last, even the bows of the foremost ships had been left behind and there was nothing to see outside her window, save for leagues of featureless ice.

She spent the next two hours conversing with the Albino Contessa and dozing on and off a bit, for she was exhausted from her ordeal and her toil at the Black Swan Inn. In the midst of one of her naps she was gently nudged awake by the contessa. "Look out your window, Victoria, for we have reached our destination!"

⁓

THE SLEIGH CARRIAGE proceeded much slower as it approached the lighted way to the Palace of Kalingalad. There were hundreds of lampposts in two parallel rows forming an illuminated approach to the gates.

Her first glimpse of the palace took Victoria's breath away. There, far out in the Great Frozen Inland Sea, the sight more enhanced than obstructed by falling snow, a fantastic structure seemed to rise up from the very ice itself—a high-walled building that was part fortress and part airy confection. It was a thing of beauty spun from stone, tile, and masonry, rather than from sugar, icing, and glaze. Spires and fantastically shaped onion domes capped the rooftops of the sumptuous palace that beckoned with thousands of illuminated windows. One wing's windows were all amber, and Victoria correctly guessed that was where the Albino Contessa had her suite.

Victoria's eyes had scarcely registered a hundredth of the beauty and intricacy of the palace when the sleigh carriage came to the end of the lighted way, drawing near a looming corner tower. The walls of the palace were massive with thick battlements at the top, but at the base they fanned out wider still, supported upon great buttresses of stone. A snow-covered ramp pierced one of the piers in the base of the corner tower and led upward through an arched gateway surmounted by ornate lamps. The sleigh carriage swept up the ramp, through the wall, and into the palace.

"This is the most amazing thing I have ever seen!" exclaimed Victoria to the Albino Contessa, who smiled at her exuberance. "It makes Summerwind look like a little cottage and even Buckingham Palace seem so plain and dour by compare!"

A moment later the carriage came to a halt in the courtyard under softly falling snow. Victoria was given a white velvet cloak to wear over the fur wrap that had kept her warm on her journey, and a pair of soft slippers. The footmen opened the door, unfolding collapsible steps. Victoria and the Albino Contessa were escorted down from the carriage, where the guards awaited them, clad in splendid coats and powdered wigs.

Directly in front of where the horses stood stamping and snorting, a long ramp sloped steeply down to the warmth and comfort of the stables. The stables were constructed deep inside the palace foundation where there was room for many horses and sleigh carriages, too—for there were frequent balls and masquerades held at the Palace of Kalingalad. Ofttimes throngs of guests were invited from all the palaces bordering the Great Frozen Inland Sea.

Just ahead two sets of stairs rose, one on each side of the stable archway. The staircases joined farther on, leading up to the palace's formal entrance doors, now held wide open by servants waiting on the upper landing.

Victoria gasped as she felt herself gently and respectfully picked up off her feet. Palace guardsmen carried both her and the Albino Contessa in their arms up the long snowy stairs. The guardsmen wore high riding boots that could withstand snow far better than the delicate kidskin slippers that Victoria and the contessa wore. Victoria rested one hand on the guardsman's shoulder and used the other to tug up the hood of her cloak. The snow was falling harder now, the flakes forming blurred halos about the lamps.

At the entrance doors they were greeted by a host of servants. Victoria and the Albino Contessa thanked the guards courteously as they put them gently down. They were escorted through a grand receiving hall. Victoria's eyes could scarcely absorb the extent of palatial loveliness all about her. The ceilings were faceted and the walls and even the arched interior doors were cushioned with gold-threaded brocade sewn in the most stunning patterns featuring starbursts and phoenixes. The windows were deeply set in the thick walls, and each stained-glass panel was a work of art in its own right. Priceless rugs cushioned the floors, and porcelain tile stoves shaped like multilayered wedding cakes banished any thought of cold.

They proceeded up a short flight of steps, then down a long corridor lit by crystal chandeliers. They walked through galleries hung with tapestries and halls with frescoed ceilings, then ascended twisting staircases wrapped about high fluted pillars. Victoria felt overwhelmed by it all long before they finally reached the door to Paracelsus' private dining room.

They were formally announced by the palace chamberlain: "Victoria Deveny and the Albino Contessa have arrived, my lord!" Paracelsus stood with his back to them, before a wide hearth where a fire crackled merrily. A table was ready with five place settings prepared upon a cloth of snow-white linen.

High-backed chairs and side tables littered with books were scattered about the room, and upon one wall was a gilt-framed painting five feet square. It was a larger version of the very same painting hanging in Victoria's nursery at Summerwind—the painting of the Faerie Queen! There was also a framed map of the Great Frozen Inland Sea, with all its features depicted precisely to scale.

And then Paracelsus, Lord of the Palace of Kalingalad, accomplished magician of ancient lineage, turned to greet them with a smile.

"I know you!" Victoria exclaimed, hardly realizing what she was saying before the words tumbled from her mouth.

For there before her, clad in a robe of midnight blue, was the old man from the Black Swan Inn, for whom she had stolen bread. His hair was white, and his thin face was etched with lines. His childlike eyes were of the clearest blue imaginable, seemingly much younger than he.

Paracelsus smiled and held out his arms as Victoria ran to embrace him. "Welcome, generous child, whose heart is awakening to kindness more and more each day! I see you have already met one of my dearest friends, the Albino Contessa."

Victoria nodded vigorously. "So you are the wicked sorcerer of the Great Frozen Inland Sea, are you?" she said fondly, looking up at him with her impish grin. "I should have known as much!"

Paracelsus shook his head. "I am not now, nor have I ever been, a *wicked* sorcerer," he said with a smile.

And then to Victoria's delight, a door beneath the painting of the Faerie Queen was flung open and Constance ran to greet her. Victoria's eyes filled with tears of joy, and Constance's did, too. They embraced and clung to each other fiercely, overjoyed to be reunited.

Chapter 19

AFTER LEAVING THE CAVE, Elliot and Deirdre moved through the hushed quiet of the early morning forest like ghosts. Elliot followed her in silence as they moved from upland glens down into hillside meadows. It occurred to him that he hadn't seen Deirdre's face in nearly two hours and he suddenly got an awful feeling that she had transformed into something ghastly—that she didn't want to turn around, for then he would see her true form. When she did turn about he gave an involuntary start. She smiled at him, and he saw to his relief that her face was as lovely and sweet as ever.

"Goodness, Elliot," she exclaimed, both impatience and concern evident in her voice. "You have been quiet all morning. Is something wrong?"

"No, I'm all right," Elliot answered, trying to sound nonchalant as best he could. "I had bad dreams all night and I didn't sleep well, that's all."

"I never have bad dreams," Deirdre declared proudly. "And no silly dream could ever scare me if I did!"

Deirdre was determined to have Elliot to her mother's cottage by nightfall, so they traveled swiftly. They were moving steadily deeper into the valley. Twice more Elliot saw vultures circling overhead.

"Do you think we'll glimpse King Venture's castle on the way to your mother's cottage?" he asked Deirdre.

"Elliot, you are quite hopeless without a map to guide you, aren't you?" Deirdre laughed. "This isn't the Vale of Tinteron; it's the Valley of Direfall. We're not the subjects of that silly old one-eyed king here!"

Elliot's pulse pounded in his ears and he experienced a welling surge of fear. Why had Sir Edrim brought him to the wrong place, then lied about it? And though Direfall did seem pleasant enough, why had King Venture and his court warned him about it?

Deirdre noticed his crestfallen expression. "Oh, Elliot," she exclaimed. "Don't tell me you listen to the old wives' tales about Direfall being such an awful place? You know better, don't you? Tell me you think better of me than that!"

Deirdre gazed at Elliot searchingly, her eyes earnest. He even thought he saw her lower lip tremble just the tiniest bit. He smiled. "Don't worry, I never really believed all those silly stories!"

Deirdre laughed, and it made him a little embarrassed when she hugged him impulsively. "Oh, I am so glad," she said.

After a few miles they crested a small rise where a picture-perfect oval of green meadow lay directly ahead. In its center stood a lovely little wood, a precise circle of old stately oaks. "It's time for us to have lunch, Elliot. We shall have truffles!

And truffles are simply the finest food you could ever imagine." Deirdre paused and smiled to herself. "Well, at least the second finest food, anyway," she added, giving Elliot a quick sideways glance.

"What are truffles?" asked Elliot.

"They are a fungus that grows just beneath the ground in woodlands hereabouts," Deirdre replied.

"I'm not sure I have an appetite for fungus just now," Elliot said doubtfully.

"Don't be foolish, Elliot Good," countered Deirdre. "You like mushrooms, don't you?"

Elliot remembered the mushroom chicken with noodles that his mother often prepared for supper and how tasty it was. "I love mushrooms," he replied wistfully.

"Well then, truffles are a kind of fungus—just like mushrooms, only better, and they'll go ever so well with our dinner."

"Okay, I'll try them if you insist," Elliot agreed.

Elliot was surprised to see Deirdre creeping forward now, bent at the waist, an expression of concentration stamped upon her face. She acted as though she were stalking game. He laughed and she turned toward him with her finger pressed to her lips—as a frown furrowed her brow. "Sshh! Be quiet, will you!" she hissed. He obeyed meekly and continued to watch.

Elliot realized that she was actually sniffing the air. He tried sniffing himself, but could smell nothing except the fresh scent of the mountain breezes that ruffled the leaves above his head. Deirdre was on her knees now, crawling forward carefully, hardly making a sound. Then suddenly she was digging, her tapered fingers forming claws as she delved through the leaves and vegetation to the soft black loam beneath.

"Oh yes! How wonderful!" she exclaimed a moment later with triumphant glee in her voice. "I've found them! And what fine truffles they are!"

Deirdre stood up and came to him, her hands brimming full of oddly shaped, wrinkled objects still caked with black dirt, and she put them in the basket. Elliot had to admit that, despite their appearance, the truffles did smell wonderful— a spicy, intriguing, exotic scent that was hard to describe— and his mouth watered.

"We will each have one raw truffle for our lunch," said Deirdre. As she began breaking them into bite-sized pieces with her filthy fingers he began to feel squeamish. She popped a succulent piece of truffle into her own mouth and offered to feed him a fragment from her dirty hand.

He tried reaching out to take it himself, but she insisted that he accept it from her fingers. "It won't bite you, Elliot! It's just a truffle—try it." He asked her to brush off the black dirt before feeding it to him, but Deirdre just laughed and popped it into his mouth. "Oh, silly Elliot Good! You are so sweet and funny, aren't you! It's best with the dirt still coating all the little ridges!" Elliot munched the truffle very warily at first and found the taste to be surprisingly delicious, especially for something just dug from out of the ground.

As soon as they left the beautiful little wood the countryside began to rise, sloping upward in a broad expanse of rolling field and meadows. It reminded Elliot of a story he once read about a field at the very edge of the world. As they walked up the last bit of rise to crest the brow of the hill, he began feeling very unwell. But when they stood atop the summit he forgot about feeling sick for a moment.

The view was breathtaking—the Valley of Direfall stretched away before them. Directly ahead was another mile or so of green meadow with little islands of forest. Not far beyond that was a rather odd brown area that even in the sunlight managed to look most unpleasant. And far beyond that, out in the haze, Elliot glimpsed the dark green of a mysterious forest.

"That forest is where my mother's cottage lies," said Deirdre. "If we hurry, we may reach it by nightfall." Elliot was feeling nauseous and unsteady again. The sick feeling came in waves and each left him weak and sweaty.

"What is that ugly brown spot between us and your mother's forest?" Elliot asked.

Deirdre answered, "That is Bogmon Moor, Elliot—and we shall have to cross it to get home."

As they continued on and approached Bogmon Moor, Elliot began to feel very wretched indeed. His stomach was extremely upset, and he felt dizzy and befuddled. Deirdre took him by the arm, helping him along at first. By now his knees were wobbling. Suddenly he shook himself loose from Deirdre's grasp, fell to the ground, and was violently sick, heaving and retching into the grass.

He knelt on all fours trembling, with tears running down his cheeks. He gasped, finally catching his breath, feeling both weak and ashamed of being sick in front of Deirdre, who was always so strong. After his head cleared he sat back on his knees. He looked up to find that Deirdre was gone!

Elliot rose unsteadily and peered about. The bleak expanse of Bogmon Moor stretched out before him for miles, rolling out into the distance like a dark stain upon the beauty of the otherwise lovely valley. And there was no sign of Deirdre anywhere.

She must have gone on ahead, Elliot thought. He was not thinking clearly. Perhaps it was the truffle that had made him ill—he was not at all accustomed to its richness.

As Elliot set out alone, a feeling of veiled menace was present in the air all about him. The moor was wide and bleak with occasional thickets of scraggly trees sporting dry branches and dead brown leaves. Gnarled crags and gaunt spires of rock rose up from the moor's broken expanse like apparitions. Elliot carefully walked about them, wondering if Deirdre was playing a prank and hiding from him. The ancient rocks reminded him of gravestones, and he moved even faster. Just the thought of spending the night out upon Bogmon Moor made his flesh crawl.

Soon the waves of nausea and dizziness returned full force. He fell to his knees and was sick once again. He didn't notice the great black birds that wheeled expectantly in the air, high above him. The next several hours were a frightful blur. Elliot was sick repeatedly, rapidly becoming weaker and disoriented. He feared that he was turned round and was heading back the way he had come. He knew he would never find the cave again, nor even the forest that contained it, without Deirdre's help. He desperately wished that Sindl would make an appearance to assist him as she had promised.

Once he even thought that he glimpsed Deirdre up ahead, for there was a patch of vivid green in the low bracken of a misty hollow. He quickened his pace eagerly, only to find that it was a clump of odd sickly plants with green bulbs. They reminded him of lady's slippers, but they were ugly and smelled supremely vile. Elliot noticed masses of flies on the underside of their leaves and he shuddered. The unpleasant smell that the plant emitted made him sick again and it was nearly twenty minutes before he stumbled on once more.

He was feeling especially dreadful when he came to a large, perfectly round pool. Its water appeared to be utterly black, almost as though it were oil. It was so dark it didn't even show the reflection of the clouds, nor the circling winged shadows wheeling high above. Elliot paused at the edge of the black pool. He was awfully thirsty, but something told him this wasn't the sort of water that one should drink. He cautiously dipped his right hand into the pool and scooped up some of the water to splash into his face. He was surprised to find it clear and cool, not inky black as it appeared.

Elliot knelt in the soft mud at the edge of the pool. He desperately needed a bit of rest. Suddenly something splashed out toward the center of the water. He jumped, sitting back on his heels.

The splash sounded again, and he saw ripples radiating from a point in the pool several feet away. Suddenly a lovely face rose smoothly up from beneath the water. It was as though someone in a reclining position just below the surface had simply risen to the top and sat up. It was a pale female face with dark expressive eyes. She would have looked more beautiful if long lank strands of hair weren't hanging limply down each side of her head, with a few stray strands plastered across her face. The person glided forward toward Elliot through the rippling waves and stopped just a few feet away from him.

Then a second face rose up from the pool to join the first. Both faces regarded him curiously, while he sat frozen in alarm, fighting down another surging wave of nausea.

"Come bathe with us!" said one of the faces. Its voice was the sweetest and loveliest Elliot had ever heard, but the teeth he glimpsed when it moved its lips to form the words were black and jagged.

The second figure laughed. "Yes, poor lad! Come in and swim with us. Our black pool will cool and refresh you, and it will soothe away all your ills—forever and ever!"

Elliot began to crawl away, scuttling backward like a crab, seeking purchase in the slippery black mud. It was almost as though the margin of the pool was widening as he went. He tried mightily to clamber to his feet—most anxious indeed to get away from the befouled water.

"Don't be a shy, foolish boy. We will carry you into the water if you are too sick to come yourself!" The figures were moving toward him now, arms outstretched beseechingly. They began to rise from the water, their veiny necks and bony shoulders now fully revealed. Their pale hands reached pleadingly out to him.

"Come swim with us!" they implored.

Elliot kept slipping and falling as he scuttled away. They were half out of the water now, coming for him, and he could see that though they were women from the hips up, they had no legs at all—rather smooth eel-like tails instead.

Long pale fingers were clutching at his boots now as the mermaids writhed, squirming half out of the water and wriggling ever nearer, their serpentine bodies grotesquely elongating and undulating. One grasped his left ankle while the other managed to get a firm grip on his right thigh. Elliot felt himself being pulled through the mud, inching nearer and nearer to the black water that they so desperately wished him to enter. Overwhelming fear caused a rush of adrenaline, and he cried out, kicking and thrashing with all his might, even punching at the wet hands that grasped him. He struggled until he extricated himself from their grasp and scrabbled backward from the edge of the pool into the thicket, heedless of the foul slippery muck.

Soon he found himself alone once again, as fading ripples ran from the center of the pool to lap fitfully against the unpleasant black mud of the bank.

ELLIOT'S JOURNEY THROUGH Bogmon Moor went on and on like an unending nightmare. He was sick again and exhausted from going far out of his way through briar thickets to give the black pool a wide berth. He stumbled on, feeling strangely detached from his unpleasant surroundings. Such was his state of mind that the next fright hardly surprised him.

Some latent instinct of self-preservation prompted him to look backward, up over his shoulder. He was shocked to discover that there in the air behind him floated a great hulking ship, high over the moorland! The black hull of the vessel appeared simply immense, mostly because Elliot was accustomed to seeing ships afloat where at least half the hull was concealed below the waterline.

Elliot didn't need to glimpse the grinning skull and crossbones of the Jolly Roger ensign rippling from the topmast to know it was a pirate ship. The whole appearance of the ship, with its gaping cannon ports and bloodred sails billowing in the wind, apprised him of that fact.

As the ship drew nearer, now half blotting out the sky, Elliot began to think it was all a fever dream. He half considered hailing the ship, calling out, and asking its crew for a ride, but he thought better of it, prudently cowering down in the bracken lest the pirates take him prisoner. For there would be no chance whatever of survival if he were forced to walk the plank off an airborne pirate ship! Elliot huddled lower, drawing his muddy cloak about himself, hoping it would serve as camouflage. He could hear the snapping of its sails, the creaking of ropes and pulleys, and the clanking of a turning capstan. He could also hear hoarse, hateful voices raised in anger, issuing commands laced with profanity—and the thud of footsteps on the decks high above.

When it began moving slowly away, Elliot glimpsed the high navigation deck above the stern gallery with its rows of ornate windows and fanciful lanterns. A tall figure, clad in a scarlet coat, sporting row upon row of bright silver buttons, stood at the stern rail and Elliot felt the menace of the figure's eyes as he searched the ground far beneath the keel of his ship. The figure wore a ponytail, tricornered hat, and silver hoop earrings. Elliot had the strong feeling that his life would end abruptly if that figure spotted him, but to his profound relief the pirate ship moved on, proceeding swiftly as more of its billowing sails were unfurled by crewmen high atop the masts standing precariously out upon the yardarms.

Finally, Elliot realized he was at long last approaching the eaves of the dark forest at the very end of the valley where Deirdre and her mother lived. The sun had nearly set. The crimson splendor was fading beyond the mountains and night was falling fast. Elliot was pleased to see that a well-tended path lay before him, winding into the depths of the wood. He saw a faint light glimmering somewhere directly ahead, just down the path, and practically ran in his eagerness to reach it.

He was only a little disappointed to find the light's source was a tall pointed lantern with a slow-burning candlestick inside. It hung from a wrought iron peg driven into the trunk of a thick oak whose canopy formed an immense shadow, towering over the smaller trees nearby. A hand-carved wooden sign with deeply recessed letters was fastened to the tree trunk beside the lantern. It read: FOR OUR GUESTS, AND FOR ALL LOST TRAVELERS. TO LIGHT YOUR WAY SAFELY THROUGH THE NIGHT AND GUIDE YOU TO OUR DOORSTEP.

Elliot took the lantern and was nearly as happy as if he had already reached Deirdre's cottage. For he knew he was almost there, now that he had a lamp to light his way.

He was lighthearted as he started down the twisting path. The wood grew denser as he progressed and the trees became much taller, their shadows taking on sinister shapes in the lantern light. Several times Elliot thought he heard soft footfalls padding upon the faintly luminous path that stretched back behind him in the gloom. But each time he spun about he saw nothing. Once he thought he spotted a shadowy half-formed shape fade quickly to blend into the trees behind, but he wasn't certain.

Elliot quickened his pace. He was seized with a peculiar thought. The last time he turned round and peered back down the path, beyond the feeble circle of yellow lantern light, he noticed something very odd. He distinctly remembered proceeding straight down a steep incline to arrive where he now stood, but the path behind him twisted sharply to the left, not leading uphill at all. Elliot wondered if some evil magic was changing the path behind him as he went.

Then suddenly he spotted a twinkling green light slowly moving toward him in the darkness. At first he thought perhaps it was another traveler in the wood, carrying a lantern similar to his own. He paused, standing motionless, taking only slight comfort in the light cast by his lantern, for its candle had burned down to a greasy lump of tallow and its flame was wavering, casting his own fantastically distorted shadow out toward the green light approaching him from the darkness. His nose wrinkled at the unpleasant smell that drifted upward from the guttering tallow.

Then he thought, with a momentary surge of relief, that it was Sindl at last coming to aid him—but then he remembered that both Aeron and Sindl were blue faeries, and their lights would not be green. Elliot recalled seeing green faeries in the court of the Faerie Queen—but this light was a different shade of green, dimmer perhaps, less lovely, and somehow almost poisonous in appearance.

Elliot's sickness had almost entirely passed about the time he approached the eaves of the wood, but now he felt odd, dizzy, and disoriented once again. The candle flame finally sputtered and went out, leaving him in near-total darkness.

Icy fingers of fear were clutching his heart, so Elliot began to run, all the while peering frantically backward over his shoulder. There were more green lights and they were gaining! There were perhaps a dozen of them now, drawing rapidly nearer from the left side of the path, with five or six more approaching from the right. Two or three others were coming from directly behind. Elliot ran for all he was worth, driven on by an intensifying fear that he didn't fully understand.

He squinted into the darkness, and saw that the lights were indeed faerie forms. They came gliding through the air alongside the path, darting and weaving among the boughs. Their faces were wild and they had long matted hair and fantastically pointed ears and wings.

Elliot began to slow down, and his alarm was just beginning to subside when he glimpsed the faeries' hands, and saw, to his horror, that they were simply frightful!

Their hands were much too large for the rest of their bodies and had long fingers and bony knuckles. Their fingernails were like claws, impossibly long and dirty. Elliot had thought he was running fast before, but now he ran even faster—fleeing for his very life.

The faeries came skimming toward him, their long hideous fingers grasping at his face and tearing at his clothing. He cried out in terror and swung the lantern in a broad arc, knocking two or three of them aside, but the rest kept on relentlessly, their hateful laughter tinkling.

Long black nails ripped holes in his clothing. The faeries were dragging him down now; several were on his back and one even alighted on his shoulders to pull his hair so hard that his eyes filled with blinding tears. Elliot stumbled and fell, the wicked faeries leaping upon him. Before he fainted, his last sensation was of searing pain as they pinched and tore at him all over.

Then it seemed as though he was coming up out of a dark and terrible dream and Deirdre was with him, helping him along. He was leaning heavily on her shoulder. She had her arm about him and carried a lantern with its tall candle burning brightly. "It's all right, Elliot!" she soothed. "Don't worry, for we are almost home!"

"How did you drive away the bad faeries?" he gasped.

"There are no bad faeries in this forest, Elliot. You have been frightfully sick and delirious the whole way. It is my fault after all, for I should have recalled that Mother says the rarest, most delectable truffles sometimes disagree with people who aren't accustomed to them."

Elliot was dumbfounded. "Do you mean Bogmon Moor, the evil mermaids in the black pool, the flying pirate ship, and the green faeries with long nails were all a fever dream?" he asked incredulously. "How could that possibly be?"

"Oh, Elliot, you are so sweet, but sometimes you are quite an imbecile!" Deirdre said with a fond condescending smile. "Only Bogmon Moor was real and I had a devil of a time getting you across it. But there are no mermaids or pirate ships there, silly. We are a long way off from the sea, you know."

"But . . ." and here Elliot held up his hand, which was scratched and bleeding in several places. "If there were no bad faeries clawing at me, then how did I get these scratches?"

"That was one of the times you went quite out of your head and ran off screaming into the bracken, cutting yourself on thorns," Deirdre explained, her eyes eloquent with concern in the flicker of lantern light. "I was worried sick until I found you again and brought you back to the path."

Elliot stumbled on with Deirdre supporting him. She was still pristine in her dirndl and kerchief, her hair perfectly in place, while his own clothes were torn and stained with black mud, and he was bleeding from a dozen scratches and cuts. "I suppose I got this smelly black mud on me when I ran off into the thorns, too," he said wearily.

Deirdre paused to ruffle his hair affectionately. "No, Elliot, that's from the times you fell down and were violently ill, throwing up in the muck!"

When they rounded the last bend in the path Elliot felt waves of relief wash over him. He saw the comforting light of cottage windows just ahead. It was a perfectly lovely little place, nestled in the forest with a cobbled path leading directly to its arched doorway. It had thickly paned windows, a steeply pitched roof, and a fieldstone chimney with smoke curling up out of it, pale against the dark sky and the shadows of the treetops. It struck Elliot odd that the wood seemed so friendly and quaint when he was with Deirdre—but that it was such an awful place without her.

Deirdre helped him hobble up to the door, which opened smoothly to emit a welcoming warmth from the room beyond. They were greeted by a woman in an apron and print dress with a dusting of flour all over her hands. Elliot practically stumbled into her arms, his face resting briefly upon her flour-dusted bosom as she eased him inside. "Goodness, Deirdre!" the woman exclaimed. "What in heaven's name has befallen our poor guest? We must see to him at once!"

Chapter 20

"Oh, Constance! You're beautiful now! I always knew you were! You're not thin anymore, and your cheeks are flushed and healthy!" Victoria exclaimed, her eyes shining with delight. "And you are safe—your bones aren't out in the darkness, frozen in the awful cold!"

"I thought that would be my fate," said Constance. "But then I saw a sleigh carriage coming, drawn by white horses, and it was so exquisitely beautiful that I thought perhaps I was freezing to death while dreaming!"

"Me, too," said Victoria excitedly. "That's exactly what happened to me!"

The Albino Contessa suggested that the girls catch up with their visiting later—they would be sharing a tower room with its own window seat. And if the clouds cleared away, they could gaze at the huge blue moon, exactly as they used to out of their attic window at the Black Swan Inn. Victoria and Constance wondered how the Albino Contessa knew about that—but she simply smiled.

And then the butler—a haughty man, immaculately clad in ivory satin trimmed with crimson velvet and sporting an impeccably powdered wig—inquired if they were ready for supper to commence. Paracelsus asked where Violet was and the butler sent another servant off to see if Violet would be joining them for dinner, or if they should begin without her. The servant returned to say that Violet had sent her sincerest apologies and that she would arrive within five minutes, so Paracelsus told the butler to wait, which he agreed to do with only the slightest sniff, and the merest twitch of long-suffering apparent about the corners of his razor-thin mustache.

Constance drew Victoria aside to talk privately, while the Albino Contessa and Paracelsus carried on a hushed conversation nigh the fire. Constance explained that Violet was the ballet instructor at the palace and that they were preparing for the single greatest performance of the entire season—to be held in just a few weeks. The ballet was called the *Saltatrix Angelus*, and the lead dancer hadn't yet been chosen.

Victoria rolled her eyes, declaring, "I am quite sick to death of ballet, and ever so glad that I have left Mademoiselle Andre and her strict ways far behind at horrid old Prosingham!"

In a moment Violet entered the room, and soon they were all seated at the table. The butler, Henriques, carefully drew back Victoria's chair. She soon found that she rather liked him, even though he was fussy, fastidious, and frequently difficult.

Violet seemed to be a strict martinet from the first. She dressed in the plainest fashion, although her garments were of the highest quality. Her hair was so black it appeared nearly blue and was pulled back tightly in a severe chignon gathered at the nape of her neck. Her eyebrows were perfectly arched over dark, penetrating eyes. Victoria was not at all sure she would get on well with the ballet instructor.

Violet seemed to be close friends with the Albino Contessa, however, and Paracelsus even held her in high regard. Perhaps a bit of snobbishness remained in Victoria, for she wondered why a ballet instructor—who was a servant, after all, though perhaps one of the very highest situation—should be sitting down to dinner with them.

Of course, Victoria had quite forgotten about Constance being a servant girl of the lowest order—utterly without family connections or pedigree—and she had accepted her most warmly. Constance did certainly appear different than the hollow-cheeked girl who had first befriended Victoria at the Black Swan Inn. She was radiant and lovely now—perhaps for the very first time in her life the inner qualities and natural goodness she possessed weren't masked by the wretchedness of poverty.

The late supper might have been a simple affair by palace standards, but it was still quite extravagant. The courses were served in a carefully prescribed order, though each was light, with portions that were sumptuous, yet not overdone. As the dinner conversation ebbed and flowed, Victoria studied Paracelsus' face with its deeply etched lines of kindness and worry. She saw that there was a story written there, and she grew certain it would prove to be a most fascinating one indeed, were it ever to be told in its entirety.

Violet was explaining how the preliminary set designs for the *Saltatrix Angelus* were coming along, and Victoria was surprised to find that the Palace of Kalingalad contained a theater that could seat two thousand guests. It had lifts, trap-doors, and wire-suspension apparatuses like the theaters in London.

After dinner, when their plates were cleared away, Violet abruptly stood up, clasping her hands tightly before her, and announced, "Victoria, I am delighted that you have joined us—chiefly because you have been chosen to perform the lead role in the *Saltatrix Angelus!*"

Ignoring Victoria's dramatic expression of absolute horror, Violet continued, "We will see much of each other in the com-ing weeks. And I do so look forward to becoming friends." Victoria was not at all certain about the friendship aspect of their relationship. She sighed repeatedly, until even Constance felt obligated to make polite gestures for her to settle down and listen courteously.

Paracelsus suggested that Violet elaborate on the story behind the *Saltatrix Angelus*. Violet explained that the bal-let was about an angel who dwelled in a splendid heavenly realm of light and peace. The tale told in dance and music how the angel descended through the ten circles of worlds into lower and lower dominions, suffering terrible peril and unforeseen danger as she sought to bring consolation to mor-tals imprisoned in the lower worlds, ever so far from light and beauty.

Violet went on to explain that the ballet would feature over three hundred dancers with exquisite costumes and complex sets. She also said that guests from all the palaces and citadels about the shores of the Great Frozen Inland Sea would be invited to attend both the ballet performance and a subsequent Yuletide madrigal.

Three emotions struggled for supremacy within Victoria. The first was mere annoyance at being chosen to dance the lead and having to subject herself to the hours of tedium—the positions, postures, steps, pirouettes, and endless repetitions that she knew must precede any successful performance. The second emotion was one of combined awe and flattery, for out of all the dancers in all of the interwoven worlds, she had been chosen for the primary role! And her third emotion was concern, for she did not see what a ballet performance could possibly have to do with her quest to wrest the blue orb from the clutches of the Ice Dragon and defeat the Shadow Knight.

Paracelsus regarded her thoughtfully. He could see she was reluctant to accept the role and spoke his mind carefully. "Child, within you lies potential for great artistry. There are many comings and goings between interwoven worlds and your talent has been noted. Though you may think such a gift a trite thing, you may find that it is of much greater import than you could ever dream. Such abilities, once honed and perfected, can in themselves work a magic of surpassing power and magnitude."

There was little Victoria could say to refute that, and try as she might, she could think of no suitable reply.

When Violet had finished laying out in detail the course of Victoria's next few weeks of life she excused herself. It soon became obvious that Paracelsus and the contessa were friends of long standing with the Faerie Queen, for they were familiar with the aim of Victoria's quest. The Albino Contessa suggested Paracelsus tell Victoria and Constance a bit about the Great Frozen Inland Sea, and where they believed the Ice Dragon's lair to be located, and what they supposed his plan to be, and for this Victoria was all ears.

Paracelsus rose from his seat, stepping to the framed map. He pointed out a high mountain—drawn in bold at the very northernmost fringe of the map. "This is Mount Shurudgrim, the dwelling place of the Ice Dragon. He is the most ancient of all the dragons in all the interwoven worlds, and the most wicked by far. He is also called the dreaming dragon, for he is especially dangerous when asleep, when the power of his enchantments is the strongest and his dreams take substance and form to walk the earth."

Victoria shuddered. "I should think! For I have dreamed of him in the darkness of a cavern. His eyes were glowing as he spoke to me in that awful voice. He told me that I should not have what is his!"

Paracelsus nodded. "He guards the Orb of Ice most jealously—perpetually fearful that there are those who wish to seize it from him." Paracelsus paused and his countenance grew sad. "When the lust for power is the only thing left to one, then it is a most pitiable state indeed!"

The Albino Contessa nodded her head in understanding, which made Victoria wonder if she was perhaps thinking of her own wicked sister, Queen Ulricke.

Paracelsus continued on, first pointing to an island in the

northwest corner of the Great Frozen Inland Sea. "This is the Palace of Valberon, where Lord Chelsambor rules."

Second, he pointed out an island in the northeastern corner of the sea, very close to the shores of the mainland. "And this is the Ice Palace, which, along with the adjoining Ice Cathedral, comprises the most beautiful structure in all the interwoven worlds. Lord Enraldorn rules there."

Third, Paracelsus noted the isle located in the very heart of the Great Frozen Inland Sea—the location of his palace, the Palace of Kalingalad.

Then, Paracelsus pointed out the location of the village containing the Black Swan Inn, in the southwest corner of the sea. "This is a place with which you are sadly well acquainted, Victoria—the village of Widdershins. And it is well named, for they have got everything backward. The rulers are the evil ones, rather than those they condemn—for they turn all that is light to darkness!"

Last he pointed to an island far down in the southeastern reaches of the sea. "And here is the Palace of Enjiloth, the smallest yet most intricate of all the palaces, for it is fashioned like a pristine jewel. Constance will be embarking by sleigh carriage for Enjiloth tomorrow morning, but we wished to be certain that you girls had your reunion first. She will return to us again for the High Yuletide festival and the *Saltatrix Angelus*. In the meantime she will be taught rudimentary spell casting by Lord Korondrath."

"So I will not be learning magic, then?" asked Victoria sullenly. For the moment she had reverted to her old petulant self. "Rather I suppose I shall be pirouetting and pointing under the strict tutelage of a tyrant!" Victoria glared in the general direction of the door that Violet had exited from just a few minutes before.

The Albino Contessa and Paracelsus regarded each other quietly for a moment. "First things first, Victoria," Paracelsus said firmly. "Never forget what I told you about the magic latent in all true artistry."

Soon after, the Albino Contessa summoned a lady-in-waiting to escort Victoria and Constance to their tower room. Thickly carpeted stairs led up to a recessed nook where Victoria found a broad window seat running the entire length of the window. It was covered with soft blankets and piled high with cushions.

That night as Victoria slept, she dreamed deeply. In her dream, she was standing in a great vaulted cathedral. The room was very cold and quite empty, save for Victoria standing all alone below the cavernous dome of its roof—clad in her dancing slippers. At one end of the room was a perfectly immense pipe organ.

One of the cathedral's windows was broken and the wind whispered in, driving glittering ice crystals before it as it sang across the pipes of the organ, resonating in a strange mystical music. Victoria began to dance in her ballet slippers, and as she danced it seemed that Paracelsus and the Albino Contessa materialized as ghosts, clutching at her with insubstantial hands that needed her help. It was then the dream abruptly ended.

At that very instant, as everyone in the palace fell fast asleep, a perilous winged shadow came gliding through the night. Even Paracelsus slept deeply in his tower, his head fallen forward, resting upon an untidy pile of star charts. His candles had burned down to stubs, dribbling fantastically shaped bits of tallow upon the floor.

The massive winged shape passed silently over the tallest spires of Kalingalad. Beneath its armored brow, its eyes glowed cold like something long dead, held fast in a glacial grip. All the sleepers in the palace caught a chill and murmured incoherently, for they found themselves troubled with horrific dreams.

Chapter 21

WHEN ELLIOT AWAKENED, it took him a good deal of
time to get his bearings. He found himself in an amazingly soft
feather bed. Two pillows had been placed beneath his head.
The bed was totally enclosed in a sweet-smelling wooden
cabinet, but its doors were propped open to give him fresh air.
He noticed the smell of the cottage. Every home has its unique
smell—most of them pleasant. This smell was a combination
of something fresh and clean—perhaps a mixture of lavender
soap and the fragrant logs on the grate—and then a smell like
an old cooking pot had been left upon the stove and not properly cleaned, with just a whiff of its prior contents still lingering.

His scratches and cuts had been cleaned and tended. Elliot was embarrassed that his only garment was a long nightshirt. He blushed to the roots of his hair, hoping that Deirdre
hadn't been present when her mother removed his clothes. He
blushed even more when he realized that he had been thor-
oughly bathed and that the grime of his journey had been
scrubbed away.

Elliot was startled when he heard footsteps in the corridor just outside the guest room. He had a brief vision of ghastly apparitions lurking beyond the door—but then he sighed with relief when it swung smoothly open to admit Deirdre and her mother. Deirdre held a brown earthenware cup in her hand and her mother bore a large pitcher. "I told you he would have awakened by now. And doesn't he look ever so much nicer now that he's all scrubbed and his hair is neatly combed?"

Deirdre's mother smiled indulgently at her daughter, then at Elliot. "Yes, now I can see that you are quite a fine boy indeed!" Deirdre laughed as he blushed and thanked her mother.

"Here now, have a nice cup of tea, well sweetened with honey and clotted cream," invited Deirdre's mother. Elliot grasped the cup, which was comforting and warm to his touch, and drained it in one long gulp.

"I'm sorry!" Elliot stammered, forgetting his manners and wiping his mouth on his sleeve to stop the tea running down his chin. "I don't mean to be impolite, ma'am—but I was so thirsty!"

"Well then, you shall simply have another cup, won't you? And then perhaps a third, if more is required to quench your thirst," urged Deirdre's mother. "But first, I advise you, young man, to lay back down, for there are some health-imparting tinctures added to this tea—powders to help you recuperate."

Deirdre smiled. "I daresay he'll soon be feeling very sleepy, won't he, Mother?" Her mother nodded and poured him another cup, which he quickly drained.

"It tastes wonderful!" Elliot declared, not caring that they had just admitted to drugging him. In fact he slept soundly until early the next morning. He awoke to the chirping of birds. The window had been thrown wide open and a warm breath of summer breeze wafted in. There was a sweet floral scent from the bright blossoms in the window box. He drew back his coverlet and got to his feet. As he left the room he felt dizzy and traced his fingertips along the wall for support as he crept down the short corridor to the kitchen. He was just in time to see Deirdre's mother carefully removing a large pan of hot blueberry scones from the oven.

They smelled simply heavenly! Deirdre's mother smiled to see Elliot looking so much better, and wished him a merry good morning, tousling his hair in friendly greeting. He was famished so he devoured his first two scones in scarcely any time at all. Deirdre and her mother watched him eat with pleasure on their faces. "Now, there's a good boy! Eat your fill. There's nothing that compliments a cook like having her food savored. Do have some more scones, Elliot—another one or two will put meat on your bones. See how the flush of good health is already replacing the sickly pallor of his cheeks. Really, Deirdre, you should have taken better care of him on the journey to our doorstep!"

Deirdre seemed excited, as though she were keeping a secret she was fairly bursting to share. After finishing her own single scone, she sat kicking her bare heels against the chair legs, wiggling her toes, and smiling. Finally she said, "Mother, I think Elliot is full. May we show him the summer kitchen? Oh, may we? You promised!"

Deirdre's mother smiled fondly and acquiesced.

"What's the summer kitchen?" he asked.

"You'll see!" Deirdre said insistently, pulling him to his feet by the sleeve of his nightshirt in her eagerness.

Deirdre's mother held the stout door leading into the adjoining room open wide for them, stepping aside as Elliot and Deirdre crossed its stone threshold. The summer kitchen was dim and quiet, with small recessed windows set high in thick walls of solid whitewashed stone. On one side of the room stood a gray stove with pots of tallow upon it. Beside it was a long drying rack for the yellow fatty candles, still wet, doubled over, and tied together by their intertwined wicks. On the other side of the room loomed an even larger stove, all gleaming chrome and black iron. It had positively immense oven doors, three burners, and a griddle. There was even a large spit for turning meat. Beside it was a stone countertop with gleaming ranks of cooking utensils all laid out in careful rows—including the glint of sharp knives of every possible description.

"Wow! I have never seen a kitchen or a stove half as big," gasped Elliot.

"It is what we must use when we entertain many guests at our dinner parties," Deirdre's mother said pleasantly.

"We also have a smokehouse, out back just beyond the dairy shed, so we can store meat through the winter," added Deirdre with pride in her voice. "And we can make dozens and dozens of lantern candles, too, for we set them on every path in our part of the forest to safely guide any travelers that happen by!"

"Oh, Elliot, by the by," said Deirdre's mother, "see that door just there—the little arched doorway—the one set deep into the brick? Do be a dear and go into the larder to get me a freshly baked loaf and a rasher or two of bacon. It's nearly time to begin preparations for our lunch. My work is never finished, it seems!"

Elliot found that the door to the larder swung open easily. He was confused when he saw there were no shelves, no sign of bacon, nor any loaves of bread. But there was a heap of straw scattered on the floor, and a bucket lay overturned in one corner, close by a broken crockery cup and a chipped bowl. There was one tiny barred window, set deep into the thick stone.

"Where's the bread? I can't seem to . . ." Then Elliot jumped with fright, his question faltering—for a barred iron inner door he hadn't noticed clanged shut behind him. He rushed back in an attempt to reopen it, but Deirdre's mother stood smiling at him beyond the bars. She finished turning a key in the squeaking iron lock then replaced it in her apron with a look of satisfaction on her face. She crossed her arms and laughed, regarding Elliot with both amusement and derision.

"Oh, Mother! Just look at his witless face!" Deirdre cried in glee. "I just know he'll be ever so succulent, won't he, Mother, now that we've fattened him?"

"Yes, dearest," Deirdre's mother said. "I'm sure he'll be exquisite. We'll start preparing him early tomorrow morning so we can serve him with truffles at our dinner party tomorrow night. Some of our more considerate guests will even arrive this evening to help with all the cooking."

Elliot was transfixed with terror in those first moments. Many things that were strange about Deirdre suddenly made a dreadful kind of sense. King Venture had been right after all. Nameless horrors *did* dwell in the Valley of Direfall— and he was in the clutches of those horrors now!

Deirdre's mother slammed the outer door of his cell closed and both her and her daughter's gloating laughter receded as they left the summer kitchen. They were going to kill him, cook him in that awful gleaming black stove, and then serve him to their friends at a dinner party! Tears stung Elliot's eyes, but he wiped them away, determined not to cry.

Then he had a sudden ghastly thought. The realization of where the tallow for the candles came from—candles that Deirdre and her mother were so fond of making—nearly made him sick. He had carried one of those foul-smelling candles in the lantern as he crept through the forest, moving ever nearer to the danger awaiting him. The thought of the lanterns set about the fringes of the forest, each with its grue- some tallow candle flickering beneath a sign that purported to kindly welcome travelers, sent chills quivering up and down his spine.

Elliot moved to the tiny window. It was only five inches square and reinforced on all sides with an iron sill, so there was no hope of climbing out. He carefully searched all about his cell. He had a brief hope of using sharp fragments of the earthenware bowl to scrape away stone and enlarge the win- dow—but after he broke it and worked futilely for an hour he realized it was hopeless. The stone showed just a faint scratch, while the fragments of the bowl were crumbling to pieces.

Elliot fought down feelings of overwhelming fear as he sat on the floor to work on the bucket and attempt to dislodge one of its binding bands. He knew the brass bands would have little effect on the stone, but it was his only chance. He would use it to enlarge the window. He knew that his hopes were dim—that his chances of avoiding the awful fate Deirdre and her mother had in store were very small indeed!

Chapter 22

THE FOLLOWING morning Victoria and Constance breakfasted with the Albino Contessa in her amber-paneled rooms. Both children were fascinated by her collections—one of faerie slippers, and another of faerie lamps, most of them tiny and ever so delicate in craftsmanship. Victoria was quite taken by a small blue and silver lamp with a cobweb pattern etched in its glass, which made it appear covered in tiny cracks.

And then it was time for Constance to set out for the Palace of Enjiloth. She appeared torn between anticipation at learning magic from Lord Korondrath and sadness at missing her friend. Victoria assisted Constance while she packed her things and helped her carry her satchels down the endless staircases from their room.

They continued all the way down to the very lowest levels of the palace, finally arriving at the vast underground stables. Victoria had been anxious for a tour. A sleigh carriage, with its attending footmen, was nearly ready. Constance and Victoria worked with the grooms to fasten the horses in their traces and attach their bits, plumes, and bridles.

Victoria had always enjoyed being around horses. The grooms quickly realized she was accustomed to them and all their accoutrements and that she required very little help assisting with the straps and cinches. She laughed, momentarily forgetting her heavyheartedness at Constance's departure. "I love fastening on their cruppers," she exclaimed, proud of her handiwork. "Look at their noble, stately tails!"

And then Constance was off, after a tearful embrace. Victoria stood in the stable below the lanterns, a lump in her throat as she watched the sleigh carriage glide up the ramp and disappear from view through the gateway.

Victoria spent time getting acquainted with the rest of the horses in their stalls and fed them each a lump of sugar provided by the grooms. Then, ignoring all offers of guidance, she attempted to find her way back to the more familiar parts of the Palace of Kalingalad by herself—but she took a wrong turn or two and ended up in a corridor that had three branches.

She chose one at random and found herself in a fabulous multileveled ballroom where gigantic chandeliers hung suspended high above her head. Then she proceeded down a second, even more ornate corridor, filled with mirrors and gilt-framed faerie paintings—until she came to a cavernous darkened room that fairly took her breath away. The walls were covered in panels of embossed blue velvet and a great rose window with thousands of facets that formed a colossal floral pattern of diffuse light high above. The window was set in one side of a dome that was colored radiant blue and painted with silver stars, each with its own brilliant jewel sparkling in the very center.

Curved balconies with satin railings contained box seats, each with its own entrance off a circular upstairs gallery. Behind Victoria, tiers of sumptuous seats ascended almost to the ceiling. The semicircular stage with its three-story-tall velvet curtain dominated the front of the room.

Soon the hush of the room was disturbed as the curtains quivered, drawing open silently. The huge room grew brighter. Victoria saw that the rear section of the stage was lit with many lamps, and there Violet was giving direction to the dancers and limelight men. There were many extras to operate the set-moving mechanisms from high catwalks, and from deep beneath the floor, where treadmill operators worked elevators and traps set seamlessly into the stage. As Victoria continued watching, a huge backdrop was slowly lowered into place. It was exquisitely painted to represent a starlit sky. A young understudy suddenly swung into view, suspended high in midair, and although Victoria knew she was being upheld by an aerial harness, the wires were too thin and delicate to be glimpsed. She swept in a broad arc, out above the other dancers a time or two. Then at length her momentum subsided and she came to a halt, alighting gracefully upon her toes.

Victoria left the amphitheater to continue her explorations. She took many random turns, one of which led her past a huge glass-domed conservatory full of tall trees and winding lamplit paths. Eventually she made her way outdoors, darting across a walled courtyard beneath a high clock tower, then ascending a long flight of steps. She flitted like a breath of wind in the snowy darkness and sped through an arched tunnel, penetrating the palace's inner wall. Soon she arrived at the door of the kitchens.

Once there, she practically collided with Henriques—the butler from Paracelsus' dining room the night before, who was supervising the serving staff in cataloging several sets of monogrammed silver. Henriques' eyebrows raised just a trifle, and his mustache twitched with apparent annoyance, but his eyes twinkled nonetheless.

"Oh dear," he said, at his eye-rolling best. "Guests and more guests come and my lord Paracelsus gives them the run of the place. The next thing I know they are underfoot and telling me how to run my kitchens."

Victoria grinned up at him impishly. "If you let me stay and watch you work, I promise to give only good kitchen-running advice."

Henriques wiped his brow in a gesture that was far more theatrical than required. "Is there no end at all to the indignities I must suffer!" he exclaimed, his face a pathetic mask of martyrdom.

But it wasn't long before he befriended Victoria, even taking the time to draw her a meticulous map of the palace's floor plan. She found that she had to keep the map with her for the first week or two to find her way anywhere at all, such was the intricacy of the Palace of Kalingalad.

To Victoria's profound delight, Henriques was able to procure both a properly made cucumber sandwich and a bottle of ginger beer—though he did seem a trifle confused when she asked him if he had ever heard of Wink soda or hot dogs. As she sat on a stool and watched the bustle of kitchen activity move about her, she began to feel a bit less lost and lonely.

Victoria visited with Henriques for quite some time, and then continued her explorations using the map he had drawn for her, until she became familiar with many of the palace's courtyards, stairs, and passages. She searched high and low for the conservatory she had stumbled upon earlier that morning, but couldn't seem to find it anywhere. During her search she ran into one of the housemaids, who told her that she was to take luncheon with Paracelsus and Violet in the private dining room.

During lunch Victoria was not at all pleased to find that her schedule was precisely laid out, and it was a very ambitious one indeed. Her days were to be spent under Violet's direction learning the choreography and steps of the *Saltatrix Angelus.*

Perhaps it was because Victoria had been ruled with an iron fist at the Black Swan Inn, but the fact that it was an honor to be chosen for the lead role in the *Saltatrix Angelus* largely escaped her. She only saw it as more drudgery. Violet's appearance reminded her of a rather cruel governess she had had as a small child. Her uncle had sent that governess away. Victoria still couldn't see how performing far more complex moves than any she had even contemplated before could possibly ever aid her quest.

And so Victoria's days blended into one another. From early

morning until midday she practiced the same ballet postures and steps over and over—with Violet likely as not explaining what she had done incorrectly, then making her repeat the steps several times. Victoria could be a challenge to work with even at the best of times, and her pained expressions of elaborate dismay as she was directed to perfect a series of moves by repeating them yet again did little to endear her either to her instructor or her fellow dancers.

The only thing about ballet practice that appealed to Victoria was the very thing that captivated the thrill seeker in her. From the first time Violet had her don the flying harness, Victoria was transfixed with the wonder of the sensation. It reminded her very much of her magical flight across Faerieland with Aeron, Sindl, and Elliot, when they had first arrived through the enchanted gate.

Evening meals were most frequently held in Paracelsus' private dining room with the Albino Contessa and Violet in attendance. Henriques would be on hand to supervise the waitstaff and he conveyed his humorous insights to Victoria with but the cleverest nuances of expression about his eyes or the merest twitch of his mustache.

After the evening meal, Victoria would often join Paracelsus in his tower study for astronomy lessons. She would follow him up the narrow winding stair that pierced the very center of the tower room. They walked carefully between the iron railings, across the arch of a precarious stone span, which led to an oaken door built into the slope of the tower roof. It opened on a high balcony, perched dizzyingly a hundred feet above the next highest tower roof. There she and Paracelsus stood, wrapped in cloaks to ward off the chill, scanning the sparse skies above the Realm of Winter Night for the approach of two planets near to each other—called a conjunction—or the apparent crossing of one planet over the other—called an occultation.

When the moon arose, huge and breathtaking in all its blue radiance, it seemed truly magical to Victoria—and she loved peering through Paracelsus' brass reflecting telescope to view the seas and features of the moon's shadowy surface.

By the time Victoria retired to her own room and fell asleep, she more often than not dreamed of repeating the same ballet moves over and over again or of trying to recall the names of all the stars in a particular constellation—and never getting them quite right.

Chapter 23

ELLIOT WORKED FRANTICALLY, continuing on hour after hour. He sipped some of the fetid water they had left for him, but he couldn't bear to eat the moldy crusts that spilled from the bowl when he had broken it. Perhaps they were leftovers from a previous occupant. But he needn't have worried about starving, for after a bit Deirdre's mother opened the outer door to place a plate of thickly buttered bread on the floor. She smiled. "We don't want you to go hungry, boy, so eat and keep your strength up." At that he completely lost his appetite and couldn't eat a bite.

As the hours crept slowly onward, he occasionally took brief respite and moved to the window, peering through the bars at the dark trees of the forest. Once he saw a girl of about Deirdre's age walking down the path. She had a pointed purple hood upon her head, tied prettily with a large bow. She carried a basket of the most lovely flowers. Elliot called out to her for help. She came tiptoeing gingerly to his little window, her expression one of compassionate concern. Her eyes widened when he told her of his peril.

She promised to go and summon help at once, though he had misgivings when he noticed that she frolicked off in the direction of the cottage's main entrance, rather than returning in the direction of the wood whence she came. His hopes— faint as they were—were cruelly dashed when she reappeared from around the corner accompanied by Deirdre. They pointed at him and laughed in mockery. Elliot experienced a renewed surge of terror when Deirdre told him that the girl was the first guest to arrive for the dinner party, and that she thoughtfully brought along a basket of wildflowers to show her gratitude—and to thank Deirdre's mother for being such a thoughtful hostess and wonderful cook!

Twice more that day he saw guests arrive for the feast. These were grown ladies—apparently friends of Deirdre's mother. Elliot was chilled at how sweet and commonplace they appeared to be, when he knew their appetites to be quite unusual.

It was nearly sundown when his bleeding fingers finally worked one of the brass bands loose from the stout wooden bucket. The rivets had proved to be especially difficult, and he had thrown the bucket hard against the wall of his prison repeatedly to dislodge the last two. Elliot stood at the grate exhausted, watching the light of the sunset cast its crimson glow over the tall treetops of the dark forest. He was in absolute despair. Even if he managed to somehow escape his cell, there was still the forest itself, teeming with evil faeries—and who knew what else—lurking along its twisting paths.

It was well after sunset and the starlight cast stark shadows through the grate of Elliot's window when he sat down upon the stone floor to rest—just for a moment. His ceaseless scraping at the corner of his window had barely dislodged an inch of masonry. There were hours of work ahead, and he didn't have that much time to live.

Elliot wondered how they planned to kill him and hoped that the method they used would be quick and painless—but he somehow doubted it. Finally, despite his determined efforts to the contrary, he fell fast asleep. He dozed for three hours, but his rest was not peaceful. His sleep was haunted by hideous dreams of Deirdre and her mother wearing aprons and chef's hats.

He awoke cold and shivering, leaping to his feet in a shock of horror. How many hours had he wasted? There was no hope at all now! He returned to his frantic scraping but his heart was leaden with dread. It was then, in very nearly the darkest moment of his entire life, that Elliot saw a quick burst of vivid light illuminate the walls of his prison. A circle of blue radiance darted out from beneath the eaves of the forest and glided across the garden toward his window. He recognized the form at the center of the circle at once!

This wasn't the sickly pale green glow of one of the evil faeries' lamps. Elliot's joy was nearly boundless as he watched her climb through the grate. "Oh, Sindl!" he cried. "Thank heaven you've come!" He was astonished to see that her tiny form could fit in the palm of his hand.

Great urgency showed in Sindl's face as she spoke. "Elliot, we haven't much time! This place is full of counter enchantments and opposing spells. Deirdre and her mother are weaving some of them to gainsay any aid that might possibly come to you. But spells that are far more potent still enshroud this entire realm like a dark impenetrable fog. Those spells originate from Queen Ulricke's fortress, the dark Tower of Pendrongor!

"Listen to me very carefully! You must . . ." And here Sindl's form wavered, dimmed, then flickered out altogether, almost as though someone had shut off a television set. When she reappeared her form was hazy and wavering—as though there was powerful interference. She was talking rapidly and he strained desperately to hear her words.

But the faerie soon faded completely. Elliot waited for a long while by the window grate, but Sindl didn't reappear again—for she could not. The interference was simply too strong. Still he had a faint ray of hope. Since Sindl had briefly materialized, the Faerie Queen must be aware of his peril. Perhaps she could do something to save him. Still, his time had nearly run out!

There were scarcely two hours remaining until dawn. Soon afterward, the door to his cell would be opened. Deirdre, her mother, and their guests would come for him. He would put up a fight, though he recalled how strong Deirdre alone had been whenever she had taken him by the arm to help him along on their journey through Direfall. He decided to spend what little time he had left sharpening the brass band from the bucket on the flagstones to fashion a primitive weapon.

Elliot sat forlornly on the cold stone floor, scraping the piece of brass upon the stones over and over again. It was then he thought that he had heard a noise out in the rear garden just beyond his window. He paused, then sure enough, he heard it again. He got to his feet and peered from the grate, his eyes wide with mingled hope and dread.

His heart leaped when he saw the form of a man clad in a heavy suit of armor ride from out of the eaves of the forest upon the back of a huge, gray, high-stepping horse. It was a knight! He was to be saved!

But then Elliot realized that it was not one of King Venture's knights at all. The device upon this knight's shield was not the tower, sword, and rose of Telvenril. The symbol that it bore was of two black swans, facing each other, locked together in mortal combat, their necks intertwined like snakes. Their mouths gaped to exhale tongues of flame that joined to form the disk of a black sun. It was a sinister device that reminded Elliot of the black star upon the Shadow Knight's shield.

The strange knight reined in his heavily armored horse and swung down from his stirrups. When the knight reached up to remove his helm, Elliot saw a harsh, battle-hardened face in profile. There was something haunted about this knight's eyes.

Then he appeared to succumb to an abrupt spell of dizziness, for he grasped the pommel of his saddle to steady himself. When the spell passed, the knight straightened once more, turning briefly to face Elliot's window in the starlight. Elliot was shocked to see that one side of the knight's face had been torn away! It appeared to be an old war wound—in fact, it had been inflicted by a battle-ax during close-quarter combat. What was left of the wounded side of the knight's face was twisted into a grotesque mask.

The knight unbuckled his sword, carefully draping his belt about his saddle bow. He removed his cloak—a garment bearing the same device of ill omen as that worn upon his shield. Next he bent to unstrap his spurs one at a time. The knight drew off both his plated steel gauntlets, then set about removing the remainder of his armor, piece by piece, without the help of any squire.

Elliot had a fear that the knight was another guest who had been invited to the awful feast, and that he was just taking off his armor to be polite. The whole process reminded him somehow of a bather at the seashore, removing his clothing item by item before wading into the surf.

Finally the knight stood still, divested of all his armor—still appearing shaky and ill. He now wore only a long doublet. To Elliot's surprise, he gave his charger a quick slap upon its flanks, whispering a single word of command. The beast whirled obediently round, its sharp hooves throwing up a cloud of dust all about as it galloped off to disappear into the wood.

Elliot could understand why the knight removed his armor if he was to be Deirdre and her mother's guest. But why should he send his horse away? Surely its reins could have just as easily been fastened to a gatepost near some tufts of grass where it could graze contentedly?

But then the knight cried out in anguish and fell heavily to his knees. Soon he had completely collapsed and begun rolling to and fro in the soft earth as though he were having a series of powerful seizures.

Elliot watched, riveted in fear, his face pressed to the grate, scarcely able to breathe as the knight's spasms became more intense by the second. His mouth opened impossibly wide in a soundless scream of anguish and Elliot saw that his hands were clutched into rigid claws as they tore up chunks of sod. Elliot glimpsed muscles rippling and convulsing in the knight's back, at his shoulders and about his neck. Even the unscarred side of his face was twisting and deforming now, appearing as something very ghastly indeed.

Low clouds swept in from the east, blotting out the starlight for several minutes. As the long moments of agonizing suspense slowly passed, all Elliot could see was a hulking shadow writhing among the plants of the garden—an apparition that slowly rose higher and higher against the backdrop of the haunted wood. He felt the tiny hairs at the nape of his neck stand on end. Then Elliot shuddered—for he heard a series of sounds that were truly inhuman and terrifying!

They were a combination of vicious snarling and squeals of absolute torment. Then came deep, unearthly grunting sounds that terminated in a low bass rumble before descending the scale even further—plummeting down the octaves until it was no audible sound at all, more of a vibration. The vibration shook the very ground before it subsided— only to begin all over again in a moment. It was then that Elliot heard an awakening commotion from the front of the cottage.

The clouds had all swept past now, and the light beyond his grate brightened to reveal a sight that left Elliot horror-stricken. A dreadful beast rose up on its haunches!

The thing was ragged and shaggy with massive forelimbs and colossal muscles rippling in its great hunchbacked shoulders. Its head was broad with a thick wrinkled feral snout and the jutting curve of two razor-sharp yellow tusks protruding. It breathed hoarsely and loudly, and the vapor of its breath surrounded its horrid head like a halo of fog about a gas lamp. The beast rose higher and began lurching closer, swaying on hugely developed forelimbs that tapered to filthy cloven hooves. Its hindquarters were extremely gaunt—almost stunted by compare to its front parts, giving it the furtive posture of a hyena.

This creature was one of Queen Ulricke's most loyal servants: the sergeant at arms of the Order of the Black Sun— Sir Lykan, the wereboar!

Elliot could feel the malice of its gaze probing into the depths of his cell. It immediately sensed him, turning its head, growling again, as he stifled a cry of terror. The maimed side of the knight's face was even more frightful in its bestial form. Behind its yellowed tusks Elliot saw its teeth grinding and clenching. Even the ripple and play of muscle tissue was visible through the jagged grimace of its torn-away cheek.

Elliot's nose wrinkled in distaste. A heavy stench of animal musk came from the huge creature as it dragged itself nearer, grunting and foaming. The bristles upon its back stood upright like the quills of a hedgehog. Despite its ungainly appearance, Elliot realized it was moving at a very rapid pace. It swept round the far corner of the cottage, pawing up great chunks of turf with its cloven hooves as it went. The thing was apparently heading straight for the front door!

Just as its gaunt slinking hindquarters disappeared from view, it gave vent to an earth-shattering, squealing roar that made Elliot fall to the floor, cupping both hands over his ears to stop the awful sound. In a moment, he heard the thud of footsteps and sudden commotion from the front portion of the cottage. Deirdre, her mother, and those guests unfortunate enough to arrive early awoke to a terrible nightmare—a nightmare that burst through their front door, splintering the thick wooden panels like so many flimsy matchsticks. A nightmare that arrived just before dawn—on the very day of their merry feast!

Chapter 24

During Victoria's free time she continually searched for the elusive conservatory with its twisting lamplit paths and dark overhead sky. But she could not find it, no matter how hard she tried. She mentioned the mystery to the Albino Contessa, who amazed her by saying that the conservatory magically positioned itself—attaching to different wings and corridors of the palace at will. The contessa added that the conservatory was enchanted—intended for visiting troupes of faerie guests—and when such folk were entertained at Kalingalad, the conservatory would shift in size and aspect, depending on which sort were visiting. Even its atmosphere would alter from one of frolicsome gaiety to something more mysterious, depending on the demeanor of its guests.

The relationship between Victoria and her tutor became more difficult with each passing day, as Violet, conscientious as ever, continually drilled Victoria until she was truly becoming a fine dancer in every sense. The other dancers—even those who were certain Victoria would never be able to perform the lead—were impressed by the scope of her burgeoning artistry.

Still Victoria took profound offense to Violet's every criticism and eventually her attitude advanced beyond contempt to outright hostility. One afternoon, when Violet asked Victoria to repeat a series of moves for the fifth time to get it exactly right, Victoria refused. She told Violet that she was being far too critical.

Violet finally lost patience. "Victoria, your *rond de jambe* is exquisite, your *tour en l'air* ethereal, your *subresant* is artful, even your *sissonne* shows promise of improvement, and your *arabesque* is perfection itself. But your *glissade* is still mechanical, your *gargouillade* is awkward, your *contretemps* is off cue, your *entrechat* graceless, and your *fouetté* a trifle lopsided!"

Then Victoria shouted at Violet, and told her that she was a tyrant—exactly like Nastya and Vidal at the Black Swan Inn.

Victoria was primed and ready for verbal warfare, facing Violet defiantly, fixing her with her second-most scathing glare, expecting anger in return and demands for compliance. She was unprepared when Violet instead turned upon her heels and stepped into the wings, saying quietly in a trembling voice that all practice was canceled for the day. Even the accusatory glances directed in Victoria's direction from the other dancers did little to dilute her heady sense of triumph. She had won!

Her elation was short-lived. On the way to her tower room, she very nearly interrupted a private conversation between Violet and the Albino Contessa. Victoria drew back into the concealing shadow of a thick drapery behind a pillar, listening to all that was said. She was surprised to see that the Albino Contessa had her arm around Violet's shoulders and was comforting her, and that Violet sounded tearful.

"Contessa, the child quite abhors me. Indeed I have not seen such loathing in a face since I dropped a tray of fresh-baked bread in the Black Swan Inn. Nastya took away my supper and my blankets that night—just as the beadle had often done at the Pomfret Workhouse after my mother died!" Victoria saw Violet half collapse into the embrace of the Albino Contessa as her body was racked with sobs of anguish.

"It must have been so dreadful, a life of loneliness and tedium to replace the ballet lessons your mother gave you in secret," said the Albino Contessa.

Victoria swallowed hard, blinking back the tears of remorse that were filling her eyes. She felt absolutely wretched. She had no idea that Violet had suffered in Widdershins as a child, hungry, mistreated, and forlorn. That also meant that she, too, had been taken out onto the ice and left to die alone in the darkness of the Great Frozen Inland Sea! Part of Victoria wanted to rush forward, fling her arms about Violet, and tell her that she was ever so sorry, but in the end she drew back and crept softly away.

And thus it was that Victoria, descending a long staircase, reached a pair of glass doors, and to her amazement, found they opened onto the magical conservatory. Tears were streaming down her cheeks as she stepped in, softly closing the latch behind her, and proceeded down the twisting paths among the thick trees. She walked on, oblivious of her surroundings. When the path led her up a little rise and around a sharp bend into a lamplit glade, she began noticing it was growing cold and she shivered a bit, glancing upward to the pointed treetops where the dark sky sparkled beyond the iron-framed panes of the dome.

And then to Victoria's astonishment, she saw a troupe of faeries coming toward her, dancing lightly down the path. They wore pristine white cloaks with fur-trimmed hoods. Each carried a blue or silver lamp, very like the lamp she had admired in the Albino Contessa's collection. The faeries drew nearer, prancing and twirling as they stepped—and suddenly there was snowfall everywhere. The flakes materialized, swirling outward from the circles of radiance cast by the lamps.

Victoria stood shivering, still tearful, but enthralled nonetheless. It was a hushed, quiet, and soft snowfall, very like the kind that comes on a winter evening to stay all night and awaken one to a transformed world. In just moments, the path was covered with snow, and the boughs of the firs were cloaked in white as were the faeries themselves.

"Why are you weeping, Victoria Deveny?" asked the foremost faerie, a lovely maiden with long eyelashes and soft dark eyes. She peered at Victoria intently from below her fur-trimmed hood.

"I am crying because I am simply a dreadful person," Victoria declared, blinking back her tears.

The faerie smiled fondly. "I am Aethryl, leader of the Yuletide Faeries, and we have come from Silverwood—a very great distance off—to see you dance the *Saltatrix Angelus* at the

High Yuletide Festival. And if I am not very much mistaken, they do not permit truly dreadful persons to dance the lead role!"

And so the faeries swept dancing past—though one did kindly give Victoria a lamp so that it might light her way back to the corridor doors through the falling snow. She treasured that lamp forever afterward, although she was disappointed that it did not create a snowfall when she lit it.

As Victoria trudged back through the snow, clutching her faerie lamp, she determined to make it all up to Violet.

The next day Violet steeled herself, forcing herself to go down for yet another practice session in the ballet theater. She fought back rising dread as she stepped out upon the stage among the choreographers, understudies, limelight men, and dancers. To her surprise, Victoria was already present, standing at the bar, one leg raised, her body bent at the waist, and her arms in perfect position. It seemed so unreal when Victoria smiled at her and said that she had been practicing for over an hour and even asked Violet if she had got it right. Violet stepped forward and made one featherlight adjustment to the position of Victoria's left ankle. When Victoria smiled and thanked her, Violet's expression conveyed a startling level of disbelief, even as her eyes misted ever so slightly.

From that point on Victoria's progress was truly stunning, both in the ballet theater and in Paracelsus' tower chamber with astronomy. She had learned to recognize all the constellations in the sky of the Realm of Winter Night.

Victoria noticed that frequently when she was with Paracelsus, high on the balcony of the Kalingalad's highest tower, gazing up at the stars, something wondrous transpired. Paracelsus seemed younger, sometimes even appearing as a young man, scarcely in his twenties—and on at least one occasion, for a brief moment, appearing as a little boy. At first she grew alarmed, being accustomed to the kindly lined face of her friend. But when she summoned all her courage to inquire if he were perhaps under the influence of some enchantment, he laughed. "Sometimes I appear young when I observe the stars," he declared. "Because by compare, I *am* young—quite less than the smallest child in age and wisdom!"

Paracelsus and the Albino Contessa listened carefully to Victoria's ideas for the accomplishment of her quest. They provided her with invaluable advice concerning the history and geography of the Great Frozen Inland Sea. Victoria shuddered when Paracelsus said, "Remember, child, that the Ice Dragon is himself an undead thing, whose dreams pose the most formidable threat. For once a person, or entire palace, is enmeshed in his dreams they join him, sinking down to a phantom existence alongside countless others who experienced the same fate long ago."

Victoria had been having strange nightmares that only fed into the theme of the dreaming dragon. In some of those dreams Paracelsus and the Albino Contessa were themselves phantoms—coming to her in insubstantial form, pleading for her help.

Paracelsus told Victoria that ages ago the palaces all formed an alliance against the Ice Dragon, sending a vast armada against him. That was when the Great Frozen Inland Sea was still called the Great Blue Sea. That battle occurred in the dragon's middle years, before he learned to wield the power of dreams. It was over almost before it had begun, for the dragon exhaled a breath of ice upon the fleet and froze them solid—turning the entire expanse of the sea to ice at the same time. That was also when the village of Widdershins became an evil place.

The palaces of the Great Frozen Inland Sea held the dragon at bay with a web of powerful protection spells, but still he sometimes attacked, in the wielding of his dark dreams even assuming an illusory human form—appearing at their gates as a stranger in need of lodging.

As Victoria listened, her heart filled with dread. "My quest is really quite impossible. If ever there was an unequal contest it will be when I face the Ice Dragon—all alone!"

Paracelsus carefully weighed the questions Victoria asked and the fears she expressed before replying with advice and counsel. It was as though he were leading her to a course of action constructed to minimize her own weaknesses and emphasize her strengths. She recognized the wisdom of it. For no matter how others might aid, assist, or advise her, the quest, after all, was hers alone in the end.

After several counsel sessions, a general course of action emerged. Following the Yuletide Festival, Victoria would journey by sleigh carriage to Lord Enraldorn's Ice Palace, which would be the staging point for the last part of her journey. For she must then proceed across the wolf-haunted taiga all alone, journeying to Mount Shurudgrim—the dragon's lair.

When this last session ended and Victoria went off to bed, ninety leagues to the north, across the coldest expanse of the Great Frozen Inland Sea a large armored shape rose from Mount Shurudgrim. It flew upon leathery wings, masked by the dark and moonless sky. The icy wind of its passage abruptly silenced a fierce pack of gray wolves who were calling to one another with chilling howls as they loped along through the snow. Then they cowered down on their haunches whining, their hackles raised, fangs bared, as the great cold shadow swept over them and was gone.

THE DRAGON FLEW on toward the Ice Palace, the largest and most exquisite architectural creation of all the palaces upon the Great Frozen Inland Sea. It rose tall upon the shore of a bay set in the far northernmost reaches of the sea, its battlements sparkling in the night.

The entire Ice Palace had been frantic with preparation, for a hundred sleigh carriages would soon depart to voyage across the sea to attend the *Saltatrix Angelus* ballet at the Palace of Kalingalad—a ballet that featured a spectacular new dancer who had come from another world.

Lord Enraldorn was seated in his throne room in conversation with his wife. Their daughters were gathered nearby, clad in white raiment decorated with opalescent moonstones. Suddenly the lamps dimmed in the great hall as a chill mist of vaporous fog swept across the polished tiles of the floor. The royal guardsmen alerted their comrades high upon the wall—as well as those standing watch at the postern doors. None of the watchmen saw a physical enemy approaching.

And then, though all seemed well, the watchmen upon the battlements were immediately seized with an overwhelming drowsiness, and before long, they fell into enchanted slumber—though in their dreams they remained vigilant. Little did they know that in reality they were sprawled beneath their fallen halberds with the palace left defenseless.

Ever so high above the tallest spire of the Ice Palace, a great winged shape with baleful eyes folded its wings and curled its forked tail across the scales of its underbelly. The Ice Dragon spiraled down, plunging thousands of feet in a rapid dive.

The creature's shadow loomed larger and larger, hurtling down over the palace. Just when a horrific impact seemed imminent, there came an abrupt flash of roiling black and purple light. The gigantic form of the Ice Dragon had vanished, and in its place in the snowy wood outside the palace, with no footprints about him, stood a tall man clad in the very finest garments. His black hair was shoulder length, and his face appeared almost noble—except for his eyes, which were eerie and sleepy. He smiled a very unpleasant smile indeed, as he waded forward through the freshly fallen snow. About his neck hung a golden chain, but whatever was suspended from it was concealed beneath the folds of his cloak.

The figure soon tired of walking through the snow, so it simply rose into the air, lifting higher and floating silently above the battlements of the Ice Palace. At last the figure stepped down upon the high steps that rose before the formal doors of the Ice Palace's entrance. He raised his hand and spoke a magic word. The doors quivered and fell silently open before him as he stepped contemptuously over the fallen watchmen.

Lord Enraldorn was now the only soul left awake in the Ice Palace; even his wolfhounds, faithful and true though they were, snored twitching upon the hearth, as if in their dreams they sensed danger but were unable to awaken and defend their master. His wife slept serenely on her alabaster throne and their daughters sprawled on the steps of the dais, their hands clasping the hilts of their jeweled daggers as if perhaps in their last seconds of consciousness they realized their peril.

He paid no heed to the sudden chill in the room as he rose to face the stranger who had entered his throne room. He recognized the overwhelming panic clutching at his heart to be spell inspired, and drove back its onslaught with supreme effort.

He silently regarded the stranger across the pedestal board of his chess set, where carved pieces of blue silver and black onyx faced each other across green and white squares. To his horror, the onyx pieces slowly began sliding across the board, taking the silver pieces one by one in a series of precisely orchestrated moves, then quickly positioning themselves with deadly strategy to checkmate his king. Lord Enraldorn noted that the onyx queen's eyes glowed an unearthly red. The stranger was quietly watching him, a dozen or so paces from the chessboard.

Lord Enraldorn drew his sword from its scabbard with a ring of tempered steel and sprang forward to do battle with the intruder. But before he had even reached the lowest step of his throne he had forgotten why he had drawn his sword at all, and he sank down, grown profoundly weak. He came to rest upon the floor with a feeble gasp. He sagged there silently for a time, his head lolling against the balustrade, his face slack-jawed—until in a few moments he began to dream. It wasn't long before a new and deadly purpose dawned darkly behind his eyes.

"Yes, I will do your bidding, for I seek only to obey," he said in a toneless voice, addressing the stranger standing before him. Then the stranger stepped forward until he was standing directly over Lord Enraldorn and vanished from the throne room in a searing crackle of energy. The very last bits of Lord Enraldorn's will were forcibly overcome by the intruder, whose wicked spirit now inhabited his noble body.

There was not a single soul about the entire palace awake. The grooms down in the stables were fast asleep; even the horses slept, their heads hanging low; the cooks, butlers, wine stewards, chamberlains, valets, and pages were all sleeping soundly—sprawled in corridors, galleries, and storerooms—wherever they happened to be when the Ice Dragon descended.

Now they were merely pawns of the ancient evil that had conquered them. And as they slept, they dreamed scripted dreams of darkness and despair.

Chapter 25

ELLIOT SAT HUDDLED UPON the floor of his prison, terrified. He covered his ears to blot out the awful sounds of horrific violence. High-pitched screams began seconds after the front door had been broken down, and now there were crashes, and the sounds of things being thrown, getting crushed, shattering and breaking as Deirdre, her mother, and their guests met their doom one by one. But the most dreadful sound of all was the bellowing shriek of the wereboar. Soon all the screams fell silent.

It seemed to Elliot that his own demise was imminent and that the great ghastly thing would come crashing in to tear him limb from limb. His fears grew when he heard a thunderous crash that sounded as if the door to the back kitchen had been ripped entirely from its hinges and flung against one of the iron stoves. He threw himself backward, bracing himself in a far corner of his cell, his legs splayed out, his trembling hands holding the sharpened bucket band as his only defense. In a moment the heavy wooden outer door shook as if a battering ram was slammed against it. After two more horrific blows the door gave way entirely and an awful hand with two long black claws extending from it groped in and tore the splintered boards out of the buckled doorframe.

Elliot found himself face to face with the wereboar. Its huge tusks, foaming mouth, and baleful eyes were far more frightful up close.

It crashed its great hunchbacked bulk against the barred iron door—all that stood between Elliot and certain doom. The entire stone-walled structure of the cell shook and trembled from the force of the onslaught. The iron bars of the door bent as the thing reared and struck full force again. Then, when it raised its tusked head to vent its bellowing roar, Elliot's nerveless fingers dropped the brass bucket band as the vision before him blurred and swam. He sagged sideways, ashen-faced and senseless, and fell upon the floor in a dead faint.

The wereboar struck the barred door again, and it groaned and creaked in its frame. Heavy though it was, it could not bear another such impact. But then, as Elliot lay still and unconscious, a wave of dizziness and sickness seemed to sweep over the bestial thing. It staggered backward, disoriented. Then it groped along the stone wall with its splay-hoofed forelimbs, seeking support as spasms racked its body, once again violently distorting its features. It finally collapsed to the floor with a crash, demolishing two stools and a sturdy side table that were directly in its path.

Elliot slowly came to his senses. It was growing faintly light. He sat up groggily. Memory came flooding back and his heart began pounding again. Apparently the beast had gone. The barred iron door to his cell looked as if a gigantic hammer had slammed against it, but still it had held fast and he was grateful. He stumbled to his feet, his head throbbing. His nightshirt was filthy, and he wished that he could wash and change.

"Ah! You are awake, I see!" came a deep voice from just beyond the door. Elliot jumped—startled and immediately alert. There before him stood the knight, restored back to human form once more and in full armor, save for his gauntlets and helmet.

"What are you?" quavered Elliot.

"Don't concern yourself with what's no business of yours, my lad!" growled the knight. "All you need to know is this— I am Sir Lykan of the Order of the Black Sun. It is an ancient knightly order established long ago by my liege lady—good Queen Ulricke!

"You, too, shall meet her, my lad, for she is determined to have you as her guest in the Tower of Pendrongor. We await only the coming of her guard—for a full detachment has been dispatched under the command of Lord Kromm. They are on their way here to escort you, for traversing these forests is a most perilous business."

"What of Deirdre and her mother?" asked Elliot tentatively, "I mean, are they . . ."

Sir Lykan shook his head. "Only a fool would concern himself with their fate, and you don't appear to be a fool, lad. They

were going to slow-cook you on a turning spit—and you inquire as to their welfare? Let's just say that they will not be
waylaying travelers in this valley again—ever. My queen will
have to rely on her other defenses."

Sir Lykan disappeared for a bit to rummage noisily about
in the back kitchen, amid a clamor of cupboard doors, pots,
and pans. In a moment he reappeared with a platter bearing
a loaf of bread, a pat of butter, a single truffle, and a blueberry
scone. There was also an earthenware cup and a small pitcher
of milk upon the platter. "It won't do to present you to my
queen in a state of weakness and near starvation," said Sir
Lykan. He took the very same key that Deirdre's mother had
used to lock the door and unlocked it.

"Eat this—you need to keep your strength up, lad. There
was smoked meat in the larder, too, but somehow I didn't like
the look of it," Sir Lykan said grimly, with a meaningful glance
at Elliot, who shuddered at the thought.

As Sir Lykan passed him the tray, Elliot noticed that even
in human form, the knight's broad-shouldered bulk nearly
filled the doorway. Elliot tried not to look at his face, for the
maimed side of it still did look frightful. Sir Lykan carefully
locked the door again, and Elliot sat down on the floor of his
cell to eat—everything but the truffle, which he regarded
doubtfully. Sir Lykan sat just outside the door, tilting back in
a sturdy wooden chair, his feet up on the single surviving stool.
He was sipping ale from a tall jug as he kept a wary eye on
his prisoner.

At last Elliot got his courage up to ask, "What will Queen
Ulricke do with me, do you suppose?"

"I haven't an inkling, lad, why she wants you. She simply does, that's all, and that's enough for me!" Sir Lykan took another swallow of his ale. "But one word to the wise, lad. For your own sake don't make her angry. My queen can be delightful, but if you cross her, then heaven help you, for you will come to a far uglier end in her deep dungeons than you ever would have here in this kitchen!"

Elliot gulped. "May I please have a basin to wash with, and may I get my old clothes back?" he asked apprehensively. The knight peered at him suspiciously. "I . . . I wouldn't want to meet your queen in such a sorry state," Elliot explained. Sir Lykan set his jug down and asked Elliot to describe the clothes he had been wearing. Then he exited the back kitchen, heading for the front of the house. In minute or two he returned with all Elliot's clothes, save for the cape, which he said was stained.

Elliot gulped, wondering if it was stained with blood from the wereboar attack. Sir Lykan also brought him a basin of soapy water and a clean cloth. After cleaning himself up and then changing back into his traveling clothes, Elliot felt much better and less vulnerable—even a bit more prepared to face whatever danger the day might bring.

As he continued drinking his ale, Sir Lykan grew more sullen. He stopped talking altogether and then soon afterward fell asleep, his chin resting upon his chest. The keys to the cell were there in plain sight—on the table at Sir Lykan's elbow.

Suddenly it occurred to Elliot that perhaps he could escape while Sir Lykan slept. He carefully tore his nightshirt into

strips, facing in the opposite direction from Sir Lykan and trying to accomplish it stealthily. Then he tied the strips together,
testing each of his knots with a firm tug before he went on
to the next. He tied the end of his rope around the center of
the brass bucket band, bending it into a U shape at each end
in order to fashion a sort of lightweight grappling hook that
he hoped would be able to ease the key from the table.

As Elliot crept quietly to the iron grate of the door, he
scarcely dared breathe. Sir Lykan appeared to be sleeping
soundly, his chest rising and falling with regularity, his hand
still clutching the handle of the jug. Elliot slowly coiled his
rope. Then he took a deep breath and tossed the end with the
bent band. To his delight, it actually landed on the tabletop!

He remained frozen, fearful the sound had awakened Sir
Lykan—but it had not. He gave the rope a series of gentle
tugs, drawing it ever closer to the key ring. Just when it seemed
he almost had hold of the keys, he pulled a trifle too hard, and
the band slid off the top of the table, clattering down upon
the stone floor. He grew pale and his heart pounded in his
chest—but still Sir Lykan slept. Elliot pulled on his rope,
steadily drawing the brass bucket band back across the uneven stones for another try. His second attempt missed the
table entirely but his third throw reached the table and put
the bucket band in close proximity to the key ring.

Sir Lykan did seem to be sleeping soundly, so Elliot took
a little courage, thinking that transforming first into a wereboar and then back to his human form once more must have
tired him greatly. Not to mention—and here Elliot's blood ran
cold at the very thought—the effort it had taken to dispatch

Deirdre, her mother, and their guests. Elliot slowly and carefully tugged on his rope. He finally managed to hook the key ring and drag it back across the table, ever closer to the edge.

Success was nearly within his grasp. The key ring and bucket band clattered to the floor. Elliot's eyes were fixed on the key ring, and he was busy wincing at every scrape it made as he drew it back across the floor—when a sudden growl stopped him in his tracks.

He glanced up at Sir Lykan, his eyes widening in dismay. It was as if Sir Lykan's face had half transformed into the frightful boar once again! His mouth gaped open and his eye-teeth had elongated and begun to curl into tusks, and his eyes were glowing red.

With a roar Sir Lykan stood up, his wooden chair tumbling behind him. He leaped forward to grasp the makeshift rope and then with a violent tug tore it from Elliot's grasp. Elliot cried out in pain, for in an instant, a rope burn had formed across the center of his palm. In another instant, Sir Lykan's face had transformed back to fully human appearance. He retrieved the key ring and heaved Elliot's rope and bucket band into a far corner behind a heap of blackened cooking pots.

"Don't *ever* try that again, lad, or I shall come and take all your clothes from you, lest you use them for rope making. Then you shall ride with Lord Kromm and his band to Queen Ulricke naked! Besides, you fool—how far do you think you would have gotten in this forest? Perhaps Lord Kromm and his contingent have managed to locate and dispatch all the peoples of the wood and perhaps they haven't.

If not, you would have simply become the main course in another similar back kitchen in another lovely cottage. But at any rate, after nightfall, the green faeries would get you and tear you to pieces!"

Elliot would have liked to argue, but he knew that Sir Lykan was right. Direfall was an evil and deadly place, after all. He crept forlornly back into the depths of his cell to sit in a far corner and think. Once again he dearly wished that his friend Sindl would reappear. Sir Lykan went back to his chair and his ale, but this time he kept a wary eye on Elliot, who did not dare attempt escape again.

The hours crawled slowly past and Elliot had nothing to do but watch the angles of shadow in the corners of his cell change direction. It was in the crimson glow of sunset—when Elliot was almost nodding off to sleep and Sir Lykan was working on his fifth jug of ale—that the sound of pounding hooves brought him to full alertness. He got to his feet, scrambling to the barred window just in time to see a detachment of nearly a hundred horsemen—Queen Ulricke's own tower guard—come riding out of the dark eaves of the forest.

The knights were clad all in black armor, with huge battle-axes suspended from their belts. The faceplates of their helms were cast as cunningly crafted iron faces—some leering and others fashioned to appear as though they were frozen in screams of anguish. Each shield bore the device of a five-rayed black star upon a gray field, separated from a black crescent moon by a bar sinister. The lead horseman carried a banner, the ensign of which was a black tower. Apparently these knights were of a different order than Sir Lykan. Elliot noticed that there was one black horse that bore a high pommeled saddle and stirrups tied high, but no rider. He also noticed that they had brought another unmanned horse with them—the gray horse Sir Lykan had dismissed the previous night before his transformation.

The troop thundered past the rear corner of the cottage and out of Elliot's sight, though he could tell by the rattle and commotion that they came to a halt before the shattered front door. Sir Lykan had already gotten up from his chair, stepped to the door of the cell, and was turning the key in the lock.

"Ah! Here they are at last! Lord Kromm and the queen's tower guard! You're going with them to the Tower of Pendrongor. Pay them mind and heed what I say: Lord Kromm is the most dangerous person you will ever meet—myself and the previous occupants of this cottage included—that is, until you come face to face with the queen herself! Lord Kromm isn't like her other servants. She reanimated him and his troop from the depths of a peat bog. They are holdovers from a battle fought long ago—at least their bodies are. I daresay the spirits that inhabit them are fouler still!"

Sir Lykan took Elliot's arm and led him out of his cell. Elliot was afraid that Sir Lykan was going to take him past the gore and destruction in the front part of the cottage, but fortunately there was a door in the summer kitchen leading directly outside. They walked to the front of the house on the gravel of the garden path. Elliot soon found himself in the center of the troop of Queen Ulricke's tower guard. Most were still horsed, but their captain, Lord Kromm, and two of his adjutants had dismounted to meet Sir Lykan. Elliot did not like their ghastly helmets at all, and shrunk from their grotesque faceplates.

Lord Kromm's voice was muffled by his helm but the sound of it still chilled Elliot to the bone. It was a cold, dead-sounding voice. It seemed as though it came from somewhere else entirely, or perhaps it was that something else was speaking, rather than the actual masked lord himself. "Ah, pleasant greetings to our comrade Sir Lykan! And I see you carried out your mission in quite admirable fashion indeed," gloated Lord Kromm, gesturing to the mangled front door that hung sagging in its frame. Visible in the shattered window close by were a broken ladder-back chair, fragments of shredded curtain, and even a pale limp arm protruding from a broken pane. Lord Kromm's adjutants and his horsemen were dead silent. For some time the only sound was the occasional stamp of their restless horses.

"Here is our queen's prize," said Sir Lykan, drawing Elliot forward by the arm with an iron grip. "See that he gets to her safely, will you, and do not treat him too harshly. He is not a bad lad, all told." Lord Kromm stepped forward directly in front of Elliot—a sinister figure full of menace. He raised the grotesque visor of his helm with one gauntleted hand as he peered down to study him closely. Elliot could not help but shudder. Lord Kromm appeared to be handsome at first glance, but what Elliot found disturbing was the waxen lifelessness of the face. It was pale and still and it bore no expression whatever. The eyes were closed as if he was either asleep or dead, but Elliot sensed they could see him somehow nonetheless. Lord Kromm's cold, dead voice spoke again, but to Elliot's horror his eyes remained shut and his lips did not so much as twitch.

"Whether he is a good lad or not is no concern of mine, Sir Lykan. He will be bound at the ankle to each of his stirrups and at the wrist to Beltane's saddle bow, and thus he will be borne to Pendrongor either willingly or unwillingly—it's all the same to me!"

Then Lord Kromm withdrew to confer with his adjutants in private. Their voices sounded nearly as awful as their captain's. Sir Lykan took the opportunity to bend down and whisper into Elliot's ear. "He only looks dead and sleepy, but he's very much alive in his own way—or something that speaks through him is very much alive. And he's incredibly powerful, so don't cross him for your own sake—see that you don't *ever* cross him!"

Elliot nodded, far too terrified of Lord Kromm and his horde to reply. Compared to them, even Queen Ulricke's wereboar seemed to be a wholesome, comforting figure.

"Well then," said Lord Kromm, "we must make haste. We have many leagues to ride before we reach Pendrongor. By the by, Sir Lykan, we have brought you your steed. It appears as though your work is finished here. If you wish to return to Pendrongor in our company you may."

"I have another errand or two to accomplish before I join

you at the court of our queen," replied Sir Lykan as he turned away, returning to the cottage. As he went, he gave a quick wave to Elliot.

Elliot tried not to look at the hideous iron faces of Lord Kromm's men as they bound his hands together. He wondered if they were as lifeless and awful looking behind their faceplates as Lord Kromm was. Then one of them lifted him bodily onto the back of the horse called Beltane. It was a wild-eyed, half-mad, foaming beast, clad in dusty black armor like all the other steeds of the troop. Beltane stamped his hooves and stepped sideways as soon as Elliot was upon his back, then he lurched, turning suddenly, his neck rearing back and his teeth bared. He was trying to bite at Elliot's legs! Lord Kromm laughed, and the sound of his heartless mirth was as cold and deadly as his voice.

In a trice both Elliot's wrists were bound to the saddle bow by one adjutant while another used short lengths of knotted cord to fasten each ankle to the stirrups. Elliot complained that the cord binding him to his saddle bow was far too short and that it hurt him dreadfully. Lord Kromm spurred the huge, lathered, wild-eyed beast he rode directly up alongside Beltane.

He bent down, looming over Elliot like a bird of prey. "Listen, you filthy little whining maggot," hissed Lord Kromm. "Do be still, that is if you know what's good for you. Your ease and comfort concern me not! My task is simply to deliver you to Queen Ulricke and in one piece. After that she may either wine and dine you as her pet monkey or slowly disembowel you in her darkest dungeon—I care not which—for it is nothing to me. Do then be kind enough to keep quite still while your betters see to the queen's business!"

THE SETTING SUN was a vivid crimson ball in the western distance when Lord Kromm raised a steel-gauntleted hand. His troop was ready to ride. And then they were off! Hoof-beats pounded the earth as the ironshod shoes of their horses nearly obliterated the lovely little herb garden where Deirdre's mother had grown flavorful accompaniments to enhance the main courses of her dinner parties. Elliot leaned forward as best he could and held on tight with his legs. He knew that he needn't worry about falling entirely from Beltane's back, because he was bound at both stirrup and saddle bow, but he feared that his spine and shoulders would be painfully wrenched were he to slip sideways from his saddle to sag against his bonds.

The horsemen careened around the corner of the cottage in a cloud of dust. They swept up onto the pathway leading deep under the eaves of the deadly forest. It grew quite dark under the brooding trees. Elliot had to bend low time and time again to keep from being dashed against overhanging boughs. Lord Kromm spared neither his horses, his men, nor his prisoner. They went all out, galloping up long slopes into the dark heart of the forest.

Elliot soon realized that if the forest paths were turning about to mislead Lord Kromm's navigation, he was compensating for it somehow, for they seemed to be making continuous forward progress. Lord Kromm was like a lodestone, heading unerringly for the far eaves of the forest, and the dark Tower of Pendrongor beyond—where his deadly queen held court.

The next several hours passed like a slow nightmare. Elliot was both hungry and thirsty. His back was terribly sore from the unnaturally stooped posture that he was forced to maintain. Beltane shied, reared, and twisted—as if he was maliciously attempting to increase Elliot's discomfort as well as unseat an unwelcome burden from his back.

The forest was frightful in the night, parts of it luminous with a pallid unhealthiness exhaling vapors of decay from rotting vegetation. The faintly glowing trees were twisted, deformed giants—the patterns upon their bark and even the tangle of their boughs and branches mimicked horrid faces that leered or gaped, shrieking silently down at them as they passed.

Elliot noticed lights far out in the forest depths. They were flitting from tree to tree, keeping alongside the troop, but maintaining their distance. He knew they were the green faeries.

There were new terrors to be glimpsed at regular intervals along the path. They passed once-picturesque cottages, now either burned to the ground altogether or gutted empty shells. Some of their largest roof timbers were still glowing crimson with coals. Most of the cottages had black pikes planted in the ground about them, leaning drunkenly every which way—Elliot could only guess what the oblong shapes impaled atop the pikes were.

They sped through the remnants of a once-tidy little village deep in the heart of the forest, where every single building had been razed. There were no signs of life anywhere. Lord Kromm and his horde—apparently while on their way to Deirdre's house—had pillaged and slain everything that breathed. The only sounds in the cobbled streets of the little village were the crackle of still-burning embers and the incongruous tinkling sound of a fountain, still cascading prettily from its spout in the center of the square.

As they passed through the village, Lord Kromm fell back from his lead position, guiding his horse up alongside Beltane. Once again Elliot found himself cringing. "Alas! What a pity!" sneered Lord Kromm. "The peoples hereabouts were once a benefit, providing our good queen with a buffer about her borderlands. But since, in their greed and desire to feast on succulent wayfaring meats, they very nearly snatched her rightful prize—you, Elliot—from her grasp, so their right to exist and draw breath has quite ceased, I'm afraid!" And with those words Lord Kromm spurred his frantic foaming horse forward in a pounding of hooves and a cloud of dust to once again take up his position at the lead.

The horrid forest went on for what seemed an eternity. Elliot had begun to wonder if perhaps its endless twisting paths had even misdirected Lord Kromm—when they abruptly came out the other side to a wide broken land of sloping barren hills and steep ravines, under thousands of stars.

As the sun slowly rose, they rode through a rolling hill country, where they were either galloping full tilt along the crumbling rims of precipitous ravines or spurring down headlong into the dark unknown depths of steep forested valleys. The horde only stopped once at midday to briefly rest and water their horses. Elliot was given a few sips of foul-smelling water from a nearly overgrown pond and a dry crust of black bread to gnaw upon, holding it with his sore rope-burned hands, before being thrust hastily back into Beltane's saddle and refastened at both bow and stirrup.

Elliot glimpsed luminescent white shapes standing on each side of the path. He strained his eyes in an attempt to see them more clearly as they passed. Whatever they were, they looked twisted and deformed. His nose wrinkled at a sudden overwhelming stench of decay and he fought the urge to be violently sick.

One of the tower guardsmen riding alongside Elliot noticed him turning pale and spoke, his voice as distant and cold as his captain's. "We have entered the glades of the corpse flowers. Aren't they lovely? And behold—we are fortunate indeed, for they are being pollinated tonight!"

Elliot squinted, peering deep into the darkness of the wood. He discerned swarms of winged shapes filling the air about the smooth stems of the corpse flowers. The pollination was being carried out by huge black moths! They had wingspans reaching nearly a foot, and their dusky vibrating wings made the air come alive with fluttering. When one flew especially close, Elliot could see a long stinger protruding from its tail. It seemed to him that there was no end to the horrors forming the bulwarks and outer defenses of Queen Ulricke's realm.

"The corpse flowers emanate a hallucinogenic gas," said the rider, now looming close by Elliot's side. "If you were to remain here, you would die in a cloud of spores while experiencing the most dreadful visions!"

Up ahead, Elliot glimpsed a towering wall of rock looming like a vast curtain of absolute blackness just beyond the dark tangle of boughs. There was no possible way that even a fleet-footed mountain goat—to say nothing of a troop of armored warhorses—could ascend it. But as they continued on, Elliot could see they were heading straight for a yawning opening directly ahead. They would not be passing over the final shoulder of the mountain, but rather through it.

The troop of Queen Ulricke's tower guard streamed under the arc of the entranceway, plunging deep into the tunnel, their ironshod hooves striking sparks upon the stones. Elliot shrunk from the two colossal statues guarding the entrance, artfully sculpted from the solid rock on each side. They had malformed, distorted appendages and howling, shrieking faces. Before all light was eclipsed in the darkness of the tunnel, Elliot could see that other carvings extended from the two original figures at the gate to form scenes of hideous vileness all up and down the tunnel's sides and ceiling.

The echoing clatter of four hundred ironshod hooves filled the tunnel with a din of awful noise until Elliot feared he was locked in some continuously replaying auditory nightmare. And then, after a long while, against a backdrop of light from far ahead, he at last glimpsed the mouth of the tunnel's exit portal looming larger and larger beyond the flowing manes of the horses and the rippling banner.

The iron hooves of the horses now rattled and drummed upon the thick oaken planks of a long crenellated bridge. A vast fortress, an impregnable citadel of truly mind-boggling proportion, loomed before them. *How will I ever escape from that?* thought an awestruck Elliot.

High watchtowers were set at intervals along the mighty outer wall. Elliot could see from the glint of spear points and plate armor high atop the battlements that each tower was heavily defended.

Above the ramparts of the outer wall were the higher walls of the inner citadel, set with dozens of watchtowers. Visible beyond and above the inner wall were the peaks, spires, and domed rooftops of armories, kitchens, dungeons, banquet halls, and storehouses. Fitful red light flickered from countless windows. Even from the windows that remained dark and blank, Elliot felt a hostile presence scrutinizing their every move.

When they were nearly halfway across the bridge, Elliot leaned backward as far as his bonds would permit, and craned his neck to peer up at the most prominent and awe-inspiring feature of all—the Tower of Pendrongor! It loomed upward, reaching a surreal, dizzying height. The pointed spires of its crown were needle sharp, standing stark against the star-encrusted sky. From the highest point of the tower the sinister black and purple pennant of Queen Ulricke's royal ensign rippled in the wind.

And floating in the air, moored to the side of the Tower of Pendrongor, Elliot glimpsed the furled red sails of the pirate ship he had seen above Bogmon Moor! He knew then that it hadn't been a hallucination after all.

Elliot noticed a cloaked figure step up into the corner tower of the outer wall, high above their heads. The figure raised a horn to his lips. The noise of Lord Kromm's troop was immediately drowned out by the impossibly loud moaning sound that issued from the horn. The awful sound seemed to shake the very ramparts of the citadel itself and echoed from the surrounding mountainsides. Elliot's wrists frantically strained against his bonds in a futile, frantic attempt to bring his hands up to protect his ears.

When at last the dreadful sound died down to slowly echo away across the mountains, Lord Kromm appeared at Elliot's side. As they passed beneath the raised iron grate of the main portal, Lord Kromm's cold voice spoke once more. "Rejoice! For we have come home at last!"

Chapter 26

THE TIME DREW NEAR for the beginning of the High Yuletide Festival. Paracelsus was already entertaining special guests and close friends at the palace, many of whom had journeyed far from the more distant areas, even before the arrival of the main throng.

The kitchens and confectioneries were abuzz with constant activity. Henriques was in a whirl, his mustache ceaselessly twitching. Despite all that, Victoria noticed that the household matters he and his staff were responsible for—from the assignment of guest rooms, to the protocols of who should be seated next to whom while dining, to the menu selection—all came off flawlessly.

Victoria was as good as her word when it came to her ballet practice. She proved to be an adept pupil, flourishing under the careful tutelage of Violet, and she caused her instructor no further difficulty. Victoria adapted well to the newest forms and postures, with an expertise born both of natural ability and newfound motivation. Many of her fellow dancers, even those who had thought her quite boorish at first but were far too polite to say so—and who were in considerable doubt as to her ability to perform the lead—now found themselves genuinely liking Victoria, even inspired by her tireless efforts. They found new enthusiasm to perform at their best alongside her.

Still, Victoria's greatest delight was to be fastened in the apparatus of the flying harness and be whisked in wide arcs out over the sets, suspended high above the stage. It made her heart soar and seemed a suitable reward, after her long hours spent at the bar, practicing the same difficult moves over and over, or working in conjunction with other dancers to finetune a series of postures while Violet consulted her choreographers to get the timing exactly right.

Very early one morning at ballet practice Victoria was disturbed after having an especially vivid dream. In her dream, a new girl had been taken from the Black Swan Inn, forlorn and alone. She was led to the assembly building, denounced by false accusations—just as Victoria had been and Constance before her, and Violet before that. The dream distracted Victoria to such an extent that she finally told Violet about it. Rather than dismissing it, Violet's perfectly arched eyebrows raised in an expression of deep concern and she declared practice to be suspended for an hour and a half. She accompanied Victoria to Paracelsus' study, where they were quickly admitted. He listened to the tale of Victoria's dream very closely.

"Victoria, my child, you did well to come to me at once, for it is through dreams that we are alerted when the village of Widdershins decides to reject another child. The Albino

Contessa's dream brought Violet here. Violet's dream brought Constance here. My dream brought you here, Victoria—as will your dream save another child, and her dream may in due course call the next.

"A sleigh carriage will be dispatched immediately. We will take every precaution so that this newly abandoned child will not long suffer exposure out upon the Great Frozen Inland Sea in the perilous night—and the child shall be taken to the Palace of Valberon to be welcomed there."

"I have a question if you please, Paracelsus," Victoria asked after a long pause, her voice hesitant.

"There is nothing you cannot ask me, child," he replied.

"You have a palace guard the size of an army and hundreds of men-at-arms. Why don't you simply invade Widdershins and free the children of the Pomfret Workhouse once and for all, rather than waiting for them to be abandoned one by one, and rescuing them later?"

"I have been asked that question countless times, Victoria," Paracelsus replied, his voice low and thoughtful, "and indeed I have asked it of myself more than once, and the answer is always the same. Our children are the only hope for the village of Widdershins—their only exposure to what is good and kind. Were we to take the children from them all at once they would be utterly lost, bereft of hope—robbed of even the possibility of redemption. Perhaps the right word may yet thaw a heart or awaken a single soul to a life far better than that which they now lead!"

And so the sleigh carriage was dispatched at once. Victoria and Violet were both relieved enough to return to ballet practice—and the quality of Victoria's dancing improved markedly now that her weight of worry had been lifted.

Victoria quite enjoyed dinner that night, seated with Violet and eighteen other guests about Paracelsus' table. One of the guests was a knight, and Victoria was quite taken with his errantry, shuddering dramatically as he told of journeying through dark forests to evil fortresses. Yet another guest was a portly gentleman in a crimson waistcoat—Lord Wilfred of Coburg—who she at first had thought would prove a pompous bore, but she found instead to be an amazing storyteller, and his tales were amusing and comical.

Each day more and more guests arrived for the Yuletide Festival and the atmosphere of the Palace of Kalingalad became one of exuberance and merriment. Henriques was in rare form—at his eye-rolling, frantically paced best. But he still made time to amuse Victoria whenever she took refuge in his kitchens.

But always, in the back of her mind like a shadow, lurked the looming danger of her quest—which she was destined to face alone.

WHEN THE LONG-AWAITED dress rehearsal for the *Saltatrix Angelus* began, Victoria did not feel ready, and the weight of responsibility she bore was very real indeed. But the Albino Contessa declared that she showed as much aptitude as the greatest ballet dancers of all time, even those in the ancient kingdoms, where ballet was considered the highest art form of all. Victoria laughed. "Well, I am somewhat ancient, you know—at least in Elliot's time. I should think that I am eighty-seven and a half by now at the very least!" she exclaimed with a toss of her head.

The dress rehearsal was intended for the staff of the Palace of Kalingalad. Every scullery maid, underbutler, housemaid, and wine steward would attend. The elaborate sets would be the very same as those used in the actual performance, and in the pit, the musicians were tuning their instruments under the scrutiny of their high-strung conductor, an eccentric wild-haired impresario who fit his role to a tee.

Behind the scenes, a great many people were employed—raising trapdoors, deploying an artificial snowfall, manning lamps and limelights, operating aerial harnesses, and even guiding a huge illuminated moon upheld by a web of wires across a starry backdrop of the bluest velvet.

When Victoria's presence was not required for a scene, she spent her time below the stage in the vast, subterranean world of guttering lamps, suspended catwalks, and elevator platforms. Scenery was raised to the stage above by assistants stepping in cadence upon huge treadmills. Dancers in costumes both lovely and frightful awaited their cues with hearts aflutter. Victoria was amazed that the complexity and the intricate choreography of what transpired below stage was at the very least as meticulous as that which went on above.

The dress rehearsal went flawlessly—except for a brief precarious dip of the moon as it traversed the starry sky. The audience was captivated. Victoria drew gasps when she flew through the air, suspended from invisible wire. Her snow-white wings were slowly beating, and her toes were perfectly *sur les pointes* in her satin slippers. However, Violet was a perfectionist. After the show she gathered the dancers together behind the curtain to give them each a final critique.

When at last the High Yuletide Festival reached its culmination, Victoria felt well prepared. Dozens of sleigh carriages at a time came twinkling in from out across the Great Frozen Inland Sea, and one by one, they rose up the inclined ramp to sweep beneath the portcullis of the corner tower. They were courteously received by retainers and footmen in the palace courtyard. There were many fond reunions beneath the clock tower, in the light of a hundred lamplit windows.

Of the first to arrive were the carriages from the Palace of Enjiloth, ruled by Lord Korondrath—and to Victoria's delight, he was accompanied by her friend Constance. When Victoria wasn't busy with last-minute costume adjustments, minor script changes, and modifications to the choreography, she and Constance became legendary for their escapades throughout the Palace of Kalingalad. The tales of their mischief and adventures may of course have been exaggerated a trifle by Henriques—who loved telling them—but they did have to be scolded by Violet three times, lectured by the Albino Contessa twice, and were even reprimanded by Paracelsus once.

The next set of carriages to arrive were those of Lord Chelsambor, from the Palace of Valberon. Lord Chelsambor was a man of profound wit and prodigious intellect. Victoria determined to be on her very best behavior whenever he was about—a resolve she wasn't always able to keep.

The third set of sleigh carriages to arrive were those of Lord Enraldorn of the Ice Palace. Lord Enraldorn was handsome and genteel, and his manners were impeccable, but there was something sleepy about his eyes that bothered Victoria. She was overwhelmed when Lord Enraldorn kissed her hand, declaring that he had planned a midnight masquerade in her honor when she arrived at the Ice Palace.

The night after the arrival of Lord Enraldorn, the formal dining room of the Palace of Kalingalad was glittering with white table linen and three hundred crystal chandeliers sparkled high overhead. The finest china and goblets of the rarest crystal were set out, and everyone had assigned places down the long rows. All of the guests were clad in their most elegant apparel and their most exquisite jewelry. Rare silks and furs were juxtaposed with fine velvets, brocades, samites, and embroidered satins as the courts of each royal house from about the Great Frozen Inland Sea wore their traditional festive splendor, striving to outdo one another.

"How astonishingly different from the bleak village of Widdershins!" Victoria marveled to Violet and Constance, who nodded fervent agreement.

More than one guest noticed something was not quite right with Lord Enraldorn, and one bejeweled contessa even declared that his eyes looked peculiar—as though perhaps he was fevered or feeling unwell. But no one, not even Paracelsus himself, realized that the entire court of the Ice Palace had been mesmerized and had slipped under the Ice Dragon's dread sway.

Chapter 27

THE TROOP OF QUEEN ULRICKE'S tower guard thundered down a long gallery that was fitfully illuminated by torchlight. Openings of cavernous archways yawned ominously on both sides. The passageway went on and on, winding ever deeper, steadily worming its way beneath the dungeon blocks and deep cisterns far below the citadel.

Elliot did not like the tunnels at all. Sometimes long stretches of corridor were left in total darkness, for the torches in their wall sconces had been extinguished. Once, they were required to pause before a colossal iron door so Lord Kromm could chant a spell to open it. When he invoked the frightful incantation, the door slowly raised, groaning and creaking upward on ancient clanking chains—and Elliot was sickened to see hundreds of rats scattering in all directions, chattering shrilly, their teeth gnashing, their pinpoint eyes glowing red.

They passed cavernous crypts, some with marble tombs set into the floors, with the effigies of their long-dead occupants sculpted atop their lids in high relief. The images depicted the departed clad in full ceremonial robes or bearing knightly swords. Other crypts were far more ghastly still, with the desiccated dead completely exposed, leaning precariously from their tall alcoves overhead, their dried and crumbling bodies kept from falling to pieces only by strung wire as they grinned eerily down at the troop.

Finally they found themselves directly beneath the foundations of Pendrongor and the passageways began rising in slow spirals. The fact that they could ride so long, often at full speed, upon the backs of their swift horses and still be making their way through a labyrinth of tunnels made Elliot realize how incredibly vast the queen's fortress was. He wondered how its construction had ever been accomplished.

In one turn of an especially narrow and fetid passageway he glimpsed a glowing vapor ooze in foul-smelling gusts from a dark side opening. He watched in horror as several dozen ragged humanlike shapes with glowing eyes came stumbling toward them from out of the gloom, whispering. Some even crawled upon all fours—others, impossible as it seemed, were scrabbling along the walls. The tower guard spurred the flanks of their armored steeds to make them go faster, and leave whatever monstrosities were coming toward them far behind.

They rode down a long gallery and alongside a lightless chasm that plummeted into the darkness, its crumbling edge scarcely inches from where their horses' hooves struck sparks from the flinty stone as they galloped past. Elliot could imagine that chasm swallowing whole invading armies into the reaches of its bottomless depths, were they ever foolish enough to invade Pendrongor from below. The old dilapidated house where he had found his magic ring now seemed so very small and safe by compare.

They rode up a spiral ramp that appeared to be taking them directly toward the ground floors—out of the darkness of the subterranean levels until they reached a vast stable. Here at least Elliot smelled oats, hay, bran, and fodder rather than the dank smell of the lower levels.

Dozens of grooms, immaculately clad in a coal black livery, stepped forward on silent felt-slippered feet to see to Lord Kromm's horses. One of the adjutants used the twisting blade of his dagger to slice through Elliot's bonds, releasing him from the saddle. His legs buckled beneath him, giving way entirely, but he was given no time to deal with the pain. Two tower guardsmen stepped forward and each took Elliot by an arm, lifting him off the ground as a contingent of a dozen or so separated from the main body to accompany their captain and his prisoner up a perilous spiral stair composed of age-old stones worn glassy smooth.

Elliot began to wonder if the tower guardsmen, in their grimacing iron helms, were men at all and not machines, for they carried him with effortless strength and ease up the long rising passageways. Elliot attempted to count the number of staircases they climbed, but lost track at seventeen—due to a sudden whir of wings combined with angry high-pitched squeaking sounds that told him a sizable colony of bats in a side corridor had been disturbed by the clamor and the smoky flare of the torches.

Elliot shuddered to think of being abandoned down in the underground passageways of Pendrongor and what it would be like to wander about in the dark until he expired of thirst and madness—or was seized by some long-forgotten horror.

Lord Kromm finally paused before a door that was reinforced with thick steel plates and iron rivets. A narrow viewing slot swished open and a password was demanded. Lord Kromm stepped forward but Elliot—although he strained to listen—could not hear what the password was. Then it swung open to admit them into the living areas and guest apartments of the Tower of Pendrongor.

Elliot realized that his custody was changing hands. A young woman with refined and noble features, wearing a long flowing gown of the richest, most luxurious green velvet, stepped forward to take charge of him. The high collar of her gown was composed of the finest lace, and her long sleeves were wide and full. She was accompanied by a dozen members of Queen Ulricke's personal waitstaff—haughty men and women elegantly clad in livery of mingled purple and black. Elliot was relieved to find that they were not frightful creatures like Lord Kromm and his horde.

Lord Kromm bowed to the young woman. "This whining cur is your responsibility now! He is of precious little use that I can see." Then he withdrew from the doorway and was gone. Elliot sighed with relief to be free from Lord Kromm's clutches.

The handmaiden stepped forward, smiling graciously at Elliot. She introduced herself as Brynn, and extended her right hand to him. It was then that his relief transformed abruptly back to horror. For the hand that emerged from the lace cuff of the handmaiden's sleeve was grotesque, with black nails, impossibly elongated fingers, and large knuckles. Of course he could not bring himself to kiss it—though he thought it was most probably expected of him. Even as he recoiled inside, he reached out his trembling fingers to politely shake the awful hand of Queen Ulricke's handmaiden.

He thought that perhaps he glimpsed a flicker of amusement in her eyes at his lack of courtly grace. "Welcome to Pendrongor, Elliot Good!" Brynn said. "This is the home of my liege, Queen Ulricke, ruler of the Realm of Lorinshar and rightful regent of the province of Telvenril—though for now a pathetic and ungrateful usurper unlawfully wears its crown!"

Elliot quailed at the powerful grip that her long filthy fingers exerted as they very nearly crushed his hand. "Thank you, ma'am," he finally managed to stutter.

Queen Ulricke's handmaiden laughed, a musical sound of studied sophistication and grace. "You are a fearful little lad, I see. But never mind. I regret to say that Lord Kromm has no manners whatsoever, and he perhaps treated you like a common criminal, did he not?" Elliot nodded, relieved to notice that she had once again hidden her atrocious hands in the expansive sleeves of her gown. "Well, I can assure you, my dear boy, that you are our honored guest, and you shall, this very night, join us at our banquet.

"Having traveled the route that Lord Kromm brought you, you must think the Tower of Pendrongor to be a vast, lightless dungeon pit, but you will soon see that it is an exquisite palace and a home to many—some who've come from other realms allied with us, and are wisely quite prepared to cast their fortunes upon the wisdom of our queen!"

As Elliot glanced about, he could plainly see that the hand-maiden was right. The living quarters that he found himself in were most graciously appointed. They had every amenity that one might hope to find. Tasseled silk tapestries hung upon the walls and deeply woven carpets softened the floor below their feet. The furniture was sumptuous and deeply upholstered, with soft cushions scattered about to add to the air of luxury and opulence.

Colorfully intricate stained-glass windows were recessed deeply into the thick walls. Logs crackled upon the grate of the large marble hearth. Folding privacy screens—featuring the most delicate and artful embroidery—were placed here and there. Trimmed silver lamps hung from the ceiling suspended from long braided chains of purest gold, and a carpeted side stair swept up to a long curving gallery from which opened the doors of several bedchambers. On the balcony, a sweet-faced young woman in a spectacularly coiffed hairstyle plucked the strings of a lute as she sang in a lovely soprano voice. The chant she recited was in a strangely complex language Elliot could not hope to understand.

Queen Ulricke's handmaiden spoke again. "You are in one of nine hundred separate guest accommodations within the Tower of Pendrongor. Our queen loves to entertain." She pursed her lips and studied Elliot and his clothing carefully.

"Oh dear! I am afraid that these filthy garments of yours are just not at all suitable for an audience with her! They simply will not do." She snapped her long terrible fingers and two footmen immediately materialized, stepping forward. "See that he is clothed properly, if you please," she said haughtily, spinning upon her heels as she turned her attention to other business.

The footmen escorted Elliot up the gallery stair, past the singing lady, and showed him to a small room where a round steaming tub of the finest silver was sunk deeply in the floor, brimming with a soapy froth. The footmen set out fresh towels for him and left him alone to bathe himself clean from the grime of the journey. He was very nearly dry, wrapped in a plush oversized towel, when they came to the door with his new suit of clothes.

Within a few minutes Elliot was dressed and his hair was properly brushed to the satisfaction of the footmen. He could tell that they were very much afraid of Brynn. Elliot was brought down the gallery stairs, past the lady who was still sweetly singing. In a moment he was standing once more before Brynn, awaiting her inspection. He was uneasy in his new outfit of plum velvet, which sported far too much itchy lace at the sleeves and throat. Brynn surveyed him carefully and nodded to the footmen.

"You have done adequately! The boy appears almost civilized," she said with an approving smile. "The black slippers and the white stockings set off the bows in his knickers to good effect, don't you think?" she inquired rhetorically of the footmen, who bowed slavishly.

Brynn stepped forward, and reached out to touch his shoulder and flick a diminutive lint speck from the velvet.

"There now! That's better!" Elliot involuntarily shrunk back a half step when the awful thumb and forefinger extended once more to almost fondly pinch his cheek. "Ah! You have turned pale, haven't you?" came the gloating observation, even as her lips curled into a malicious expression that was part smile and part sneer. She plainly enjoyed frightening him.

He was commanded to sit quietly in a chair and wait until the handmaiden was ready to escort him to the banquet. He waited miserably, filled with apprehension. The chair was too tall for him and he kicked his slippered heels against its gilt legs in time to the monotonous ticking of the mantel clock. The singing had ceased.

He took comfort in the fact that his ring was still upon his finger, though obscured by the Faerie Queen's enchantment. Thinking of his magic ring made him miss Victoria a great deal, and he desperately wished she was with him now and wondered if her adventures were proceeding well and if she was safe. Then his thoughts turned to his mother and a deep sense of grave foreboding distressed him.

Finally it was time, and as the clock chimed the top of the late hour, Elliot followed Brynn out through a different door than the one he had entered. He noticed that the footmen kept very close by, one on each side, and he felt he was more prisoner than guest. He swallowed hard. Soon he would find himself standing face to face with Ulricke, the dread sorcerer queen of the Realm of Lorinshar!

The high passageways they traversed were dazzlingly opulent. Just as the lower levels of the Tower of Pendrongor had been hideous, so were the upper levels surpassingly lovely.

There were paintings and sculptures hanging from the walls and within nooks all down the sides of the corridors. Even the hanging lamps must each have been worth a king's ransom.

Finally they crossed a long gallery extending out like a bridge to join a spiral stair that plummeted down through the center of a huge dome. The underside of the dome formed the ceiling of the gargantuan room far below. Brynn paused before they descended the stair. Once again Elliot couldn't keep from shrinking back as her long ghastly fingers fussed with his collar and hair—performing last-minute adjustments to make certain that he was presentable.

Then they proceeded down the staircase, turning round and round repeatedly as they went. When they reached the bottom, Elliot found himself in the splendor of a vast banquet hall. A huge table ran about the circumference of the wall so that each guest had an unobstructed view of every other guest in the circle.

Elliot swallowed hard. Queen Ulricke of Lorinshar was seated haughtily between two pillars, clothed in black garments trimmed with purple. She sat upon a high-backed chair, facing the foot of the stairs where he stood tongue-tied and awestruck.

"Do be kind enough to bring the lad to me," said the queen, her voice as smooth as silk. "I wish to meet our guest, who has bravely come so far and at such cost!"

Elliot stood still, his heart thudding, his feet like lead as he stood rooted to the spot. "Go! The queen herself has summoned you, you witless fool," hissed Brynn while pointing forward with a long bony forefinger.

He stepped forward, moving slowly across the polished black marble floor. The eyes of the queen's curious guests were watching him intently. He noticed Lord Kromm was seated in a prominent place, his face waxen and pale. Elliot wondered if he ever ate or drank, and he shuddered at what the vivid red liquid might be that filled his crystal goblet. Sir Lykan sat to Lord Kromm's left, and his elegant court clothes made the contrast with his gaping wound seem more surreal. Elliot kept moving forward as he was bidden, and then Queen Ulricke's commanding presence overwhelmed all else.

Elliot felt as though—even from across the huge room— Queen Ulricke's incredibly powerful personality had stepped forward to take his chin in hand and study him. His eyes locked upon her face, and he couldn't tear his gaze away.

Queen Ulricke was physically much smaller than he expected and more youthful. Her face was fastidious and sweet and she wore her raven hair straight, and it hung to her waist from its central part, eloquently framing her porcelain white face. But it was the queen's bloodred eyes that held Elliot spellbound. Before he knew it, he approached her table and his feet stopped of their own accord. He felt like a mechanical toy whose windings had all run out. He stood gazing upward, wide-eyed and astonished, into the queen's lovely face. She was a most compelling figure indeed!

Queen Ulricke raised her right hand in a courtly gesture of welcome and smiled radiantly at him. Elliot saw that her hands were quite normal—even dainty. He was much relieved, for he had been afraid that she would have long terrible fingers like her handmaiden. Elliot noticed that Queen

Ulricke wore rings fashioned of a strange black metal upon each of her fingers and her thumbs as well. He was startled when the rings began to writhe as if they were living things experiencing some dreadful torment.

Presently Queen Ulricke permitted herself another smile. "I bid you welcome to my court as my personal guest, Elliot." She glanced down at her twisting rings, which had him so transfixed. "My rings have sensed the kindred presence of similar magic, and are reacting accordingly."

Elliot was truly dismayed when—after feeling an abrupt sensation of quickening in his finger—he looked down to see that his own ring's disguise had been overcome by Queen Ulricke's magic. It was now visible in its true form, as an intricate silver band adorned with a vivid red jewel!

Behind him the spiral staircase slowly turned on its axis as it rose to disappear into a quickly closing gap in the center of the domed ceiling. He swallowed hard when Brynn—at Queen Ulricke's command—took his quivering hand to escort him about the circumference of the chamber, introducing him to the most notable guests.

"When I present you, bow politely—and see that you do it properly," Brynn commanded. Elliot cringed when he felt the black nail of her long forefinger groping up his sleeve to scratch at the underside of his wrist.

Lord Kromm and Sir Lykan he already knew—all too well, in fact. Brynn introduced him to other knights who were in attendance. None of them appeared to be the sort of knights who would make good Knights of the Round Table. Rather they were the sort that damsels in distress would require rescue from—those who most probably had imperiled the damsels in the first place.

And then Elliot was presented to a sneering man in a powdered wig, who wore a brilliant red coat graced with double rows of sparkling buttons. The crimson weal of a dueling scar traced down the length of his right cheek and nearly matched his coat. Elliot recognized him at once, for this was the captain of the airborne pirate ship of Bogmon Moor. "Elliot, meet Captain Ransom," said the handmaiden smugly. "He and his crew are our queen's honored guests—and his flying ship is moored to the side of Pendrongor!"

Elliot was introduced to only a small fraction of the many other guests in the banquet hall. The contessas, ladies-in-waiting, and duchesses seemed as deadly and devious as the males. Elliot wondered if some of the gem-encrusted rings so gracefully set upon their tapered fingers might contain deadly poisons hidden in tiny reservoirs.

The most positively alarming member of Queen Ulricke's court—other than the queen herself—was Lord Sarton. Elliot noticed the guests sitting nearest him had their chairs offset to each side and he wondered why. Lord Sarton was a handsome, clean-shaven man, but his eyes were very peculiar. One eye was a different color than the other and he seemed to have difficulty focusing his gaze upon Elliot as introductions were made.

Brynn whispered into Elliot's ear. "Lord Sarton is one of the queen's favorites. He is an astral shape-changer. He spends much of his existence as an apparition—partially in the astral realm and partially in the physical. When in changeling form, he exhales a deadly blue vapor!

"But it tires him exceedingly to remain on the physical plane for occasions such as this, so he draws warmth from the room nearby, sucking it from the air in his close proximity—and in this manner obtains the energy he requires to remain materialized on the physical plane." Elliot drew back, shivering.

The awful long-fingered hand pulled him closer still, its grip merciless. "Come!" commanded the musical voice at his ear. "You must be properly introduced, mustn't you?" Already Elliot could see his own breath condensing in the cold air that surrounded Lord Sarton, and he understood why even the jaded members of Queen Ulricke's court seated on each side—accustomed as they were to all manner of horror and depravity—had cringed and moved away. He trembled at the sudden chill as Lord Sarton made as if to bow. Elliot bowed stiffly in return, mumbling a quick "How do you do" before backing quickly away to sneering smiles of amusement from the court. He felt his cheeks flush, and he knew he was being made sport of, but there was nothing he could do to prevent it.

Finally, he found himself standing before Queen Ulricke once again. "Elliot, you must be simply famished after so long a journey. Come and sit as my honored guest, here at my left hand!" Queen Ulricke's voice was as smooth as silk as she addressed her second handmaiden. "Sutton, do kindly slide down just a bit to make room for Elliot!"

Elliot saw the ring of the table open silently as Brynn guided him up a short flight of steps. Footmen appeared as if by magic with a velvet-cushioned chair and a fresh place setting for him. Brynn took her place in turn, and as Elliot was seated, the ring of the table silently closed upon itself once more, now showing no gap whatever in the snow-white tablecloth.

And then, moving quietly on satin-slippered feet, dozens of servants arrived in pairs from a hidden spiral stair leading upward from the circular pattern in the center ring of the table. Trays of silver and gold were piled high with the most decadent dishes. Elliot had thought King Venture's feast to be amazingly lavish, but this extravagance made that seem the plainest fare.

Elliot was in awe, both of the captivating queen and her close proximity. She proved to be a gracious hostess—for she sat patiently explaining to him the proper techniques of eating the odd delicacies set before him. She demonstrated how to make proper use of the unfamiliar utensils, even at one point turning toward him to carefully cut his food with her own hands. All the while her gaze was directed fondly upon him, and she smiled at him as though they had been friends forever.

At first Elliot thought the queen's crimson eyes alarming, but that was before he realized how perfectly lovely and caring they were. He wished that children of his acquaintance back in Alton Bay could see him now. Queen Ulricke made the summer court of good King Venture seem trite and silly by compare—and she made Elliot feel as though she was the only person in the world who genuinely liked and understood him.

Little did he realize that powerful enchantments were weaving subtle spells about him like tangled webs. His mind was no longer his own. Each time that Queen Ulricke fixed him with her gaze, spoke to him, or smiled at him, it had a potent and calculated effect.

And so the feast continued with a dazzled, tongue-tied Elliot completely overwhelmed by the sorcerer queen. He found it becoming more and more difficult to believe the awful things he had heard about her. He was quite certain that all her naysayers were mistaken—unless perhaps they had stooped to maliciously crafting such fictions out of plain jealousy. Surely Queen Ulricke had never shown them the kindnesses she bestowed upon him.

When the last course had been served, Queen Ulricke laughed like a child and clapped her hands. "And now, my dear friend Elliot," she said, smiling bewitchingly, "I have business elsewhere at this moment, but rest assured, I shall join you presently!"

Elliot was startled when the queen abruptly vanished in a clap of thunder, a burst of light, and a puff of sweet-smelling smoke.

The ghastly black-nailed fingers of Sutton, the second handmaiden, firmly grasped his shoulders. "You have had a long day, Elliot Good," she hissed. "A guestchamber has been prepared for your repose."

He was escorted from the banquet hall and led along a bewildering maze of passages. Near the top of a long stairway, Sutton stooped to unlock a recessed door. He was guided through a dim candlelit chamber and escorted to a soft bed. He sat down as she bowed mockingly and backed from the chamber as if in deference to royalty. As she went she snuffed the candle flames, one by one, with her grotesque fingers. Elliot sat in the darkness, far too overwhelmed with all that had befallen him to even think of sleep.

Though Queen Ulricke had made him feel welcome in the Tower of Pendrongor, he still missed his home in Alton Bay. Hours later, as he was lying quiet, though still wakeful, he glimpsed a vivid light dawning just beyond the balcony window of his chamber—but it was not yet dawn. It was as if a great moon was slowly rising—changing and shifting the degree of light throughout the room.

Elliot stumbled to the balcony doors, struggling to open them with unsteady hands. He was just in time to see a pale ghostly apparition materializing in the darkness. There, gliding through the air in front of the backdrop of an enormous blue moon, came ten pale horses, their manes flowing in an unearthly wind. The horses formed a ghostly team drawing a carriage that glowed with lurid internal light. At the front of the carriage sat two spectral drivers guiding the reins, their faces as still as death.

The carriage descended toward Elliot in utter silence, its horses treading upon the very air, manes flowing, hooves silently stamping. Elliot could tell they were neighing, but no sound came from their mouths. The horses appeared both vicious and terrified, as though they neither understood nor appreciated the power that bore them aloft.

The carriage came to a stop as it drew abreast of his balcony rail. The horses reared, their eyes wild and frantic. Two footmen stepped down onto the balcony, unfolding a short set of ivory steps from a compartment beneath the carriage door.

The first footman opened the door while the second placed a cushion of red velvet upon the step. Then they stood to the side, bowing low.

A small, exquisitely jeweled, impossibly high-heeled slipper stepped down from the carriage to rest upon the velvet cushion—and thus it was that Queen Ulricke of Lorinshar arrived upon the balcony of Elliot Good's guestchamber. She wore the most elaborate and outrageous gown he had ever seen. It had a high rounded collar and voluminous sleeves flowing with lace. It was composed of the palest ivory, decorated with the most intricate patterns of milk white moonstone mingled with bloodred rubies. The pale-skinned, dark-haired queen looked both frightening and beautiful as she swept down the carriage steps.

Elliot's heart first skipped a beat and then seemed to stop altogether as Queen Ulricke moved toward him as if she were floating above the floor. She took his face between her palms and smiled.

His knees buckled beneath him as his vision blurred and swam—just as the queen spoke to him. "And do you, my newest and dearest friend, Elliot Good, approve of my entrance?" she inquired.

The response was torn from his very soul. "Oh yes, my queen," he cried adoringly.

She gazed upon him intently. "I know what it is to feel homesick," she said, as if she had read his mind. "The illusion I just produced was my rendition of the moon in the Realm of Winter Night, where I was born long ago." The queen sighed and gazed out the window. Then she turned back to Elliot.

"What is it that troubles you, my friend?" she asked softly. "What is it that most distresses you?"

And then as tears filled his eyes he went on to ask the question that had tormented him day and night since the Shadow Knight's attack. "What of my mother?" he asked. "Is she still alive?"

The queen's captivating eyes turned liquid with kindness and pity. She stepped forward to embrace him. "Oh, my precious boy!" she said as she cradled his head on her shoulder. "You must be very brave indeed. She is gone, gone forever— and you must let her go!"

Elliot cried himself to sleep as the queen attempted to soothe him and promised to take good care of him.

Chapter 28

THE DAY FOLLOWING the banquet was the day of the evening performance of the *Saltatrix Angelus*—the single event that, along with the Yule log lighting, would serve as the culmination of the High Yuletide Festival. Paracelsus told Victoria that a traveler from her world came to the Realm of Winter Night long ago and brought with him traditions, like the Yule log, that seemed strange at first but grew increasingly popular—becoming adopted as local custom in due time.

And so the evening found the ballet theater full of elegantly clad guests, all wearing their finest, most formal apparel. The seats were overflowing. Along the sides rose the semicircular balustrades and black velvet railings of the box seats—each sporting its proper coat of arms—where Paracelsus, the Albino Contessa, Lord Chelsambor, Lord Korondrath, Lord Wilfred, and Lord Enraldorn sat surrounded by their families and the most distinguished members of their retinues. Constance was a guest in the Albino Contessa's private box. High at the rear of the theater, above the topmost balcony, behind arched windows that showed the merest trace of frost, could be glimpsed the sparkle of blue light from the silver lamps of the Yuletide faeries who were also in attendance.

At last the theater lights were dimmed and the chime sounded. The muted glimmer from the great stained-glass window, high in the cupola at the very top of the dome, was far outshone by the bright incandescence of the side lamps, as they were directed upon the opening curtain.

First the curtain wavered, then parted to reveal a stunning set with a storm-wracked backdrop, where armored knights upon horseback clashed in futile warfare and grim fortresses loomed, while pitiless lords oppressed their people. But a brave prince stood alone against the chaos of the tower realms. He fought valiantly until he was taken captive and imprisoned in the dark tower of the most evil lord of all—who pretended to be his people's benefactor.

Real warhorses were used in the scenes of pitched battle. Actual knights in full armor were combined with the grace and expressive elegance of ornately costumed dancers. Limelights were kindled and focused to highlight the drama.

In the second act, the stage was transformed into a heavenly realm where a lovely young angel, clad all in blue, danced gracefully as she offered to descend through the circles of the lesser worlds to bring aid and comfort to the imprisoned prince, surrounded as he was by perils and dangers of every kind. She implored that she be sent, and at last her request was granted—though reluctantly.

The transition to the grim realms of the lower worlds, with their battles and strife—where the prince stood alone against evil upon every side—was in stark contrast to the elegance and splendor of the heavenly courts, where seraphim and angels dancing *sur les pointes* compassionately sought to bring relief to the suffering mortals below.

Victoria glided down through the circles of the darkling worlds, clad as a radiant blue angel, with sparkling snow-white wings. She descended through the starry realm with its breathtaking constellations. She dropped farther still, past the moon that rose vast and shining, turning the cloud tops below her feet translucent with silver light—then sweeping above the artfully contrived fields and villages.

Victoria swung out in high dizzying arcs over her audience, suspended from her aerial harness. When she had swept upon the farthest pivot of her arc, her trajectory brought her high above Lord Enraldorn's box. She was so disconcerted by the eerie and sleepy look of his eyes that she failed to notice the quick flicker of vivid light that stabbed out from the gemstone of her ring.

The set was to be rapidly changed in the cover of darkness below. But when the footlights rose to full luminescence once more, Victoria found, to her shock, that something was terribly amiss. The dancer who played the prince, with whom she was to dance in the upcoming scene, was slumped inertly upon the stage.

She realized also that the music from the orchestra pit had ceased completely! Victoria stood alone, her head swimming. Nothing so drastic had occurred before—and nothing at any of the rehearsals could have prepared her for this.

The theater was eerily silent. Victoria peered out into the audience, her vision obscured by the bright lights focused upon her. She drew her hand to her forehead in an attempt to block out the glare so that she could focus properly. It was then she realized with a start that the stone of her ring was flaring, just as it had in other moments of great danger! Her hand trembled as she directed its beam into the wings. She was horrified to see the dancers who waited there, sprawled upon the floor, sound asleep. She swept the beam out into the audience, and saw that they, too, were slumped in their seats, eyes closed.

Victoria felt only a momentary stab of indignation. She couldn't possibly have lulled her audience to sleep, could she? But soon her mounting dread overcame all else—for she realized that a diabolical enchantment was at work.

Chapter 29

Elliot came to his senses slowly, to find that he was resting comfortably, his head upon an immense pillow of the very softest down. He sat up on his elbows to glance about the sumptuous room. His circular chamber was situated in one of Pendrongor's tallest spires.

Beside his bed stood a tray, upheld on four ivory legs. The tray bore a silver pitcher full of ice-cold water, bunches of both green and red grapes, and the most succulent-looking plums that he had ever set eyes upon. There was even a small loaf of fresh-baked bread, and to accompany it, a beaker of honey, a saucer of strawberries, and a frothing cup of fresh milk.

A voice from close by startled him.

"Good day, Elliot! I must confess that I was sick to death with worry. But I see that you are looking well this morning." Elliot was surprised to see Queen Ulricke standing beside his bed, her lovely face exhibiting the deepest concern. He was astonished at how slight and small she was, for she was scarcely taller than his friend Victoria, and there was something about her that appeared childlike and almost innocent. The idea that she was hundreds of years old was far too absurd to even seriously consider.

The queen wore a simple white unadorned gown, and Elliot noticed that her rings had changed. Rather than writhing and twisting, they appeared only as plain bands of gold, set upon all her fingers. The queen reached out her hand to gently touch his forehead with soft cool fingertips. "Ah, that is well indeed." She smiled. "You have no fever, Elliot. I see that the elixir my physicians concocted for you has done you a world of good!"

Queen Ulricke drew up a chair close beside his bed. "I was so worried," she said softly. "I stayed up nearly the entire night and used a cloth dipped in cool springwater to bathe your feverish brow. You seemed as though you were having the most dreadful dream. You called out the name Victoria several times and then murmured the name Deirdre as well. And then it was as though in your dream you were imprisoned in a cage while both girls were piercing you with pins, and it seemed that Deirdre wanted to eat you for her supper and that Victoria was mocking you and calling you a weakling and a coward.

"I must confess that my heart nearly broke, Elliot, when in your delirium, tears poured down your cheeks, for it seemed that this Victoria—whoever she may be—declared that she had always secretly despised you!"

And here Queen Ulricke gazed down at him with a smile of such bewitching tenderness that it fairly took his breath away. "Strange that Victoria should call you such things, for I see neither a coward nor a weakling before me, but rather a stalwart lad of indomitable bravery!" Elliot swelled with pride as he gazed up into the dearest face it seemed that he had ever glimpsed, the face of the Queen of Lorinshar.

"But come," said the queen graciously, patting his arm with her small beringed hand. "Put on your dressing gown and sit with me. For I have eaten nothing and would like to break my fast with you. I have prepared a little treat for us to enjoy together, and if you desire anything, you have only to test my magic—for I shall gladly obtain any whim for you!" Queen Ulricke was even gracious enough to step behind a tall folding screen as Elliot climbed out of his bed to put on the dressing gown. Then she took his hand and led him to one of the scroll-armed settees.

She sat beside him and snapped her fingers. He watched awestruck as the bedside table and its heavily laden tray levitated soundlessly to float across the room, its ivory legs suspended four feet in the air. It came to rest gently beside them. Queen Ulricke laughed the carefree laugh of a child. "I must confess that I always love doing that!" she said, with a mischievous wink.

After enjoying breakfast with her, Elliot felt so at ease with the queen that he apprised her of his quest. "Permit me, Your Majesty," he summoned the courage to say. "I feel that despite what I've heard, you are kind and true. The object of my quest is an orb of fire possessed by a dragon. Have you ever heard of either the Fire Dragon or his orb?" Queen Ulricke glanced quickly at Elliot's face, then grew thoughtful, pursing her lips.

While preparing her response, she handed him a piece of the fresh-baked bread, which was dripping with rich golden honey.

"The last fire dragon died ages ago," she replied at length. "And that was just as well—for the fire dragons are nearly all desperately evil. Villages, towns, and whole countries even have all turned to ash under their flaming breath. But the ice dragons were of another sort entirely. They were good and kindly—just the sort to take one under its wing and teach one about the world," said the queen.

"Now there is but one ice dragon left, and he lives in a realm far away—the Realm of Winter Night, where he works ceaselessly for the benefit of all mankind. He was once my mentor, Elliot, and I miss his gentle insights very much indeed!" Queen Ulricke looked as though she was about to cry and Elliot tentatively reached out to pat her hand.

The queen blinked back a tear or two as she gave him a dazzling smile of gratitude in return for his courtliness. "Oh, Elliot," she declared. "You are so very dear!" Then she was quiet again for some moments while he nibbled self-consciously at the last remaining crumbs of his bread. "To the north, just beyond the far reaches of my realm, across the Silent Sea, I am told there is a dragon pinnacle. It soars to quite an unimaginable height and in the light of the setting sun it will sometimes attain a vivid red hue. But alas! I fear that it is a dragon pinnacle in name only, for never in all the years of my reign have I heard of there being an actual dragon in residence there."

Perhaps it was Elliot's crestfallen look that moved the

queen, for she smiled at him and took his chin gently in her hand. "Don't worry overmuch, my brave and true friend," she said. "All the resources and wisdom of my realm shall be placed at your disposal to aid you in your quest, and I myself shall speak to my lords and chamberlains this very day to see if they perhaps have heard any lore—no matter how ancient and obscure—that may prove of benefit to you."

And then Queen Ulricke grew merry and mischievous and Elliot laughed aloud, for he found her mood infectious. "Come," she urged. "Test my magic. There must be something you desire, perhaps some trifle from your own world—some treat or trinket I can obtain for you. You have only to ask for it, Elliot!"

The Queen of Lorinshar placed her arm about his shoulders to pull him close and kiss his tousled hair as though he were a cherished little brother. Elliot thought and thought, and the queen chuckled at the expression of concentration upon his features.

But I really can't ask for what I'm thinking of, thought Elliot. *You would have to be from my world to know what it is, and you would have to have tasted it!*

He was startled when the queen appeared to have to read his mind. "I journey to many worlds, having just recently returned from a sojourn to your very world and time, Elliot. I understand you far more than you think, for it was I in the form and likeness of another who appeared before you, to rescue you from those despicable louts who pursued and mistreated you in the wooded lane!"

Elliot was astounded at this new revelation. Why had the

Faerie Queen let him believe a falsehood? "You mean that it was you in disguise, and not the Faerie Queen at all?"

Queen Ulricke laughed. "Of course, my dear friend. It was I who saved you, for if those boys kept you near your doorstep you would never have had your adventure, nor found your magic ring, which brought you to me!"

He was stunned. The queen smiled at him and continued. "You know, Elliot," she said very softly, "magic rings can be a heavy burden—this I know from experience!" She lifted up her fingers and once again, for but a single moment, her rings transformed back into the strange bands of black metal, writhing and twisting upon her fingers. "I myself am quite accustomed to the care and keeping of them. So know, dear boy, that if yours ever becomes too much of a weight to bear, you may simply entrust it to my care—temporarily, of course—for you may come to me and claim it whenever your need may arise!"

Elliot was so dazzled with subtle enchantments that he suspected nothing but kindness in the queen's offer. "I humbly thank you, Your Majesty," he said. "And I may take you up on it someday. But for now it's a burden I must bear alone." He thought perhaps—for just the tiniest moment—a brief flash of anger smoldered somewhere deep behind the tenderness in the queen's eyes.

"It is no matter, Elliot," she said with a gracious smile. "Such things are but trifles between us."

And then the queen grew mischievous once more. "Do test me, Elliot!" she demanded with an expressive pout. "Do please test my magic! Let me prove the wonders I can work on your behalf. Tell me what it is that your heart desires!" Once again Elliot thought for a moment, and then blurted out his wish at last. "How about an ice-cold bottle of Wink?" he asked hesitantly. "It's a lemon-lime soda."

Somehow he had rather feared that the Queen of Lorinshar would be angry with the simplicity of his everyday request. But she laughed and laughed, the unaffected and musical notes of her mirth conveying only joy. She snapped her fingers and then simply remained seated, her arm about his shoulders, as they waited for the magic to unfold. Soon, Elliot heard a door open of its own accord somewhere close by. He was astounded to see a soda machine floating through the air. It stopped scarcely a foot before him, hovering in midair, three feet above the floor. The pictures above all the selection knobs on the machine depicted only frosty glass bottles of Wink!

Queen Ulricke grinned at him impishly. A dime appeared between her fingertips as if by magic. "I told you that all worlds are interwoven, Elliot." And with that Queen Ulricke put the dime in the slot and pulled the selection knob. There was a clattering thud and a green bottle appeared in the trap. The queen bent forward to retrieve it, smiling at Eliot as she presented it to him, vaporizing the cap with a snap of her fingers. She blinked her left eye slowly and deliberately. "Wink— the sassy one!" she murmured. Elliot was amazed, for she had spoken the exact words of the television commercial!

Elliot reached out to take the bottle with a trembling hand. "You will find that it is all you expect—and perhaps a bit more besides!" said Queen Ulricke. He slowly brought the bottle to his lips. "Wait!" exclaimed the queen, feigning annoyance. "Some gentleman you proved to be, Elliot!" She snapped her fingers yet again and a tray with a dark green bottle and a crystal glass glided into the room to pause hovering at her knee. "I wish to enjoy some refreshment along with you!" she announced.

Elliot studied the label of the queen's bottle. It depicted a lovely faerie with brilliant green wings hovering in pale moonlight, but she had a wicked mocking smile. The image reminded him of the faeries who had accosted him in the woods of Direfall.

Elliot studied the label. "Green Fairy A-B-S-I-N-T-H-E! What is absent?" he asked.

"Almost, but not quite correct," replied the queen patiently. "It is absinthe, a quaint concoction I developed an appreciation for when court business took me to Paris in 1890!"

She poured a bit of the vivid green liquid into her glass, stirring it with her fingertip until it foamed and churned, all at once frothing pale and milky. "A toast," she declared, "to my dear sweet friend, Elliot Good!"

"And to Your kind Majesty, the Queen!" he replied as they clicked their drinks together.

Queen Ulricke sipped from her glass, smiling with satisfaction as she watched Elliot. A few swallows later, his pupils began to dilate. He paused as his momentary surge of alarm was dimmed with the lethargy and stupor conveyed by a powerful elixir. It seemed to him that the entire room had first begun spinning rapidly and then turned topsy-turvy and rolled upon its side. He fell sideways drooling, his head coming to rest on the queen's lap.

As if in a dream Elliot felt the Queen of Lorinshar stand him up and put her arms about him, propping his head upon her shoulder as she led him back to his bed and laid him gently down. As his eyes blurred and his vision swam he became conscious of only two things: the loveliness of the queen's face and the bewitching power of her gaze as she smiled fondly down upon him.

She spoke softly. "Within a few hours you will change, my dear boy," she said. "For I offer you a temporary treat— a taste of power, the like of which you have never known or dreamed of. When you have fully transformed you may cross the bridge and descend into the Garden of the Night. And there, upon the mountainside, you may relish the experience which I have bestowed upon you."

She reached down to take Elliot's ring from his finger, but then she thought better of it. After all, she would soon be making him an offer he could not refuse—and then both the ring and he would be forever hers!

Hours passed and Elliot lay motionless in the darkened chamber. The queen had gone elsewhere to see to other business and he was all alone. It was in fact well that he was unconscious, for his body had begun a series of violent convulsions that eventually resulted in his throwing himself from the bed altogether—such were the intensity of the spasms.

As the hours crept slowly past and the shadows in the chamber lengthened, the convulsions and seizures grew more violent still. Elliot's rigid body jerked, twitching in frightful paroxysms, jittering and skidding across the polished floor—so great was the force of his upheaval. His eyes rolled, his hands grasped at the carpet like rigid claws, and his mouth began foaming profusely as first his teeth grew alarmingly long, and then the central portion of his face, including his upturned nose—the very nose his mother had loved to kiss at bedtime when he was very small—began to elongate grotesquely.

It was plain that the drink the queen had given him was no ordinary lemon-lime soda after all. Rather it was a draft of evil magic, a potion, both extremely potent and highly dangerous—for it was slowly turning Elliot Good into a wolf!

Chapter 30

VICTORIA WAS RUNNING, tucking up her skirts as she went, her radiant garments streaming out behind her like a mist. The silent stage seemed to have grown vastly larger and more frightening.

She ran whisper quiet among the sets and backdrops that were now suddenly stark and far more sinister, weaving through the obstacles presented by fallen dancers, knights, and even their horses. She flitted along the footlights like a ghost, heading for what she knew was the very source of danger—for her ring was directing her straight to a spot below the tiers of box seats.

Victoria paused, unsure of what to do next. Suddenly, a dreadful voice addressed her from Lord Enraldorn's private box. It was a voice she recognized from a terrible dream. "I have summoned you, Victoria Deveny," it said. Victoria trained the beacon of light from her ring in the direction of the sound, and was not entirely surprised to find that the person addressing her was the peculiar Lord Enraldorn. His sleepy eyes had grown far brighter now.

She steeled herself and replied in a haughty voice, "Why, Lord Enraldorn, couldn't you wait until I visit the Ice Palace to work your enchantment upon me?"

"I am someone *far* greater than he," the figure countered, and Victoria was shocked when she, still in her flying harness, was abruptly jerked from the ground to be left dangling high in the air above the stage. She peered upward to see if one any-one was controlling her harness, but there was no one on the catwalks.

"They have all fallen into a deep sleep, Victoria," murmured the menacing figure cloaked in Lord Enraldorn's likeness. "No one can aid you now. No one but me." Suddenly, Lord En-raldorn's body slumped back into his seat and underwent a series of violent convulsions. Victoria watched horrified as she hung helplessly in the air. From Lord Enraldorn's body came a misty phantom, shapeless at first, but growing ever larger as it took on the form of the terrible Ice Dragon. He hovered over the sleeping audience, growing ever larger, yet still appearing confined, as the proximity of the rising tiers of seats impeded the beating of his huge wings. His great tail swept round, knocking the jeweled chandelier to the floor with a tremendous crash. "This simply won't do," he mur-mured, closing his heavily lidded eyes.

Victoria felt herself growing disoriented and profoundly sleepy. She fought to stay awake as she was gently lowered to the ground and her harness magically unfastened. Instead of landing on the stage, she found herself standing on a cold marble floor in the midst of a cavernous cathedral. She was utterly alone.

The Ice Dragon overshadowed Victoria, his head towering far above her. He was a vast, cold, dead thing of unutterable age emanating the most dreadful power. The very air around him breathed menace and peril. Victoria clutched her cape tightly about herself, for she felt chilled to the bone and close to fainting.

"What have you done with everyone?" Victoria asked, noticing that a vivid orb was suspended from about his neck on a chain, dangling above her.

"They were insubstantial, my dear," the dragon answered smoothly as his tail coiled, repositioning itself soundlessly back in the shadows of the cathedral's nave. "It was a simple matter to make them disappear. After all, I am a very great sorcerer."

And as he spoke his eyelids drooped momentarily, as though perhaps he had lapsed briefly into dream slumber once more, and in that brief interval Victoria sensed that the phantom terrors of his dreams were congealing thick in the air about her. Suddenly it became very difficult for her to think clearly. She was strangely taken with a mad urge to cast herself down upon the cold stone floor before the Ice Dragon and beg him for mercy.

He addressed her once more with a velvet-smooth and reasonable voice. "How would you like to come away and learn magic from me? I sense that you are gifted, and when it comes to spells and arcane lore I could teach you much. I could make of you a potent sorcerer renowned all through-out the interwoven worlds. After all, I have done such a thing before, long ago!"

Victoria steeled herself to reply and was dismayed at the tremulous tone of her own voice. "I desire only one thing from you, and that is the Blue Orb—the Orb of Ice." As soon as the words departed her lips, Victoria had second thoughts and wondered if perhaps she hadn't wisely chosen her words—for it was probably not a prudent thing to say such a thing so directly.

"Ah, yes, your silly little quest for my orb." The dragon laughed coldly. "I came here to save you from being eaten by wolves on a futile journey to Mount Shurudgrim—and to tell you that the orb is my property alone!" As Victoria watched, the orb changed from a bright transparent blue to a milky, cloudy hue.

"The Faerie Queen asked me to obtain it, and that's what I shall do," Victoria declared defiantly, though certain that she was probably breathing her very last breath.

"The Faerie Queen is very wicked and not at all to be trusted, and neither is Lord Paracelsus! Do you not see, sweet ignorant child? They are in league with Lord Primvet, Clericor Demyin, and Nastya. It was all a treacherous plot to make you do the dirty and dangerous part of the business—to manipulate you into stealing the orb on their behalf."

The Ice Dragon's carefully modulated voice became even more reasonable and sympathetic. "And were you to succeed, you would either finish your days in misery at the Pomfret Workhouse, or be left to languish at the Black Swan Inn, slaving your life away—in either case a very unfortunate end indeed, for you see, my child, they would simply have no further use for you!"

Bewitching phantoms and evil thoughts began to take shape in Victoria's mind, and they swirled about her in disorienting clouds of confusion, illustrating the Ice Dragon's lies with uncanny clarity. Victoria actually found herself believing him. Feelings of anger, hurt, and betrayal rose up in her—and even a vivid hatred, too—which the Ice Dragon sensed at once, relishing it and seizing upon it with glee.

The great horned head came down lower still, until its eyes were level with her own. "Then join me, dear child," the Ice Dragon urged. "Join me, and we shall make short work of them, and something frightful will befall each of those who has so misused you!"

His voice was so reasonable that for a moment Victoria's bewitched mind was filled with poisonous—yet still somehow delicious—visions of doing horrible things to people, visions that had somehow forced their way in upon her consciousness from the outside and cleverly masqueraded as her own thoughts. When the visions subsided, Victoria asked the Ice Dragon about the fate of Lord Enraldorn.

"Alas, Lord Enraldorn could have simply sworn an oath of loyalty to me, but instead he chose to fade away—slowly dwindling to become a living ghost under my dream spells. Now he and his court will forever haunt the abandoned halls of their precious Ice Palace!

"Swear an oath of loyalty to me, Victoria Deveny, and you shall prosper, and I will lend you my Orb of Ice and you may use its formidable power to destroy your enemies—for all that's mine will be placed at your disposal, in obedience to your every whim. And then you may assist me in destroying each of my foes one by one, and when that transpires you will truly find your destiny as my protégée—for I will teach you many wondrous and terrible things!"

The Ice Dragon's compelling face was just inches from Victoria's now, and his voice was silken smooth in its subtle persuasion. Intoxicating visions of herself as a sorcerer queen of unfathomable power danced through Victoria's mind. She saw herself with worlds at her feet, adored and feared by multitudes. She also saw herself generously rewarding those who were loyal to her and having unspeakably wicked things done to those who would not submit to her rule.

Little did she know that the very same vision had completely bewitched another child, one of two sisters, ever so long ago. The one with black hair and red eyes was taken in and fell beneath the Ice Dragon's deadly influence, but the one with the alabaster skin, snow-white hair, and amber eyes had resisted bravely—all alone. Thus was the origin of wicked Queen Ulricke and the Albino Contessa—Victoria's steadfast friend.

Suddenly, the gemstone in Victoria's ring flared to life once again, penetrating through all the delusions and enchantments of the Ice Dragon, and she saw that Clericor Demyin, Lord Primvet, and Nastya were truly wicked, while the Albino Contessa, the Faerie Queen, and Paracelsus were her stalwart friends. The counterspell from the faerie ring illuminated all the dreadful darkness of the Ice Dragon's enchantment.

And then Victoria saw the human misery, the tears and the rivers of blood that would flow as battles raged at her command, and whole kingdoms succumbed to her vast armies and tattered multitudes were led away to lives of slavery and toil. She recoiled from that vision in utter repulsion, where, alas, little Ulricke—to her own detriment—had not.

Victoria then recognized that she was confronting an expert mesmerist, for she had seen such a one at work, when on holiday at Portobello Pier. The mesmerist had the most commanding eyes and used his consummate skill and the nuances of subtle expertise to convince a dignified lady that she was a giggling schoolgirl. The mesmerist told her the most flagrant falsehoods, which she believed absolutely—for she tittered, blushing with coy adolescent embarrassment when he asked her who she secretly adored. But the mesmerist Victoria now faced was far more skillful than any Portobello Pier showman, far more ancient—and infinitely more wicked. She determined to resist him with all her heart and all her might.

"No!" shouted Victoria, summoning up what little flagging courage she had left. "No! *You* are wicked and *you* are my enemy. Paracelsus and the Faerie Queen would never befriend Clericor Demyin or Nastya—that lot are more likely to be *your* friends! Now give me the Blue Orb! Give it to me at once or I shall . . ." She paused, trembling, her courage flagging.

The Ice Dragon's head reared upward, now more serpent-like than ever, high into the arch of the cathedral's ceiling. His eyes were flaming with absolute hatred.

"Or you shall what?" hissed the Ice Dragon.

Victoria replied in a faint little fearful voice, "Or I shall take it from you by fo . . ." She then found herself unable to finish the sentence, for the blast of malice that came from him smote her like a heavy weight and drove her quivering to her knees, her head reeling hopelessly.

"Or you shall take it from me *by force?*" the Ice Dragon mocked, finishing Victoria's sentence for her. "You? A mere stupid child! Take it from me!" And his cold laughter, a scornful venomous mirth that tore at her very soul, echoed and pealed through the phantom cathedral.

Then the Ice Dragon spoke slowly and softly, his voice positively dripping with spite and contempt. "No, you ungrateful little wretch! First, I shall show you the truth, for it is truth, not dreams, that most devastates! Dire things have befallen you, child, but like a simpleton you still cling to your illusions. And second, you shall dance for me, for dance I am told is the last parlor trick you know, and you keep it up your sleeve as a bulwark to fend off reality—to prevent it from crashing in upon you!"

A sensation of mounting horror clutched at Victoria's heart. Even as she stood transfixed it seemed that the pillars of the cathedral about her fluctuated, grew dim, and melted away. In their place it seemed she stood out upon the Great Frozen Inland Sea, surrounded by a fleet of ice ships. Their dark towering shadows loomed all about, and in the ruin of sterncastles, rigging, and ice-rimed sails she saw how the illusion of a cathedral had presented itself to her senses. The Ice Dragon's eyes bored into hers, mastering her completely, and to her shock she found she was covered with matted snow and her hands were blue with cold.

"It is time for truth, child," whispered the Ice Dragon, peering at her from close proximity as the coils of his body drew near, surrounding her with a still greater chill. "Shall I tell you the truth?"

Victoria tried to speak but no sound came. She was trembling violently, both with cold and fear.

"In your heart of hearts you know that you are dead, child," said the Ice Dragon, the light in his eyes growing more eerie still. "You perished alone out upon the Great Frozen Inland Sea, scarcely a hundred yards from where they abandoned you."

Victoria fell to her knees, clutching her ice-cold hands over her ears. "No!" she cried. "I am alive! I asked the Albino Contessa if I had died when she rescued me in the sleigh carriage and she assured me that I hadn't!"

The Ice Dragon laughed. "Paracelsus and the Albino Contessa lived in the Palace of Kalingalad in peace many years ago. But unwisely, they decided to make war on me—they and those from the other palaces attacked as I slept under Mount Shurudgrim. Alas, they were no match for me and they all perished in battle. Their palaces are in ruins now. You have been playing with ghosts and phantoms, child—because you are one yourself!"

Victoria remembered the strange disturbing dream she had where Paracelsus and the Albino Contessa were sad spirits seeking her aid. She was also reminded that, just moments ago, the Ice Dragon had caused an entire theater audience to disappear before her eyes. Could they really all have been ghosts?

The Ice Dragon's gaze bored more deeply into Victoria's. "You are dead, my child; you perished all alone out upon the ice—as did your friend Constance before you. Look down at your feet!"

Victoria's heart lurched. She didn't want to look, but something compelled her. An involuntary scream was torn from her throat, for there, at her feet, protruding up from the ice and snow, the slender frozen hand of Constance reached up in a gesture pathetic and forlorn, seeking assistance that never came.

Victoria burst into tears and knelt in the snow to ever so gently brush the flecks of ice and frost from her friend's cold, dead hand. She was shivering violently as she held it tenderly.

The Ice Dragon waited a bit before speaking again. "You are one of my phantoms now, child. I shall restore the illusion of the cathedral if it brings you comfort." As Victoria got to her feet, wiping away her tears, she saw the towering ships about her fluctuate and transform once more into the hushed dimness of the cathedral. But now she could see the cathedral for the insubstantial illusion that it was—its very walls almost transparent.

"Dance for me, child," commanded the Ice Dragon.

Chapter 31

When Elliot came to his senses, he was immediately aware of new and delightful smells. Oh, the smells! The simply divine smells! How had he ever existed—or even managed to experience joy—without smells such as these? There were dozens of smells, rather hundreds—no, the number of intriguing smells was countless. His long black snout twitched in its eagerness to experience them all, longing to investigate each and every one of them in turn.

Elliot smelled mouthwatering food cooking in Pendrongor's kitchens, dozens of floors below. He smelled the fresh blood that flowed in the veins of the watchmen, just outside his door, and he detected the unpleasant, tainted smell that infused the blood scent of one of Lord Kromm's sinister tower guardsmen who commanded them. Elliot could smell that one of the handmaidens was close by—as close as several chambers away—and that her scent was strange, in fact, not fully human at all. He lowered his great wolf head to sniff the scratches on his forearms left from the attack of the green faeries—and he found that they had healed and that he was sniffing big gray wolf paws instead.

But where the scratches had been, the faintest trace scent of the faeries lingered, and he could tell that it was a kindred scent to that of the handmaidens. He wondered if perhaps Queen Ulricke had captured an evil green faerie or two, enlarged them with spells, removed their wings, and made them swear allegiance to her—and in this he was more correct than he could possibly have known.

Elliot sniffed the air for the scent of the queen herself and finally identified it—finding it a strange mixture of spice and poison. It was a scent both wild and sweet, but there was an element of decay about it, too. He was surprised to find that, in wolf form, smells that would have sickened or disgusted him as a human were mere matters of curiosity to his sensitive, twitching nose.

He opened first one eye and then the other. He could make out the details of the tower chamber with great clarity, but everything seemed a trifle strange, as if his depth perception had been altered. Some things seemed flatter and less three-dimensional than before, while other distances seemed to achieve even greater depth. He gulped and licked his lips, and to his surprise, he felt a long tongue sweep across rows of razor-sharp canine teeth.

He heard the scrambling noise of claws upon marble and wondered if perhaps some beast were creeping up on him. Then he realized he was sitting up now, on his wolf haunches. Elliot's fear was mingled with an exultant feeling of power and a nearly limitless sensation of freedom. He felt his hackles rise

and his ears drew back close against his head as he snarled—
a vicious deep bass sound that would have completely un-
nerved him when in human form, a far cry from his pathetic
attempts to howl when playing wolf as a little boy.

Elliot got to his feet with a surge of energy, and after a few
hesitant steps, began to run in circles about the tower chamber. He nearly fell three or four times as his sharp claws skidded on the marble floor—after his antics had disarrayed and
rumpled the carpets, pushing them into the far edges of the
room. When he came face to face with a cheval glass he was
in for a shock, for in it he saw a great ghastly wolf with hor-
rendous fangs and glowing green eyes. Elliot would have
laughed aloud if he still had human vocal cords—he was
simply astonished that the frightful apparition facing him was
in fact himself!

He leaped over both settees and then he ran round and
round the room loping faster and faster till he was panting
with exertion, his long red tongue lolling from his mouth. Finally he sat down upon his haunches again to rest. Then Elliot felt as though he must howl; in fact, the urge was quite
irresistible, and so he threw back his head and did so.

The blood of chamberlains, margravines, scullery maids,
and minstrels all ran cold in their veins when they heard the
sound. Apparently their queen had created yet another mon-
strosity. In the ring gallery just below the queen's balcony, the
were-beasts sent forth answering howls, grunts, baying, and
growls—save for Lord Sarton, whose chains simply disappeared into the glowing blue portal of the astral realm.

And seated upon her throne, brooding wickedness in her

crystal room—her lamp gown aflicker with its seething lights, rings squirming upon her fingers—Queen Ulricke smiled and clapped her hands with glee. "Ah! My dear friend Elliot Good!" she purred exultantly. "Let us see what doors now open wide for both of us!"

Elliot leaped up and padded silently to the chamber door. His wolf heart was overjoyed to find it partly open before him. He thrust his muzzle into the narrow opening to nudge the door further ajar with a creaking groan. The watchmen were under strict orders to allow him access anywhere. They drew back, cowering against the stairwell wall as the great wolf swept past.

He took the ancient steps two at a time, soon leaving his guestchamber far behind. He came to another door whose guards also drew back in horror. And then he was out alone in the cool of nighttime upon a high dizzying bridge leading out onto the Garden of the Night. It was a large walled enclosure set high upon the mountainside—in Pendrongor's very shadow. The garden was a private place, and it was off limits to everyone but the queen or those favored to receive her permission.

Elliot used loping strides now, panting as he went, his tongue lolling, his eyes glittering balefully beneath untold thousands of red stars. His wolf's heart pounded with joy and a heady sense of newfound freedom. As he passed watch posts, perched atop the parapets of the bridge, he leaped high into the air, snapping and snarling. The halberd-bearing guards in their coats of chain mail stepped quickly backward to give him a wide berth.

At the highest central span of the bridge Elliot paused, lifted his werewolf muzzle heavenward, and gave another long piercing howl. Then he ran all out, nearly drunk with an unaccustomed sensation of limitless power, relishing his mastery of speed and distance. His paws were silent as he bounded down the final descent of the span, rushing at last out onto the freedom of the mountainside and the Garden of the Night.

The Garden of the Night was a dangerous place, situated high atop a craggy outcropping. The grass was a smooth carpet of pallid gray, and strange nocturnal flowers speckled its rolling lawns. These were foul-smelling orchids that unfolded only to the light of stars and moon and closed their fetid blossoms in loathing from the sunshine of day. The stooping trees formed gaping faces composed of knot and bough, and their branches appeared to terminate in grasping hands. Set all about the garden were pedestals of granite and marble upon which stood poised statues that were at first lovely to look upon—but upon closer inspection, the onlooker would find they possessed some dreadful deformity, or were involved in scenes depicting ghastly atrocities.

But the changed Elliot cared naught for this. He was a werewolf now, a predator, and he had never felt more alive. The quiet boy who had often fled in fear of bullies once more turned his muzzle skyward, sat back on his haunches, and howled once more until there came an answering cacophony of baying, roaring, snorting, and grunting.

Elliot got to his feet and ran like the wind, going round and round between the leering statues and dashing through dark thickets of fir. His very blood fairly sang with a rush of power and the urge to howl and hunt. The starlight above him seemed twice as near and vivid as it had ever appeared to him as a human, and the sounds were sharp—carried from far away to his sensitive ears.

He could plainly hear even the tiniest sigh of wind through the petals of the moonflowers, and he heard the scrabbling of a collapsing crag high upon the mountainside above. He detected all manner of sounds from within Pendrongor itself, despite its thick walls of stone: the commonplace sounds of human habitation, the panting breath of bellows forcing air into weapon forges, and the hopeless tears of weeping captives.

Elliot leaped and ran tirelessly, snapping his great fanged jaws at nothing at all, pausing to growl at a whim. He scoffed at anything and everything that would have made him cringe with fear when he was just a boy. He spent hours in the Garden of the Night, exploring its every glen, dip, and hollow until he felt that it was his own private domain. At last, however, a strange dizziness befell him, and though he was not at all tired, he felt beset with illness. His head soon hung low, his tongue lolling from the side of his mouth, his eyes grown dim.

Some latent instinct drove him on, and he moved as quickly as he could to the bridge. At last he found it and crossed it slowly, his wolf's head sinking lower still. The guards nonetheless took no chance, for they quickly stepped back into their sentry posts, their halberds set firmly between themselves and him. Elliot had just crossed the threshold of his chamber when his legs buckled beneath him and he fell onto his side upon the floor, foaming from his muzzle.

Brynn and Sutton had been awaiting his return in the darkened room. They stepped forward, their faces alive with delight to watch his agonizing transformation back into a boy. First it was as though a large dog lay upon its side, paws twitching as it whimpered in its dreams, then the convulsions began in earnest. Nearly two hours later it was not a wolf that lay drenched in sweat and deathly pale at the handmaidens' feet, but a boy.

The handmaidens laughed, the tones of their amusement musical and sweet. "I never tire of that spectacle," exclaimed Brynn.

"It is simply a delight to behold!" Sutton agreed. And then they stooped to carry a senseless Elliot to his bed once more. They lit the lamps, so that the room would not be in darkness when he awakened. They built a fire in the marble hearth as they had been instructed.

"I am certain that she will soon tire of this pathetic thing," said one handmaiden to the other. They both laughed merrily as they left the room—locking the door fast behind them.

Chapter 32

THE ICE DRAGON HAD commanded her to dance for him—and strangely, defiant as she was, something deep inside Victoria compelled her to do just that. It was not so much that she was cowed by him—though she was—rather it was a subtle nudging from deep within her heart, that to dance was not only the right thing to do, but that it was the *only* thing to do.

So all was lost. She was dead and had failed in her quest. There was no hope at all. Victoria considered a happiness and a beauty that never were to be far better than dismal reality. So she stood up on the very toes of her dancing slippers there in the silence of the cathedral, and carefully positioned her arms and toes to begin a sequence of formal steps.

Victoria was uncertain how long she would be able to continue her dance without musical accompaniment. She always danced to music of some sort, both at Prosingham and at Kalingalad.

Her steps were tentative at first, but then her confidence grew and she determined that she would make this her best performance ever—whether or not she were a living dancer. She would not dance for the Ice Dragon at all, but rather for all her friends whom she would never see again.

And as Victoria danced, she appeared as an ethereal form, flitting about the floor of the vast cathedral. Ever so slowly, the Ice Dragon's sneer of contempt faded, and he grew quiet and still as he watched the artistry of her form and the beauty of her steps.

The gems upon the toes of her dancing slippers sparkled blue-green in the faint light as she spun and pirouetted. And then the great blue moon of the Realm of Winter Night came out from behind its cloud concealment, and its vivid light swept radiantly across the floor to illuminate Victoria as she danced the most skillful steps she had ever performed in all her life. She danced lightly up and down the steps of the chancel, then, reaching the polished floor once more, twirled high in midair, spinning to alight in a low sweep, arms gracefully outstretched.

What Victoria did not then know, as she swirled on her toes, was that a magic far greater than the deathly power of the Ice Dragon was at work.

The night outside was very still and cold, and from the broken corner of one high stained-glass window, the wind howled in through a shattered pane as it propelled a scintillating cloud of ice crystals along before it. Some of them whispered across the floor to spin and sparkle about Victoria's feet, while others went airborne, sighing about the silver gleaming pipes of the cathedral organ.

And thus it was that Victoria's dance now had accompaniment, for the ice crystals flirted softly about the pipes, and then slowly, very slowly—almost inaudibly at first—tones and notes were coaxed from the organ, though there were no visible hand upon the keyboard and no visible feet upon the banks of pedals. It was here that the Ice Dragon experienced his first surge of alarm. For these were not elements of his design.

Victoria danced tirelessly, weaving in and out about the side chapels and the columns of the transepts, twirling among the huge weight-bearing pillars of the nave, and thence she proceeded up the chancel steps, then back and forth beneath the darkened lamps suspended from the high dome, far above the apse. She danced as light as the wind while skillful fingers of ice and frost played about the pipes of the organ, bypassing its keys, until a symphony of wonder and magic echoed profoundly through the Ice Cathedral—its impact magnified by the power of her faerie ring.

And as Victoria raised her arms for her next pirouette, she saw the stone of her ring gleam more vividly, and it seemed somehow to remind her that all the countless drills and practices, the same sequences repeated over and over again, were the real magic she had been sent to learn. And it was the strength of this magic—ability developed with much toil and effort—that was now itself enchanting the most dreadful sorcerer that had ever existed in all the interwoven worlds. For the icy phantom was himself succumbing to the mystical power activated by Victoria's dance and the whisper of the wind playing across the pipes.

And slowly the Ice Dragon began to see the inside of things as clearly as the outside. He glimpsed Victoria as a radiant being of wondrous beauty, and at the same time he dwindled in his own perceptions and unwillingly saw himself as a small and vile thing, having tremendous might only upon the outside—but within, he was weak and spiteful and mean-spirited.

The Ice Dragon was shocked to see the walls and pillars of the cathedral solidify and grow real. It was no longer just an illusion of his creation. He bent his will to the task of undoing the counterspell—but found he could not. He felt a gnawing fear, that as the Ice Cathedral turned real about him he would be imprisoned forever.

"I must go at once!" said the Ice Dragon. As the dragon drew back, his head rearing high as he sought escape, Victoria boldly stepped onto one of his icy coils and grasped the chain from which the orb was suspended about his neck.

"Not till you give me the orb! You shall not escape until you relinquish it forever!"

Victoria was shocked at what she saw in the Ice Dragon's eyes in that moment. First it was rage and spite, but then fear gained mastery. For his part the Ice Dragon glimpsed something in Victoria's eyes, something he could not bear, and it shook him to his very core: It was pity mingled with contempt, and he knew then that his strength was dwindling rapidly and that he must flee at once.

And as Victoria watched, still grasping the chain, the great armored bulk of the Ice Dragon wavered, flickered, and then grew slowly dim. The Ice Dragon faded to finally disappear altogether. His smoothly uncoiling tail was the last part of him to vanish.

All at once the music stopped, and the flecks of frost and bits of ice swirled about Victoria to lower her gently down, for neither the Ice Dragon nor his coils were there to support her any longer.

And there, suspended from the chain she clutched in her hand, was the blue Orb of Ice, shining with the utmost resplendent clarity.

Chapter 33

ELLIOT SPENT THE REMAINDER of the night and nearly all the next day in a deep leaden slumber. When he finally awakened, he felt as though he had been poisoned, which in a manner of speaking he had been, for the potion Queen Ulricke gave him in the guise of lemon-lime soda was a most perilous elixir possessing toxic properties.

He rolled over, clutching his head in his hands. His temples pounded awfully. His mouth was so dry it felt as though it had been stuffed with cotton wool. He managed to find a pitcher of water and then drank his fill. He sat up slowly, hoping to get his strength back. After a bit, he finally took a chance and stood up. The pulsing pain in his head grew so intense that he reeled, stumbling backward, but found support against a marble pillar just in time, as the spell slowly passed. His joints ached and his muscles felt as though he had fallen down a long flight of steps. He was profoundly relieved when he glimpsed the sparkle of his ring on the floor where it had fallen during his transformation and he slipped it back on at once.

By now it was dusk again, and a muted crimson light filtered colorfully in through the etched windows. He stumbled to the door, tested the latch, and found it secured from the outside. He would have been surprised to have found it any other way.

He stumbled back to the settee and held his head in his hands as the fearful pounding slowly subsided. He recalled a good deal of his experience as a wolf and was repulsed by the tremendous upheavals that must have befallen his body as it transformed. He hoped that he had suffered no permanent injury. Yet he also recalled the experience with a sense of pride. The sensation of nearly limitless power was something that he could become quite accustomed to. His senses had been so acute that every sight, sound, and smell was keen and vivid. Now that he was a boy again, it seemed that his faculties had all diminished, and that he was only half alive, in a world conveyed to him by dull perceptions.

He lay sideways on the settee, his head on the arm until at last he felt a bit better. He had begun to relax a little, and did not hear a key slip into the lock. Neither did he hear the barely audible squeak of hinges as the door to his chamber swung wide to admit two figures.

The handmaidens crept furtively into his room. They were hoping to give him a good fright—which in fact they did. Elliot jumped and cried out when four ghastly, long-fingered hands darted noiselessly from over the back of the settee to grasp and pinch at his face and shoulders. He shuddered and struggled to sit up. He turned round to look and noted once more the contrast between the handmaidens' sweet, gracious faces and their horrid, filthy hands. They laughed musically at his expression of dismay.

"Queen Ulricke has summoned you to her chambers, so prepare yourself at once," commanded Sutton.

"Yes indeed, our queen wishes to chat with you! And who can tell, perhaps she will even permit you to live." Brynn laughed.

Elliot was dragged to his feet, his flesh fairly crawling to feel the power in the grasp of those hands. They propelled him forward, steering and guiding him with pinches, digs, and shoves.

After traversing several long corridors they reached a doorway of black obsidian that seemed as though it had once been an actual opening that had been sealed long ago, for there was no sign of either latch or keyhole upon its smooth, featureless surface. A black flaming lamp guttered from deep recesses at both sides. One of the handmaidens flicked her long-nailed fingertips at the door as she whispered a sibilantly malignant spell. The door wavered, then in a moment dissolved—and there in front of them, a dim lamplit stair twisted upward into the darkness. Round and round they turned, ascending the stair quickly, until another spell door dissolved to admit them, and Elliot found himself in Queen Ulricke's private chambers.

Brynn pinched his cheek and Sutton laughed while admonishing him. "See that you mind your manners! Be quiet and respectful—and be sure that you touch nothing. Our queen will be with you as soon as she is able!"

Then the handmaidens exited the chamber. Once again Elliot heard the hissing of a spell, and the door materialized again, solid as a block of granite—sealed fast.

At the very center of the black marble floor was a sort of circular fire pit, with high tongues of red and black flame burning from its depths licking and scorching the domed ceiling overhead. The ceiling was upheld by black pillars carved in the likenesses of grotesque monstrosities. To one side was an arched door, seemingly suspended in the wall, fifteen feet above the floor, its borders carved with a flowing script. But there was no stair leading down from the door.

The walls of the chamber were covered with charts and incomprehensible diagrams, which had strange symbols incised upon them. There were odd instruments displayed along the walls, most resembling archaic astrological devices perfected long before the telescope. Directly opposite stood a stone table covered with disorganized clutter. There were dozens of leather-bound volumes—some with covers so ancient they were crumbling, while others were filthy, befouled with mold and mildew.

Scattered among the volumes were glass vials, retorts, and spiral-necked distillation flasks. Nearly all were full of a phosphorescent green liquid that foamed out over the lip of its container. The liquid spread across the tabletop and dripped upon the floor, where Elliot saw it had eaten steaming holes in the black marble.

Onyx lamps hung from chains about the room—each topped with a twisting black flame, wavering and undulating like an evil genie. Fixed atop wall sconces running about the circumference of the room was a startling collection of bleached skulls. Elliot noted with relief that most of them appeared not to be human. Nor were they the skulls of commonplace beasts—rather the remains of monstrous things, frightful creatures conjured by spell and potion. Incredibly long fangs gleamed from unhinged gaping mouths, and deadly horns spiraled from ponderous, heavily browed foreheads. Spines with vertebrae still attached extended downward from some of them, as though she who collected them was determined to amplify every gruesome effect.

He noticed that to one side of the chamber was a raised dais following the form of the wall. Upon it stood nine massive suits of black plate armor atop granite pedestals. He hoped there weren't actual knights in them—or worse, some ghastly entities lurking inside, peering out through their visors, ready to pounce. He studied the suits of armor warily and at last determined that they were not inhabited. Behind each of them arced the blank face of a door like the one he had come through to enter the room. Elliot wondered if each door led to the tomb of the knight who once possessed the armor. Each close-visored suit of armor held a black sword in its gauntleted hand. Black flames flickered up and down each blade—save for the last.

At last Queen Ulricke made her entrance. The spell door suspended high above the floor wavered and dissolved in a crackle of magical energy. A black waterfall came cascading down out of the opening, pouring from the portal to fan out along the floor. Then it was as if the liquid began instantly freezing in place—and as more came down, it thickened, changing form until a black staircase appeared, each tread evenly and elegantly spaced. A serpentine rail formed even as Elliot watched, with banisters tapering downward. Finally, with a glacial crackling sound, the form of the stair became completely solid.

As Queen Ulricke descended the stair, Elliot could not take his eyes from her—such was the captivating majesty of her presence. She wore a black gown that seemed at first to be composed all of tatters as it fanned out upon the stair at her feet, writhing and undulating along the floor like a living thing.

Her cuffs were black as coal and her high formal collar rose dramatically in the back. Her hair piled high on her head. Queen Ulricke wore her black orb suspended from a chain of woven silver about her neck, flecks of purple fire flickering from its depths. The queen swept smoothly across the floor, her feet concealed beneath the hem of her gown.

She held out her immaculate little hands and took Elliot's hands affectionately into her own. "Dear Elliot," she said solemnly, her eyes at once serious and full of caring. "This very night is your moment of truth. It is now that your short life may—if you dare permit it—take such a turn as will astound you!"

Elliot did not understand precisely what Queen Ulricke meant. She smiled at him. "Perhaps if I but show you," she said. "Come this way, up the steps if you please, onto the dais—to the suits of armor."

In a moment they were standing before the first suit of armor. Queen Ulricke placed her hand upon Elliot's shoulder and steered him gently to the spell door behind the pedestal. She pointed her forefinger directly at its surface and whispered a magic word. The door wavered, dissolving into nothingness, to reveal a small candlelit chamber beyond. Along the walls and at the rear stood rows of black candles, each rank of precisely graduated height. The room appeared to shift subtly in dancing shadow.

In the very center of the crypt floated a pale, glowing sphere. A shadowy shape swam about within the sphere, moving this way and that, twisting and turning on currents of liquid half-light, sometimes fading to nearly disappear altogether and then brightening once more. Elliot got the skin-prickling sensation that the shape was not only very much alive, but that it was intelligent and aware of their presence, for it grew darker as it coagulated and thickened. It moved to their side of the glass, and flushed alternating black and crimson, growing in intensity while it studied them.

"Elliot, meet one of my eight Shadow Knights! This is Pietr," said Queen Ulricke. "I would more formally introduce you, but I may not speak their secret names aloud, for those names can only be invoked when I am in deep trance—in the course of the most exacting incantations."

Elliot's blood ran cold. So here was his answer at last! The Shadow Knight who had killed his mother and terrorized both him and Victoria was one of the queen's own creatures!

And Queen Ulricke had shown him such sympathy when he had wept to her over the death of his mother. Despite his fear he felt himself become angry at her duplicity.

"Each of these, my ever stalwart knights, was once a boy like you—some from other times, and some from different worlds. They each came to Pendrongor as my guests, and to them—as now with you—I offered power undreamed of. Each of these eight wisely took me at my word, for they put their trust in me and have become my most loyal servants. They each have their tasks to carry out, and they ride on coal black steeds to perform my bidding—for I seek change and betterment all throughout the interwoven worlds, and the good of all peoples weighs heavy on my heart!

"At preordained times, they each may obtain my counsel, so I summon their spirits here, and join them in their crypts to converse with them. If they are faced with any quandary that they know not how to unravel, they may call out to me, and I shall come to them. Thus, they are never truly alone, though oft their noble work exposes them to peril!"

Elliot could bear no more and interrupted Queen Ulricke. "But the Shadow Knight is wicked! He killed my mother— you said so yourself! And he mercilessly pursued my friend Victoria and me, and his horse has a horrible forked tongue and—"

"Be still, child, if you please," chided the queen, holding up her hand to quiet him. Her lovely face grew grave. "Seven of my knights remain true and do only my bidding, but one strayed, grasping for power that was not his due, seeking doors between worlds that I did not open unto him. He shall be dealt with presently, and in due course each of his wrongs shall be mended. That I promise you!

"For my command was for him to take only those magic rings that were not in rightful hands, and return them to their proper places. It was never my intent for him to wrest your ring from you, or Victoria's ring from her. But come! You must meet him! When in human form he was called Trevelyan, a difficult boy, one of the youngest—and now that he has become one of my knights, he has, I must confess, proved most troublesome!"

She led Elliot from the first Shadow Knight's crypt, down the row to the eighth suit of armor. Once again a softly spoken word dissolved the dark spell door. And there, before Elliot's astonished gaze, was a crypt that lay all in darkness. The black candles had guttered and gone out. The floating sphere, however, loomed much larger than the first, and was more intensely illuminated from within, but its light was more fitful and sinister.

The shadowy shape inside the sphere was darker than the other, and larger still, as it swirled about in rapid circles, as if impatient to escape its confines. Queen Ulricke stood behind Elliot now, resting a hand upon each of his shoulders to guide him forward. When he drew close, the shape in the sphere reared backward, then propelled itself forward, lunging toward the inner surface of the sphere and striking it hard. He couldn't help but cringe when the shadowy shape fell back, then reared again, striking with all its might. There was no mistaking its malignant intent. Had Elliot not been transfixed, he would have seen a look of alarm spread briefly across the queen's face.

"Perhaps you have seen quite enough of your old nemesis," Queen Ulricke suggested almost anxiously as they turned to leave the crypt. "But rest assured, Elliot, that any wrongs done by him to you and yours were not of my command nor by my bidding. Come," said the queen, her tone once again gracious, "for I have one more crypt to show you!"

The last suit of armor stood fully as tall as the rest, but the blade of its sword bore no black flame. When Queen Ulricke spoke the magic word, Elliot was surprised to find the crypt beyond was in total darkness. The hundreds of black candles had not yet been lit, and the sphere within was empty.

Queen Ulricke of Lorinshar bent down to fix Elliot with her most bewitching gaze, even as her lips slowly formed an enticing smile. "This can be yours, Elliot! That suit of armor, there upon the pedestal, can be your very own, and that sphere can serve as a perpetual link between you and me, allowing us to communicate, even as you begin a new life of adventure, the like of which you have never dreamed of! For Elliot, I desire you to be my ninth Shadow Knight!"

Conflicting emotions took possession of him then, each struggling for supremacy. Fear was there certainly, but pride was mingled in as well, for by far the most powerful and compelling person he had ever met desired to employ him in her service. There was also anticipation, the thought of the limitless might that a Shadow Knight would possess. He determined that he would not be an evil Shadow Knight, but a good one, seeking wrongs to right in whatever interwoven world the queen dispatched him to.

Queen Ulricke read Elliot's mind then, for her smile softened and grew more lovely still. She pulled him closer, her arm protectively about his shoulders. Her voice was hushed as though she were conveying a great confidence. "You are destined to be the one, Elliot! So forsake your absurd quest, your toy rings, your simpering faeries, and your little childish games!"

The orb upon the silver chain about her neck expanded all the more, and the purple flames within fluctuated hypnotically. "Simply swear an oath of loyalty to me and give up your trinket, for only then can I open the gates of countless worlds to you, and bestow nearly infinite power upon you!"

Elliot was deep in thought, faced with the most momentous decision of his life. He hesitated. The queen paused, her forceful gaze once again locked upon his own. "Well, Elliot, have you come to a decision?" she asked presently, her voice smooth and persuasive. The room was filled with swirling spells—a fog of magical incantation that dampened his resolve and perplexed his mind.

"Do not fear the process," intoned the queen. "After suitable incantations I shall simply hold out my hands to you, and your etheric double will step out from your body as if it were an old suit of clothes! Nothing could be easier!"

Elliot's eyes eloquently expressed his anguish, for he was torn. "I can't! I just can't! Don't you see, Your Majesty," he blurted at length, his anguished voice finally breaking from the emotions that were overwhelming him. "I will not forsake Victoria. She is on her own dangerous quest because of me!"

Then the queen smiled sadly, her voice aggrieved, yet still understanding. "So you cannot forsake your friend! This same Victoria who mocks you and makes rude sport of you with her newfound companions! This same Victoria who calls you a weakling and a spineless fool—who imitates your every mannerism to amuse her new friends, who, I fear, have sadly replaced you in her regard!"

Queen Ulricke waved her elegant hand before his eyes and a swirl of pale mist appeared. It grew to take the form of a flattened circle. "Elliot, she has forsaken you—for she has carelessly abandoned her quest!"

And there, taking form and shape in the circle of mist, Elliot saw a snowy village scene where houses with diamond-paned windows, chimney pots, and high gables all nestled together in the softly falling snow. Then, his point of view shifted to the interior of a building, going past a sign that read BLACK SWAN INN.

At a table fairly brimming with good things to eat sat a burly man in an apron, a sharp-faced woman, and a portly man with a fringe of white hair. They were talking and laughing with Victoria like old friends. In a moment Victoria got up from the table. "And this is how Elliot embarks upon adventures!" she said, laughing as she assumed an expression of fearful timidity. "He's far too lazy to run, of course, that is, unless he senses danger—then he can run very well indeed! That's but one reason I despise him so!" Then she bowed as her companions laughed and clapped their glee.

The circle of mist dissolved into thin air, vanishing abruptly with a flick of Queen Ulricke's fingertip. "There is more as well," she said sadly. "But I haven't the heart to show you. Suffice it to say that Victoria and her new friends call any timid person they meet an 'Elliot'—and say to someone whom they deem cowardly, 'Don't be an Elliot!' hoping that the insult will shame them to bravery."

Tears were running down his cheeks, and his heart was leaden, but something rose within him, something that he had never dreamed he possessed. He bowed his head, attempting to recover himself.

"No!" he cried at last, blinking back his grief. "No! I don't believe you! And I don't want to swear loyalty to you—for you are wicked! Those little rooms are tombs, those boys who said yes to you are all dead, and you have imprisoned their spirits in those spheres! And I don't believe that it was the real Victoria in the mist, either!"

Elliot was not done. "And I think that the Shadow Knight—I mean Trevelyan—was just following your command, to get all the gemstones from the magic rings, and I don't believe that it was his idea to get Victoria's and mine, but that *you* told him to! The Faerie Queen told me that you don't want anyone else to have the power to cross between worlds! But I do believe that he is willful and strongminded—that once he tasted power he rebelled against you, and wanted the gemstones for himself because, unlike you, he needs those rings to cross between worlds!"

Queen Ulricke rose to a formidable height, and the light

in her orb flared menacingly. Her face was livid with fury. "So then, you filthy little brat, I have your answer at last! Then you deserve no token of my regard whatsoever, you spiteful little beast!" She fairly spat her words, her hands curling into claws, her eyes filled with hatred.

"You little churl! Victoria and all the others are right to despise you for the craven weakling you are. Even your own mother, before she died, often wished she was the mother of any boy but you. One day, down by the newsstand, she saw Stevie St. Michael with his mother, and she envied her for being the mother of a real red-blooded boy!"

Elliot knew his life was now likely forfeit. His voice was sad as he said, "You have my answer, Majesty. It is no!" Then he turned his back upon her, moving down the marble stairs from the dais.

The queen's rage grew as cold as ice. As he waited by the spell door, it dissolved of its own accord and once again he was in the clutches of her handmaidens, who, well gauging their sovereign's mood, gleefully scratched, dug, and pinched him with their filthy nails, clawing and raking his back, stomach, and sides as they took him once more into custody.

"Take him to the highest tower and feed him nothing but bread and water!" commanded the queen, her crimson eyes flaming. Then abruptly her voice softened, her eyes once again growing almost tender. "However, Elliot," she purred, "I am a forgiving monarch and not unreasonable. I will ask you again in the morning, for perhaps you will have come to your senses by then!

"And if you don't exhibit good judgment," said the queen softly, "a lingering death in my dungeons will be the best that awaits you!" Queen Ulricke waved her hand to dismiss Elliot and her handmaidens. Brynn and Sutton whispered awful things to him as they led up twisting staircases, taking him higher and higher to his tower prison.

Chapter 34

THE ICE DRAGON FLED blindly. With each stroke of his once-mighty wings he felt his strength ebbing. The power that enabled him, an undead thing himself, to maintain his physical likeness was fading. His only thought was to place as much distance as possible between himself and that terrible child. His darkness and coldheartedness were being counterbalanced by an ancient magic, activated by the artistry of Victoria's dance and amplified a thousandfold by the ring she bore.

He was rapidly approaching the village of Widdershins. The Ice Dragon's batlike wings were faltering as he peered below, glimpsing his own huge shadow darting over the moonlit rooftops. He circled the village a time or two, viewing from his great height the crooked streets, the homes and shops—scenes revealed most clearly in the round pools of light cast by the streetlamps. It was very late and candles shone in only a few windows. The Ice Dragon was feeling truly wretched now and his strength was failing fast. He determined he would fly over the Pomfret Workhouse, for it invigorated him to glide through the cloud of human misery that floated up from its dismal courtyards. It was then he first noticed that all was not well with the aerodynamics of his flight.

The Ice Dragon's vast shadow loomed larger and larger over the rooftops in the moonlight as he wheeled round, spiraling in ever tighter circles, descending lower toward the clustered buildings, his bulk all the more colossal by compare. The rooftops were suddenly very near indeed.

A GRAND FEAST was in full sway in the banquet hall of the Pomfret Workhouse. Clericor Demyin and Lord Primvet were clothed in their formal robes for the occasion—garments trimmed in scarlet and gold. Vidal and Nastya were among their guests, as were the heartless owners of the bakeries, inns, and butcher shops that employed orphans as free labor, exploiting them perpetually in indentured servitude.

The feast they were celebrating was called the setting feast, in which the taskmasters were rewarded. Even now, lots were being cast to see which child would be chosen from the haggard throng to toil at the Black Swan Inn, then when the time was right, perhaps be chosen for sacrifice for the betterment of all Widdershins.

Vidal and Nastya were seated in the choicest places of honor. All the guests were sumptuously reclining upon cushions of the finest satin and plushest velvet. Braziers of fragrant wood burned in the corners, banishing the chill. There were food and wine aplenty and the guests had been amusing Clericor Demyin and Lord Primvet with tales of the deprivations to which they subjected the children entrusted to their care.

Suddenly, Nastya paused, her cunning face expressing momentary alarm. She had raised her glass to her lips—but she did not drink. Instead she turned to her husband.

"Vidal, did you hear that?" she asked. Vidal paused; he was eating a flavorful stew of mussels and prawns boiled in a sauce composed of heavy clotted cream, white wine, and scallions. It had been served from a silver tureen and he dabbed at some of the sauce that had gathered at the corner of his lips with his lace napkin before replying.

"I thought that perhaps I did hear something, my love," he rumbled agreeably.

Seated across the table from Vidal and Nastya were the butcher from the Red Boar Inn and his gimlet-eyed wife—a heartless twosome who had very nearly worked three of their orphans to death. They thought they heard something as well, perhaps a whistling, rushing sound, as if a storm was bearing down upon them from the depths of the Great Frozen Inland Sea.

Lord Primvet beamed indulgently at their foolishness and Clericor Demyin guffawed. "Bah!" he sneered. "I would say that it's simply the wretched workhouse brats blubbering because their food rations have been reduced yet again—if our banquet hall were not situated across the courtyard, well away from their noise and smell. For times are hard, as you know well, and when even the best of us find it necessary to make certain sacrifices from time to time—why shouldn't those wretches experience want?" And with that he winked his praise to the Red Boar butcher and his wife as he took a large bite of succulent lamb.

The governor of the Pomfret Workhouse was seated beside his pampered wife, her pudgy little hands sporting ruby and emerald rings and her fine bonnet alone worth four times the combined monies spent to feed and clothe the occupants of the workhouse. He helped himself to another scrumptious piece of breaded veal, while his wife purred, "It will serve them well! For they are so ungrateful despite all we do!"

She beamed delightedly at a pale green escargot jiggling upon her tiny fork, dripping lemon butter as she held its fat rounded shell in her other hand, clasping it delicately in engraved silver tongs. She popped the snail into her mouth with a beatific smile of satisfaction.

"And we have the perfect gift for you, Nastya! I do so hope that our candidate's lot is cast." The governor's wife chortled gleefully, while smiling fondly at the table where her daughter Darcy sat haughtily between her two best friends, Hortense Demyin and Tasha Primvet.

"She is a skinny, sallow-cheeked little thing that our Darcy was good enough to take in hand and attempt to do something with—to no avail, of course. It seems that the nasty creature is still cross with Darcy for taking the framed portrait of her father—a ne'er-do-well who died of consumption this winter past—but really there is no place for distraction at the Pomfret Workhouse, is there? And besides, our Darcy needed the frame to display her etchings!

"Despite whatever measures we take with the girl, she just becomes more recalcitrant—though we endeavor to instill . . ."

Here she stopped in midsentence, her voice fading in sudden alarm, for now the sound was unmistakable. Nobody in the Realm of Winter Night had ever heard a train, but if they had, the sound would have reminded them very much indeed of a large freight—the kind requiring several mammoth locomotives to draw it up a long grade. Whatever it was, it bore down upon them at a very high rate of speed!

The sentries hurried for the doors as the room fell silent. The only sound was a mighty rushing that was soon shaking the huge building to its foundations. Fine vessels of silver and porcelain clinked and trembled as they skittered across the tablecloth. Wine sloshed from toppled goblets.

And so it was that the Ice Dragon finally lost the ability to maintain flight—for his power was utterly undone. He tumbled head over claw from the sky, veering into a steep and uncontrolled dive. He was now hurtling with tremendous velocity directly down toward the tarnished copper dome high atop the largest structure in the enclosure that comprised the Pomfret Workhouse.

Just above the moonlit dome of the banquet hall, he used his last ounce of strength to spread his wings once more—but he waited a moment too long. Chairs tumbled over as panic-stricken guests sprang to their feet, unsteady on besotted legs. The building was shaking as though it was undergoing an earthquake, and toppling candlesticks were setting table linens ablaze. The last thing Nastya ever did was open her mouth to scream.

A split second later the bulk of the Ice Dragon crashed upon the roof with cataclysmic force. A horrifying roar sounded for miles, cascading through the narrow twisting streets. The noise seemed to go on and on forever. From the lamplit quay—whence they had taken Victoria out to die— the sound echoed like a thunderclap out into the breadth of the Great Frozen Inland Sea, to reverberate back and forth again in a succession of hollow booms.

The building was utterly demolished, even its thickest timbers broken like matchsticks. What had been the banquet hall of the Pomfret Workhouse became a sinking molten crater from which black flames writhed and twisted, roaring heavenward in showers of glowing sparks—until at long last there was naught left to consume. The conflagration slowly subsided, collapsing inward upon itself—strangely without its eager flames or even the falling embers ever once touching the workhouse dormitories, nor the many shops and houses nearby, where pale, sickly children lived, forced to work long and hard for meager sustenance.

As Victoria stood gazing at the orb in amazement, she became aware that the phantom cathedral had transformed again into the ballet theater, packed with guests who were slowly regaining their senses. To Victoria, standing alone on the stage, they appeared lost and bewildered. The gravity of what she had just accomplished overwhelmed her—and she fell down in a dead faint.

When she came to, she was reclining on a couch in Paracelsus' study with Henriques, Violet, Constance, the Albino Contessa, and Paracelsus himself gazing down at her anxiously. She wondered for a moment if her unexpected triumph over the Ice Dragon was just a dream, brought on by anxiety about her performance in the ballet. But then she spotted another face peering down at her—it was Aeron, still small of stature and perched upon Constance's shoulder. He flew toward Victoria on bright translucent wings. She greeted him affectionately, welcoming him with great relief.

"You have done well, Victoria," he exclaimed, pride in her evident in his voice. "You have fulfilled your quest and obtained the Orb of Ice!"

Victoria sat up hurriedly. "The orb! Where is it?"

"Be calm, child, for you have just been through a great ordeal," the Albino Contessa said gently.

"Your orb is safe," said Paracelsus, handing it to her. As she held it, they all beheld the orb in awe, for it was constantly changing hue—from a pale, almost transparent blue to vivid cobalt. It also fluctuated in size, shrinking from a diameter of three inches to barely the size of a marble, and then as they watched spellbound, it grew larger again until it was the size of an apple, weighing heavily upon Victoria's palm.

Aeron smiled. "It is quite impossible to carry a magic orb in a knapsack or in one's hand, Victoria, so I'll show you the best way to accommodate it. Some magic rings and some orbs are actually made for each other, and it's no coincidence that this technique often works very well."

"Do show me at once, please!" Victoria begged, with just a tinge of impatience creeping into her voice. "For it is getting heavier with each passing second!"

Aeron instructed Victoria to hold her ring hand flat, palm downward, so that the stone in her ring faced up. Then he told her to position the orb above the stone in her ring, and to simply let go of it. She eyed him suspiciously, fearing the heavy orb might damage the gemstone in her ring after bouncing from her knuckles to shatter upon the floor. But Aeron was insistent, and she complied at length, gingerly holding it above her ring, and reluctantly releasing it. She was braced, ready at a moment's notice to catch it before it plummeted to the floor—but there was no need. There was a searing flash and Victoria saw that the orb had vanished!

"Where is it, Aeron?" she asked anxiously. "Do tell me what has become of it! Is it safe?"

"It has been temporarily absorbed into your ring's gemstone, which functions as a sort of matrix for storing magical energy," Aeron replied.

"But why does my ring feel no heavier?" Victoria inquired, wiggling her fingers doubtfully.

"Hold your hand above the gemstone, and you will see— No, not like that, rather hold it cupped and ready for grasping!"

Victoria did as she was told. There was another flash and the orb was resting in her grasp once again. This time she did not hesitate, but let go of it a second time and it fell to disappear, magically reabsorbed into her ring.

"There's someone else who wishes to speak to you, Victoria," announced Paracelsus, and the group gathered round her parted to reveal Lord Enraldorn, looking much recovered from the ravages of the Ice Dragon's spells. He bowed low and thanked her profusely for saving him, his court, and his kingdom.

Victoria remembered the manners she had been taught at Prosingham Academy and curtsied in return, declaring that although she didn't really know the mechanism of its accomplishment, she had done it gladly and was delighted to be of service. Then she made all of the concerned onlookers smile when she declared she was positively famished and if it would not be rude to ask, might she possibly have a bit of supper?

Henriques gladly fetched some of her favorite things from the kitchens. As meddlesome as this child could be, she was his favorite of all their guests and he was overjoyed that she was alive. After all, it was all due to Victoria that any of them had survived the evil that had menaced them.

Chapter 35

ELLIOT STAGGERED as the handmaidens gave him a shove propelling him through the doorway of his tower prison. The door clanged shut behind him and the key grated in the lock as they sealed him in. The cell was bleak—spartan in the extreme, with walls and floor composed entirely of close-fitting stone blocks. There were pillars looming all about the circumference of the cell, and in one corner a heaping pile of straw served as a bed. Beside the bed stood a wooden stool with a dented basin containing drinking water. The crooked handle of a dipper protruded from the basin. An iron ring, suspended from a chain, dangled from the center of the domed ceiling.

A thick clump of rushes, dipped in tallow and bound together, had been thrust through the ring and lit to serve as a crude lighting fixture. The rushlight wavered and smoked, dripping bits of hot tallow on blackened fragments of old rushes littering the floor below. Elliot could tell the cell had been used to hold other prisoners. He wondered if perhaps the boys who had chosen to become Shadow Knights had spent their last night in human form in this very cell, before yielding to the queen's demand. Elliot also wondered if other boys still had spent their very last night here, remaining courageous—refusing to submit to the queen's service—and what fate befell them.

What had gone through their minds as they watched the rushlight sputter, casting surreal shadows in the gloom? Elliot finally succeeded in pushing such thoughts from his mind and he went to the basin to splash water on his face and hands. Brynn's and Sutton's filthy nails had pinched, prodded, and tore at him all the way to his cell, and he felt soiled and befouled. After he had washed, he felt a good deal better— "pounds better straightaway"—as his friend Victoria Deveny would have said.

Elliot thought that he heard high-pitched squeaking noises, and he strained his eyes, peering upward into the darkness. At last he finally glimpsed bats wheeling among the pillars and alighting upon the inner surface of the dome. He watched them scramble awkwardly, upside down, across the stone to a tiny gap through which they escaped into the night. It made him fervently wish that he could so easily cheat fate!

He inspected his straw bed, and saw from up close that it was damp and filthy. He doubted that his jailers ever bothered to change it. He brushed away the uppermost bit of dirty straw, and to his horror, saw large black beetles scurrying rapidly, worming deeper into the crumbling mass. Elliot shuddered in disgust, but he might have done more than shudder had he known they were flesh-eating beetles! It was going to be a very long night indeed.

Elliot peered about his cell in the dancing shadows cast by the rushlight. In a futile gesture he moved to the door and tried the latch, but of course it would not budge, not even the slightest bit. He abandoned the idea of sleep and paced about his cell. He was very nearly three-quarters of the way round when he discovered a small doorway with a pointed capstone of carved stone, hidden behind a thick pillar. To his disappointment, the doorway was sealed solid with brick and mortar, but as he probed it with his fingertips, something amazing occurred. For the stone of his ring flared brightly on his finger, and as it did, the bricks and mortar melted away. His magic ring had opened a way of escape before him!

He had to stoop very low to slip beneath the arch, and he crept forward slowly, feeling the way cautiously with his hand outstretched so he wouldn't collide with anything. He went very carefully, groping forward with his leading foot in case the passage led to a gaping pit.

Even at this great height—in one of the topmost spires of Pendrongor—Elliot was astonished to find that the wall was incredibly thick. The curve of the passageway penetrated it in a flattened S shape that was especially narrow at the curves. The floor of the passage was uneven as well, and he stumbled several times before finding himself—to his surprise and delight—standing out beneath the stars upon a tiny stone balcony.

When he peered over the parapet his hair very nearly stood on end. There would be no escape that way! Nearly one thousand feet below lay the walls and pinnacles of the lower citadel. Off to one side high above loomed the smooth stone curve of Pendrongor's central spire. On the other side, nearly six hundred feet below, was the broad expanse of the Garden of the Night, the pallor of its trees and statues unmistakable.

Beyond the dizzying precipices of the craggy mountainside lay a vast dark sea. It was quiet and still, like a mysterious shadow in the near distance. One of the smaller moons was waning, and it lay upon its side, low on the horizon, casting just enough light for Elliot to see some of the sea's features. He could glimpse tiny bits of light reflecting off the distant ebb and flow of its waves, but all about its shores was only desolation.

The great expanse of water that so transfixed Elliot was the Silent Sea. No swimming fish, no shellfish, and no plant could live in its depths or about its shores, and no life-form whatever dared drink from it, for the Silent Sea had been blighted—rendered lifeless long ago by Queen Ulricke's spell of doom. She regarded the Silent Sea as her northern bulwark. Its waters were so poisonous that were any invaders to attempt passage by ship, they would be overcome by deadly vapors long before reaching the other side.

Indeed, it is said that such ships are adrift still, out upon the far reaches of the Silent Sea, their crews stone-cold dead upon their decks—overcome by the deadly sea, long before they could ever reach the borders of the queen's realm and attempt her overthrow.

Elliot summoned all his courage to peer over the balcony railing once more, this time leaning well forward. He thought he had glimpsed the lantern-topped tip of a mainmast when he first peered over; now he was certain. Three hundred feet below bobbed the rakish black hull and furled red sails of Captain Ransom's pirate ship—the very ship he had first seen while in the throes of fever out on Bogmon Moor.

The pirate ship was fastened to an aerial mooring post protruding from a lower balcony, which also served as its docking pier. Elliot saw some of the crewmen moving about upon its decks. The sails were furled to the yardarms now, but the Jolly Roger ensign still waved from high above the crow's nest on the topmast. The pirate ship swayed at its mooring as the wind changed direction to whisper and swirl in turbulent crosscurrents about the spires of Pendrongor.

Elliot sat down in a corner of the balcony, resting his elbows on his knees as he gazed mournfully out over the Silent Sea. In the lopsided moonlight, under the crimson stars, it did somehow retain some of its old beauty—beauty it had long ago when it was a lovely living sea and had another name.

He watched the ripple of its distant waves far below, swelling upon tides that still moved and expanded the lifeless waters. He watched until, despite his fear and apprehension, his eyelids grew heavy. At last his head sagged forward and he fell fast asleep. In the room behind him, through the stone passage, the rushlight burned out in a puff of black smoke and falling ash, leaving his empty cell in darkness as beetles squirmed and writhed in the filthy straw mattress.

Elliot was troubled by harrowing dreams featuring dank dungeons, where long clawlike hands constantly scratched and tore at him. And then it seemed he heard voices and a hubbub of commotion, and he sensed a looming shape above him. A familiar voice kept repeating his name. "Elliot! Elliot!

Wake up! We have precious little time, and we must make our escape! Do wake up. Oh, please do! You must!"

He came groggily to his senses. When he cautiously raised his head to brush the sleep from his eyes, his heart gave a leap of joy, for Sindl was there beside him! Her lovely voice was welcome to his ears, though her expression was one of worry and dismay. A soft blue radiance was cast all about her and her wings vibrated, trembling in the air, as if she was ready for instant flight.

To his surprise he noted she was of full stature and not tiny as she had been at the window of Deirdre's cottage. But her voice and manner still conveyed great urgency. "It seems that the spells Ulricke cast around her realm have been weakened—for Victoria has succeeded in defeating the Ice Dragon, thus lessening the power of his protégée," she explained. "That is why I have been able—at long last—to finally struggle through to you."

"Oh, Sindl!" Elliot cried, joyfully rising up on his knees to embrace her. "I thought you had forgotten me!"

Sindl was tugging at his sleeve. "I would never purposely abandon you, Elliot, and I tried several times to aid you, but Queen Ulricke weaves a powerful web of enchantment all about her realm! But come! We haven't much time and we must get away!"

As Sindl helped him toward the railing, an incredible sight met his gaze. A snow-white ship was moored there waiting! It was a small ship and Elliot could tell by its extreme loveliness and the graceful lines of its construction that it had been fashioned by faerie shipwrights. It had fluid sweeping curves, a high swan-shaped prow, and tall stern decks. It had but a single mast and he noticed a very strange thing about its sail.

The sail hung slack and limp, even though strong winds were now whipping about the sides of Pendrongor. The winds moaned across the stones and through the balcony railings, streaming Sindl's hair across her face. But apparently the faerie ship's sail responded only to the winds of the Faerie Realm, and was not subject to the breezes or the tempests of any other.

Elliot had been terrified that anyone awake upon the deck of the pirate ship below would spot the faerie ship. But now, scarcely one hundred feet below the hull of the faerie ship stretched a featureless floor of fog. He also worried that his escape would be glimpsed from windows in the spires above—but beyond the top of the faerie ship's mast lay a thick ceiling of cloud. It had a slight crimson cast, due to the red stars illuminating the night sky beyond.

A vast aerial wonderland stretched out over the Silent Sea, before Elliot's incredulous gaze. Obviously a powerful magical enchantment was at work, for an endless white expanse lay before him, its ceiling composed of cloud and its floor fashioned of fog, with occasional towering pillars of mist joining them out in the far distance.

The faerie ship bobbed gently, floating just above the railing. A single white gangplank angled steeply up to an entrance port in its bulwarks. Sindl practically dragged Elliot to the gangplank in her urgency, but when they reached it he paused. It was so narrow and there was a yawning chasm on each side. So the faerie took flight, hovering behind Elliot, reaching down to grasp him under the arms, and flew him onto the ship so quickly he barely had time to be startled.

They quickly pulled the gangplank up after them—but at that precise moment there was a loud clamor back within Elliot's cell. "They must have been warned that I have come to rescue you!" Sindl's eyes were wide with consternation as she darted quickly back across the deck to the helm.

Elliot heard the sounds of the dungeon guard searching his cell and he knew it would not take the guards long to find the entrance to the balcony passage. He was despondent at the thought of being snatched away to undergo some horrible fate—just when rescue was imminent. But the two mooring lines magically uncoiled, whisking silently up onto the deck of the faerie ship and allowing them to make their escape.

Sindl took up the helm, and as soon as she gave it a turn, the ship responded instantly, gliding away from the balcony, pointing its swan-shaped prow into the night, away from the Tower of Pendrongor. Even though the wind blew from the opposite direction, the sail of the ship bloomed full of enchanted wind from Faerieland. And then they were off, sailing silently and rapidly away, just as the enraged handmaidens, accompanied by members of the dungeon guard, appeared upon the balcony.

Elliot had moved back to the high sterncastle to be close by Sindl, and as he peered behind them, he saw Brynn and Sutton raise their arms, curling their awful hands into threatening claws. He could tell from the angry expressions transfixing their faces that they were chanting spells—summoning dark incantations in an effort to drag the faerie ship back into their clutches.

The faerie ship quivered, then paused, slowing its progress through the air. Sindl was dismayed when she felt themselves being drawn ever so slowly backward. And then Elliot's enchanted ring flared to brilliant life, for its stone shone like a beacon, and the lamps upon the stern brightened as though a powerful counterspell had been unleashed. The ship strained and struggled against the force that was pulling them back, and all at once it broke free, its sail once again ballooning full of wind.

When Elliot glanced back again he was amazed to see that the Tower of Pendrongor had already grown small, dwindling away, needle sharp in the distance. Sindl asked Elliot which direction they should take to fulfill his quest and he thought carefully for a moment, as the deck of the white ship heaved beneath their feet. At length he decided. "We will make for the dragon pinnacle in the uttermost north," he declared, grown suddenly firm and resolute.

"Very well then," she replied, adjusting the tiller a few degrees to starboard. "We're off! To the dragon's pinnacle we shall go!" And so they went, their course leading them straight out across the Silent Sea.

The ship sped round them, gliding in long curving sweeps between fields of cloud stalactites. The silver lamp upon the topmast appeared as a diffuse blue illumination, scraping along the underside of the fog. Occasionally they could see the sparkling waves of the Silent Sea through rare gaps in the floor of fog, and rarer still, breaks in the ceiling of cloud above would open to permit intermittent glimpses of red stars in the vault of the heavens. Sindl remained at the tiller, her face serious as she expertly guided the lovely ship through the night, its single sail brimming full of enchanted wind.

Elliot began to feel a bit more at ease on the high stern deck, as it heaved and bobbed beneath him. They had just made a broad arcing turn, to sweep round a majestic pillar of cloud, and he was gazing backward out beyond the stern lamps when the sight that met his eyes filled him with fear.

The sleek black hull of the pirate ship was visible in the distance! It was in hot pursuit, and its bloodred tiers of sails were as full of wind as the faerie ship's own. Elliot tugged urgently on Sindl's sleeve. She turned round to look, and her eyes widened in alarm. "It's Captain Ransom's pirate ship," he said heavily.

Sindl sighed. She had seen the other ship moored at the Tower of Pendrongor and had worried it might follow them. She grew quiet as she concentrated on her work at the tiller, steering their ship artfully into a vast pinnacle of towering cloud. Both ships were moving swiftly, betwixt the clouds and fog. "Hold on, Elliot! It gets turbulent in the cloud pillars and I don't want to lose you!"

He gave heed to her warning as the faerie ship abruptly entered the tower of cloud with a heart-stopping plunge, a buffeting sensation, and a series of bumps as changes in both air and temperature made their ride anything but smooth. Long tendrils of fog swept wraithlike across the deck of the faerie ship until even the lantern high atop the mast disappeared altogether, and the stern lamps appeared as vague circles in the thickening fog.

And then, out they sped into the open night once again, racing along through a forest of great cloud pillars. Elliot kept careful watch behind them and had just begun to say, "I think we've left the pirate ship behind," when the dark interloper tore out from a towering pinnacle off to their right and bore straight for them.

He clung to one of the stay ropes, his knuckles white as the deck of the faerie ship tilted sharply when Sindl performed a series of evasive maneuvers. "We'll lose them yet, Elliot!" she called, shouting over the sound of the wind as it sang through the rigging and billowed in the sail.

She gave the tiller a quick turn to port and the faerie ship dipped downward, attaining a steep angle of descent. Elliot hung on for dear life, but as frightened as he was, he was worried still more by the dark deadly shape that swerved to plunge low and match them, and it was gaining fast!

They suddenly entered a cool and quiet world down in the layer of fog, with long tendrils clinging to the mast and also to both Elliot and his faerie companion. Then, directly below, scarcely two hundred feet down, the sparkling waves of the Silent Sea materialized, and Sindl pulled sharply up on the tiller to slow their descent. "I don't dare take us too low, for the waters of the Silent Sea are poisonous—and merely inhaling the spray from those breakers would render us senseless if we get too close!"

Elliot risked a look over the rail to see the shadow of the faerie ship darting over the waves. And then he involuntarily ducked low, because the black hull of the pirate ship materialized as a menacing shape of distorted shadow, directly above and behind them. It was swiftly drawing closer, and Sindl was fearful that the pirates intended to ram their mast and snap it off altogether. The faerie ship heeled hard to starboard again as she steered it into a rapid climbing turn—and once more all was muffled and gray as they rose up through the layers of fog. They then found themselves again in the vast aerial cathedral among surreal layers of fog and cloud, darting betwixt tall vaporous pillars while the pirate ship rose up behind them in pursuit.

Suddenly the pirate ship heeled hard to port, and all its sails went slack and limp. Elliot didn't have long to wonder what had happened, because he heard Sindl call his name, her urgent voice sounding fearful amid the whisper of the wind in the rigging and the loud billowing of the sail overhead. Her eyes were wide with dismay and she was pointing out beyond the swan prow of their ship.

There, well out ahead, poised motionless in the air, waited a hovering formation of at least fifty phantom ships!

They were ragged, ancient, their sails all tatters, yet luminous still. Their sleek hulls seemed to have only half materialized and Elliot could see pale banners snapping from the tips of their mainmasts and even the ghostly forms of crewmen standing vigilant watch upon their decks. At first Elliot thought that hope was lost, for if the pirates didn't apprehend them the ghost ships would, but then he remembered that the pirate ship had abruptly ceased its pursuit when it saw the spectral fleet looming ahead.

Sindl grew very quiet at the helm, as though she couldn't quite decide if the ghostly fleet was friend or foe. But then she made up her mind at last, and daring all, steered the swan prow of the faerie ship straight for the ethereal ships. Elliot held his breath and waited as they drew nearer.

To his profound relief, the ships parted before them. Their faerie ship was permitted to glide through the very center of the ghostly fleet.

The pale forms of the officers and crewmen, still in ancient naval uniforms, gazed down from the high decks of the ghost ships, regarding them with intense curiosity. Both Elliot and Sindl cringed under the penetrating scrutiny of their undead gaze. And then, in a few moments, they swept safely past, moving well beyond the fleet, as its ranks closed once again— this time composing a defensive formation to shield the way behind them.

Elliot's heart pounded as he watched the ghost ships fade into the pillared distance of the aerial cathedral. "Perhaps these casualties of the Silent Sea consider any enemy of Queen Ul-ricke a friend to them," Sindl said thoughtfully.

And so the faerie ship continued on due north toward the dragon pinnacle. When dawn came crimson, the fog and the clouds quickly vanishing, they flew onward under the light of the sun. Sindl steered the ship on its course, its shadow tiny with distance as it darted across the deceptively sparkling brightness of the Silent Sea, now thousands of feet below their keel. There was no longer any sign at all of the pirate ship that had pursued them.

Chapter 36

VICTORIA WAS FEELING surprisingly well after her encounter with the Ice Dragon, and her mood was further improved by tidings that some of the children of the Pomfret Workhouse had taken to the streets of Widdershins and were liberating the other children.

She danced the *Saltatrix Angelus* to completion the very next evening, and was met with a standing ovation following the performance—applause that was as much for her banishment of the Ice Dragon as for the extraordinary grace of her technique.

Afterward the Yuletide Ballroom was opened, and all down the archways of the grand entrance hall the chandeliers were lit, one by one, and the throngs exited the ballet theater to stream merrily down the lamplit stairs beneath the falling snow to its cavernous open doors. The dancers were carried by liveried retainers as they entered the ballroom, still in their makeup and costumes—to the praise and accolade of the guests—though the dancers who portrayed the cohorts of the wicked lord took off their sinister masks, and it was deemed necessary to remove the angel dancers' large feathered wings in the press of the crowd.

At one end of the Yuletide Ballroom, a great log was ignited to crackle and blaze in the huge hearth. The fireplace was graced with the coats of arms of both Paracelsus and the Albino Contessa—carven skillfully, combined in the stonework. At the other end of the hall, a ninety-foot-tall living yule tree stood splendidly beneath a glass cupola set in the roof so it could grow unimpeded. It was illuminated with colored lamps and decorated with faceted jeweled ornaments—which added a magical quality to the sparkling bursts of light.

And so the dancing began, lasting well into the wee hours, and Victoria was deliriously happy, surrounded as she was by her dear friends. She forgot for the moment about the peril soon to come.

The next morning her elation abruptly ended, for Paracelsus announced solemnly over breakfast that she must leave the Realm of Winter Night that very day. She was relieved to hear that according to a messenger of the Faerie Queen, Elliot was near completion of his quest—but dismayed by the news that awful things had crept into Elliot's world, and the Shadow Knight was many times more powerful than when they had last faced him. Constance shuddered with horror at what her friend must face.

It was decided that Paracelsus, Constance, and the Albino Contessa would bring Victoria to the southern end of the

Great Frozen Inland Sea—where the faerie gate first materialized above Widdershins. But only Aeron would accompany her through its portal to Faerieland.

Scarcely an hour later Victoria stood in the courtyard of Kalingalad, ready for departure. Violet and Henriques had already said their affectionate good-byes, and both had tears in their eyes as they watched the jeweled sleigh carriage draw away from the palace. In a moment it was out upon the ice of the sea.

Aeron placed a powerful enchantment upon the carriage that would speed them safely to their destination. Of course Victoria could not guess at the consequences when faerie enchantments mingled with the magical powers of her ring and the tremendous mystical properties of the Orb of Ice.

The sleigh gathered speed, its horses tossing their manes as they fell into a synchronized stride. Victoria was in the middle of marveling to Constance at how majestic the thunder of their hooves sounded upon the ice—when she saw a puzzled look sweep across her friend's features. She leaned forward, listening intently. Victoria realized that she no longer heard hoofbeats and at first she thought they had stopped altogether, or that they had entered a field of deep drifts that muffled all sound.

Victoria experienced the most peculiar twinge in the pit of her stomach and turned to look out her window. To her astonishment, she saw the trackless ice of the Great Frozen Inland Sea far below them—for the sleigh carriage was airborne!

Victoria grew concerned for the horses, wondering aloud if they might be frightened, and she insisted upon opening the door, even considering stepping precariously out onto the high curving runners to check. She pretended not to hear the Albino Contessa's suggestion that they send Aeron on a quick flight about the carriage to report back, and she alarmed them all greatly when she leaned far out, the wind tearing at her cloak and whipping her hair about her face. Aeron braced his feet on the edge of the doorway, holding on to her for dear life—desperately hoping she would regain her senses and come in again before the wind plucked them from the carriage!

Victoria practically tumbled back in through the door as the wind slammed it shut behind her, only to be lightheartedly scolded by Paracelsus.

"The horses simply adore it!" she exclaimed, her cheeks flushed and smarting, her eyes bright and watering with wind tears. "They are still prancing proudly, and although their hooves are in contact with nothing but thin air, they are still magically drawing the carriage along and keeping us on course!"

Victoria and Constance sat fascinated, perched upon the edge of their seat, their eyes glued to the scenes flashing by far below. It wasn't long before Victoria saw something that astounded her. They were flying high above the fleet of petrified ships now, their shapes highlighted in stark relief in the deep contrast of moonlight. She gasped, unable to believe the evidence of her own eyes. For now—as impossible as it seemed—there were living crewmen aboard the ships!

As they watched in silence, they saw hundreds of men swarming the upper decks, out upon the yardarms, and in the crows' nests at the summit of the masts. Even the ice alongside the ships was dotted with tiny forms who had clambered down the rigging or lowered nets to descend onto the ground. They had kindled large bonfires and were waving at the magical sleigh carriage that turned in the moonlit air high overhead, its speeding shadow flitting over them like a swallow.

The carriage responded to an unspoken command, veering from its course to circle twice more about the fleet. Victoria and Constance gasped in wonder as the tiny forms far below doffed their hats and leaped into the air, while ever so faintly upon the wind came the sound of distant cheering.

"The fleet assembled ages ago to make war upon the Ice Dragon and he defeated them, but his destruction has lifted their enchantment," Paracelsus explained, "and many others have been set free as well."

"Victoria, they realize you are the one who conquered the Ice Dragon," observed the Albino Contessa. "For you have saved them—and though they don't know your name, they are grateful and will never forget!"

Victoria sat riveted, peering out her window. "I sensed something truly ghastly beneath those ships as I passed," she said softly. "They were full of phantoms after all. I am so glad they have come back to life and are flesh and blood once more!"

She paused thoughtfully before inquiring. "But why doesn't the sea thaw now that the Ice Dragon has been defeated?"

Aeron was silent for a time. "Now I think I understand what Queen Edwina once said," he said softly. "The Great Frozen Inland Sea is his only beautiful creation."

And so as the sleigh carriage swept round the great fleet for the last time, Paracelsus declared that he would dispatch a rescue party for the crewmen from the ships, and give them homes, perhaps dividing them among all the palaces. Indeed many of them eventually found homes in the village of Widdershins and adopted the orphans there.

As they drew near the place of Victoria's abandonment, she had a lump in her throat. "Will I ever be your guest again, do you suppose?" she inquired of the Albino Contessa with a catch in her voice. "And will I ever see my friends Violet and Henriques again?"

The Albino Contessa reached down to gently take Victoria's ring finger in her hand. "And what do you imagine this is for, child?" she asked, smiling softly, gently tapping the stone of Victoria's ring. "I have no doubt that you shall be our guest again, but perhaps we shall be entertained in your world first, for all gates between interwoven worlds open from both ends!"

By now the jeweled sleigh carriage was flying like the wind through the night as the leagues of distance sped past beneath them. The horses neighed, prancing with elation. Victoria, caught up in the spirit of the moment, felt her heart racing. It wasn't long before she saw the village of Widdershins and the lamplit ramp down which she had ridden to what she believed would be her certain doom.

And there far below, in the very center of the village, lay a large dark ring that still smoldered precisely where the banquet hall of the Pomfret Workhouse had once been, for there Vidal, Nastya, Clericor Demyin, and the Ice Dragon had all met their end.

The carriage was spiraling higher now. Victoria couldn't recognize the rooftop of the Black Swan Inn in the jumble of hundreds of high gabled buildings among the narrow twisting streets. If the Ice Dragon had still been alive, flying where they were now, he would have taken no pleasure in the air of the village—for what wafted up from its streets was now an atmosphere of happiness and joy.

At length they glimpsed the gate from the side window, its pristine white steps and high carven arch appearing like something from a dream. The sleigh carriage drew close alongside and came to a stop, its horses standing suspended in midair.

Victoria stepped down first, onto the stairs of the gate, closely followed by the contessa, Aeron, and Constance. Paracelsus brought up the rear. The guards welcomed them, relieved to see their kinsman Aeron once more.

And then came a moment of tears when a lump formed in every throat and hearts were heavy. Victoria reluctantly released the hands of her friends and ascended the last steps with Aeron. She paused before the archway to turn and wave. Then Victoria and Aeron stepped forward to vanish in a brilliant burst of light.

One really never gets used to this at all! Victoria thought as they abruptly changed worlds once again.

Chapter 37

"I think we've come to the end of the Silent Sea at last!" Sindl announced. She lashed the tiller in place with a length of mooring cord and they both went up into the prow, directly behind the swan's head, to stand lookout between its swept-back wings.

Sindl's faerie eyes were far keener than Elliot's, and certainly more suited to penetrating great distances—for at first he could see nothing. But within a few moments, he, too, spotted what appeared to be piles of red tinted cloud, off in the far distance. The scarlet sun of Lorinshar was lying low upon the horizon and suffused everything with a startlingly unearthly glow. Elliot realized that what he had taken for red clouds were actually great pinnacles of rock. Huge spires and sharp peaks loomed as they drew nearer the far shore. Soon the shadow of the faerie ship was hovering over the crumbled boulders and crags of the coast.

When Elliot glimpsed the dragon pinnacle it was certainly unmistakable! It loomed directly ahead, towering to an impossible height. Its sides were sheer, composed entirely of vertical cliffs and frightful precipices. The topmost spires strongly resembled an enormous red dragon rearing back upon its haunches, its tail wrapped about its feet, its wings uplifted behind, still partially folded. Its head was held high as though it were about to breathe a blast of flame.

Elliot gasped at the sight of it and stared closely, afraid for a moment that it was a live dragon, waiting there in place, ready to pounce. But as they drew nearer he could readily discern the combination of rock formations that made it appear so lifelike.

Sindl returned to the stern, while Elliot remained in the prow. He could tell they were very high indeed, because the air felt thin in his lungs and it was noticeably more difficult to draw breath after any exertion. He kept close watch as they slowly followed the curve of the pinnacle, sweeping rapidly around it. Sindl exercised the utmost care in her maneuvering—for she knew that were their delicate ship to collide with a jagged spur, it would spell disaster.

Elliot almost despaired of finding a ledge suitable for mooring. But then, when they were nearly three-quarters of the way round he glimpsed a stone pier extending out from the side of the pinnacle, directly ahead. It was nearly dark now, and he was surprised to see the pier illuminated with dozens of tall golden lamps burning with scarlet flames.

The pier even had stone mooring posts, set at precise intervals all along its length, and each post was fitted with an iron ring, apparently designed for flying ships to tie alongside. A long flight of smooth stone steps led up from the pier to an ornate archway—opening onto a partially enclosed stair gallery circling about a rocky crag before disappearing into a tunnel that had been bored through a bulwark of solid rock to penetrate into the unseen depths of the pinnacle.

Elliot shouted back to Sindl, excitedly pointing to the pier. She carefully steered up alongside, and the sail went slack, bringing them to a gentle bumping halt. The enchanted mooring cords slipped across the deck to knot themselves securely about the iron rings at bow and stern.

They stood at the railing, ready to step across to the pier, when suddenly a black shadow careened into view from round the pillar, dropping down upon them like a stone, plunging at high velocity, its ghastly red sails ballooning full of wind.

There was no time to flee in the faerie ship. Sindl clutched Elliot's hand and cried, "Jump, Elliot! Now!" and together they leaped across the dizzying space between the railing of the ship and the edge of the stone pier. Sindl's vibrating translucent wings compensated for the distance or Elliot would have missed his footing entirely. Barely a second later there came an awful crash as the heavy iron keel of the pirate ship smashed down onto the lovely faerie vessel, striking it a catastrophic blow amidships.

As Sindl and Elliot watched horror-stricken, the faerie ship crumpled and plunged down from the side of the stone pier, plummeting toward the distant base of the pinnacle. The magical mooring lines even uncoiled themselves from about the pillars to swirl down through the air, following after the broken hull as it disappeared from view.

But there was no time for mourning, for the pirate ship turned about and swept sharply round again—now making straight for the pier. There was only one thing for them to do and that was to flee. Sindl ran alongside Elliot, arm in arm, her wings radiant in the glow of the deepening sunset. As the pirate ship moored to the pier behind them, they heard shouting and cursing as its heavy gangplank trundled forward to crash onto the stones. Elliot and Sindl ran for all they were worth up the long flight of steps in the light of the red lamps. Elliot could tell the steps were ancient, for they were worn glassy smooth by the footsteps of centuries and the polish of countless storms.

It seemed as though the steps stretched on forever before them as the stairway curved, following the arc of the pinnacle. They passed through an archway nearly eighty feet high whose lintel posts were carved in the likeness of two warring dragons intertwined in high relief. The sound of cursing, the clatter of heavy boots on the stairs, and the ring of cutlass steel on the railings told them that the pirates were gaining rapidly. Once again Sindl grasped Elliot and lifted him into the air. She flew along, bearing him at a high rate of speed.

The passage turned abruptly and brought them up short before a door composed of hard black stone and covered with the closely spaced lines of a strange fiery script, each letter sparkling from deep within its engraving. Elliot and Sindl paused breathlessly before the door. The pirates were almost upon them now.

"It must be a spell door of some sort," said Sindl in dismay.

"I shall try to recall all the opening spells I know!" But even she feared it to be hopeless. Within seconds they would be in stabbing distance of two dozen pirate cutlasses.

Suddenly the stone door pivoted open of its own accord with an earthshaking rumble. The way deep inside the dragon pinnacle now lay open before them. Quick as a flash, both Elliot and Sindl darted inside, just as the door pivoted shut, closing in the pirates' faces.

A high corridor lined with lamps led upward before them. The rock walls of the passage took in the red lamplight and reflected it back again, scattering its rays in vivid spectrums of golden highlight. Elliot and Sindl walked onward, their voices hushed with awe. Neither of them knew what lay ahead and neither had any idea whatsoever how they would ever descend from the pinnacle without the aid of their faerie ship—for though Sindl could fly, it wasn't wise to traverse the skies of Lorinshar without additional protection.

Presently the passage began rising even more steeply and as it did a series of corkscrew turns began, twisting up into the very center of the pinnacle. At last they reached a great round doorway. They paused for breath, then with thudding hearts, stepped over the threshold to enter a vast cavern. Its high ceiling was upheld on mammoth pillars. In its center loomed a hoard of treasure, an enormous pile of coins, jewels, and gemstones of every type, size, and style imaginable.

And there, high above them, upon the very summit of the treasure hoard lay coiled a huge red dragon! Its long, heavily scaled body was wrapped about the peak of the pile at least three times. The dragon's tail was coiled about a pillar and its sharply pointed tip terminated just yards from where Elliot and Sindl stood in awestruck stillness.

The dragon's head was rearing high and its face with its elongated snout did in fact remind Elliot of a cross between a horse and a sea serpent. It had several horns protruding from its brow ridges and others below its chin gave it a bearded appearance. Its scales looked as smooth and impenetrable as plate armor. Both its hind feet and forefeet were equipped with massive claws, each a good deal thicker than one of Elliot's arms. Its black and red tinted wings were raised up behind its head, as if ready for immediate flight.

Elliot and Sindl stood stock-still, transfixed with fright, half expecting to be incinerated with a roaring blast of flaming dragon breath. They waited for the beast to move, but it did not. Soon they found themselves feeling foolish, wondering if perhaps it was simply a colossal carving.

They took a few tentative steps forward, when a small avalanche of goblets, crowns, and platters cascaded down one side of the pile. Sindl had barely uttered the words "Elliot, do be careful! I believe this is a living thing after all!" when the long serpentine neck abruptly extended and swept downward. The twenty-foot-long head of a live dragon tilted toward them. Its eyes were mingled crimson and pale yellow as it fixed them with a stare that was frightening to behold.

"What preposterous foolishness indeed," said the dragon. "Of course I am alive, or at least I've always suspected I was. And do be good enough in the future not to talk about one who is present as if he were an inanimate object!" As the dragon spoke, Elliot and Sindl were very grateful that it thoughtfully turned its head to one side, for smoke and crackling tongues of scorching flame accompanied each syllable it uttered.

"We are sorry, sir," Elliot said haltingly, "but everyone told us that there were no living dragons left, and so we despaired of ever actually meeting one. But we hoped you were real—real and alive—and well, too." He sincerely hoped he was not giving offense, or violating any dragon etiquette.

The dragon once again turned its neck to point its fire-breathing head to the side as it replied. "Dragons are not flighty creatures like most others—humans and faeries included. But time moves slowly for us, and when we reach adulthood we forsake the fire-breathing, pillaging ways of our youth to rest upon our treasure hoards and watch the ages of the world unfold. Do they expect me to take a constitutional each day just to prove my existence? If so, then I'd much prefer not to be believed in at all!"

Then the Fire Dragon lowered his head to scrutinize his visitors. Elliot and Sindl could hear the rumble of his breath and noticed that it smelled of hot coals. They realized at once that it would not do at all to lie to a fire-breathing dragon.

"And so," said the dragon. "What is your purpose here?"

"If you please, sir," said Elliot. "My world is under threat from a dreadful apparition. We call him the Shadow Knight. He began as one of Queen Ulricke's creatures, but his power grew until even she can no longer control him, and I believe she has actually come to fear him herself!"

The dragon shook his head. His motion was slow, so as not to startle them. "Such are the pitfalls of dark magic." He sighed. "And you would think that its practitioners might learn their lesson—but do go on!"

The dragon noticed that Sindl smiled at Elliot and laid her hand gently upon his arm as he continued. "He was stalking my friend Victoria Deveny and me, and when he came to seize us, my mother attempted to delay him so he threw a black orb at her and she was sucked in—and I'm afraid she is dead!"

Elliot couldn't go on, so Sindl finished for him. "Elliot's quest is to obtain the Orb of Fire." And here she hesitated for a moment before continuing. "We had heard that it belongs to you, sir, or has been entrusted to your guardianship. My queen tells us that the Orbs of Fire and Ice combined may wield enough power to defeat the Shadow Knight!"

"I know the Orb of Fire well," replied the dragon. "But I esteemed it to be but a trifle, a plaything—and you say it has great power? I must confess that I am astonished at this news. Imagine that! But of course you are most welcome to it, for all decent and reasonable dragons share freely of their treasure hoard—that is, if one is simply good enough to ask politely.

"I am certain that the Orb of Fire is somewhere close hereabouts. In fact, I recall glimpsing it, lying between a golden goblet and a ruby-encrusted tray, scarcely more than a hundred years ago when I last uncoiled for a nice stretch. If I recall correctly, it may lie quite near that pillar over yonder—no, just a bit to the right—yes, over there, close by the tip of my tail. Perhaps if you will be good enough to allow me." And here the great bulk of the dragon shifted, and he adjusted his position slightly, causing a minor avalanche to come tumbling down until Sindl and Elliot found themselves up to their knees in a king's ransom.

"I beg your pardon," said the dragon politely as his enormous head extended to overshadow them once again. Then he bent round, peering downward to where his tail was coiled about the pillar. The dragon dug with the claws of his hind leg, sweeping heaps of sparkling treasure aside until he penetrated down several feet into his hoard. "There! If you dig a bit more in that cleared area, perhaps, I think you will not be very far off," he observed cheerfully.

Elliot and Sindl gingerly and with many "beg your pardons" scrambled over the top of the dragon's tail, sliding down into the hollow he had created. They carefully moved aside gemstones, diadems, pendants, bracelets, silver bars, gold doubloons, pieces of eight, and many rings.

After nearly ten minutes of patient digging—with the dragon's head poised above them, gazing down intently—Sindl found it. "Here it is!" she cried triumphantly, raising her hand to hold a small red orb aloft. It flashed fire all about the immense chamber, turning its crimson hue all the more vivid. Even the semicircle of red lamps flared more brightly as she held it high in her upraised palm.

"Simply amazing!" exclaimed the dragon. "And you are most welcome to it, for as you can see, I have more treasure than I know what to do with!"

Quickly, even as the orb began expanding in size, Sindl showed Elliot how to store it in his ring. Elliot was astounded when he let it slip from his fingertips and saw it absorb into the ring's gemstone.

"There," said Sindl. "That's done. See how easy it is with a magic ring?"

"It is well that you didn't wait until it was three feet across, for it would have been a task indeed to lift it," remarked the dragon, arching his thickly armored brows.

Elliot was delighted to have completed his quest and obtained the Orb of Fire for battling the Shadow Knight. But he was reluctant to leave the presence of a real live dragon, and a friendly one at that. Realizing he'd likely not have such an opportunity again, he decided to ask the dragon a few questions.

"Sir, why are there so many lamps along the entrance pier and up the stair gallery?"

At length the dragon replied. "Well, if there are ever any faerie ships about, I desire them to come and moor at my pier to keep me company with news and tales of the world. As you have seen, my door is always open to faeries. But come to think of it, none have visited for ever so long. Perhaps the ancestors of the faeries living today knew of me, but at long last they simply forgot to tell their children's children. And they quite likely forgot me themselves and in time I was reduced to myth."

"Why are there so many lamps here as well?" Elliot inquired, ignoring an uncharacteristic warning glance from Sindl. "You could just breathe fire when you needed light, you know," he went on to suggest helpfully.

The dragon nodded, lowering his huge armored head down very close indeed, before replying in an almost sheepish tone. "That is true—but you see, I am just the tiniest bit afraid of the dark!"

Elliot was stunned that such a vast and powerful creature could have fears so like his own. Sindl changed the subject diplomatically, for she didn't want the dragon to be embarrassed, so she asked him her own question.

"Please, sir, we have no way to return across the Silent Sea, for a pirate ship rammed our vessel—and as far as we know, they may still be moored at your pier waiting for us."

The dragon replied readily. "You may both ride upon my back if you like, for I do so need the exercise. It's been nearly three hundred years since I last took flight, and if I don't fly again soon I may get rusty and crash into things as I go."

Both Elliot and Sindl were awestruck at both the dragon's generosity and the thought of what it would be like to ride upon his back. "And as for any pirates," the dragon went on, his voice suddenly becoming very sinister indeed, "why, they will quite rue the day they attacked my friends—of that you may be certain!"

At length it was time for them to depart. The dragon warned them to stand well back. They were glad they heeded his advice, for the uncoiling of his body caused a major avalanche to come spilling down all about them—even though they were now standing much farther away.

The dragon stretched his legs, raking his claws along the pile of treasure that had partially collapsed. Elliot and Sindl smiled to see him lower his head and scratch his chin upon one of the steeper piles—shutting his eyes and grunting with pleasure like a colossal hound. Elliot noticed tendrils of smoke curling up out of both his nostrils.

After he finished scratching and looked round, he gave vent to a deep rumbling growl of satisfaction and said, "I suppose I shall just have to rearrange all this when I return. But in fact I have been rather uncomfortable of late, for my bed has required adjustment for the last eighty years or so!" Then he opened his great batlike wings, which, when unfolded, practically filled the entire upper portion of the cavern.

Then the dragon lay flat, so they could climb upon his back. Of course Sindl had no difficulty, for she could fly, but Elliot found he needed to clamber up a high teetering treasure pile to use it as a sort of ladder. First the dragon told them they were sitting too far back, and that when he flapped his wings they would be instantly tumbled about, so he had them move up and sit astride the narrowest part of his neck, directly behind his head. Sindl sat behind Elliot, wrapping her arms about his waist, while he held on to one of the dragon's small twisted horns with both hands.

"Hang on tightly," warned the dragon as he crawled forward, causing cascades of treasure to fan out across the floor, spilling out into the shadowy galleries beyond the circle of pillars. Then he paused to utter a single magic word. Elliot and Sindl saw a door open silently before him in the rock, revealing the gaping mouth of a deep shaft, which sloped steeply downward into the darkness. Hot air came blowing up out of the shaft, and the scorching wind ruffled Elliot's hair and streamed Sindl's out behind her.

"Here we go, then!" said the dragon, pushing himself forward until he lay poised at the opening. Then, with a stomach-fluttering sensation of rapid, uncontrolled descent, they were off!

The dragon simply dropped, plummeting into the depths of the shaft, his batlike wings folded like a diving osprey. Elliot and Sindl both clung for dear life in the swooshing rush of their passage through the darkness. Finally they plunged out into the open air through a cavernous vent.

The dragon's enormous wings were beating fast, and their descent finally slowed as they leveled off barely a hundred feet from the boulder-strewn base. It was night, and the larger of the two moons had risen, casting its eerie light upon the landscape below. Sindl and Elliot hung on tightly as he flapped his wings in steep ascent, and then, as he gained altitude once more, he banked in a tight sweeping turn, swooping round the pinnacle, its sheer rock walls speeding past with a hiss of wind. When they were three-quarters of the way around they glimpsed the lamplit pier, but there was no sign of the pirate vessel.

The dragon inquired where they desired he take them, and Sindl asked if he would perhaps be good enough to bring them all the way to the portal of the high faerie gate, located above the southern mountains, where Elliot had first entered Lorinshar. The Fire Dragon nodded agreeably.

"Ah! Then it is to be just a short flight, you say. Well, I shall continue on for another two or three hundred leagues after I drop you off before I turn round. I daresay I feel much better already from the exercise!"

The Silent Sea passed rapidly by under the dragon's wings

as he flew tirelessly onward, the beat of his pinions and his breathing smoothly synchronized in a cadence of even rhythm. Elliot and Sindl were amazed at how little time it took them to recross the sea. It seemed scarcely an hour later they were fast approaching the coastline, for even though the faerie ship had been swift, nothing could match the velocity of dragon flight.

They decided it would be wiser to fly over the far shore, well south of Pendrongor, so that they would be concealed from Queen Ulricke's scrutiny by a spur of tall mountains.

By sunrise Elliot was almost growing accustomed to the sensation of being upon a dragon's back, and from his high perch he gazed down into heavily forested valleys nestled deep in the folds of mountains. He even thought he recognized the Valley of Direfall far below.

Then they crossed over craggy peaks that were higher still and it grew frightfully cold for a time—in fact, Elliot was shivering violently as he watched the dragon's shadow rush across pristine fields of snow. The dragon flew lower when passing over the next valley to give Elliot a chance to warm up. There he actually glimpsed the summer encampment of good King Venture. He could just make out the pavilions of the royal court, appearing as tiny specks upon the vivid green of the valley floor. Elliot pointed them out to Sindl and she wondered aloud what the knights would think, if they happened to be looking upward at that moment, to see a flying dragon. He wondered what Sir Edrim would think of his survival despite the betrayal.

Elliot was just about to say that they must be near the location of the faerie gate—when from around a jagged peak, just off to the west, sped the sinister black hull and bloodred sails of the pirate ship!

Elliot's heart thudded with alarm, but Sindl wasn't as concerned as he, for she knew a bit more about the capabilities of dragons.

The dragon laughed. "There are those upstarts now! Imagine thinking that they can land at my pier anytime they wish without asking—and then terrorize my guests! They are a frightfully insolent lot and I shall make short work of them!" The rhythm of his wings increased apace as he flew in great powerful strokes, turning to veer toward the approaching vessel.

"I am amazed that they are here waiting for us, for they are not that swift, despite the rake of their hull and the amount of canvas they carry," sneered the dragon.

As they drew closer, the pirate ship heeled hard to starboard. Its sails billowed as it righted itself. When it did, Elliot and Sindl saw its gunports were all gaping open, and that dark cannon muzzles had been trundled forward and staged on both its decks. A hoarse voice from its high sterncastle barked out the command, "Fire as you bear!"

Dense white puffs of smoke rolled evenly down the port side of the vessel—and a second later, they heard the cacophonous roar of the volley. Elliot cringed, knowing that cannonballs, still molten from their propelling charges, were hissing through the air toward them. They felt a scorching wind sweep over them as the first cannonballs whipped past overhead, much too close for comfort. The dragon folded his wings, lowered his head, and dropped like a stone into a steeply angled dive. Elliot found himself looking straight downward, beyond the dragon's snout, at a swiftly approaching expanse of mountainside. He gritted his teeth and hung on, his knuckles white. His heart felt as though it had been left behind, along with his stomach. More cannonballs hissed through the air, though now they passed harmlessly high above.

Next the dragon made a sharp turn, flying up the length of a steep alpine valley to plunge inside a cold layer of mist shrouding the highest peaks in the range. For a time they flew in a featureless white fog, but the dragon knew exactly what he was about. When next he folded his wings to plummet downward, they abruptly dropped from out of the bottom of the cloud, and Elliot spotted the crow's nest of the pirate ship and its bloodred sails directly below.

"We shan't give them a chance to turn their cannon on us a third time," declared the dragon. Elliot and Sindl felt themselves being drawn upward and backward as the dragon reared, arching his back, and then he threw his head forward. With a thunderous roar, reverberating from mountain to mountain, he breathed out a great blast of consuming fire. It roiled, smoking as it went, billowing from his gaping mouth like a raging inferno.

The tongues of fire writhed crackling through the air, arcing downward to engulf the masts and rigging of the pirate ship. Its sails dissolved in a conflagration of roaring flame, as its burning masts sagged and drooped. Elliot watched the pirate ship heel hard to port and rapidly lose altitude, its sails turning to glowing embers and blowing sparks of ash. Soon what remained of its rigging, shrouds, and spars blew away in a cloud of black smoke.

The dragon followed the pirate ship down, as it crashed in an alpine snowfield high on one of the spectacular peaks. Its hull was intact, but its sails and rigging were gone. Elliot glimpsed the tiny antlike figures of its crew leap over the railings and slide down the bulwarks to land in hip-deep snow alongside their vessel. Some shook their fists at the dragon as he wheeled high above them, but most just gazed upward, their faces wary, hoping he wasn't going to dive, to breathe fire upon them again.

After leaving the pirate ship behind, the dragon flew outward in ever expanding circles, searching above the mountains for the faerie gate. Elliot wasn't sure that the gate was always materialized, but Sindl assured him that at least it would be now, as his imminent return was expected. At last they saw it a good distance off, floating high above them. When they drew close they were able to make out the vigilant guardians posted upon its steps, the wind whipping their hair out behind them. The dragon flew up close to the gate, so close in fact that even the faerie sentries appeared alarmed by his overpowering vastness.

And then for a magical moment, all forward motion ceased, and the dragon hovered beside the gate. Elliot and Sindl patted the dragon's scales affectionately and thanked him earnestly for his assistance. He said that it was nothing really—only the sort of thing any decent chap would do.

As they slid down his sides to alight safely upon the steps of the gate, the dragon bade them farewell. Elliot and Sindl watched, standing quite still upon the steps, as he wheeled round once more. They waved to him and he acknowledged by bowing his head. His wings increased their tempo and in moments he was gone, a colossal shape fading into the haze of the distance.

The sentries of the gate guided them up the lamplit stairs. Elliot took a deep breath and joined Sindl as they stepped through the portal hand in hand.

Chapter 38

VICTORIA AND AERON materialized upon the steps of the high air gate, far above the palace of the faerie kingdom. The sentries stood silent, under the tall lamps in the starlight. Victoria glanced about—but there was no sign yet of Elliot.

The captain of the gate pointed downward, over the railings into the night and announced, "Our queen has left her palace and is on her way to meet you!" Victoria rushed to the railing and peered down. There, ascending through the starry night, having just cleared the highest treetops of the palace wood, a sparkling faerie lamp darted swiftly toward them. Seconds later the Faerie Queen alighted upon the stairway of the gate.

She and Victoria stood side by side, the cool nighttime wind tugging at their clothes. "Do not fear, Victoria," Queen Edwina said presently. "Elliot will not fail. A kind providence is directing his steps and watching over him—just as it watches over you."

Nevertheless, time passed slowly until nearly an hour had

crept by, and there was yet no sign. Despite the Faerie Queen's assurances, Victoria felt a gnawing fear. She worried that something dreadful had befallen her friend.

But suddenly the gate behind her opened once more, and she experienced a surge of relief—as she felt rather than saw the vivid flash back over her shoulder. She spun about, just in time to see Elliot and Sindl materializing below the archway. Her heart soared as she ran lightly up the staircase to greet him.

Elliot and Victoria embraced each other, overjoyed to be reunited. Victoria was blinking back her tears, and Elliot kept clearing his throat and holding his mouth in a funny way—as though he was endeavoring not to cry. Victoria rested her hand affectionately on his shoulder and smiled.

"I have endured adventures both marvelous and frightful, Elliot," she said softly.

He nodded vigorously. "I'll say! Do I ever have tales to tell you!" he cried.

Then Queen Edwina interrupted their happy reunion. She smiled graciously, but when she spoke, her voice was serious and grave. "The power of the Shadow Knight has become perilous, for it is now distorting the boundaries of the interwoven worlds. He's using the magical properties of the gemstones he possesses to form unstable portals into other planes and permitting vile things to creep through and wreak havoc. He desires to lure you both back to where he awaits, so that he may seize the stones in your possession. Then his power will have grown so vast that he will no longer require Ulricke's magic to move between worlds."

The Faerie Queen stepped forward to hold hands with the children. "The Shadow Knight that we would face if we wait until the morrow would simply be a hundred times more dreadful—so we must make haste! We must return at once to the gate at the opposite end of Faerieland, which opens directly into Elliot's world."

After the children said their earnest good-byes to Aeron and Sindl, the Faerie Queen joined them upon the lowest step. The three of them held hands and stepped off the staircase as one. Their journey began with a heart-stopping swoop—out into the night, soaring high over the hills and forests of Faerieland.

Perhaps it was the thought of the impending confrontation with the Shadow Knight that darkened their hearts, but as they sped above the forests, glens, and dales of Faerieland, the children thought only of the scariest tales they had ever heard. It seemed that the entire realm was darkened, rendered unpleasant with a nightmare taint.

As Elliot's thoughts tormented his beleaguered mind he turned to Victoria for respite, but saw to his dismay that her face also showed evidence of horror. But when she sensed he was looking to her for solace, she turned and smiled courageously. He returned her smile gladly. Then each turned away once more, lost again in a tumult of their own fears, as the leagues of Faerieland passed by below their feet.

They continued on, speeding out across rolling meadows that lay still and quiet in the starlight. They passed over walled villages, their fortifications now required to hold the dark terrors of the night at bay—terrors unfolding just beyond their safe candlelit windows. And then in the far distance they saw the cliff top with its perfect row of trees and the vale gate in the fold of the hills. Moments later they alighted softly upon the lawn and were striding rapidly forward through the dewy grass.

Elliot and Victoria felt chills flicker up their spines as they were drawn by the Faerie Queen toward the lamplit stair. "Come," she said, "we must not linger here!" Then with her arms about their shoulders she led them to the portal. They stepped through and vanished in a sparkling eruption of light.

When the peculiar disorienting sensation of twirling and tumbling had subsided, Elliot and Victoria found themselves still hand in hand with the Faerie Queen, descending rapidly through a palpable gloom. Queen Edwina glanced at Victoria, her eyes conveying her grave concern. "Child, didn't you say that the portal of the gate upon Elliot's side opened onto a meadow?"

Victoria nodded, finding herself just as confused and disoriented. "I haven't the slightest idea where we are!" she cried, shouting over the sibilant hiss of a chill wind that sprang up from nowhere to sigh and whisper about them in the darkness.

"The power of the Shadow Knight has altered the placement of the gate upon this side," said Queen Edwina at length, clutching both children's hands in hers.

For his part, Elliot was peering as best he might through the mist that seemed now to be reaching up and grasping at them. For a time he was not even certain he was in his world at all, for he couldn't locate a single point of reference to get his bearings. But then as he concentrated, peering through the

churning darkness, he finally recognized where they were—
they were being steadily drawn toward the water of Alton Bay.

But what profoundly disturbed Elliot was the fact that
though it was not night, it was certainly not day, either—for
a dark pall had settled over the surrounding countryside. Victoria found it even worse than the thick eerie type of fog they
called a "London Particular" in her own time—the kind of
fog that made hansom cabs appear as strange beasts in the
cobbled streets, just beyond the warmth and light of her uncle
Dexter's town house windows.

"It is far worse than we imagined!" exclaimed the Faerie
Queen. "Powerful enchantments are all about us! Keep holding hands. Under no conditions should we permit ourselves
to become separated!" She was nearly shouting now, just to
be heard above the roar of the wind.

Victoria and Elliot were startled when the wind suddenly
increased in volume to blow even harder, for now it was whipping at their clothes and howling along between them, as
though it was hell-bent on separating them. The Faerie Queen
shouted something to the children, but neither of them could
possibly have even hoped to understand a word of what she
uttered, and in another moment a forked tongue of lightning
crackled down the sky off to their left, accompanied by a deafening thunderclap.

The tendrils of mist were now resolving themselves into
ghastly gape-mouthed faces that screamed at them with the
voice of the howling wind and snarled at them with each crash
of thunder. Elliot shuddered as he felt the cold fingers of dank
mist close about his neck, and beside him Victoria thrashed

and kicked hard at something. She was fighting a morbid apparition that Elliot could only half see.

And then, a moaning face of mist materialized before them, looming directly in their path. It blew at them with all its might—and it was like being in the funnel of a tornado, for there was no comprehensible sound or sense at all, save for a continuous cacophony of mad shrieking. To the children's horror, the Faerie Queen was torn violently from their grasp—blown up and backward, tumbling head over heels, away into the gloom.

The children miraculously managed to grab hold of each other's hands and clung to each other with a determination born of despair—lest they be wrenched apart, each left alone to face the consuming vileness that was awaiting them below.

They were passing low across the waters of Alton Bay, and the cold splashes of mist and spray that spattered against them smelled foul. As they skimmed across the wave tops they saw hundreds of pale fish bobbing lifelessly upon the surface. Dark streamlined shapes were leaping from the water to accompany them on their way. Their hearts briefly leaped with hope, for they supposed them at first to be porpoises— even though both Elliot and Victoria knew better, of course, for porpoises are saltwater creatures. But then they realized that the shapes cavorting about them were not friendly at all, for the long serpentine necks were bending to lunge upward, bringing their smooth glistening heads with savage jaws brimming full of sharply pointed teeth almost into biting and tearing range of the children's defenseless limbs. Elliot and Victoria cried out, kicking at the snapping fangs.

And then they were fast approaching the head of the bay, where the bathing beach still lay before them. They saw that it was stark and empty of swimmers, though an atrocious fifty-foot-long thing—very much like a gigantic snail—had clambered up from the depths of the lake and dragged itself ashore to perish. Both Elliot and Victoria wrinkled their noses and were very nearly sickened from the overwhelming stench of decay drifting cloyingly upward from the decomposing sluglike body.

Elliot was shocked to see that the buildings beyond the bathing beach all appeared ancient now, and were crumbling to ruin, sagging and overgrown with tangles of vines, among dark dead trees. All the streets and sidewalks had become nearly unrecognizable.

"Elliot, what has happened? Alton Bay is even more decrepit than that old abandoned house!" Victoria shouted, horror-stricken at the nightmarish changes that had befallen the picturesque Alton Bay.

And then both children gazed out ahead of them, for they were rising now, heading directly for the wooded hill where Elliot's house stood, nestled in tall evergreens. And just beyond, toward where the abandoned house loomed in its dark wood, the children saw a towering cloud of thick, palpable darkness. It roiled and churned, continually collapsing in on itself as it awaited their arrival. Purple lightning crackled and flickered from deep within it, accompanied by earthshaking rumbles and earsplitting peals of thunder. Both children knew that they were being drawn to the very source of all the ghastly changes that had befallen the once-beautiful little town on the shore of a once-lovely lake.

WORLDS AWAY, deep in the Realm of Lorinshar, in her dark Tower of Pendrongor, Queen Ulricke grew very alarmed indeed, for an uneasy wind arose from nowhere to blow about her chamber, hissing into its darkest recesses and whispering about its furthest corners. The wind knocked over two of her retorts and rapidly fanned the pages of her spell books—as though it was searching them for something. Queen Ulricke arose from her seat and glided to the stairs. She quickly ascended to the dais. Black flames were squirming furiously, writhing down the blade of one of the swords in a tempest of fire. It was the very one belonging to the Shadow Knight Trevelyan. Queen Ulricke spoke a secret word in a hushed voice and Trevelyan's spell door opened silently before her. The queen was disturbed to see that his sphere had now grown to vast proportions, expanding to nearly completely fill the crypt.

The dark shape within thrashed and raged, twisting and lunging, hurling itself against the inner surface of the sphere as though it was determined to break free and have at her. Queen Ulricke kept her wits about her—for she wasn't truly horrified until her own orb rose up to tug and pull at its chain about her neck. It was being steadily drawn toward Trevelyan's sphere. Queen Ulricke's eyes widened in dismay. She spun about on her heels, leaving the chamber at once, grasping her orb protectively in both hands as she descended the steps.

Moments later Sir Lykan and Lord Kromm were summoned to Queen Ulricke's chambers with the utmost urgency. They found her in the torchlit corridor outside the door, shaken as she waited there with Brynn and Sutton, appearing even more pale than usual.

"Set a watch upon that door, both of you—see to it personally on the very pain of death!" she hissed. Then, accompanied by her handmaidens, she swept down the spiral staircase, the shadows of the trio elongating and distorting as they flickered along the stones.

THE MAGIC OF THE FAERIE gate set Elliot and Victoria gently down in Elliot's driveway. The lovely Victorian home was now scarcely visible at all through the tangle of trees grown so close beside it. Its clapboards were green with mold and mildew, its corner tower wrapped in vines, and its roofs were sagging. The windows of the house were simply black gaping holes.

The pavement of the driveway was broken up by long grass and dense bushes in hundreds of places and the garage had collapsed completely. Elliot guessed his mother's car must be rusting in the woods just where they had abandoned it—it seemed ever so long ago now!

The children crept forward, hand in hand, their hearts thudding with fear. Elliot very nearly stumbled over some rusty piping that lay in the middle of the driveway, half concealed in the grass and weeds. Victoria stooped down and picked one of the pieces up. "Look at this, will you, Elliot," she said, dismayed at what she had found. "It's part of your velocipede!" Elliot got a very queer feeling indeed in the pit of his stomach when he saw that what she said was true. He recognized the C and the two P's from the word *Chopper* that had once been painted on the thickest bar of the frame.

"It's a nightmare, Victoria," he declared, shaking his head as he took the bit reluctantly from her fingers to examine it more closely. "It's like one of those dreams where everything safe and familiar becomes frightful!"

"I know exactly what you mean," she replied gravely.

And then the thunder rumbled and crashed all the more, and a crackle of lightning divided above them to splinter a branch from an old oak tree. It plummeted down from directly above their heads, and as they scrambled for safety, Elliot saw that the sharp end of one branch had scraped Victoria's cheek and that she was bleeding.

The earth shook and trembled beneath their feet and the great black cloud, with vivid lightning deep inside—the very same cloud they had glimpsed from the air—bore rapidly down upon them from out of the wood. Entire trees were being torn up from the ground, roots and all, to be flung aside like toys, as the cloud roared onward.

The cloud approached until it was directly in their path. It was black as night and seemed to consume what little light there was, intensifying the deepening gloom it cast all about itself. Victoria stood still, hand in hand with Elliot, her free hand pressed to her bleeding cheek.

Both children turned in sudden alarm as the front door of the house squeaked open upon rusty hinges. "Elliot!" called a familiar yet somehow terrifying voice from deep within the overgrown, decaying home. "Elliot!" the voice called again, drawing nearer this time, as though it had almost reached the door.

Victoria took Elliot by the arm and spun him round to face the looming cloud instead, now wreathed in lightning as it expanded in size to grow more colossal with each passing second. "Don't look, Elliot!" she shouted, holding him tightly and pointing him forcibly away from the house. "Don't you dare look! It's not her! It's not your mother at all! It's just the Shadow Knight doing it to scare us, that's all!" And though all his instincts urged him to retreat to the house, Elliot knew that Victoria was right and he listened to her and stood grimly, facing the churning darkness of the cloud instead. Still the voice called for him again and again, and then shuffling foot-steps crossed the veranda and descended the stairs.

Victoria would have done well to listen to her own advice, for she glanced back over her shoulder just for a moment the second time that the voice had called, but she blanched at the ghastly sight that met her eyes. She turned from it in horror, her flesh fairly crawling.

And then a form came to them out of the dark cloud, for a vast and potent shadow, blacker still and denser than the cloud itself, detached at length, and there before them rode the dread form of the Shadow Knight. The steed upon which he was mounted had transformed into something hideous—

something almost prehistoric now, bloated and smooth, squelching like a slug, and deathly pale besides. It was hardly horselike now, and it had no eyes, but it seemed to sense where the children stood—for it lunged at them, its long gray forked tongue flickering as it screamed from its toothless mouth.

Chapter 39

THE SHADOW KNIGHT DISMOUNTED, sliding down from the back of his foul steed. He towered over the children as he strode toward them, his horned helmet and masked face terrible to behold. The awful black star in the very center of his shield pulsed and wavered as it radiated yet greater gusts of darkness into the world.

He held his dreadful black orb in his right hand, and both children could see that the hilt of the sheathed sword at his hip featured the crimson radiance of the enchanted gemstones he already possessed. And they glimpsed the two empty sockets—where he meant the stones from their rings soon to be.

The tones of his voice when he spoke were but a menacing whisper—a whisper that seemed to originate but an inch from the children's ears.

"Give me your rings of your own free will—or I shall simply take them by force, and then you shall each perish horribly, while your own worst nightmares eternally unfold all about you over and over again, without end!"

Victoria and Elliot stepped forward bravely and stood hand in hand, both trembling, before the Shadow Knight. "Never! You may not have them!" shouted Elliot, his voice quite nearly breaking.

"They are not yours to possess!" shouted Victoria in agreement. "And you shan't have them."

Then, perhaps guided by some instinct or some compelling magical power that aided them, Elliot and Victoria extended their hands to point their fingers straight at the Shadow Knight—even as he stood looming over them, crowned with menace. He slowly raised his orb and both children's hearts sank, as once more Elliot experienced the grim recollection of his mother being sucked into the orb and devoured.

"Stand fast, Elliot!" exclaimed Victoria. The Shadow Knight drew back his gauntleted fist and flung his black orb with all his might, straight at the children. As it hissed through the air, it expanded hugely—and both Elliot and Victoria knew something dreadful was about to befall them.

However, at the very last moment, brilliant forks of light shot out from the gemstones in the children's rings—a rapidly pulsing red flash from Elliot's, combined with a blinding bolt from Victoria's. The lightning thundered and crackled with magical energy as the lights met to join forces in midair, arcing out to crash and flare against the orb thrown by the Shadow Knight. The vivid bursts of magical energy from the rings, charged as they were by the orbs of ice and fire, shattered the black orb of the Shadow Knight in a brilliant flash of white-hot incandescence. The molten hot fragments of the Shadow Knight's orb plummeted to the ground, igniting the grass and weeds where they fell. Foul-smelling flames and black twisting clouds of smoke rose from the fragments as they burned, casting off sparks into the grass until they were all consumed and finally disappeared altogether.

The dark cloud that the Shadow Knight had stepped out from now turned blacker still and rose into the very heavens. The crashes of thunder from deep within its depths were continuous and deafening. The cloaked and helmeted shape strode forward, and with a ring of well-tempered steel, drew its sword from its scabbard—its blade flaming with tongues of dark fire. Victoria clutched at Elliot's sleeve. Apparently destroying the Shadow Knight's orb had simply infuriated him, and both children were ready to turn upon their heels and flee for their very lives—even though they sensed that it would be futile, and behind them stood the decaying horror that had once been Elliot's mother.

Suddenly the immense shape paused and staggered, then fell to its knees and dropped its sword. The earth shook and trembled beneath its armored bulk. It clutched its helmeted head and rocked back and forth, as frightful tearing crashes of thunder resounded all about and lightning seared downward, destroying several of the trees closest by as they dissolved into billows of white-hot flame.

The Shadow Knight raised the visor of his helmet and vivid rays of intense black light stabbed out from the eyeholes and the leering mouth portal. It was as though he began falling to pieces then, for gaps and tears appeared in his armor everywhere—and the white-faced children could see that rather than there being a physical person inside, there was only a mass of black light, churning very like the cloud out of which it had arisen. As the Shadow Knight's armor rapidly disintegrated, more and more vivid stabbing flashes of unlight flickered outward, until his outer physical form was gone entirely.

The brief sense of relief that Elliot and Victoria felt for a second or two was overwhelmed by a new horror, for the form of the Shadow Knight was still there, after all, though it now had no armor or even physical substance at all. It was now very like the black gaping star in the center of its own shield, for the Shadow Knight had become simply a man-shaped hole— a tear in the very fabric of place and time, an enlarging void that, even as the terrified children watched, began to draw in and consume everything in its proximity.

Then the burning leaves of the nearby trees that the lightning had ignited were stripped from their limbs and branches in an abrupt shower of sparks and embers to be drawn into the man-shaped hole like a flickering cloud of fireworks. Elliot and Victoria clutched at each other in desperation, for they felt the great power of the sucking wind that came out from the vortex.

"Run, Elliot!" screamed Victoria, and they tried to flee for all they were worth—but against their will they found themselves being pulled inexorably backward.

The Shadow Knight's own mount, even though now revealed in its serpentine form, was soon drawn in as well, its forked tongue flicking in and out as it gave one last screaming neigh.

From above the great din of noise came a sound very like the wind rapidly turning the pages of an open book—and the children saw that nearly all the mildewed shingles from one entire side of the roof of Elliot's house were being drawn into the void. Next, with a tearing squeal of rusty nails, entire lengths of clapboard from the nearest side of the house were pulled away to vanish, followed by choking clouds of plaster and splintering fragments of rotten lath. Still the hole raged and grew, sucking and consuming more and more.

Victoria and Elliot were on their knees now, being drawn forward, sliding across the ground, as they clung to each other in utter despair. It was then that a thunderclap sounded with such overwhelming volume that both children were temporarily stunned and completely disoriented.

Elliot thought—for a very brief moment, just before his senses reeled and he lost consciousness altogether—that he saw a circle of flaming letters form in the very air about them, then the circle began to spin, revolving more and more rapidly as it grew dazzlingly bright.

Victoria felt as though perhaps she was hallucinating, for it seemed to her that she glimpsed her friend Paracelsus, his lined face haggard with exhaustion and titanic effort, his eyes closed tightly. A blue flame danced in the very center of both his upheld palms—and as the flames rose higher still, they began to spin and form a blazing circle of fiery letters.

Both children then experienced a sensation far more violent and tumultuous than any they had known before, even when traveling through the magical portals between interwoven worlds. It seemed that they were spinning head over heels, in the midst of a pandemonium of noise and light.

When at last they came to their senses, they were astonished to find themselves lying sprawled upon their backs in disarray, beneath the peaceful starlight, under the lattice gate, close behind the old house.

Victoria was certain that the form of Paracelsus stayed with them for a few moments and he smiled and spoke to her. "I have changed the point of origin in the paths of time, and sundered the causes of ill effect. Things that ought never to have been are undone. It is my gift to you, precious child who saved us when all was lost!"

And as his form finally faded, she glanced up in wonder to see a meteor slide down the sky, to burst in a shower of light somewhere over the distant treetops. Victoria and Elliot watched as fireflies moved haphazardly about the eaves of the evergreen wood, close by the old abandoned house that now somehow seemed like a comforting and familiar friend.

A sound from directly behind them startled the children, and made them quickly sit up and turn round. Edwina the Faerie Queen stood lightly on her toes in the dewy grass. The children rose and rushed to ask her what had happened—for they both were more than a little confused by the cataclysmic events they had borne witness to.

Edwina laid a gentle hand upon each of their shoulders. "You have done splendidly, my children," she declared solemnly, "for you have defeated the Shadow Knight. You have overmatched his might, shattered his deadly orb, and vanquished him!"

"But what of those awful things we saw?" Elliot asked. "Were all those real?"

The Faerie Queen nodded. "They were once terribly real, but now they are real no longer, for the event path that was formed by the Shadow Knight's onslaught was closed when you defeated him, and my friend Paracelsus redirected it to where it would have gone had it never been interfered with. And now it is very nearly as if the Shadow Knight had never been at all." Edwina smiled fondly at Elliot and Victoria—her great affection for them evident in both her expression and her voice.

"This chapter in the tale of your adventures is finished," she declared, "and you must go home now, Elliot."

He looked up at her with haunted eyes. "But will my mother be there? Will she be alive?"

"She is both alive and well, and she does not know that you and Victoria have even left your rooms, so she may be rather cross with you for being out so late past your bedtimes without her permission!"

Elliot laughed. "She can even take television away from me— I don't care—even for a whole week!" he declared happily.

"And what of me?" inquired Victoria. "What shall I do now?"

"You may spend one last night in Alton Bay, Victoria, for I know you must be tired from all of your adventures. Then, tomorrow, you'll go back through the gate to your own time."

Victoria and Elliot looked at each other, teary-eyed.

"I will gladly accompany you both back as far as the house, for there are some loose ends that I must tend to," said Queen Edwina.

And so they walked back together under the starlight, moving silently through the whispering trees surrounding the old mysterious house, past the rusted lamppost, and soon came to Elliot's mother's automobile with its headlights still on—exactly where they had left it. Elliot reached in to shut off the lights. The children discussed the problem of the automobile and decided that it would perhaps be best for Elliot's mother to believe that pranksters had driven it out into the woods behind the house, and had abandoned it there in the trees—and to leave the story at that.

As they all went through the meadow together, over the embankment, and down the lane, the Faerie Queen moved to walk alongside Elliot. She gently took their hands in her own. "Children, I think that additional tasks await you, for the rings that you and Victoria bear are your very own to keep—and they are never bestowed lightly. There are more evils to be fought in the interwoven worlds and more dangers to be faced still than either of you may yet know or have any inkling of! For Queen Ulricke's design was to obtain all the rings so no mortal could move between worlds to summon help, which means her plans for ill are still unfolding, though the Shadow Knight Trevelyan did present her with a twist when he desired them for himself."

As they reached the driveway, alongside the lighted windows of his home, Elliot was a trifle saddened to see that his Chopper was still in pieces. The Faerie Queen moved at once to begin searching for something in the grass alongside the edge of the drive. She searched carefully, bending low as she went, exclaiming aloud as she began to find what she had been looking for. Elliot and Victoria knelt to help her, and within a few minutes, they had assisted in the recovery of all the faerie gemstones that the Shadow Knight had stolen from their rightful bearers and proper hiding places.

Victoria and Elliot both shed a tear as they embraced Edwina the Faerie Queen, who vowed they would meet again in due course. Then they stood together waving as she faded into the night, disappearing into the softly sighing trees.

MEANWHILE, high in her dark Tower of Pendrongor, Queen Ulricke at last summoned up her courage and had Lord Kromm and Sir Lykan step away from her chamber door. Her handmaidens whispered anxiously together, reluctantly accompanying her as she cautiously reentered her chamber. Holding one hand over her own orb to keep it safe and secure, she crept inside. She soon sensed that somehow the danger had passed. She went up the stairs to the dais and stepped to the Shadow Knight Trevelyan's crypt. The armor had all crumbled away to flakes of rust and the blade of the sword had finally been consumed entirely by its own black flame.

Queen Ulricke spoke the word that opened the spell door and there inside, upon its pedestal, she found that the sphere of her most powerful and deadly Shadow Knight lay quiet and empty!

AT THE VERY MOMENT that Queen Ulricke turned paler still in her rage, Janet Good was sleeping fitfully on the sofa in her living room. She suddenly awakened with a start and she sat up in alarm. Her hair practically stood on end and a peculiar sense of dread seized her when she heard a footfall upon the veranda—and with fear-widened eyes she watched the doorknob slowly turn.

She drew back with a gasp, struggling quickly to her feet. She found herself trembling despite her best efforts to remain brave as the door slowly opened, creaking loudly upon its hinges. It was thus with profound relief that she saw Victoria and Elliot standing hesitantly on the veranda before her.

"Goodness, you two!" she exclaimed at length. "You gave me quite a fright, I must say! I didn't even know that you were outside—and you shouldn't be either at this hour. You should both be up in bed sound asleep!"

Janet Good found herself quite surprised indeed when Elliot and Victoria rushed to her and hugged her fiercely, clinging to her for all they were worth. She also noticed that both children were blinking back tears and that Elliot's lower lip was trembling. Elliot's mother had a good mind to scold them soundly and send them both back up to bed at once, but the earnestness of their embrace, combined with the concern for her evident in their eyes, compelled her to relent. Instead she had them sit beside her on the sofa and she threw an arm affectionately about their shoulders.

"I must tell you of the strange dream I was having before I woke up," she said. "I just have to tell someone before the memory fades. I dreamed that I heard heavy footfalls outside on the porch, so I rushed forward to quickly lock the door. I drew the bolt just in time, too, for something truly horrible was trying to get in. But then a gauntleted fist smashed through the side pane and reached in to unlock the door from the inside. The front door was flung open with such violence that it was literally torn from its hinges. The commotion awoke you both and you came to the stairs. The horrid thing was looming upon the threshold. It looked like a huge knight, and I could sense that it wanted both of you—or something that you each possessed.

"I told you to run for your lives, but the intruder started coming up the stairs after you and then it threw something at me because it was enraged that I was barring its way. Then I had the most awful folding and collapsing sensation, and I felt myself spinning downward into a black abyss. When I came to my senses, I was in a dark place—but I was not there alone. A little boy named Trevelyan was there with me. He was dressed in very quaint old-fashioned clothes.

"At first he tried his best to frighten me—and there was something scary about him, too, for his eyes were black and featureless and that took getting used to. But after a bit I realized that he wasn't really a truly wicked boy in his heart, but rather that he was lost and all alone. He simply wanted his mother and was angry because he could not find her. I tried my best to comfort him, and after a bit I think I succeeded, for when we sat down to rest, he sat beside me and rested his head upon my shoulder and his eyes turned blue again.

"We sat there like that for the longest time, until suddenly we weren't in the dark place anymore at all. We stood in a lovely linden wood and the most exquisite carriage was coming down the raked gravel road. Trevelyan got to his feet and shouted joyfully—and the carriage ground to a halt. Then a sweet-faced woman stepped down from the carriage and ran to him with tears of happiness streaming down her cheeks. He turned to wave and smiled radiantly at me—and then they drove away. That's when I awakened on the sofa, and it was as though the bad parts of the dream were beginning all over again, for I saw the handle of the door turning and I was frightened before realizing that it was just the both of you!"

The children's eyes met, and they glanced at each other meaningfully for a long moment. Neither Victoria nor Elliot nor his mother felt like going to bed just then so they all went into the kitchen and Janet made a pot of tea and served them cookies. Victoria said that Elliot put far too much cream in his tea and that it was better without any cream at all, or perhaps with just the merest pinch of lemon. He laughed and told her to see to her own tea making and to mind her own business—so Victoria was required to stick out her tongue and then she made a face at him. She called him an enormous nuisance and fixed him with a scathing glare, but it was only her least most scathing glare, because she wasn't really cross with him at all.

∾

JANET GOOD NOT ONLY finished the faerie painting of Victoria, but proudly exhibited it in an art show in a nearby town. A wealthy woman who simply adored Victorian-style faerie paintings was completely captivated by Janet's work. She insisted that Elliot's mother paint her an entire series of them.

That series—others of which also featured Victoria—was eventually exhibited both in New York City and Boston galleries as part of a prestigious art show. Several of the paintings actually sold for very large sums of money—for the wealthy woman who had befriended and encouraged Janet Good had endlessly raved about them to all her influential friends.

Elliot's mother earned more than enough money to buy him a new Chopper and completely repair their automobile, for she said that it was a perfectly good one, and why bother going to the trouble of purchasing another? She had their house painted as well, and even the little overgrown garden just below Elliot's window was now no longer neglected. It was carefully tended until it became really rather lovely.

But that was all in the future. The very next day Victoria knew she must leave Alton Bay and return to her own time. Both children had nodded politely when Elliot's mother declared that she was simply dying to meet Victoria's uncle Dexter, just as soon as it could be arranged. Victoria and Elliot were subdued as they walked slowly back to the magical gate late in the afternoon. The sunset was turning the sky a deep crimson, high above their heads. Victoria was back in her best dress and in her fine lace stockings, without any shoes—just as she had arrived.

"At least I shall have the satisfaction of interrogating my uncle Dexter as to why his portrait hangs over the mantelpiece in the old tumbledown house!" she declared determinedly.

"First ask him if he is perhaps acquainted with someone named Mr. Murchison," Elliot suggested diplomatically.

When they reached the lattice gate, all overshadowed by the row of tall trees along the very edge of the meadow, Elliot and Victoria both had lumps in their throats. They clung to each other tightly, cried a bit, and were not ashamed—not even a little. Then Elliot said good-bye to his best friend. Victoria declared she would miss him dreadfully. He watched as she stepped forward alone, and they kept waving to each other until she abruptly disappeared in a dazzling flash of light.

On his way home Elliot found himself feeling a bit better, for after all, he was just a short walk from two doors between worlds—and both he and Victoria now possessed magic rings capable of opening either of them!

Victoria was amazed when she arrived back at Summerwind to find that she had been gone only for several hours and not for months and months as it had seemed to her. She had barely closed the bookshelf door that concealed the staircase leading to her secret room when Ellen, Mrs. Hampstead, and Sheffington came bursting in. They did what adults often do when they have experienced a bad fright: They became really rather cross and gave her a good sound scolding.

Victoria stood so meekly when they admonished her that they soon relented and embraced her and told her that she mustn't ever disappear again. Then they sent Ellen running downstairs to tell Victoria's uncle Dexter that she was accounted for and safe and sound after all.

And so things returned to normal in England as well. That is, normal for a time—until one of the doors between worlds opened once more.

Epilogue

EARLY ONE EVENING scarcely three weeks later, a strange black hansom cab turned off King's Cross and headed out in the direction of Hampstead Heath. Passersby on the cobblestone sidewalks doffed their top hats and bowed their heads—for the cab was closely followed by a splendid horse-drawn hearse, one of the finest the city of London had ever seen.

Inside the hansom cab, a young girl of perhaps eleven, clad in an elegant mourning gown of black velvet and fine brocade, sat sobbing quietly. Beside her sat an equally elegant woman, also clad all in black. The woman's face was veiled. She reached out a small, gloved hand and shook the girl's shoulder. "Do stop your sniveling, will you," she demanded. "Sometimes I almost regret that I had Sir Lykan save you at all! Your mother is gone, and you'll just have to get used to that fact, won't you, my dear? For I simply cannot have her continually robbing me of my rightful prey, now can I?"

Deirdre looked up, her eyes shining. "Oh, that's not what I am crying about, my queen," she sobbed. "For you are like a kind mother to me, and you feed me such lovely things. It's just that I am still a bit queasy from that awful feeling I got when we came through the black gate and floated out over the waters of the channel."

The veiled woman nodded sympathetically. "Now that I understand!" she replied. "I always become ill when crossing over water. But take heart, my dear. We shall stay in a lovely town house that one of my handmaidens has already procured. And we shall have servants to order about, and many delightful plans to make."

Deirdre pouted a little, but even so she brightened visibly. "And that astral man, that blue vapor-breathing shape-changing thing who slumbers in the coffin back there in the hearse—he frightens me so!"

"Ah, Lord Sarton!" Queen Ulricke smiled fondly. "Well, he frightens everyone! But he is my ace in the hole, for I mean to wreak vengeance upon those sniveling brats. Then I shall be done with the lot of them! The girl who destroyed my mentor, the Ice Dragon, will be whining soon enough—and she'll go running to summon the boy, and they shall both come into my clutches and be my fair prey at last!"

"Mine, too, don't forget," exclaimed Deirdre, punctuating her pout with one last dramatic sniff for good effect. "For remember you said I might have the boy, when all is said and done, for we have unfinished business between us—he and I!"

Queen Ulricke nodded and stroked Deirdre's head affectionately. Passersby were alarmed to hear the sound of laughter from inside the hansom cab that led the somber funeral procession.